"Count on Vicki Lewis Thompson for a sharp, sassy, sexy read."
—Jayne Ann Krentz

Praise for the Novels of Vicki Lewis Thompson

Wild & Hexy

"Each book that Vicki Lewis Thompson pens is an experience that will have you laughing from the start. The world is well-built, the characters are charming, and the story line is simply delightful. *Wild & Hexy* is a zany adventure in romance and magic. Readers won't be able to resist another visit with the inhabitants of Big Knob."
—Darque Reviews

"An excellent addition that makes me eager for more! . . . You never really know what might happen in the small town of Big Knob, but you won't want to miss a thing. A must read!"
—Fallen Angel Reviews

"There was so much going on in this book that I really didn't want it to end . . . wonderfully fun . . . a keeper for sure!"
—Fresh Fiction

"If you thought *Over Hexed* was phenomenal, wait until you read *Wild & Hexy!* . . . A rip-roaring good time."
—Romance Junkies

"Get ready for a truly *Wild & Hexy* ride . . . brewing with lots of magical fun, mishaps, and most important of all—romance! . . . Vicki Lewis Thompson has penned a fun paranormal tale."
—Romance Reader at Heart

"Pure FUN from first page to last!"
—The Romance Readers Connection

"Sassy, fun, and magical, *Wild & Hexy* is pure delight from the first page. . . . This novel is one you'll want to read in one sitting, and then you'll want to read it again."
—Romance Reviews Today

"A fun book to read from start to finish."
—Once Upon a Romance Reviews

continued . . .

Over Hexed

"A snappy, funny, romantic novel."
—*New York Times* bestselling author Carly Phillips

"Filled with laughs, this is a charmer of a book."
—The Eternal Night

"The same trademark blend of comedy and heart that won Thompson's Nerd series a loyal following."
—*Publishers Weekly*

"Thompson mixes magic, small-town quirkiness, and passionate sex for a winsome effect." —*Booklist*

"A warm and funny novel, you find yourself cheering. I would definitely recommend it."
—The Road to Romance

"This novel was brilliant. I laughed until I cried and it was a very fast read for me. This genre is the beginning of a new series for Thompson, and if this novel is any indication of the following books, then Thompson has hit the jackpot." —Romance Reader at Heart

"Vicki Lewis Thompson has a true flair for humor. Pick up *Over Hexed* and be prepared to be amused, delighted, and satisfied as Vicki Lewis Thompson takes you on an unforgettable ride." —Single Titles

"Vicki Lewis Thompson sure delivers with *Over Hexed* . . . a lighthearted tale that won't soon be forgotten." —Fallen Angel Reviews

"With her wonderful talent of lighthearted humor, Vicki Lewis Thompson pens an enchanting tale for her amorous characters, steeping it in magic and enough passion to scorch the pages." —Darque Reviews

"Vicki Lewis Thompson has created another romance blended with humor to make you beg for more."
—Once Upon a Romance Reviews

CASUAL
HEX

Vicki Lewis Thompson

AN ONYX BOOK

ONYX
Published by New American Library, a division of
Penguin Group (USA) Inc., 375 Hudson Street,
New York, New York 10014, USA
Penguin Group (Canada), 90 Eglinton Avenue East, Suite 700, Toronto,
Ontario M4P 2Y3, Canada (a division of Pearson Penguin Canada Inc.)
Penguin Books Ltd., 80 Strand, London WC2R 0RL, England
Penguin Ireland, 25 St. Stephen's Green, Dublin 2,
Ireland (a division of Penguin Books Ltd.)
Penguin Group (Australia), 250 Camberwell Road, Camberwell, Victoria 3124,
Australia (a division of Pearson Australia Group Pty. Ltd.)
Penguin Books India Pvt. Ltd., 11 Community Centre, Panchsheel Park,
New Delhi - 110 017, India
Penguin Group (NZ), 67 Apollo Drive, Rosedale, North Shore 0632,
New Zealand (a division of Pearson New Zealand Ltd.)
Penguin Books (South Africa) (Pty.) Ltd., 24 Sturdee Avenue,
Rosebank, Johannesburg 2196, South Africa

Penguin Books Ltd., Registered Offices:
80 Strand, London WC2R 0RL, England

First published by Onyx, an imprint of New American Library,
a division of Penguin Group (USA) Inc.

First Printing, March 2009
10 9 8 7 6 5 4 3 2 1

To Josette Quesnel, who is a genius at French manicures and a font of information on the French male psyche, and to the staff of Hotel Henri IV Rive Gauche in Paris, who made a huge city feel warm and cozy. *Merci beaucoup.*

ACKNOWLEDGMENTS

Finishing a book always fills me with gratitude. Hey, I managed to put together another one! But not without plenty of help. I'm grateful for my editor Claire Zion's continued faith in me, and the wise advice of Robert Gottlieb and Jenny Bent at Trident Media. I couldn't have created a French hero (I'm not kidding!) without the trip to Paris planned and executed by my amazing assistant Audrey Sharpe. I also need to thank Klaus Badelt, whose score for *Pirates of the Caribbean, The Curse of the Black Pearl* powered me through the last few chapters. Most excellent writing music, Mr. Badelt.

Prologue

Tie game, bottom of the ninth, bases loaded and the Mariners' designated hitter was up at bat. Seated directly behind home plate between two of the hottest babes in Seattle, Prince Leo sipped his ice-cold brewski and smiled. Late September, and his favorite team was still in the running. Life didn't get any better than that.

Then his cell phone rang. Worse yet, it was his mother. He could let the call go to voice mail, claim the ring had been drowned out by the roar of the crowd. But Queen Beryl wouldn't buy it. Fairy princes, of which he was one, had incredible hearing.

Because of that ability, he'd overheard this morning's conversation at the palace between his mother and one of her oldest friends, a witch from San Francisco named Isadora Mather. Very odd, that conversation. Unless his mother had been joking, she was having second thoughts about handing over the kingdom to her one and only son. Yeah, she was probably joking.

Still, the discussion had made him briefly consider giving up his primo seats and the company of the Dempsey twins this afternoon so he could stick around and get the 411 on what he'd thought was a done deal—his becoming King of Atwood in the near future. In the end he hadn't been able to make himself miss the game.

Besides, he had every confidence he'd end up on the throne. He'd reached the required age, so all he was waiting for was his mother's decision on a good coronation date. He'd tried on his late daddy's crown, a little dusty after sitting around all these years, and it fit just fine. Soon he'd be the big boss in the forested kingdom of Atwood, a misty island at the far reaches of Puget Sound.

True, his mother had the power to deny him that job, but she wouldn't disinherit her own flesh and blood, even if she was irritated with him these days. So what if he liked to party? Was that a crime? And maybe he hadn't put much effort into those charitable projects she was so big on, but there would be plenty of time to get serious once he was king.

She'd probably known he was listening and had wanted to give him a little scare when she'd told Isadora that she might pass the crown to a commoner. He didn't believe for a minute that she'd do such a thing, but just to hedge his bets, he answered the phone.

"Hey," he said. "Let me call you back after the game."

"I'm afraid not." His mother had adopted her imperial tone. "This is of utmost importance."

Leo sighed. "What's up?" He couldn't imagine anything of more importance than a game-winning home run, which would put the Mariners in the playoffs and cause the very stacked Dempsey twins to leap out of their seats and jump up and down, which would promote major jiggle. He watched the pitch come in.

"The time has come for you to prove yourself worthy of the crown," his mother said.

Swing and a miss. Damn. "I don't remember hearing anything about that before." He had to watch what he said. The Dempsey twins thought he was just another sexy guy with excellent moves. When dealing with nonmagical women, he kept his fairy status a secret.

Letting it be known would only cause problems. For one thing, people assumed all magical fairies were tiny. Tiny was an option, one he didn't use much. Still, at full size, if he suddenly announced he was a fairy, it would be misinterpreted, to say the least.

"You're hearing about it now," his mother said. "I have an assignment you must complete first."

"This is sounding like *Mission: Impossible*." Leo winced as the batter missed another fastball.

"You'd better hope it's not impossible." His mother was obviously in a mood. "You're perilously close to losing your birthright."

Leo rolled his eyes. Oh, the drama. Meanwhile, the Red Sox catcher called a time-out and loped to the mound to confer with the pitcher. If Leo hoped to finish this phone call before the next pitch, he'd better play along. "All right. What's the assignment?"

"I'm sending you to Big Knob, Indiana, where—"

"Big Knob?" Leo felt the twins' attention on him and realized he'd said that a little too loud. He gave them both a lazy smile as if he'd been referring to himself. "Oh yeah. Big Knob." He hoped to hell his mother wasn't expecting him to deal with George, the juvenile delinquent dragon living in the woods near that Podunk town.

"Your assignment involves a young woman by the name of Gwen Dubois. She owns the local florist shop, Beaucoup Bouquets."

Now, that was more like it. A woman. Maybe even a French woman. "Is this a rescue situation?" He could get into that, especially if she happened to be gorgeous. He didn't want to have to fight any dragons, but from all reports, George didn't like to fight. Leo turned his attention to the game as the catcher hunkered down behind the plate.

"It's sort of a rescue," Queen Beryl said. "She lacks self-confidence with the opposite sex."

Just his luck, she'd be ugly. "And why isn't she self-confident?"

"She doesn't consider herself particularly attractive."

Bingo. "Mom, I don't think—"

"I want you to give her the kind of attention that will change her self-image and make her feel sexy."

Leo preferred his women to be sexy from the get-go. "I'm not really into stuff like that."

"Which is exactly why I'm assigning you this task, Leo. You're to ignore your obsession with external beauty and consider someone else's feelings for a change. You must prove yourself capable of a selfless act."

That hurt. "I can be selfless."

"I've seen very little evidence of it. Oh, and when you go, stay out of the Whispering Forest and away from that dragon, George."

Earlier Leo had hoped not to be assigned to George, but he hated being told what to do. "Why?"

"The dragon is Dorcas and Ambrose Lowell's project."

"Mm." Leo had heard of the witch and wizard who'd been banished to Big Knob because they'd screwed up some spell or other. Leo was curious about that, too, but not enough to make a trip to some piddly small town. "There must be some other assignment you can give me."

"I'm afraid not. Do you want the crown or don't you?"

He wanted it, and apparently he'd have to jump through hoops to get it. He sighed. "Yeah, okay. I'll do it." The pitcher went into his windup. "When do I have to go?"

"Next week."

With a crack of the bat, the hitter sent the ball over the center field fence. Leo jumped to his feet and cheered while the Dempsey twins leaped around and bumped into him with their generous assets. Sweet. "Sorry, Mom!" he yelled into the phone. "Next week is out."

"Why?"

"We're in the playoffs! We might end up in the World Series! Maybe I could go in November."

"Won't work. You'll need plenty of time, and Gwen's closing the shop mid-December to spend the holidays in Arizona with her parents."

If it hadn't been for his acute hearing, Leo wouldn't have picked up on that last sentence. Pandemonium ruled at Safeco Field, and the Dempsey twins became orgasmic in their joy. He looked forward to capitalizing on that in his hotel suite tonight.

"January, then!" he shouted into the phone. "Gotta go, Mom! Bye!" He snapped the phone shut and shoved aside all thoughts of his assignment. Party time!

Chapter 1

In his luxury apartment in Paris's Latin Quarter late that evening, Jean-Marc Chevalier sent one last e-mail to Gwen Dubois in Big Knob, Indiana. Powering down his laptop, he instantly missed the connection they had shared for three weeks.

But if he failed to get off the Internet, he would never be packed for the early morning flight that would take him to meet her. Technically he was going to Chicago for a botanical conference, and Big Knob was only a side trip prompted by an unusual plant sighting. He no longer cared at all about the conference and not much about the plant, either.

He should care about the plant. If it was not a hoax, finding a tropical plant growing in Indiana in the dead of winter would rival anything he had discovered in the Amazon or the Kalahari. Right after New Year's he had received his first e-mail from Gwen about a bromeliad growing on the snowy floor of the forest near Big Knob. She had agreed to keep the discovery a secret while he researched the possibility of such a phenomenon.

Keeping that secret had been easy for him, but not for her, apparently. She had concocted an excuse for his visit, something about a long-lost French relative.

Fortunately the plants were growing in a forest that residents believed was haunted, so nobody went in there, especially during winter.

Being a practical sort, Gwen scoffed at the haunted forest theory and had been sneaking out in the early morning to make sure the plants were still alive. Maybe it was her pluck that drew him, or the intelligence she had shown as they had moved away from the topic of plants and debated everything from the value of hybrid cars to the excellence of California wines.

He had started out calling her Mademoiselle Dubois, as any proper Frenchman would. She had quickly insisted on Gwen, and he was given no choice but to go with Marc. The use of first names made their e-mails seem more intimate, and he had grown to like that. Gradually the botanist had taken a backseat to the man.

The attraction could hardly be physical because they had not exchanged pictures. He had no idea what she looked like and was enjoying the mystery. She could turn out to be homely and plump, but he doubted that. This meeting had a feeling of Fate about it.

Months before she had contacted him, he had decided to attend the conference in Chicago and get his first taste of the U.S. Fortunately, Chicago was within six hours' driving distance of Big Knob, and he had easily changed his flight to come in a few days early. That seemed more than coincidence.

Was Fate throwing him in the path of scientific discovery or romance? Or both? By tomorrow night, he would have the answer to that question.

Taking his suitcase out of the closet, he swung it onto the bed and began to pack. After zipping the suitcase, he stared at it for several long seconds. What if she was as amazing as he expected? What if the chemistry he sensed through their e-mails was the beginning of a major attraction? In other words, should he take condoms?

No. That would be cheeky, taking condoms on a visit to a woman he had never met. He set the suitcase on the floor. Then he hoisted it back onto the bed and unzipped it. Condoms took up little room. No one would have to know he had them unless they became necessary.

Oh, hell, he should not take them. Despite the e-mails, what did they really know about each other? Jumping into bed directly after meeting her reminded him of that horrible American custom the one-night stand. He preferred a more romantic approach. He zipped the suitcase.

Then again, she was used to American men, and he would hate to seem hesitant by comparison. They were not strangers who had met in a bar. She had confided her worries about her mom's arthritis, which had precipitated her parents' move to Arizona. He had mentioned the loss of his parents ten years ago and had confessed his frustration with his younger sister, Josette, who seemed to have no idea what she wanted to do with her life.

On paper, or rather, in e-mail posts, he knew Gwen about as well as or better than he had known some women he had taken to bed. The condom issue might be irrelevant, though. He might not have that box in he bathroom that he vaguely remembered. He should check.

On his way into the bathroom, his BlackBerry rang. Retracing his steps, he grabbed it off the nightstand and looked at the readout. Josette.

He answered and continued on into the bathroom, where he opened the mirrored cabinet over the sink.

"I hate law school."

This was so typical that he had to stop himself from laughing. "You have only started pre-law. Stay with it more than a couple of months, okay?"

"I have been there almost five months, not counting Christmas break. I am not cut out for the courtroom."

"You have never been in the courtroom." Tucking the phone against his shoulder, he opened the condom box. Nearly full. Not surprising. There had been no one since Blaise LaRoche.

"I was today. My professor made us act out a mock trial."

"So soon?"

"He believes in weeding out the misfits. That would be me."

"Josie, it is too early for you to—"

"While I was presenting my opening arguments, I puked all over him. I think they call it projectile vomiting."

Marc squeezed his eyes shut. Poor kid. Sometimes he forgot that she was twenty-two because she acted younger than that. "It was probably something you ate. It could happen to anyone."

"No, it was paralyzing fear. Well, not paralyzing, or I would not have puked, would I? I dropped out of all my pre-law classes."

"But you signed up for something else, I hope?" He saw the money from his parents' trust fund being sucked into the void of Josette's indecision.

"Not yet. I was so horrified that I spent the rest of the day taking Victor and Hugo for a long walk along the Seine. I finally worked up the courage to call you tonight."

Marc prayed for patience. "You need to get into some other courses. How about accounting?"

"Kill me now."

"But math is one of your strong suits." He gazed

at the box of condoms and wondered whether to take a few instead of the whole box. "With accounting, you could avoid getting up in front of people, so there would be less risk of puking on them."

"That would be a benefit." She was silent for a moment. "Do accountants have their own private offices?"

"Sometimes." He decided to take the whole box, just in case.

"I could have a cute little office all to myself and take the dogs as mascots."

"Well, maybe." He was unsure of that. He would much rather see her wind up in an accounting firm with lots of employees, because she tended to be too solitary, but he hated to bring that up and risk alienating her completely. She needed to settle on a steady career before she exhausted all the trust fund money.

Josette sighed. "Maybe I will try it. Oh, I went on a date last night."

"You did?" She hardly dated at all, and he had no ideas for dealing with that, either. She was pretty and smart, but she held herself somewhat aloof.

"Surprising, I know. But he wanted to have sex right away, so I told him to drop dead."

Marc swallowed his first response, which was to demand the bastard's name so he could flatten his nose. "American?"

"No, Italian."

"Well, you made the right decision." Marc had so many questions, questions he lacked the nerve to ask. When she had turned seventeen, he had braved The Talk with her, which had embarrassed them both. He might be ten years older than Josie, but he was still her brother, not a parent. If only their mother were here to guide Josette through this time. . . . But she was not.

The doorbell rang. "Hold on, Josie. Someone is here." He stepped into the hall and opened the door. There stood Blaise, a burgundy velvet cape setting off her platinum hair and a crystal wineglass balanced between two fingers.

He and Blaise had parted ways several months ago, and he had no second thoughts about the split. The social whirl she called a life was not his style.

"I have to go, Josie."

"A girl is at the door, right?"

"Um, yes."

Josette sighed. "Girls always run after you. Apparently you are the social success and I am the geek."

"Josie, you are not a—"

"But I am. So what? Have fun in Chicago. Call me when you get there so I know you arrived safe." Then she hung up.

Wishing he had handled the conversation better, he clicked off the BlackBerry and laid it on the hall table. "Hello, Blaise."

"Hello, yourself." Blaise gave him the once-over, paying particular attention to what he had in his other hand. "I was coming home from a party and saw your light. Do you have company, or is this my lucky night?"

He glanced at the box of condoms. Not much chance of finessing this one. "I . . . I have to pack."

Her carefully groomed eyebrows arched. "For a rendezvous, I assume." She edged her way into the apartment. "Do I know her?"

"No." If only he had left the condoms in the bathroom. He would rather not explain himself.

"So there is someone new." She gestured with the wineglass. "I expected that. You are marvelous in bed."

"So are you."

"Then what went wrong?" She nudged the door shut with the toe of her satin pump.

He smiled. "You wore me out."

"Why not say so? I thought you liked it fast and hot. I can do it slow." She reached for the braided loop holding her cape closed. "Let me show you."

He moved back a step. "In bed you were fine. As I said many times, it was all the parties."

"Funny that you can spend a week in the jungle sleeping in tents, battling snakes, bugs and God knows what else, but one late-night party exhausts you."

"Blaise, I see no point in rehashing this." He paused. "I really do need to finish packing."

"Packing your condoms, you mean." She unfastened her cape and set her wineglass on the hall table. "What if we test-drive one and see how they fit?"

Not long ago he would have taken her up on the offer. A couple of hours of intense sex and he would sleep like a baby on the plane. But that would be unfair to Blaise, and it would be unfair to him, too.

He shook his head. "No."

"Are you sure?"

"Yes."

Pouting, she picked up her wineglass. "You used to be a lot more fun, Marc."

"Sorry to disappoint you." He opened the door.

With a sigh, she walked through it. "You were the only man I could get to do it in Daddy's private box at the opera house."

He remembered that well, and they had come close to being caught, too.

"Good-bye, darling." At the last minute, Blaise turned, clutched him by the back of the head and pulled him down for a kiss.

Only a clod would resist a beautiful woman's at-

tempt to kiss him, and Marc was no clod. Blaise gave
the kiss all she had, supplying plenty of heat and lots
of tongue.

She pulled back, her gaze smoky. Reaching up, she
stroked the cleft in his chin, the one that made shaving
a bitch but seemed to intrigue women. "Still sending
me away?"

Aroused despite his resolve, Marc allowed himself
a few seconds to picture rolling around on his bed
with Blaise. Then he thought about the potential he
sensed in this new relationship with Gwen. "Yes," he
said. "I am."

Gwen's business at Beaucoup Bouquets tended to
slow down in January. Good thing, because she had
something besides flower arranging on her mind these
days. Specifically, a man.

Closing Beaucoup Bouquets at four, she totaled the
register receipts and put on her coat, scarf and boots
in preparation for walking to Click-or-Treat, Big Knob's
Internet café. She'd been ending her day at Click-or-
Treat ever since New Year's.

The Internet was her connection to a certain French
botanist who'd decided to arrive early for his Chicago
conference so he could drive down to meet her. He'd
be in town around seven tomorrow night.

Gwen locked the door and started toward the Internet café, owned by her friend Jeremy Dunstan. Her
route took her past the police and fire department
building, and this time of day she usually ran into
police chief Bob Anglethorpe on his way back to the
station from his afternoon snack of pie and coffee at
the Hob Knob.

She would have planned to meet Marc there tomorrow night, except the restaurant closed at six. That
left two potential scenarios—he could come straight

to her house or she could direct him to the Big Knobian Bar. Because she'd never met him, she'd picked the bar. Assuming he didn't behave like a potential serial killer, she'd invite him home for dinner.

As she passed the police station, the chief came toward her, bundled in a parka and wooly cap with earflaps. "Tomorrow night, isn't it?"

"That's right." Comings and goings were common knowledge in a town of 949 residents.

"Did I hear he'll be staying at the Holiday Inn in Evansville?"

"Uh-huh." Big Knob had no hotel. Everyone thought Marc was a long-lost cousin, but he was still a single man. If he slept at her house, tongues would wag.

"They're predicting snow," Bob said. "If the roads get bad, he should stay in Chicago and drive down Thursday morning. You don't want your newfound relative splattered all over the freeway."

"I'm sure he'll be careful, but thanks for the advice. See you later." She waved and continued on her way.

Weather was an issue this time of year, no question. She'd already warned Marc not to take any foolish chances on the road. He'd laughed off her concern, which hadn't surprised her. Through Internet research she'd discovered he was the plant world's version of Indiana Jones, a guy who thought nothing of swimming across a barracuda-infested river if he could locate an undiscovered plant species on the other side.

A snowy highway wouldn't intimidate him, but if the roads were truly bad and he made it here, anyway, she'd be forced out of good manners to put him up and ignore the gossip. The possibility of a man in her guest room had apparently tweaked her libido, because she'd been having erotic dreams lately.

A blond guy with hot blue eyes and an athlete's physique appeared in various guises—as an officer in uniform, a lifeguard, a cowboy in tight jeans. Her imaginary lover seemed so real that she'd wake up trembling in the aftermath of an orgasm. Was she in such desperate need of a boyfriend that her subconscious had created a virtual one?

If so, her subconscious had done a damn good job of it. Thinking of one particular part of his anatomy, she glanced toward the large granite outcropping that had inspired the early pioneers to name the town Big Knob.

Dusted with snow, it rose 192 feet into the overcast sky, and some claimed it gave people *ideas*. That hadn't been true for her until this past week, but now whenever she gazed at Big Knob, she had plenty of ideas.

She would soon be reading Marc's e-mails, though, so she guiltily squashed those fantasies. No doubt once he arrived, her imaginary lover would disappear, which would mean she didn't have to consider seeing a shrink. For now, though, she couldn't seem to help what she dreamed, and if she woke up in the middle of the night feeling sexually satisfied, that wasn't all bad.

As she cut across the town square, her boots crunched through the frosty grass. The Christmas decorations had come down two weeks ago, and now all that was left was the life-sized bronze of the pioneer woman who had helped settle Big Knob, Isadora Mather.

As Gwen approached the intersection that bordered Click-or-Treat, a red scooter carrying Dorcas and Ambrose Lowell came putt-putting toward her, heading in the direction of Highway 64. Ambrose drove the little scooter, which struggled for traction on the icy street, and Dorcas hung on looking none too happy.

Both wore silvery down jackets with fur-trimmed hoods and black leather gloves. They looked like a couple of upscale Eskimos. Gwen still hadn't figured out why an attractive, middle-aged couple like the Lowells had moved here from Sedona to set up a matchmaking and marriage counseling business. The matchmaking hadn't drawn too many customers, but the marriage counseling was a hit, much to Gwen's surprise.

"Gwen!" Ambrose waved, which temporarily made him lose control of the scooter. Dorcas yelped and hung on as Ambrose straightened his course and brought the scooter to a shaky stop beside Gwen.

Although Gwen was eager to get to the café and read her e-mail, she decided to stop, at least for a minute. She had the Lowells to thank for making the connection with Marc, although there'd been absolutely no matchmaking involved in that, fortunately. She wasn't into such things, but she was grateful to Dorcas and Ambrose for helping her make the initial contact.

The connection with Marc had been all about plants. Because the Lowells were from out of town, they didn't believe the Whispering Forest was haunted and they liked to spend time there. One day they'd stumbled upon several strange plants and had dug one up to see if she could ID it. When she'd drawn a blank, Ambrose had suggested checking Internet sources, which had led them to Marc.

"Hi, there," she said. "Isn't it a little chilly riding on that thing?" That was another oddity about the Lowells—they made do with a scooter instead of buying a car like normal people. During the winter months they sometimes borrowed a car from their assistant, Maggie Madigan, but Maggie probably needed it more now that she had a two-month-old baby.

"Brisk," Ambrose said.

"Freezing," Dorcas said. "We'd intended to use Maggie's car, but it's in the shop."

"Which is silly," Ambrose said. "I could have fixed it for her."

Dorcas cleared her throat. "She's probably remembering the last time, when you managed to reverse the gas- and brake-pedal functions."

Gwen worked hard not to smile. Ambrose was something of a lovable goof, and she could easily imagine him screwing up car repair. "How's Maggie's baby?"

"Wonderful." Dorcas's eyes shone. "Little Daisy is such a joy. When Maggie comes back to work full-time in a couple of months, she'll be bringing Daisy."

Ambrose whipped around on the scooter seat, nearly dislodging his wife. "Daisy? In the office?"

Dorcas patted his arm. "It'll be fine. So, Gwen, is the potted plant still healthy?"

"Yes, but it should be, protected in the house. Amazingly enough, the ones in the forest still look perky, too, even after the freeze we had last night. Are you headed out to see how they're doing?"

"Yes," said Dorcas. "We'll let you know if they're still okay. We don't want Monsieur Chevalier to get here and see a bunch of dead plants."

"No, we don't." Gwen found it intimidating to hear Marc referred to by his last name. She supposed technically he should be called *Doctor* Chevalier, but he'd never used his title in his e-mails, and now he was simply Marc to her. She sometimes forgot he was such a big deal to those in his field.

"Are you excited about his visit?" Ambrose asked.

"Sure." She kept telling herself that Ambrose and Dorcas couldn't possibly have engineered this meeting with Marc. It wasn't as if they'd caused the plants to appear in the Whispering Forest.

But they were matchmakers, so logically they would be interested in this meeting even if they'd had nothing to do with it. She'd briefly considered consulting them for advice when Marc had announced he was coming, but she didn't have extra money for that. Besides, she'd vowed not to manipulate the situation with Marc. Either it would work out between them or it wouldn't.

"Frenchmen usually appreciate a fine wine," Dorcas said. "We have an excellent vintage we brought from Sedona. Why don't we give you a bottle to share with Monsieur Chevalier?"

Gwen had heard of this wine that the Lowells kept in their cellar. She knew of two couples in town who had each enjoyed a bottle of it and were now married. That had to be a wild coincidence, and Gwen wasn't usually superstitious, but she decided to decline the offer.

"Thanks for being willing to share," she said, "but I picked up a couple of bottles of good California wine in Evansville." She'd done that on purpose, because she and Marc had gotten into this silly debate about French versus California wines, and she wanted to make sure he at least tasted some she considered decent. Assuming he seemed harmless and she invited him home to dinner.

Ambrose cleared his throat. "I don't like to brag, but Mystic Hills wine beats any wine I've ever tasted. If you don't believe me, come by tonight and we'll give you a sample. It'll blow you away."

"That's very generous, but I think I'll stick with what I have." She hesitated. "You know, I'm probably a fool not to hire you to help me, but I . . . want to see if things will develop naturally."

"Do you think we're trying to meddle in your relationship with Monsieur Chevalier?" Dorcas's amber eyes grew wide.

"I'm sure you wouldn't. But you might think you could help, especially because I'm not the most experienced girl when it comes to relationships."

"Nonsense," Dorcas said. "You'll be fine."

"Well, the way I figure it, either Marc and I will get along or—" She shrugged. "We won't."

"So it's *Marc*, then?" Dorcas smiled.

Gwen felt her cheeks warm. "We've e-mailed quite a bit, and it seemed silly to keep using—"

"I think it's wonderful," Dorcas said. "Well, Ambrose, we need to be off before it really starts snowing. I felt a couple of flakes. Have a good evening." She tapped Ambrose on the shoulder and the little scooter wobbled off, the wheels slipping on the slick road.

Talk about a couple of flakes. But they were lovable flakes, and Gwen was sure they meant well. She would have been worried about their safety riding around on that ridiculous scooter, but traffic was nonexistent right now. Traffic was nonexistent most of the time in Big Knob, which was why they had no stoplight in town.

Gazing after the departing couple, she sighed. They might have given up for the time being, but it was increasingly obvious they were dying to step in and demonstrate their matchmaking skills. She didn't plan to let them. Once Marc arrived, she'd closely monitor his interaction with Dorcas and Ambrose Lowell.

Chapter 2

Dorcas leaned forward and spoke into Ambrose's ear so he could hear her over the noise of the scooter. "So much for that wine maneuver."

"We'll think of something else," Ambrose said over his shoulder.

She didn't know what, and time was running short, but more conversation with Ambrose was a bad idea. That one over-the-shoulder comment had resulted in another skid. She held her breath as he brought them out of it.

Stupid scooter. She'd never liked the thing, not from the day he'd brought it home more than a year ago. But they couldn't risk traveling on her broom in broad daylight, and walking all the way to the Whispering Forest in the winter was even less fun than riding on the scooter. She was ready for a car, except the terms of their banishment forbade traveling more than five miles away from Big Knob, so a car seemed like an unnecessary expense.

Fortunately it had stopped snowing. The big storm wasn't due until sometime tomorrow, maybe after Jean-Marc Chevalier had hit town. Dorcas hadn't ever tried to mess with the weather. Weather changes had more far-reaching consequences than she wanted to be responsible for. The snowstorm, if it should strand Jean-Marc in Big Knob, would be a happy accident.

As they passed Sean and Maggie's stately Victorian on the way out of town, Dorcas glanced over with a sense of pride. She and Ambrose had engineered that match, and now the house seemed to glow with happiness. She pictured little Daisy inside, sleeping or nursing, and wished there was time to stop.

But it would be dark soon. They needed to revitalize the plants and get them ready for another freeze tonight, plus see if they could make contact with George. She'd been so encouraged by the New Year's resolutions he'd dictated to Ambrose on January first. She pulled the list from her pocket.

1. Stop playing poker with the raccoons.
2. Patrol the forest at least once every eight hours.
3. Stop scaring people with the disembodied eyes trick.
4. Stop whining that life is unfair.

Until about a week ago, he'd kept those resolutions.

Then recently she and Ambrose had found evidence of late-night poker games, although George insisted he'd been asleep by nine. Just yesterday Jeff Brady, owner of the Big Knobian Bar, had snowshoed into the forest and claimed to have seen a pair of eyes floating in the trees. That was classic George.

The dragon had denied all knowledge of that, too, and he'd compounded his transgression by complaining that life was completely unfair. When he forgot to patrol every eight hours, he blamed his supposed case of ADD. Dorcas was at her wit's end with him.

If George failed to earn his golden scales, the Wizarding Council would require Dorcas and Ambrose to stay in Big Knob indefinitely to monitor his progress. That was no longer Dorcas's biggest concern, though. Primarily, she wanted George to grow up and accept his duties as Guardian of the Forest, because his refusal to do so was disrupting the natural order of things. She hated when that happened.

Ambrose swung the scooter left into the snow-covered dirt road leading into the forest. At once the scooter's front tire plowed into a drift and the motorized part of the journey came to an end. Ever since the first snowfall, they'd been parking the scooter at the end of the road and walking in.

Yes, they could have melted a roadway through the snow if they'd wanted to, but that seemed like a selfish and unnecessary use of magic. The plants they'd introduced into the forest were enough interference with nature, but they hadn't been able to figure out any other way to get Monsieur Chevalier to Big Knob.

Last summer, their scrying had revealed him as Gwen's soul mate, but his place of residence had presented quite a challenge to the matchmaking. They'd caught a break when he accepted the invitation to the Chicago conference, and they'd leaped on the opportunity.

Ambrose turned off the motor and lowered the stand before climbing off and helping Dorcas down. "Did you remember your wand?"

"It's inside my parka." Last week she'd managed to forget it, and the trip had been wasted. She hadn't been able to bolster the plants' immunity to cold or charge George's iPod. The plants had survived, but George had been p.o.'d about his iPod. She hoped he wasn't so childish that he'd used that as an excuse for breaking his resolutions.

"I'm worried about this meeting between Gwen and Jean-Marc," Ambrose said as he began trudging along the path their boots had created in the past few days.

"At least they're on a first-name basis. And being soul mates should count for something, even if we haven't been able to work with Gwen. I just wish she'd do something with her hair."

"Actually, she's going in for a haircut tomorrow at four. I heard her tell Jeremy that while I was in Click-or-Treat yesterday. She talks to him more than any-body, I think."

"I'm not surprised. They're a lot alike, both on the geeky side." Dorcas caught a flutter of wings from the corner of her eye. She turned, but didn't see a bird. There were only a few this time of year, mostly blue jays and cardinals.

"And they both miss Annie," Ambrose said. "Jere-my's not one to complain, but he and Annie are still almost newlyweds. I'm sure it's tough to be separated."

"Sure. And Gwen doesn't have any other close girl-friends besides Annie." Dorcas heard the rustle of wings but still couldn't spot a bird. Strange, because with the leaves gone and snow blanketing the ever-greens, a blue jay or cardinal would stand out. Dorcas shook her head and continued walking. Maybe she was imagining things.

"Speaking of Annie," Ambrose said, "we've been at a major disadvantage with her off researching the Loch Ness Monster. I'll bet she could have convinced Gwen to come and see us before Jean-Marc hits town."

"I think so, too." Dorcas sighed. "Bad timing."

"If only Gwen had agreed to take the wine. That would have been something to jump-start things."

"You know, Ambrose, I'm afraid word is getting out about that wine."

"But we've only used it twice."

"And that's a lot in a town this size," Dorcas said. "The wine now has a reputation, and Gwen hasn't cultivated her spirit of adventure. But there has to be a way to influence that first meeting."

Ambrose shook his head. "I don't know how. I'm running out of ideas. I don't have much faith in the Bob and Weave's ability to transform her, either."

"Darling, you're a genius! That's it!"

Ambrose stopped in his tracks. "What?"

"The hair appointment! I'll see if I can book one at the same time as Gwen's."

Ambrose gazed at her in horror. "You're not actually going to let them do your hair, are you?"

"Why not?"

"When the shop owner's hair is four different colors, I'd say you'd better watch out. I like your hair the way you do it."

Knowing how men felt about a woman changing her hairstyle, Dorcas didn't comment. But the casual brunette bob she'd worn for years had recently begun boring her to tears.

"You won't let them do anything drastic, will you?" Ambrose looked worried.

"Of course not." Which in woman-speak meant that anything short of shaving her head was okay with her. "But if I get an appointment, I won't be around to remind you to turn on the exit sign. You won't forget, will you?"

"Don't worry. I'll remember."

"Maybe I should set a timer."

"Dorcas, I'll remember, okay?"

"If you say so." But she worried about it, anyway. When they'd first moved to town Ambrose had decided to bespell the exit sign on the interstate to control access to the town. With the sign off, no one could find the exit, and Ambrose had loved that concept. He'd insisted they didn't want surprise visitors when they were trying to rehabilitate a problem dragon.

In a town as small as Big Knob, they usually heard when friends and relatives were expected, and Ambrose would turn the sign back on. At least he would most of the time. Once he'd forgotten and a belly dancer hadn't showed up for a bachelor party, but that had worked out. Tomorrow night, though, it was critical that the sign be on for Jean-Marc.

The road into the forest became more clogged with drifts, which slowed their progress. Finally they reached a small trail leading off to the right. Glancing around to make sure they hadn't been followed, Dorcas started through the trees. They'd chosen a remote spot for the plants with the hope that no one besides Gwen would be able to find them. The local belief that the forest was haunted helped the cause.

"Every time we come I expect them to be dead," Ambrose said, following behind her.

"They only have to last for a couple more days. The catalogue said they could be maintained in a hostile climate for up to a month, so I think we'll make it." She rounded a bend in the path and there were the tropical plants, five of them. With their waxy leaves, they looked fake, as if someone had stuck plastic luau decorations in the snow as a joke.

Each one was about two feet high, with dark green outer leaves and a red spiky center. The wizarding catalogue had described them as *a magical bromeliad copy that will fool the most dedicated gardener into thinking a winter miracle has taken place.*

The plants were supposed to be a practical joke, but one that only a witch or wizard would appreciate. Jean-Marc wouldn't know what they were, and while he was busy analyzing them, he would be spending time with Gwen. Now, if only Dorcas could work a little miracle of her own in the beauty salon tomorrow, she'd—

"This dragon was born to dance!" In a swirl of smoke, George appeared in the clearing, all two thousand pounds of him. "What Georgey-Porgy needs is a partner!"

Before Dorcas could protest, the green-scaled dragon had snatched her up and spun her around in time to the music he heard through the earbuds of his white iPod. She gasped and opened her mouth to complain, but Ambrose beat her to it.

"George, put her down."

Dorcas thought he sounded irritatingly calm, but then he wasn't the one being held eight feet in the air, legs dangling. "I appreciate your enthusiasm, George," she said, "but one of your claws is poking me in the back."

"And besides that," Ambrose added, "you're about to trample the—oops, there goes one now."

"The bromeliads!" Dorcas rapped him on his snout. "Stop dancing. You're squishing the bromeliads."

"The whosit?"

"The plants we put in to attract Gwen's soul mate!"

"But he's coming, right?" George twirled her around again. "So the bromo-whatsis don't matter now."

"Yes, they do." Dorcas managed to extract her wand from under her parka and tap the iPod. "If you want that thing recharged, you'd better cool it."

"So you've decided to be Dorcas Downer today." Rolling his eyes, George set her on her feet again. "I was gonna show you the move I learned from the raccoons. They've been watching *Dancing with the Stars*."

"How?" Dorcas had an image of several extension cords strung together and hooked up to the nearest house, which would be Maggie and Sean's. The raccoons weren't above stealing a TV and jerry-rigging an antenna, either.

"The same way they watch anything," George said.

"They set up a bench outside somebody's window so they can peek in. It's not fair that they can do that and I'm stuck here in the forest."

Dorcas held up four fingers. "And what resolution did you just break?"

"I can't help it! It's *not* fair. The raccoons have it so easy."

"But they don't have a duty to guard the forest, and you do. I wish you'd—"

"Dorcas, you'd better bring your wand over," Ambrose said. "We'll need a spell to repair this plant."

She turned to find Ambrose crouched beside a flattened bromeliad. "Bacchus's britches," she swore softly.

"What's the big problemo?" George lowered his head and peered at the plant. "Just dig it up and toss it. You still got four."

"Yes, but Gwen saw five this morning." Dorcas blew out a breath. "If one's suddenly gone, we'll have to explain it." She searched her memory for a spell that would revive a crushed magical plant. Nothing was coming to her.

"I can handle this." George cleared his throat. "Stand back."

Ambrose looked up. "What are you—yikes!" He leaped out of the way as George torched the bromeliad.

"There you go." The dragon brushed his claws together and gazed at the smoldering and blackened leaves. "You can start the praise any time now."

"What's to praise?" Dorcas glared at him. "You burned it to a crisp. I might have been able to uncrush it, but there's no way I can bring it back now."

George continued to look smug. "Yeah, but you can blame it on lightning."

"Except that there's been no storm." Dorcas stared at the blackened plant.

"You could make one." George sounded excited by the prospect.

"No. I don't like fooling with weather."

"Sheesh, it's one little bolt of lightning," George said. "A few megawatts. What's the big deal?"

"I'm not doing lightning."

"Then how about this?" George scooped up a boulder the size of a grocery cart and dropped it on the plant, spraying them all with snow.

Ambrose wiped the snow from his face. "Can't see the plant anymore. I'll give you that."

Dorcas decided they'd fooled with this problem enough. "Okay. We'll tell Gwen a deer ate one of them. But you'll have to do something about your dragon prints all over the place, George."

"Love to." George swished his tail, almost knocking Ambrose to the ground. "Happy now? And don't forget to power me up." He held out his iPod. "Do it to it, dudette."

Dorcas pierced him with her most intimidating stare. "George, I need to know once and for all. Are you playing poker with the raccoons?"

"For the millionth, trillionth time, no, negative, not on your life."

"We've found evidence of games going on," Ambrose said. "And they only play when they think they can win something from a nonraccoon, which would be you."

"It's not me."

"But who else . . ." Ambrose groaned. "I hope Isadora's not back in town. That witch is a pain in the tuckus."

"She's not back," Dorcas said. "I'm sure I'd know."

She studied George and had to admit his righteous indignation rang true. "All right, let's not worry about this any more tonight. Give me the iPod and I'll charge it up for you."

The charging took less than five minutes. Then she placed a warming spell on the remaining four plants, said good-bye to George and started back down the path with Ambrose following right behind.

"Something's going on," Ambrose said as soon as they were out of George's hearing.

"Yes, I know. But I don't think George is the one responsible this time."

"The raccoons don't play poker for the hell of it, only if they see some potential gain."

"I know that, too." Dorcas thought about the bird she'd been unable to see, even though she'd caught a glimpse of something flying and heard the flutter of wings. "We need to make another trip out here at midnight, and this time we'll take the broom."

"It'll be colder than a pair of frozen testicles tonight."

"I don't look forward to it any more than you do, but I think there's another magical creature living in the forest."

Although Gwen worried that she didn't look glamorous or sophisticated enough for Marc, she had no doubt he'd love her little house. Her father had come to this country at the age of six, carrying fond memories of the French countryside. After settling in Big Knob with Gwen's mother, Rachel, he'd re-created the cottage where he'd been born. He'd told Gwen so many stories of living there that she'd developed a passion for anything French.

Now that the house belonged to her, she'd lovingly preserved the atmosphere. Fragrant bouquets of herbs and flowers from the greenhouse dangled upside down from rough-hewn beams. Textured walls and sturdy furniture contributed to the look, as did copper-bottomed pots hanging in the kitchen. Although the appliances were thoroughly modern, the kitchen gave the impression of rustic living, complete with hand-made pottery stacked on open shelves.

But the bedroom was Gwen's favorite room in the house. A four-poster she'd inherited from her parents was made up with high-thread-count sheets that she'd aged with tea, softened with many launderings, and hand-embroidered to look like heirloom linens. She'd added a feather bed topper to the mattress and mounds of goose-down pillows. She loved going to bed every night and had always slept soundly.

Until this week. These days she put on her night-gown and slipped between the sheets with a combination of anticipation and anxiety. With Marc showing up tomorrow night, she intended to pay close attention to what happened and try to analyze exactly what was triggering her erotic dreams.

She used the word *dreams*, and yet they seemed so much stronger than that. *Hallucinations* was more like it. And she had orgasms. Dear God, did she have orgasms—two, three, and one night a grand total of four.

Although her phantom lover had a specific face and body build, he didn't look like anyone she remembered meeting. He wasn't a stand-in for any of the movie stars she liked, either. He might vaguely resemble Brad Pitt, but Gwen had never been a huge Brad Pitt fan.

Colin Firth was more her type. She'd watched *Pride and Prejudice* more times than she cared to admit. Logically she should have created a fantasy with Colin Firth in the starring role.

Her blond dream guy had a swimmer's build—lean hips and broad shoulders. His smile could turn from angelic to deliciously wicked in a second. He also insisted on calling her by her full name, Gwendolyn, and every time he said it, she trembled with lust.

During the dream she would swear he was really there in her bed, but each time she woke in the middle of the night, her sheets soaked with sweat and her own orgasmic juices, she was alone. She'd gone so far as to get up and check all the locks, but they'd been secure.

Tonight would be different, she vowed. Tonight she'd stay in control. Closing her eyes, she allowed herself to sink deep into the feather bed. A plump pillow cradled her head and the soft sheets slid over her ivory silk nightgown.

Although she didn't count on becoming sexually involved with Marc, especially during this first visit, she hadn't ruled that out, either. She'd owned the silk nightgowns for years in anticipation of someday having a torrid love affair. Torrid love affairs did exist in Big Knob, but she hadn't been lucky enough to participate in one.

A torrid love affair with a Frenchman would be far more than she'd ever hoped for. She wanted to be prepared. She wanted Marc to think she wore silk every night, and that she had more sexual experience than her one youthful affair during her college days.

Holding the thought of Marc firmly in her mind, she drifted toward sleep.

Her dream came swiftly as her blond lover appeared at her bedside, dressed as a pirate. Tight breeches showed off his considerable package, and a loose white shirt hung open to his waist, revealing his powerful chest. Miraculously, his blond hair was longer tonight, more in keeping with the costume he wore.

His tricornered hat sported a feather and was decorated with the traditional skull-and-crossbones insignia.

Gwen's blood heated, as it always did when her dream lover appeared. But she didn't *want* to want him. She should leave her heart and mind open to the possibility of Marc.

The briny scent of the sea wafted through the room as the man tossed his hat on the bedpost and leaned over her. "Gwendolyn, may I make love to you?"

She tried to resist the lure of him, but he was so sexy, so confident. In the end, she lost the battle with herself. "Yes," she murmured.

Chapter 3

Prince Leo hadn't expected to enjoy himself so much, but he could get used to having sex with Gwendolyn every night. She was one hot chick. Or at least she was once she took off her dowdy clothes and ugly glasses. The silk nightgowns were a nice touch, too. He always left them on, bunching them up around her neck during their hot sessions, then pulling them back down before he left her bed.

He'd arrived in Big Knob a week ago, transporting himself by the normal fairy method. He'd simply stood outside the castle at Atwood and imagined himself in the Whispering Forest. The whole process had taken about five seconds. In times like these, when he heard humans complaining about the hassles of plane travel, he was grateful that he had an alternative method for getting around.

Although he disliked minimizing himself, he'd done it when he first arrived in order to flit around and scope out the situation. Being small and airborne had worked for every situation except when that witch and wizard were around. He needed to keep track of them and their scheme to bring some damned Frenchman to town for Gwen. She didn't need a Frenchman when she had him.

He'd been eavesdropping on the Lowells this afternoon and had almost been spotted. Good thing he could maneuver like a stunt pilot. The witch, Dorcas, might have thought she'd seen something, but he'd flown away before she could be sure.

He'd decided early on that invading Gwendolyn's dreams would be the way to conduct this campaign, and after a week he was positive he'd made the right decision. At night her defenses were down, and besides, she had that awesome bed.

He'd perfected dream sex years ago and was proud of his skill. Too bad it wasn't something he could mention to his mother, so she'd know he wasn't a complete slacker. But he and his mother didn't discuss sex.

He'd mastered slipping into a woman's dream dressed as one of her fantasies. If she was especially responsive, and Gwendolyn certainly qualified, then he could give her several orgasms before inevitably one would be so powerful it would wake her up.

Leo was an expert at knowing when that would happen, and his own climax was exquisitely timed to match her last one. To that technique he'd added another, this one even more difficult and exceedingly valuable.

At sixteen, upon discovering a trap door into a dusty, long-forgotten chamber deep within the castle, he'd come across a trunk containing old books. His father's name had been inscribed inside the cover of *Sexual Secrets for Fairies*, so naturally he'd started to read. On page ten, he'd hit gold.

The ancient fairy trick had required hours of solo practice, but as a hormonal teenager, he hadn't minded at all. When the practice had ended, he'd learned to vaporize his semen. From his first sexual encounter to these nights with Gwendolyn, his partners had been left with nothing but memories.

This ability had served him well over the years, primarily as birth control. But it had also made him quite popular with the ladies. He was free to reveal his secret to the magical ones, who claimed the puff of air greatly enhanced their orgasmic experience.

Nonmagical women couldn't be told about his powers, of course, so they credited him with amazing self-control. As for oral sex, magical women were more than willing to indulge him since all they had to swallow was a little air. He'd had to forgo the experience with the nonmagical ladies, however. They just wouldn't understand.

He was so proud of this feat that he'd considered offering classes to other male fairies. Two things kept him from doing it. If he taught others, then he would cease to be special. And then there was his mother. Somehow he couldn't see her being thrilled with such classes, even though they'd perform a charitable service far greater than anything she'd dreamed up so far.

Still, instead of constantly criticizing him for being such a party animal, she might take the time to notice that he'd created no unwanted pregnancies, no little bundles of peasant joy to embarrass the throne. He had one small concern. He'd been vaporizing for so many years that he wasn't sure if he could reverse the process. A fairy prince would be expected to produce an heir.

Plenty of time to worry about that, though. At the moment he had the luxury of concentrating on the voluptuous Gwendolyn, who was responding to his initial caresses with her usual abandon. She'd begun to moan and beg him to take off his clothes. She believed in his pirate disguise and he was glad he'd taken the time to use a sea-scented cologne to make the experience more vivid.

So much for that Marc character. Leo wasn't about

to let some guy from Paris horn in now that the program was going so well. He'd bet his retractable wings that another week of good sex would transform Gwendolyn into a babe on the outside, too. She'd have her confidence; he'd have his crown. It was all good.

And this . . . this was *very* good. He had an erection the size of the Space Needle. He climbed from the bed so he could shuck his breeches and shirt faster.

Then he was back in that cozy bed with a woman who was already halfway to her first orgasm. Tonight he was tired of bunching the nightgown at her neck. He wanted her completely naked.

"Lift your arms," he said softly.

She obeyed, and he slipped the nightgown over her head. He'd put it back on later when she was limp with satisfaction. "You're incredible," he murmured in her ear as he reached between her thighs and slid his fingers inside her wet vagina.

Her question came in a breathless rush. "Who are you?"

"A friend." *And this is what friends are for.*

"I need to know." She writhed against the sheets and gasped as he brought her to the brink. "Please."

"This is all you need to know." And he sent her over the edge. "Am I right?"

"Yes!" She arched in his arms, lifting her glorious breasts.

He feasted on them as he withdrew his hand and moved over her. She was still skimming the waves following her first climax, and more than ready for another. Relinquishing the pleasure of her breasts, he entered her quickly and pumped fast, taking her up to the heights again.

"Come for me, you sassy wench."

She did, making the bedroom ring with her cries.

As the spasms rolled over his aching penis, he gritted his teeth to keep his own orgasm in check. He prided himself on being able to climax on cue, and not a moment before. But when he was buried deep in this woman, he had trouble holding back.

With a groan of surrender, he came. He would have loved to stay and enjoy the aftereffects of his climax, but that would be idiocy. If she woke up and realized he was a little more real than she'd thought, she'd probably start screaming and pop him in the nose.

No, he had to leave, no matter how much he was enjoying this soft bed, and return to his less well-appointed cave in the forest. Grabbing his pants, shirt and pirate hat, he slipped out of her dream a split second before she woke up panting and slick with moisture. He'd go scare up those raccoons and play poker for the rest of the night. He felt a winning streak coming on.

As always, Gwen sat up with a jolt, her body trembling from her recent orgasm. Cool air hit her bare breasts, and she realized she was naked. Had she peeled off her nightgown in her sleep?

Still flushed, she leaned over and switched on the bedside lamp. Her nightgown lay on the bed beside her in a crumpled ivory heap. The covers were in a jumbled mess, and she felt terrific, but a little worried, too.

The blond guy had shown up again, despite her best efforts. Her subconscious must have dredged him up from somewhere, some chance meeting that she'd forgotten. Now she was fantasizing about him in her dreams, and apparently . . . this was the part that made her blush . . . pleasuring herself in her sleep.

She hadn't known such a thing was possible. Wouldn't it take more coordination than a sleeping person possessed? Or maybe it was like sleepwalking, only this was sleep-masturbating, complete with ripping off her nightgown and giving herself several orgasms.

She hoped such a thing wouldn't happen when she was with a real man, like, for instance, *Marc.* Dear God, she'd die of humiliation if someone caught her doing this. Maybe she'd have to see a shrink, after all.

What a time to have a potential boyfriend coming to town. At least he was French, and they were supposed to be more open-minded. Still, she couldn't imagine how any man would react if he witnessed something like that.

She took a deep breath in an attempt to calm herself. The air smelled of the sea. *The sea?* She was hundreds of miles from the sea. Was she truly going nuts, or was someone sneaking into her house wearing sea-scented cologne?

Scrambling from the bed, she took time to pull on her nightgown before making a thorough search of the house. The locks were secure, but they always were. She checked every closet, behind the sofa, behind the drapes, in the shower, behind every door, and under the bed.

The cottage was empty.

Slowly she returned to the bedroom and took another sniff. The scent was fainter, but still there. She'd been to the ocean once with her parents, and this was exactly how it had smelled. Nothing in her house would account for that aroma, either.

But how could anyone slip into her bedroom without her knowing, have wild sex with her, and then disappear? She tried to remember if anyone had a key. She'd had no reason to give one out. Her parents had the only other key, and they were careful about such things. They would never allow a copy to be made.

Locks could be picked, of course, and she supposed these were old enough to make that easy for a professional. Still, anyone picking her locks would have to have amazing skill to get in without her knowing, night after night, and leave with the same stealth. And for what reason? To have great sex with her?

The hairs prickled on the back of her neck. She'd told no one about these dreams because she'd considered them a figment of her imagination. But her imagination had never produced something as realistic as the fresh sea air.

She tried to see herself reporting this to Bob Anglethorpe. Bob was middle-aged, married, and on the conservative side. Gwen pictured walking into the police station with her complaint.

Hi, Bob. I'd like to report a case of breaking and entering. Actually, they didn't break anything, but they sure did enter, giving me multiple orgasms in the process. This last time, after they left, I could swear I smelled ocean air.

No, she couldn't make that report. The only person she could imagine confiding in was currently on assignment in Scotland. Her best friend, Annie, was writing a scientific series on mythical creatures and was currently investigating supposed sightings of the Loch Ness Monster.

Annie would listen to Gwen and not judge or think she was crazy, but her friend wasn't here. That meant only one option remained—to hope that once Marc arrived, these nightly episodes would end.

Gwen glanced at the clock and discovered it was midnight. Automatically she calculated the time difference between Big Knob and Paris, something she'd been doing ever since making contact with Marc. In a few short hours, Marc would board a plane for Chicago.

He'd arranged to rent a car after he landed, so he could drive down to Big Knob. Gwen had been nervous about meeting him, but after this incident with sea air, she welcomed his visit. She had no idea what would happen, except that having Marc show up would change things.

After all, his last name meant "knight" in French. Somehow, some way, he would fix this situation. She just knew it.

Dorcas managed to get a hair appointment that coincided with Gwen's haircut and manicure. At four on the dot, Dorcas walked into the Bob and Weave and discovered that Francine had started on Gwen, which left Dorcas with the only other stylist, Sylvia Hepplewaite.

Although Ambrose had been scandalized by Francine's multicolored hair, Dorcas would have taken Francine over Sylvia, a flashy blonde who had a reputation for talking about her sexual experiences during appointments. Dorcas liked sex—a lot—but she wasn't crazy about discussing orgasms while she was having her hair done.

Her preferences didn't matter, though. Francine was the more competent stylist, and Gwen needed a good haircut more than Dorcas did. If Sylvia ruined Dorcas's magically created look, she'd go home and cook up a brew to fix it. At least that was the theory. She'd never had to repair a beautician's work before, so she didn't have the spells and potions handy.

That was the least of her worries, anyway. It seemed they had a fairy prince living in the Whispering Forest.

After a chilling ride out there at midnight, she and Ambrose had prowled through the trees as they followed the sounds of a poker game in progress. From the cover of the evergreens, they'd observed the raccoons playing with a handsome blond guy dressed like a pirate. The fact that he sat in the clearing with no coat on gave him away. Fairies were impervious to heat and cold.

Fairies also had extremely acute hearing. Unfortunately Ambrose had stepped on a twig. The prince had immediately reduced his size to a height of six inches, sprouted wings and escaped into the darkness. Of course, that had been the fluttering she'd heard yesterday afternoon, too.

Even with such a quick look, Dorcas thought she'd recognized the prince. Leo of Atwood was a notorious playboy, though, and Dorcas couldn't figure out what he was doing in an isolated place like Big Knob. Because it had been pointless to try finding him in the dark now that he knew they'd seen him, they'd gone home.

Just what they didn't need—a playboy prince living in the forest. But she had to put Prince Leo out of her mind for now. Her mission today involved convincing Gwen to try the beautifying facial masque Dorcas had spent the day making. She'd assigned Ambrose the job of researching the prince while she brewed the masque from a tried-and-true formula.

As she walked to the counter, Francine looked up from the shampoo bowl where she was washing Gwen's hair. "Hi, Dorcas. You'll be with Sylvia. She's due back from her break any minute. Go ahead and take off your coat and have a seat. Can I get you coffee?"

"I'm fine, thanks." Dorcas hung her coat on one of the hooks by the front door. Then she chose a wicker chair in the front of the salon and debated which issue of *People* to read. Ambrose might be addicted to My-Space, which he accessed every day at the Internet café, but Dorcas's secret vice was tabloids. She never tired of celebrity gossip.

Besides, reading a magazine would make her appear relaxed and part of the beauty salon scene. She wanted everyone to believe she'd come to have her hair done, not to foist her facial masque on Gwen. Coaxing Gwen to try it would require careful timing.

She had another trick up her sleeve, or rather, around her neck. Although this was the zero hour, so to speak, she still had ways of influencing this coming meeting between Gwen and Marc. Ambrose had done his part by bringing them together on the Internet. Now it was up to her to make sure the first encounter went well.

She opened the magazine and flipped to an article that caught her interest. Then it occurred to her that in a beauty salon, she could discuss it, unlike when she was with Ambrose, who abhorred celebrity gossip. That was a beauty salon benefit she hadn't thought about before.

"Oh, good grief," she said. "Can you believe the latest about Britney Spears?"

"She's a newsmaker, that one." Francine rinsed the conditioner out of Gwen's hair. "Do you remember when she was hitting the nightclubs minus her underwear?"

Sylvia breezed in through the back door and took off her parka. "No underwear? That's not a big deal. Guys love it when you show up for a date with no underwear, right, Gwen?"

"Never tried it," Gwen said from the depths of the shampoo bowl.

"You should," Sylvia said. "A French guy like Marc might expect those kinds of surprises. So, are you ready, Dorcas?"

"Sure." Dorcas put down the magazine and walked over to Sylvia's station. "Thanks for taking me on such short notice." She set her purse on the counter and sat in Sylvia's swivel chair.

"No problemo. What a gorgeous pendant. What's that stone?"

"It's Larimar." The translucent blue-green stone was said to be connected to the lost city of Atlantis, and Dorcas could testify to its power. When she wore it, she was filled with feelings of love and invincibility. She hoped that before the afternoon was over, she'd be able to bestow its powers on Gwen.

"I've never seen anything like it." Sylvia started to tuck under the collar of Dorcas's daffodil yellow blouse. "This is silk, isn't it?"

"Yes."

Sylvia pulled back the collar, peeked at the label, and whistled. "We're not risking this little number." Opening a drawer, she took out a teal smock and handed it to Dorcas. "You can use the bathroom to change."

"All right." Dorcas would have worn something less expensive, but she didn't own any ratty outfits. If a person lived a long life, that person had more time to acquire fine clothes. Being stuck in Big Knob meant she had to order from catalogues these days, but she'd become quite proficient at that.

Soon she was smocked up and back in Sylvia's chair.

"Much better." Sylvia clipped a towel around her neck. "You've never been in before, have you?"

"No. I've done my own hair for years, but I thought it would be fun to let someone else handle the job today."

"You've come to the right place." Sylvia snapped a purple plastic cape around Dorcas's shoulders.

Dorcas decided not to mention that she'd come to

the *only* place, unless she'd chosen to have her hair cut at the barber shop.

Sylvia ran her fingers through Dorcas's chin-length hair. "How about something different today, something daring?"

"I'll consider that. But before we start on my hair, I have a huge favor to ask." She reached for her purse. "I just ordered this new facial masque, and I'd love to have you apply it before my shampoo. That should give it enough time to work."

Sylvia took the red jar Dorcas handed her. "Wow, this looks like a high-end product. I've never seen such a gorgeous jar. Where did you get it?"

"It's a very exclusive shop. It's pricey. But it works miracles." She glanced over at Gwen, who was sitting up having her hair towel-dried. She looked very interested in the masque. So far, so good.

"Miracles, huh?" Sylvia opened the jar and sniffed. "Probably too rich for my blood, but it smells wonderful."

"It sure does." Francine began combing out Gwen's hair. "I can smell it from here, like a roomful of roses. How much is it?"

"Almost five hundred dollars." Dorcas had deliberately set the price high because she didn't want anyone trying to order it. She'd never have the time to make it in marketable quantities.

"Whoa!" Sylvia set down the jar as if it had burned her fingers. "Maybe you'd better put it on yourself. If I do it, some could ooze off into the sink and there would go fifty bucks' worth down the drain."

Gwen and Francine seemed similarly impressed by the price tag.

"It must be really good." Gwen sounded wistful.

"It is good," Dorcas said. "But there's one drawback to it. The ingredients are so delicate and fragile that once the jar's open, you have to use the contents within three hours before it spoils."

"Yikes!" Sylvia quickly screwed on the lid. "If I'd known that, I wouldn't have opened it. Couldn't you order a smaller amount?"

"It doesn't come in a smaller amount." In actuality, Dorcas hadn't been able to figure out how to make less. And the part about spoiling was true. The recipe had stated clearly that the potion wouldn't keep longer than three hours once it was exposed to air.

"You must really like the stuff," Francine said. "I can't imagine spending that much on something that doesn't last."

"It's an extravagance," Dorcas said, "but I decided to treat myself. I knew most of it would go to waste, unless . . . oh, you probably wouldn't want to do this."

"Do what?" Gwen leaned forward in her chair.

"If we all had facials, then we'd use up the jar and I wouldn't feel as if I'd thrown away so much money. But you probably don't want to—"

"Hell, yes, I want to," Sylvia said. "Let's have us a spa party!"

Francine glanced at the clock. "Why not? You and Gwen are the last two appointments for the day. But, Dorcas, you are so not paying for your hair appointment if you're letting us share your five-hundred-dollar facial masque."

"And I'm giving you the works," Sylvia said. "I think we need to do a weave on your hair, plus a mani-pedi, an eyebrow wax, a neck and shoulder massage, whatever you want. I'd do a Brazilian wax, but we don't have a private room for that kind of thing. Most women in Big Knob don't know what that is, let alone want their privates waxed."

For once, Dorcas was grateful for the lack of sophistication in this tiny town. Ambrose had never asked her to get a Brazilian and she wasn't about to accustom him to such things.

She turned to Gwen. "Are you up for a facial?"

Gwen smiled, which transformed her somewhat ordinary features, making her quite pretty. "I would love one," she said.

Dorcas barely managed to keep herself from pumping her fist in triumph.

Chapter 4

Two hours later, Gwen couldn't stop giggling. She hated to put on her glasses and ruin the effect, so she leaned forward to get a good look at herself in Bob and Weave's large plate-glass mirrors. Wow.

The babe gazing back at her bore no resemblance to the old Gwen. Her brown hair was filled with golden highlights. When she tossed her head, the layers Francine had created bounced and shimmered, so she tossed her head again, relishing the transformation. She'd never had hair that looked as if it belonged in a shampoo commercial.

Her hair wasn't the only difference, either. Whatever had been in that facial had softened and brightened her skin. Her eyes sparkled and her teeth seemed whiter, which she attributed to the new shade of lipstick.

Francine had talked her into a different brand of makeup, and Gwen had to admit the results were dramatic. She'd never dared wear a lipstick this red, and before today she'd ignored eye makeup completely, thinking there was no point if she wore glasses. She hated the thought of putting them on now.

"You look fantastic," Francine said.

"We *all* look fantastic." Sylvia applied dark red lipstick with a brush and pursed her lips. "I could almost have an orgasm just looking at myself."

Francine blew out a breath. "Thanks for sharing, but I'm sure we'd all rather you held off until you're in the privacy of your own home."

"What a spoilsport." Sylvia grinned. "Listen, Dorcas, it would be worth a hundred and twenty-five apiece to do this again sometime."

"It takes about three months to fill an order," Dorcas said. "But we can consider it, if you want."

Gwen glanced at Dorcas, who still wore the smock she'd put on earlier. Dorcas kept turning her head this way and that while peering in the mirror. Sylvia had convinced her to go much shorter and had styled the cut into a spiky arrangement that emphasized Sylvia's other alteration, a series of burgundy streaks.

As a final touch, Sylvia had dusted the entire coiffeur with silver sparkles. It was quite a departure from Dorcas's normally understated do, but the facial had taken years off, so maybe the new look fit, after all.

As for Francine, her complexion glowed from the effects of the facial, and she'd been inspired to try some different makeup colors, which brought out the beauty of her brown eyes. "We are four hot babes," Francine said. "I'm going to start saving my money for another jar of that stuff, if you'll order some for us, Dorcas."

"So everyone wants to try this again?" Dorcas continued to gaze at herself in the mirror, as if she couldn't quite believe it was her.

Gwen understood the feeling. "I would try it again," she said. "I love the way I look. I almost hate to put my glasses back on."

"Then don't," Sylvia said. "Or at least wait until

after you meet your French guy. It's not as if you have to drive anywhere, and you know this town like the back of your hand."

"That's true." Gwen straightened the collar of her white Oxford shirt and tucked the shirt more firmly into her navy slacks. "And speaking of my French guy, he should be here in another hour or so." The butterflies that had disappeared during the facial and hair styling came back with a vengeance.

The makeover was a double-edged sword. A man would expect more worldliness from a woman with golden highlights and ruby-red lipstick. Her inside no longer matched her outside.

"Is that what you're wearing?" Dorcas asked. "I mean, it's a nice outfit, but—"

"Paris is the land of haute couture," Sylvia said, blunt as always. "You need a little more pizzazz."

Gwen made a face. "I don't own a single piece of clothing with pizzazz," she said.

"I have an idea." Dorcas hurried into the bathroom and returned with her silk blouse still on its hanger. "I'll bet we're the same size. Wear this."

Gwen backed up a step. "Oh, no, I couldn't. I can't see the label without my glasses, but from Sylvia's reaction, I'm sure it's designer."

"You bet your sweet gardenias," Sylvia said. "It's a—"

"Who cares?" Dorcas held out the blouse. "It's only a blouse, and I have a closet full of them. Humor me and go try it on. We can trade."

"It would go great with your new hair color," Francine said.

When Gwen continued to hesitate, Sylvia put her hands on her hips and gave her a stern glance. "Girl, do you want to give him a boner or not?"

Yikes. Gwen felt the heat in her cheeks. "I—"

"Take the blouse."

"Okay." Her cheeks hot, she accepted the blouse and hurried into the bathroom. Apparently the silk was a higher quality than her nightgowns, because she couldn't help the sigh of pleasure as the material slid over her skin.

She'd never cared much about clothes, but fastening the pearl buttons of the blouse was such a tactile experience that she began to understand why some people loved fashion. Sylvia was right. Paris was the hub of fashion, but fashion was about the only thing related to France that Gwen had never found interesting.

Marc would be used to women who knew how to dress, though. She was grateful for the loan of this blouse. Tucking it into her navy slacks, she took a quick look in the bathroom mirror, but it was too high to give her much of a view. She hung her cotton shirt on the hanger and walked back into the salon.

Francine gave her a thumbs-up. "Fits like a glove. Very nice."

"Except you've buttoned it too high." Sylvia stepped forward and quickly unfastened a button.

"Wait." Gwen reached to button it again.

"Stop that." Sylvia batted her hand away. "Let's do one more. There. Now *that's* sexy. Good cleavage display. His tongue will stick to the roof of his mouth, guaranteed."

"I have to agree." Perched on Sylvia's swivel chair, Dorcas gave Gwen the once-over. "But now you need this." She unclasped the pendant and walked toward Gwen.

"Hold on." Gwen raised both hands in protest. "The blouse is one thing, but there's no way I'm borrowing a piece of valuable jewelry."

"It's not all that valuable, and you really need a necklace." She turned toward Sylvia and Francine. "Doesn't she need a necklace, girls?"

"Abso-freakin'-lutely," Sylvia said. "That necklace is killer."

"And Gwen's the most responsible woman I know," Francine added. "Your necklace will be perfectly safe."

"I'm sure it will be. Come on, Gwen. Just try it." Without waiting for a response, Dorcas slipped the pendant around Gwen's neck and fastened the clasp.

The stone nestled in her newly revealed cleavage, warm and soothing. And Dorcas was right—the necklace looked wonderful with the blouse. Gwen felt her resolve weakening.

Dorcas nodded in approval. "Perfect."

"It does look great, but I—"

"Then wear it with my blessing." Dorcas smiled at her.

"All right."

"Yay!" Sylvia clapped enthusiastically. "This is like getting Cinderella ready for the ball. By the way, where is the ball? Where are you meeting him?"

"I told him I'd be at the Big Knobian by seven."

Sylvia nodded in approval. "Smart. Then if he's a toad or a creepy guy, you can still escape." She glanced around at the other women. "I don't know about the rest of you, but I'm feeling a Girls' Night Out coming on. What say we all go over to the Big Knobian and give our Cinderella some fairy godmother backup?"

"Great idea," Dorcas said immediately. "I'll change out of this smock and let Ambrose know I won't be home for a while."

"I'm in," Francine said. "No point in wasting this expensive facial treatment on my cat." She turned to

Gwen. "Unless you don't want us to? Maybe you'd rather go over by yourself."

"I'd love the support." Gwen did feel a little like Cinderella, and in the past couple of hours she'd become bonded to her unlikely fairy godmothers. "I'm sure Marc's not dangerous, but I wouldn't mind having a posse with me to help make that judgment before I invite him home to dinner."

"We've got your back, girlfriend," Francine said.

"Thanks. Besides, without my glasses, I'll need someone to lead me around."

Ten minutes later, bundled up against the cold, all four women left the salon.

Francine glanced up at the sky. "At least it's not snowing yet. Your guy shouldn't have any trouble with the roads."

"No, fortunately." Nervous as she was, she wouldn't have wanted a snowstorm to keep him from getting here. She was as ready as she'd ever be for this meeting.

She dropped back to walk with Dorcas and lowered her voice. "Did you check the plants today?"

"Yes, and one's missing."

"Either missing or flattened. I could swear there was a plant where there's now this big boulder. If I didn't know better, I'd think we had a bear in Whispering Forest. Nothing else could move a rock that size."

"Maybe there is a bear," Dorcas said. "The government has all these wildlife recovery programs going on. One could have wandered over from Ohio. Well, here we are!"

All thoughts of boulders and bears disappeared as Gwen walked into the Big Knobian behind Francine and Sylvia. The bar wasn't very crowded tonight, which meant she could easily hear the jukebox playing a Tim McGraw song. A quick look around told her she knew everyone there, so Marc hadn't arrived ahead of her.

As she took off her coat, a wolf whistle cut through the music.

Sylvia preened and sashayed over to the pool table to the left of the door, where Johnny Harshaw, manager of the Knobby Nook Department Store, had a game going with Hank Leiber, the mechanic at the gas station. "Why, thanks, Johnny," Sylvia said. "You're looking buff yourself."

"That was for *her*." Johnny pointed his pool cue at Gwen.

Taken completely by surprise, Gwen swallowed and gulped in air at the same time, which made her choke. Terrific. Her first wolf whistle and she was asphyxiating herself over it.

"Get the lady a drink," Hank called out to Jeff Brady, owner of the Big Knobian.

Jeff came out from behind the bar with a glass of water. "You okay?"

Unable to speak, she nodded. Tears streamed down her cheeks, no doubt leaving mascara tracks, and she'd bet her red face could light up the entire bar. She took the water and began drinking slowly while she tried to hide her embarrassment behind the glass. Thank God Marc wasn't here yet. She needed to get a grip.

"Pump her arm up and down." A loud woman's voice came from the right side of the door, where the booths were located. Gwen knew it had to be Clara Loudermilk, and sure enough, there sat Clara, clutching her Chihuahua, Bud.

Clara's husband, Clem, sat across the table from her. "I don't think that really works, sweetie," he said. A structural engineer, Clem had made a fortune with a patented bra he'd created for his generously endowed wife. Clem was by far the richest man in town, but he still dressed in bib overalls and usually deferred to Clara.

"Of course it works, Clem." Clara glared at him. "This is exactly what I'm talking about. You question everything I say these days."

So that was why they were in marriage counseling with the Lowells, Gwen thought.

Dorcas walked over to the table. "I'd be happy to mediate this discussion."

Clara bristled. "Not if it's costing us money. Right, Bud?"

The Chihuahua whined and wiggled in her arms.

Appreciating the diversion, Gwen exchanged a smile with Jeff, who still hovered nearby.

"You doing better?" he asked.

She nodded.

"Go ahead and finish the water while I get you a glass of wine. These first meetings can be tough."

"No time for the wine." Francine stepped closer and put her arm around Gwen's shoulders. "But Mister Tall, Dark and French just walked in the door."

On cue, Gwen inhaled the rest of the water and went into a second spasm of coughing.

"I didn't mean to make you do that." Francine started pounding her on the back.

"Pump her arm!" Clara yelled out.

"Breathe, girl," Francine said.

"I'm trying," she said around the spasms.

Jeff glanced toward the door. "Can we help you, buddy?"

"I hope so. I am supposed to meet Mademoiselle Dubois here."

She couldn't hear perfectly because the coughing made her ears ring, but she caught enough of the accented baritone to know Jean-Marc Chevalier sounded exactly as she'd imagined he would. Francine had already implied he was gorgeous. This moment could have been so beautiful.

"You're the guy from Paris," Johnny said. "So that's why she got the makeover. I was wondering."

Gwen closed her eyes and wondered if she could possibly be more humiliated. Now Marc would know she'd updated her look for him, which wouldn't be so bad if she didn't presently look like a raccoon having a fit.

She had a brief fantasy of running into the bathroom and getting herself back together, but then she'd be acting like a vain coward. She was a vain coward, but she didn't want Marc to know.

"Distract him, Sylvia." Dorcas had returned to her side and gave the low command.

"My pleasure." Sylvia was almost purring.

Gwen opened her eyes. Wait a minute. She didn't want Sylvia getting friendly with Marc. Marc was Gwen's e-mail friend, and—

"Look up." Dorcas whipped out a handkerchief and began dabbing under Gwen's eyes. "Turn your head to the left." She ran the handkerchief under Gwen's eye and over her cheek. "Now to the right. Good."

Gwen's face tingled where the handkerchief had touched it.

"Mademoiselle Dubois?" The dreamy French voice was right behind her. Maybe Sylvia's tactics hadn't worked, after all. "Is that you?"

"You're okay now," Dorcas murmured under her breath.

Gwen had to take her word for it. Slowly she turned. As awful as this moment was, at least she'd finally be able to put a face with his oh-so-French name. Well, sort of. Without her glasses he looked a little blurry.

But what she could make out looked pretty damn good. She squinted a little to bring him into focus, and he still looked wonderful—deep blue eyes, a strong nose, a sensuous mouth, and an adorable cleft in his chin.

No doubt about it, this was her French fantasy come to life. His expression was concerned, as well it might be considering that people had been hovering over her from the minute he'd walked through the door. No doubt the poor man was at a loss for words. She couldn't blame him.

It looked as if she'd have to break the ice. Maybe she could impress him with her courage under fire. Yeah, that was the way to play it. Classy and in control, able to handle public embarrassment without losing her cool.

Clearing her throat, she thrust out her hand. "Yes, it's me. Welcome to Nig Bob."

Chapter 5

And Marc had thought *he* was nervous about this meeting. Yes, he was sweating a little under his leather jacket, but Gwen looked terrified. He did what any normal Frenchman would do to make a woman feel better.

Taking her hand in both of his, he leaned forward and brushed a kiss on each of her cheeks. "I am glad to be here, mademoiselle." Mm. He caught the scent of roses.

She gasped in obvious surprise. In fact, the whole room seemed to draw in a collective breath.

He leaned back to gaze down at her. "Is something wrong?" Her cheeks had turned as pink as a Paris sunset. He loved her hair, and wondered how big a change she had made.

"N-no, nothing's wrong." She gulped. "I mean, I'm glad you're here. How was the trip?"

"Fine, except—"

"You had problems? Was it the luggage?"

"No, I had some trouble finding—"

"The right freeway, I'll bet."

"No, the exit for Big Knob." He wanted to stop the nervous chatter and find a way to get Gwen out of here, away from the crowd that seemed to be hanging on every word. He wanted to gaze into her eyes, which he thought were brown, although it was difficult to tell because she kept squinting at him.

"You couldn't find the exit?" A brunette with burgundy streaks and sparkles in her hair frowned.

"I wonder how I missed it." Marc blamed jet lag, because after he turned around and came back, the sign was there in full view.

"Excuse me a minute." The brunette dug in her purse for a cell phone. "I need to make a call." She moved to an unoccupied booth.

"Gwen, aren't you going to introduce this gorgeous guy around?" asked the aggressive blonde who had been so intent on buying him a drink when he first came in. She had mentioned she could tie a knot in a cherry stem with her tongue. For one scary minute he thought maybe *she* was Gwen.

Gwen blinked. "Of course. Excuse my bad manners. Everyone, this is Monsieur Jean-Marc Chevalier. Monsieur Chevalier, let me introduce my friends."

Marc did his best to pay attention, but he was not good in these situations. Monsieur Harshaw was the person who had embarrassed Gwen with the remark about her makeover, and Monsieur Brady owned the bar. He immediately forgot who the other pool player was. Mademoiselle Hepplewaite was the blonde, and the one with quadruple hair colors was Mademoiselle Edington? No, Edgerton.

He found it difficult to care, both because he was dead tired and because Gwen looked so approachable and soft that he wanted to concentrate on her. The way she had buttoned her blouse made it easy to see . . . He snapped his gaze back to her face, not wanting to be caught studying her breasts.

The attractive, middle-aged woman with the sparkles in her hair had returned from making her phone call, and Gwen introduced her as Dorcas Lowell.

That name rang a bell. Madame Lowell and her husband had been the ones who had discovered the bromeliads in the forest. According to Gwen, Monsieur Lowell had suggested finding an expert on the Web, which had brought them to him. He had the Lowells to thank for this connection with Gwen.

But he could not mention that, because the plants were still a secret shared only by him, Gwen, and the Lowells. He was aware of Madame Lowell gazing at him intently, though, and he gave her a smile in return, hoping she would know it was a smile of gratitude.

About that time, the couple with the Chihuahua came over, and after Gwen had introduced them, the husband handed Marc a card.

Marc glanced at it. CLEM LOUDERMILK, SUPERIOR SUPPORT SYSTEMS was engraved in red on a gray background. "Do you manufacture metal braces?" he asked.

"I'm into bras."

"Oh." Even with an adequate amount of available brain cells, Marc would have struggled to respond.

"Here's the deal," Monsieur Loudermilk said. "Years ago, I invented a bra with excellent structural integrity for my wife, Clara, here, and a major company picked it up. Now I have plenty of money, but I'm bored."

"Clem, I *told* you we could travel," his wife said. "We can buy an RV and take Bud."

"Don't want to travel," Clem said to Clara. Then he turned back to Marc. "See, we've been getting marriage counseling from her and her husband." He pointed to Madame Lowell. "They think I'm bored because I haven't invented anything new lately, so I've decided to design a bra that's a little more interesting."

"Interesting?" His wife glowered at him. "You mean indecent!"

"You don't know anything about it, Clara," her husband said. "I'm an artist. I need to expand my range." He gazed at Marc as if expecting a response.

Marc nodded. "Sounds logical."

Clem beamed at him. "I knew you'd appreciate my situation, you being French and all. I've done my research, and the French are all about women's underwear. I thought you might have some ideas."

"Well, monsieur . . ." Always inclined to be truthful, Marc had to admit an interest in the subject. Any Frenchman worth his salt had ideas about women's undergarments. Marc tended to prefer silk over lace because lace could be scratchy, whereas silk was the closest thing to a woman's bare skin, yet it preserved the mystery. He wondered what kind Gwen liked.

"Oh, Clem, for pity's sake." Madame Loudermilk held the Chihuahua under one arm and clutched her husband by the sleeve with her free hand. "Leave the poor man alone. You have too many ideas already. At the next counseling session I'm telling the Lowells you're turning into a sex fiend."

In bib overalls? Marc tried not to smile as Madame Loudermilk tugged her very round and supposedly oversexed husband toward the door.

"Call me!" Monsieur Loudermilk threw over his shoulder before Clara yanked him outside.

"I will try, monsieur." Despite himself, he was intrigued. He had never met a brassiere inventor before and he was curious. How did the man do his research? What sort of testing would the garments require?

"Sorry about that," Gwen said. Her cheeks had

flushed even pinker as she gestured toward the curved wooden bar. "Would you . . . like something to drink?"

He had not eaten anything since getting off the plane. The threat of an impending snowstorm had crowded out all other concerns except getting to Big Knob before the snow hit. He always carried energy bars, a habit he had developed while traveling in primitive conditions, but energy bars could only carry a man so far. He was starving.

If he put alcohol in his very empty stomach, he would be drunk in no time. Not a good way to start this visit. "I would love some food. Is there someplace I could buy a hamburger and fries?"

She stared at him. "You want a burger and fries?"

"But of course! Americans are famous for this, *non*? What is nearby?"

The guy named Jeff laughed. "Nothing, buddy."

"The diner's closed," said the woman with several streaks of color in her hair.

"Oh. How about in Evansville? I have to go there, anyway, for my hotel." He hated to leave Gwen, though. Maybe she would like to take a drive.

"Nonsense," said Dorcas. "If a burger and fries is what you want, I'd be more than happy to make it for you and Gwen. Our house isn't far, so why don't we—"

"I can manage a burger and fries," Gwen said. "And my house is closer than Dorcas's."

So Gwen was inviting him to her house for dinner. He took that as a positive sign. When she had suggested meeting at the bar, he had assumed she was using caution before committing herself to alone time. He had thought the same way, but now that he had met her, he was ready for a little more privacy so they could get to know each other.

Besides, if they went to her house, he would be able to see the bromeliad. The potted version would not prove much, but at least he could start studying it before he went with her into the woods tomorrow.

He turned to Dorcas. "Thank you, madame, but if you do not mind, I will have dinner with my . . ." He struggled to remember what relative he was supposed to be.

"Cousin," Gwen said. "On my father's side."

"*Oui.* Cousin. We have much catching up to do."

"I understand." Dorcas gave him a knowing look, as if she could guess that he was already having carnal thoughts about his supposed cousin. "*Bon appétit.*"

Once Gwen had established that Marc was coming home with her, she didn't see any point in delaying the trip to her house. Bidding everyone good-bye, she accepted Marc's help with her coat and walked out the door with him. She'd never left with the best-looking guy in the room before, and she had to admit to a sense of triumph.

"Should we drive over?" Marc asked.

"No reason to. It's just down the street."

"Then let me get something out of the car." He clicked the keychain to open the passenger door. Opening it required a hard pull because of the ice collecting around the edges. "I brought you a small gift," he said as he emerged with a package and handed it to her.

"Goodness, you didn't have to do that." But she was thrilled to know he'd thought of her. The present was inside a paper bag decorated with a map of France. It had been taped shut. "Shall I open it now?"

"We can wait until we get to your house."

"Good idea. It's cold and you're hungry." She tucked the gift inside her coat pocket, where it nestled like a sweet promise. He'd bought her something, which must mean he wanted her to remember this visit. As if she'd ever forget it.

On one level, she couldn't believe this was happening. Twenty-four hours ago they'd been Internet buddies only, separated by an ocean and the anonymous nature of cyberspace. Tonight he'd be eating in her country kitchen. And he'd brought her a present.

"Which way?"

Apparently she'd been standing gawking at him like an idiot while he grew more chilled by the minute. His leather jacket couldn't possibly be warm enough for this weather. "Did you bring a scarf or a hat?"

"No."

"Then we'd better get going. It's this way." A breeze cooled her hot cheeks as she started walking down First Street toward Beaucoup Bouquets. Her little house was located behind the florist shop.

"The town square is not quite a square, is it?"

"I suppose not."

"More of a pentagon."

"Yes. Even the gazebo's a pentagon, so it matches, but we still call it the square. You couldn't have the July Fourth weenie roast on the town pentagon."

Marc laughed. "No, probably not."

His laugh was easy to listen to. Not everyone's was. Walt, the town's barber, had a laugh like a barking seal. Gwen would never rule a guy out because he had an obnoxious laugh, but knowing Marc didn't made him all the more appealing.

He might be freezing, but he looked damned sexy as he trudged along the slushy sidewalk wearing his black leather jacket and no hat. The cold breeze ruffled his thick hair, which made him look even sexier. She hoped he wouldn't end up sexy-looking but sick as a dog. That thought reminded her to check his feet. Sure enough, he was wearing very wet, very trendy loafers. "I didn't notice that you're not wearing boots, either. We should have driven, after all."

"This is fine."

"Your shoes are going to be ruined."

He shrugged. *"C'est la vie."*

She couldn't stop her little sigh of pleasure at hearing him speak French.

"Are you really worried about my shoes?"

"No, I . . . like hearing French."

"J'aime écouter toi parle anglais."

"You like hearing me speak English?"

"It works both ways. French might be exotic to you, but English is exotic to me."

"But English is so ordinary, while French is the language of—" She stopped abruptly before saying the word, which only made her comment more awkward than it would have been if she'd just said it.

"Love?" he finished for her.

"Right." The word shouldn't be so loaded, considering they barely knew each other. But when the word was said with a French accent caressing each vowel and consonant, what woman wouldn't feel a little weak in the knees?

She took a shaky breath and searched for a way back to casual conversation. "You mentioned the pentagon, and I didn't really explain why we have one."

"And why do you?"

"Because the streets are laid out in the shape of a five-pointed star, which forms a pentagon in the center." Thank you, Miss Dubois. You may go to the head of the class.

"I have never seen a town grid like that."

She'd appointed herself tour guide, so she might as

well finish the job. "The town's founder laid the streets out that way as a tribute to his wife, who was his shining star."

"How nice."

"Her statue's over there." Gwen pointed toward the gazebo. "You can't see it from here, but it wouldn't matter, anyway. I'm sure it's pretty well covered in snow. Her name was Isadora Mather."

"Mather? Would you spell that for me?"

She spelled it easily. Every first grader in Big Knob learned how to spell that name. But she couldn't understand why he was so interested. "It's not French, is it?"

"No, but it is a famous name. On my way to majoring in botany, I took a course in herbal healing. The textbook discussed the witch trials both here and in Europe, because many of the women accused were accomplished herbal healers."

"So you're talking about that judge in Salem, Cotton Mather." On some level Gwen had realized the last name was the same as the town founder's, but she hadn't thought anything more about it.

Marc nodded. "Yes, the very one."

"It's probably a common pioneer name."

"Perhaps. But a five-pointed star surrounded by a circle is the symbol for the nature-based practice of Wicca."

"Is it? I'm not really up on that kind of stuff."

"Non?" He glanced at her in surprise. "With your love of plants, I would think a belief system focused on the natural world would interest you."

"I was never exposed to it. I use herbs to cook, and that's about it. If I'm sick I go see Doc Pritchard." This whole discussion was making her uneasy. She wasn't particularly religious, but she'd spent her life attending services every Sunday at the Big Knob Community Church. The conservative folks of Big Knob were about as far from witchcraft as you could get.

"I would love to know if the Mather name can be traced back to Cotton."

"Even if it could, it wouldn't prove anything." Or more accurately, Gwen didn't want it to prove anything. "Anyway, there's no circle around Big Knob." But as soon as she'd said that, she thought about the walking path connecting the five points of the star.

That was just a coincidence, though. She'd used those paths all the time as a kid. A path from point to point made logical sense as a shortcut. Once you got out to the end of a point, you didn't want to retrace your steps all the way back to the center of the star, so you'd cut across. Everyone did it, and the path had become a wide rut after people had used it for nearly two centuries.

"Isadora Mather nursed the first settlers through a horrible smallpox epidemic." Gwen continued to recite the information she'd learned in school as if to guarantee there was no misunderstanding about the founders of Big Knob. They were upstanding citizens who had nothing to do with witchcraft. "Without Isadora there wouldn't be a town. That's why the Big Knob Historical Society raised money to put up a statue of her."

"And how did she cure people? With her knowledge of herbal remedies?"

"I don't know." She'd never questioned how Isadora had battled the smallpox epidemic. Her teachers had implied that she'd done it through sheer grit. "I suppose she might have known something about herbs, though."

"I am sure she did."

"That doesn't make her a witch." She turned down the walkway leading to her house.

"Not in the sense you mean, but she might have been Wiccan."

"No, no, she wasn't. I'm almost positive that she was Presbyterian, or maybe Methodist. She might have been Baptist. Yes, I think that was it. Baptist." Finding the keyhole wasn't easy without her glasses, but she finally managed it.

"Forgive me if I have upset you."

"Oh, you haven't." First chance she got tomorrow, she was calling Jeremy's mom, who was president of the historical society. Lucy Dunstan would clear up this Cotton Mather story in no time, and then Gwen could forget all about Wiccan symbols and magic.

"I have upset you. You could barely get the key into the lock, you were so upset."

"That wasn't me being upset." She flipped the switch that turned on the hall light and closed the door, which felt like a very intimate thing to do.

"Are you nervous?"

She looked up at him. He was still blurry, but blurry didn't ruin the stunning effect. Marc's blue eyes made her think briefly of the imaginary man who visited her at night, but the eye color wasn't even close to the same. Her dream lover had light-colored eyes that at times seemed almost silver. Marc's eyes were the velvet blue of deep twilight.

Now he was studying her with those amazing eyes and waiting for an explanation for her fumbling at the lock of her very own door. She could admit to wearing glasses or she could admit to being nervous. Both were true, but owning up to bad eyesight seemed like unnecessary honesty.

"Yes, I'm a little nervous," she said. Huge understatement. Walking across the square was one thing. Standing here with him inside her little house was a whole other thing. "You don't seem nervous at all, though."

"Perhaps I hide it well." He gazed at her, his hands shoved in the pockets of his jacket. "From the moment I saw you, my heart has been racing."

Once he confessed that, her own heart rate jacked up considerably. No man had ever said something so revealing to her before. Apparently the makeover was a success.

He cleared his throat. "I realize we have only just met."

"In person." She took a shaky breath. "We sort of met three weeks ago."

"And you cannot imagine how much I looked forward to your e-mails."

"I . . . me, too. Looked forward to yours, I mean." She'd lived for those e-mails.

"I am sure this is too soon, but—" He paused and gazed up at the ceiling. "I told myself to take this slow, but I have such an urge to kiss you."

Her heart beat so loud in her ears she was almost deafened. "Is that a request?" She couldn't believe he was asking. Anytime she'd been kissed before, the guy had just done it without so much as a by-your-leave. Not a single one of those former kissers had been a tenth as hot as Marc.

Marc was the sort of man who could throw her to the braided rug at their feet and she wouldn't object even a little. Instead he was asking politely if he could kiss her. If he was a typical Frenchman, they sure were different.

"It is a request," he said with a half smile that curled her toes.

"You don't want to see the plant first?" She heard the words come out of her mouth and wanted to gulp them back. A French god wanted to kiss her and she was geeking out about a stupid plant. "Forget I said that."

"All right, I will." He took her by the shoulders and drew her close. "We have yet to call each other by our given names."

"I know. I was waiting for you." As she gazed into his eyes, her senses sharpened, giving significance to the smallest things.

The soft tick of her mantel clock counted the seconds before he lowered his head to kiss her. The imprint of his fingers through the material of her coat made her wonder what his fingers would feel like on her bare skin. Drawing in a shaky breath, she caught the scent of his exotic aftershave.

"I am glad to be here. . . . Gwen."

Somehow he turned her ordinary name into a French-accented endearment. She gulped. "I'm glad, too. . . . Marc." Holy cow. All they'd done was exchange first names, and she was a bonfire. She couldn't imagine what would happen when he kissed her. She might have to break out the fire extinguisher.

Chapter 6

This is unlike me, Marc thought as he closed in for the kiss he had craved ever since his first glimpse of Gwen's full lips. *I usually take my time getting to this point.*

But he had fought the urge to gather her into his arms from the moment they had met. The French custom of two quick kisses on the cheek had only increased his desire to touch her.

Brushing back the lapels of her coat, he slid both hands behind her neck and up into her scalp. He registered the silky mass of her hair sliding between his fingers, the scent of roses wafting from her skin as he leaned toward her slightly parted mouth. Her eyelids drifted downward until her dark lashes rested against her cheek.

He had kissed many women in his life, but he had never anticipated a kiss more than this one. Without understanding the impulse driving him, he felt powerless to resist. Kissing her took priority over everything—food, sleep, even scientific curiosity. He needed this melding of lips, had to have it or something inside him would wither from lack of contact.

Struggling for a civilized approach, he gave her a butterfly-soft kiss. It failed to cool the heat in his

veins. Instead it stoked the fire and gave him an intox-
icating taste so familiar he would swear he had kissed
her a thousand times. Her velvet mouth seemed made
to fit against his, and her languid sigh shredded his
control.

A wild sense of urgency roared through him. With
a groan he tilted her head back and plunged his
tongue deep. Had he not been a man of some experience, the sensation of thrusting into her hot mouth
would have made him come. As it was, his erection
strained against his jeans and his mind filled with im-
ages of tearing off her clothes and taking her right
there on the floor.

No! By God, he would not behave like some savage.
He had standards. Summoning what was left of his
restraint, he pulled back, released her and stepped
away, breathing hard.

Her eyes were still closed and she swayed a little.
Her lips glistened from his kiss, and color suffused her
cheeks. Slowly she opened her eyes.

He saw the passion there. If he pressed his cause,
she would not resist. She wanted him as much as he
wanted her.

But he was not that kind of lover. He worked to
tame his breathing. "I . . . apologize."

"Why?" Her question was low and throaty, filled
with tightly leashed passion.

"I overstepped."

"I didn't mind."

He reminded himself she was an American woman.
Judging from Hollywood movies, plenty of American
men skipped the romance and went straight for the
sex. Gwen would not question such behavior.

She had no knowledge of his style, could not know
that he never lost control this soon in a physical rela-

tionship. But he knew it, knew what he expected of himself, and it was not this.

Gazing at her affected him in ways no woman ever had, and he was confused by that. She was beautiful, but no more so than other women he had kissed. Yet her lips drew him like a moth to a flame, and looking into her eyes made him think of naked bodies and perfumed oil.

But when he tried to see her objectively, which was difficult, he failed to pinpoint any outstanding physical attributes. Maybe he was dealing with pheromones. He had read of them in the animal world, but had thought that deodorants and perfumes kept them from being a factor in human sexuality.

Yet what else could be going on? Pheromones would explain why he wanted to bury his nose in the curve of her neck and breathe her in. When he was close to her like this, pheromones must be working like a powerful magnet pulling him closer and closer until he became mesmerized once again by her plump lips. . . .

He drew back with a soft curse. He had caught himself leaning toward her, ready to repeat his first offense and perhaps go on to commit others even more heinous. His condoms were in his suitcase two blocks away. Time to focus on something safe.

Shaking his head to clear the lust from his brain, he heaved a sigh. "The plant," he said. "Let us go look at it."

She blinked. "Okay." She hesitated, as if trying to remember where the plant was.

He could understand that kind of confusion. He was having trouble remembering his own name.

"Right. The plant. It's in the kitchen." Still wearing her coat and boots, she started toward a door to their left. Then she turned back to him. "Would you like to take off your coat?"

"Yes. *Merci.*" He had been so preoccupied with getting his hands on her that he forgotten to take off his coat or help her with hers. His mother would have been ashamed of him.

Courtesy demanded that he assist her with hers first, but he was afraid if he got that close, he would lose control again. This was ridiculous. He longed for a computer so he could do some serious research on pheromones. Maybe jet lag had something to do with it.

Although it assaulted his sense of good manners, he allowed her to remove her own coat. She unbuttoned it, but before taking it off, she leaned down to take off her boots.

Dear God, now he remembered how seductive that yellow blouse was. He became mesmerized by the tantalizing peek at her cleavage. He wanted more. How easy it would be to slip the pearl buttons free and slide the blouse down over her creamy arms.

Once her boots were off, she straightened and shrugged out of her coat. When she hung it on a coat tree by the door, something in the pocket knocked against the pole. "Oh." She reached inside the pocket. "Your gift."

He had forgotten that, too. The man who had chosen it while strolling down the Champs-Élysées was not the same pheromone-infected person who now stood in Gwen's hallway. That was fortunate, because pheromone-man would have bought her matching silk underwear. In black.

"Shall I open it?"

"Yes." Anything to distract him from the lure of her body. He snapped out of his daze long enough to remove his jacket. Following her example, he hooked it over a peg adjacent to hers.

"This is so exciting." She worked the tape loose. "I've never had a gift from a foreign country before, unless you count Canada, which I don't because it's attached."

He decided not to watch her mouth while she talked, because that made him want to kiss her again. "It is only something small."

"But you thought of me." She opened the bag and pulled out a box the size of her fist. "It may be small, but it's heavy."

And not good enough. He longed to grab it away and promise her something better. Had he known he would feel this way about her, he would have spent more money and time on this gift. He might have chosen jewelry, something that would nestle against her soft skin the way the pendant did.

Gwen pushed back the hinged lid of the box and gasped. "Marc, it's *beautiful.*" Carefully she removed the lead crystal paperweight, cradling it reverently in her hand as if he had given her the Hope diamond.

Its facets glittered in the overhead hall light. Maybe he had found the right gift, after all. She seemed really happy with it.

Holding it closer, she peered at the smooth face of the paperweight. "What's that in the middle?"

"A fleur-de-lis."

She squinted at the glass design embedded in the middle of the paperweight. "So it is!"

He was beginning to suspect she wore glasses and had decided to leave them off for this first meeting. How endearing that she wanted to look her best, but he had a feeling that glasses would not have dented this overwhelming attraction.

"Fleur-de-lis," she repeated. "Otherwise known as *Iris pseudacorus*." She gave him a proud smile, looking exactly like a little girl who had just handled the toughest word in a spelling contest.

He was lost beyond all hope. Somehow he knew she had learned that fact just for him and was pleased to display it so early in the visit. Once again, he fought the urge to kiss her breathless.

"It's a beautiful paperweight." She returned it gently to the box. "Thank you."

"A beautiful woman deserves beautiful things."

She glanced at him. "That's nice of you to say, but I feel like a fraud."

"A fraud? Why?"

Setting the box on a little table in the entryway, she turned to him. "You heard Johnny back in the bar. I went to the Bob and Weave and got all dolled up this afternoon. Normally I don't look like this. My hair's different, my makeup's different, and even my clothes are different. I borrowed this blouse and the necklace from Dorcas."

"How flattering that you would go to so much trouble."

"I *needed* to. If you'd met me looking the way I did earlier today, you wouldn't have been so hot to kiss me."

"I doubt that."

"I'll prove it." She picked up her purse from the table and rummaged through it. "Get a load of these peepers." She put on a pair of the ugliest glasses he had ever seen.

Laughing was probably a mistake, but it had been a long day, and the glasses *were* ridiculous.

"I look awful in these, don't I?"

"You could never look awful. Are those even yours?"

"Sadly, they are. They represent the real me, and I think you deserve to see that."

It might be tempting Fate, but he walked over and took her by the shoulders. The silk blouse, warmed by her skin, felt like heaven under his fingertips, and her rose-filled scent reached out, taunting him with the thought of another kiss. "If those glasses represent the real you, then I am Napoleon Bonaparte."

"They do." A fine tremor passed through her as she gazed up at him. "I'm not cool like you."

"Cool? I am not even slightly cool, *cherie*."

"Oh yes, you are. And I'm not. You need to know that going in."

He had kept his equilibrium until she pronounced those last two words. Instantly he had a vivid image of what *going in* could mean, and he wanted that. He wanted it with a vengeance. Fortunately, his condoms were in the car. Still.

And because they were, he needed to stop touching her. "Gwen, I cannot seem to think about anything except kissing you." Actually, he could think of something else, like making love to her.

She drew in a sharp breath. "Nobody's ever . . . that's not the kind of thing men usually . . ."

"It is simply the way I feel." With great regret he lifted his hands from her shoulders. "But if I kiss you again, we will not go into the kitchen and look at that plant."

"Which is what you came for."

He chose not to respond, because that was not true now and maybe never had been.

"It's in here." Turning, she led him through a doorway into a room that reminded him of a kitchen from his childhood. He and Josette still owned the vacation cottage in the country, but they never went there.

He tried to appreciate the quaintness of Gwen's

kitchen, but he was too busy thinking about the astounding effect she had on him. He was probably expected to comment on the house, which seemed to be lovingly decorated. Vaguely he remembered that the living room had the same sort of French farmhouse feel.

"You have a nice home," he said. Not a particularly imaginative assessment, but it was the best he could do considering he was pumped up on pheromones.

"Thanks." She smiled at him. "My father had it built as a replica of his boyhood cottage back in France. I thought you might feel at home here."

He did feel at home, but it was not the house. The truth hit him hard. It was Gwen.

"I can't believe you forgot to turn on the exit sign." Dorcas took the martini Ambrose handed her.

"I can't believe you let them do that to your hair. It's *spiky*."

"I happen to love it. I needed a change."

"Maybe I should get a Mohawk, so we can match."

"Now you're just being silly." Dorcas was still irritated with her husband over the exit sign. He'd almost created a disaster. She went over to join Sabrina, their black cat, on the sofa.

That was the other sore subject—Sabrina. Ambrose had recently given her an expensive collar that obviously used to be someone's bracelet. The platinum links were connected with diamonds, and it was loose enough to work as a collar, but it was too pricey for a cat.

Ambrose had bought the bracelet/collar online at a wizard site called eCharm. He'd bought it without asking, and the cat had become impossibly vain about it. At the moment she'd arranged herself on the purple sofa so that the diamonds caught the light from the nearby lamp.

She'd also begun demanding to take part in happy hour. Eyeing Dorcas's drink, she meowed.

"Sabrina wants her martini." Ambrose set his glass on the mantel. "I'll get it."

"I think we should break her of this little habit," Dorcas said. "It was cute the first time, but I'm worried about my stemware."

"She's never broken anything," Ambrose said over his shoulder as he headed for the kitchen.

"And you'd better not." Dorcas looked into the cat's green eyes. "I paid a pretty penny for those glasses."

Sabrina met her stare and flicked her tail as if to say she deserved pricey stemware as much as anyone.

"I think it's that collar you're wearing," Dorcas said. "It's giving you delusions of grandeur."

"It's not the collar." Ambrose returned carrying a martini glass filled with sparkling water. And he was sporting a Mohawk.

Dorcas didn't want to laugh and give him the satisfaction, but she couldn't help it. "Fix it back," she said between giggles.

"Just making a point." He set Sabrina's glass on the coffee table. "Your drink, madam."

Sabrina rose with a lazy stretch and hopped to the table, where she began lapping the water.

"I think it is the collar," Dorcas said. "Did you check to see if it had an entitlement spell on it?"

"The wizard I bought it from guaranteed it was spell-free."

He looked so ridiculous with the Mohawk that she had a tough time keeping a straight face. "So if it does have an entitlement spell on it, you can get your money back?"

Ambrose picked up his drink and sat in the red wing-backed chair next to the fireplace, where a cheerful blaze crackled and popped. "The collar is spell-free. I have a certificate."

"But if it's not, you can get a refund from this guy?" Dorcas could predict what her husband's answer would be. He was one of the most gullible wizards she'd ever known. Now he was a gullible wizard wearing a Mohawk.

Good thing he could change it at will. She could change her hair at will, too, but she wanted to leave it this way for a while. She didn't dare make any drastic changes, anyway, or Francine and Sylvia would get suspicious.

"I'm sure I could get a refund," Ambrose said, "once Sherman gets back from his trip to Mongolia. He won't be online for another six months or so. But it doesn't matter, because there's no spell on that collar."

Dorcas made a mental note to check the collar when Ambrose wasn't around. Sabrina had always had attitude, but lately she'd behaved as if she ruled the household. That happened to be Dorcas's position, and she didn't intend to give it up.

"My hair feels weird this way," Ambrose said.

"It looks weird that way."

"Will you change yours back if I change mine?"

Dorcas shook her head.

"All right." With a sigh, Ambrose muttered a few words and his hair returned to its normal conservative cut. Then, as if wanting to change the subject, he raised his glass. "Here's to Gwen and Marc."

"To Gwen and Marc." Dorcas raised her glass, too. "And a heavy snowstorm coming up in the next hour." After a generous sip, she leaned back against the red throw pillows arranged along the back of the sofa. "What did you find out about Prince Leo?"

"He's not at Atwood."

"Well, we knew *that*. We saw him in Whispering Forest."

"We didn't make a positive ID."

"I did." Dorcas took another swallow of her martini and hoped the mellowing effects of the gin would kick in soon. Whenever unexpected events threatened to interfere with her plans, she got peevish.

Sabrina lapped up the final drops of her sparkling water, and to the cat's credit, she didn't move the glass even a millimeter while doing it. When she was done, she turned toward Dorcas with an expectant expression in her green eyes.

"Now she wants you to plump up a pillow for her," Ambrose said.

"You know, Ambrose, she used to be content to lie on the sofa without all this fuss."

"So she likes a little extra comfort these days. So do I. I was thinking we should order a pillow-top mattress." He winked. "More bounce to the ounce."

She couldn't help smiling. "You're funny."

"No, I'm horny." He smiled back. "We've both been working too hard."

"There's plenty to do." But she liked that he was always interested in having sex with her, even after all these years.

"Would it be so bad to fluff Sabrina's pillow?"

"I think we're spoiling her, but what the Hades." Dorcas vowed this would be the last time she'd go through this routine. At the first opportunity, she'd check the collar for an entitlement spell, and she just knew she'd find one.

Laying the pillow down, she wedged it into the corner of the sofa. Sabrina minced from the coffee table to the sofa to the pillow. Then she curled up on top of it and gazed at Dorcas with a satisfied smirk.

"This pampering will not last," Dorcas murmured under her breath.

"What was that, love?"

She turned back to her husband. "Just thinking out loud." She'd spent enough time worrying about the cat. They had more pressing matters to deal with. "Were you able to find out why Leo's here?"

"Not exactly." Ambrose swirled his drink in his glass. "But it's no secret that his mother, Queen Beryl, hasn't been happy with his behavior and is considering giving the throne to a commoner."

"From what I've heard, I wouldn't give it to him, either. I'm not happy that he's in the forest playing poker with the raccoons. It's only a matter of time before George gets sucked back into that routine." She had a sudden thought. "Do you suppose he's after George's treasure?"

"I don't think so. Atwood is a rich kingdom. No, the rumor is that Queen Beryl has given him some task to accomplish that will qualify him to become King of Atwood."

"A task he's supposed to accomplish *here*?" Dorcas didn't like the sound of that one bit.

"It would seem so, wouldn't it?"

"Can you get in touch with Queen Beryl?"

"I've tried. She's taking a much-needed vacation and is out of pocket."

Dorcas drank the last of her martini. "Wonderful. Then it's up to us to get him by the ear and demand to know what he's doing messing around in our woods."

"*Our* woods?" Ambrose stared at her. "I've never heard you sound so possessive before."

"I can't help it. We've put a lot of work into this place."

Ambrose gazed at her. "Are you becoming attached to Big Knob, Dorcas?"

"No, of course not. Perish the thought." But that's precisely what she was afraid of. She was beginning to love this crazy little town.

"So I suppose we have to go back into that cold forest again tonight." Ambrose shivered.

"Yes, Ambrose, we do." She winked at him. "But I'll find a way to warm you up once we get home."

Chapter 7

Stupid, stupid, stupid. As Gwen took Marc into the kitchen, she berated herself for that little speech about being uncool. He hadn't kissed her as if she was uncool. He'd kissed her as if she was freaking Angelina Jolie. It had been the best kiss of her entire kissing history thus far.

Given that amazing liplock, why had she felt the need to point out her shortcomings and put on her glasses, which she now couldn't take off without looking vain? Why couldn't she have continued to play the role of desirable, sexy lady for a few days and enjoy whatever attention came her way?

The answer wasn't difficult. She didn't want to settle for a few days, and anything longer than that would surely reveal her lack of sophistication. She wanted to know beforehand how Marc might react to that. Such a preview wasn't possible, but that didn't stop her from wanting one.

"It certainly resembles a bromeliad." Marc walked over to the bay window where Gwen grew herbs year-round.

She'd temporarily moved several into her greenhouse to make room for the potted plant that Dorcas and Ambrose had brought from the Whispering Forest. She'd wanted to keep a close eye on the plant.

But at the moment she didn't give a damn about the plant. She was too busy keeping a close eye on Marc. "You're still wearing those wet loafers. I need to get you some heavy socks."

"Believe me, wet feet are not a problem. I have dealt with far worse than that."

"I've read on your Web site about your trips up the Amazon." She could picture him in khaki shirt and shorts, paddling a dugout through dangerous rapids, his skin tanned from the hot sun, his shirt plastered to his chest. . . .

He smiled. "I make the trips sound as thrilling as possible so I can keep receiving grant money."

"Even so, a trip to Big Knob to look at a bromeliad species must seem pretty tame."

"Not so far." He held her gaze.

She gulped. She'd never been with a man who specialized in saying exactly the right thing. Now that she was wearing her glasses, she could see the heat in his eyes, too. He wasn't making idle conversation.

At this rate she'd never be able to concentrate on cooking hamburgers. And she definitely wanted to feed him. It was the least she could do after he'd given her the kiss of a lifetime.

She gestured toward the plant. "Go ahead and examine it while I start on dinner."

"May I help you?"

"Are you a cook?" Panic shot through her at the thought that he might be a gourmet chef. That sort of thing was probably part of every Frenchman's DNA.

"Not much of one, but I could slice vegetables or something."

Thank goodness he didn't whip up soufflés in his

spare time. "I'd rather have you study the plant and tell me what you think." Then maybe she'd have a decent chance of getting dinner on the table without burning down the house.

Turning away, she opened the refrigerator and pulled out a package of hamburger. Fortunately she'd picked some up yesterday, or she wouldn't have been able to satisfy his dinner request.

"If you are certain you do not need help."

Oh, she needed help, all right. She needed help navigating the unfamiliar waters of having a man who looked like Marc interested in her. "I have it covered." She took a couple of potatoes out of the bin at the bottom of the refrigerator. "Seriously."

"Very well. Then let me take a closer look at this plant." He unclipped a BlackBerry from his belt. "I stored several pictures of unusual bromeliads, so I could compare them with this one. I—uh, oh."

"What?" She glanced over her shoulder. Damn, but he looked good standing in her kitchen. His white dress shirt, unbuttoned at the neck, looked as if it might be silk. "Is something wrong?"

"I had a call from my sister, and I missed hearing the ring."

He sounded so guilty that she wanted to comfort him. "It's easy to miss when you're driving in heavy traffic. And the bar was noisy, too." *Then you were kissing the living daylights out of me. Speaking for myself, I wouldn't have heard the entire Mormon Tabernacle Choir singing the* Hallelujah Chorus.

"I promised to call when I arrived."

"I'm sure she'll understand. You've had a lot on your mind."

"But she has no other family besides me. I need to try to reach her."

Gwen was used to calculating the time difference

between Paris and Big Knob. "Wouldn't she be asleep?"

"I can text her first, although she may be up. She has insomnia." He stared at his BlackBerry and murmured something that sounded like a French curse.

"What is it?"

He glanced up. "I remember you said that cell phone reception is unreliable in Big Knob. I should have called from the airport."

"You could give it a shot, anyway. Sometimes we get lucky with reception."

He continued to study the screen and shook his head. "Not promising. Is there any room in the house better than the kitchen?"

"My bedroom." The suggestion sounded seductive, although she hadn't meant it that way. Nothing she could do about that. It was the truth.

Indecision lurked in his eyes. He glanced at the BlackBerry again and sighed. "Very well. I really need to attempt this call. Where is your bedroom?"

"This way." If he hadn't kissed her, this little trip wouldn't be so loaded with tension. But he had kissed her, and she was extremely aware of his footsteps on the hardwood floor as she led him down the hall past the guest room to the back of the house.

At the bedroom doorway she reached inside and flipped the switch that turned on the bedside lamps. She'd replaced the boring shades her parents used to have with Tiffany-style stained glass. The lamps filled the room with jeweled light that she loved, but tonight they seemed like overkill, as if she'd deliberately set the stage to lure him into her bed.

The whole room looked that way, now that she saw it as he might. The four-poster became phallic, and the plump mattress and pillows cradled within those four sentries promised sensuous delights.

But if he wanted better cell phone reception, this was the room for it. She stepped back out and gestured for him to go inside. "I don't use my cell often, but when I do, this is the best place."

"Thank you." He glanced into the room and took a deep breath. "Inviting."

She wasn't sure how to respond. "Thanks. I like it."

He hesitated, as if reluctant to step inside.

"You can try somewhere else if my bedroom makes you uncomfortable."

"Au contraire." He gazed at her with those deep blue eyes, which gradually darkened until they were almost navy. "I am afraid that I will feel entirely too comfortable."

He wants to kiss me again. She knew it with a certainty that she'd never experienced with a man, as if she could read his mind. If she moved a step closer, he would pull her into his arms, gently remove her glasses, and go for it. The thought gave her goose bumps of pleasure.

But she wouldn't step closer. He'd feel even guiltier if he didn't get in touch with his sister, and Gwen didn't want to be responsible for that. "I'll leave you to your call." Heart pounding, she turned and walked down the hall.

"Gwen?"

"Yes?" She turned back. If she'd thought he looked good in her kitchen, he looked even better in the doorway to her bedroom. And she loved the way he said her name.

She wanted him. No point in denying it. If he held out his hand, she would walk back down that hall and deal with guilt about his sister later.

"You implied in your e-mails that people in Big Knob like to gossip," he said.

"They do, but—"

"I will work hard not to damage your reputation."

She'd been about to tell him she didn't give a hoot in hell about her reputation now that he'd kissed her. But she decided against saying so and possibly appearing too willing to be a bad girl. "Thank you," she said. "By the way, how do you like your hamburger?"

"Juicy."

Of course he did. She swallowed a whimper of desire. If he liked his women that way, too, then she'd be exactly to his liking. The more time she spent with him, the juicier she became.

Back in the kitchen, she tried not to think of him lounging in her bedroom. She had a chair in there, but it was a fussy little antique not sturdy enough for a grown man. He'd either have to stand up or sit on the bed.

When she thought of him sitting on the bed, she had to fan herself. The guy was too hot for his own good, and he'd *kissed* her. For some unknown reason he seemed extremely attracted to her small-town, unsophisticated self. That must have been some makeover.

She got to work, but it wasn't really work because she was doing it for Marc. Forming hamburger patties and slicing potatoes had never felt so sensuous. Gwen found herself humming under her breath while she prepared dinner. When was the last time she'd made a meal for a guy? She couldn't remember.

The conversation with his sister was taking a while, which she could understand. Well, actually, she couldn't. She'd never had a sibling.

Annie was the closest she'd ever come to one, and even they had grown apart when Annie had moved to Chicago. Fortunately Annie was back and the friendship had picked right up again.

Gwen wished Annie could be here for some old-fashioned girl talk, but that was a selfish thought. Annie had been thrilled with the grant that allowed her to live in Big Knob except when she was traveling to research her series. If that job hadn't come through for Annie, she and Jeremy might be living in Chicago while she continued to work at the *Tribune.* Then Gwen wouldn't see much of her best friend at all.

When the patties were seasoned and on the electric grill and the potatoes sliced and ready for the deep fryer, Gwen set the table in her cozy little kitchen. She debated using candles and decided against it. She was not out to seduce Marc. If he decided to seduce her, however, she wasn't about to resist.

Marc still hadn't returned by the time she was ready to start cooking. She hated to dive in until she knew he'd be available to eat the food. He'd asked for juicy hamburgers, which meant he had to eat them straight off the electric grill.

Going to the bedroom door to summon him didn't feel right. He obviously was very close to his sister, and Gwen wasn't about to interrupt their conversation and risk having Josette resent her. She wondered if she'd ever meet Josette. So much depended on the next three days.

On impulse she got out some white cheddar cheese and sliced some to go on the hamburgers. She nibbled on an extra piece and realized she was getting hungry. Earlier she hadn't been able to think of food, but her initial nervousness had mostly disappeared. She looked forward to sharing a meal with Marc.

Except he was making the longest trans-Atlantic cell phone call in history. Maybe she should simply go to the door and give him a little wave, so he'd know she was about to start cooking dinner. Maybe he planned to talk until she called him to come and eat.

That made sense. As she was about to head down the hall, the phone in her kitchen rang. She picked it up.

"I had to call," Francine said. "How's it going?"

"Great."

"Is he right there, or can you talk?"

"He's in the . . . other room, making a call to his sister in Paris." How elegant that sounded.

"Oh, God, Gwen, he's incredible! That accent is to die for, and he looks so . . . French!"

"He does." Gwen couldn't help smiling. And he was here, in her house, and he'd already kissed her once. But she wouldn't tell Francine that. She might have told Annie, but Annie wasn't here.

"So have you had dinner yet?"

"We're about to."

"Good, because it's started snowing."

"Really?" Gwen glanced at the green glass panes of her bay window and discovered they'd iced up. She must have been really distracted not to notice that.

"Yeah, but if you two are about to eat, it shouldn't be a problem. It's not too bad yet. Listen, I'll let you go, but I just had to call and say attagirl. He's gorgeous."

"Thanks, Francine." Gwen was still smiling as she hung up the phone. Women had never envied her a boyfriend before, and it felt nice.

She really should go get Marc if the snow had started coming down. As she headed off, her phone rang again. Probably Sylvia this time, or maybe Dorcas.

Feeling giddy with happiness and in an uncharacteristically playful mood, she picked up the phone and didn't even bother with hello. "Is Marc a hottie, or what?"

"I'm not a good judge of stuff like that," said a male voice that sounded suspiciously like Bob Anglethorpe's.

Gwen was so embarrassed that the roots of her hair tingled. "Uh, Bob. I thought you were someone else."

"Thought so. Listen, have you taken a look outside lately?"

"You mean the snow?" She wasn't ready to admit that she'd been so absorbed in what was happening inside the house that she'd been completely unaware of anything going on outside. Now that she took the time to listen, she could hear the wind blowing.

"The snowstorm hit about thirty minutes ago, and it's a doozy. It's not quite as bad right here, but I've been on the scanner and Sixty-four is a mess—vehicles off the road, a couple of fender-benders, folks needing a tow."

"I see." Her pulse rate kicked up. It looked as if her reputation might be in danger, after all.

"I took a look out on the square and saw your—ah—*cousin's* vehicle is still parked in front of the Big Knobian."

She decided to ignore the jab. Until someone questioned her directly, she'd stick to her story. "Cousin Marc's still here. We've been catching up on family news, and right now he's talking to his sister back in Paris." She loved throwing a mention of Paris into a conversation. It sounded so cosmopolitan.

"You can't let him drive to Evansville in this. I can't remember if you have an extra bed over there or not, but if you want, I could put him up. We'd just move one of the boys to the sofa and let your cousin have a bunk bed."

So there it was, a chance to save her reputation by having Marc go sleep over at Bob's house. In one of his kids' bunk beds. She thought of Marc with his silk shirt, leather jacket and expensive loafers, sleeping in a bunk bed and brushing his teeth in a bathroom filled with plastic army men, Tonka trucks and wet towels. He'd probably get Cheerios for breakfast.

Or he could stay here in her guest room, which had a double bed and a bathroom across the hall that would be exclusively his. The towels were hung neatly on the rack and the sink was spotless. She'd cleaned it yesterday, just in case. And she'd make omelets in the morning.

She had to keep him here, for his sake. Yeah, right. For Marc's sake. What a laugh.

"Thank you, Bob," she said. "That's really generous, but I have a spare bed, so you don't have to displace either of your boys."

"It's really no trouble. Patsy said she'd love to talk to a person from Paris, France."

Gwen hadn't thought of that angle. Marc's impending arrival had been the talk of the town, and now that he was here, everyone would want to rub elbows with the French guy. So would she, although she wanted to rub more than elbows.

"Marc'll be around for the next three days," she said. "I'm sure Patsy will have a chance to talk with him. The guy's exhausted, though, so maybe it's better if he just stays here tonight."

"If you're sure." Bob sounded disappointed. "I was also thinking of your reputation. You know how people talk."

"I know they do." Gwen fingered the smooth stone pendant Dorcas had loaned her as she considered the prospect of inspiring juicy gossip. Instead of being worried, she found herself smiling. "But they've never talked about *me*," she said. "Maybe it's about time. Good night, Bob." Still smiling, she replaced the phone in its cradle.

Now she had an even more pressing reason to interrupt Marc's phone call. She needed to inform him that he wouldn't be leaving tonight, after all. He might want to trudge back across the square and get his suitcase out of the car.

On her way down the hall she didn't hear his voice, so he must still be texting. Silence reigned in the back of the house. As she approached the doorway, she made out a soft, rhythmic sound. Snoring?

Sure enough, when she peeked inside the room, Marc was stretched out on her bed, fast asleep. He'd slipped off his shoes, but otherwise he was fully clothed. His head rested on one of her feather pillows, and his BlackBerry lay on the comforter where it had obviously slipped out of his hand.

She walked over and cupped his shoulder. Nice muscle definition. She shook him gently. "Marc."

With a groan he rolled away from her.

"Marc, wake up."

No answer. Walking to the other side of the bed, she crawled onto the mattress and peered into his face. "Dinnertime, Marc. Juicy hamburgers just the way you like them."

His eyelashes fluttered, but he made no sound other than his steady breathing. He was completely out.

Bracing her chin on her hands, she gazed at him. He had dark lashes any woman would kill for and the kind of cheekbones that meant he'd grow more handsome as he aged. She wondered if he'd shaved in the airport bathroom, because his beard was only now starting to show.

This close she could see where he'd nicked himself near the dimple on his chin. That would be tricky to shave, and he'd been in a hurry. In a hurry to see her. She couldn't ignore the fact that he'd been eager to get here.

Maybe that had colored his perception and made him think he wanted her more than he actually did. He might see the situation differently after a good night's sleep. He had a head start on that, and unless she wanted to resort to throwing cold water in his face, he probably wouldn't wake up until morning.

All righty, then. She needed to make him as comfortable as possible. In romance novels the heroine was somehow able to undress the hero even when he was sound asleep and pretty much a dead weight. Although undressing Marc appealed to her, she couldn't imagine how that worked in real life.

At least she could take off his damp socks so his feet could warm up. He didn't stir as she peeled them off. He had long, aristocratic toes sprinkled with dark hair. With a flutter of sexual awareness, she found herself imagining how the rest of him would look naked.

Moisture collected in her mouth as she fantasized stripping him down, inch by inch. She wasn't planning to actually do it, but that didn't mean she couldn't think about it. She might want to cool her jets, though, or she'd never sleep tonight.

Job number one was getting him covered up, including his sexy toes. In the end she decided to retrieve the down comforter from the guest bed and put that over him. When she went to bed she could use some of the old blankets stored in the cedar chest. They might be a little musty, but they'd be okay for one night.

Covering him awakened all sorts of tender feelings to pair with the lustful ones. She thought about his sense of obligation to his sister and wondered if he'd reached her. If not, then tomorrow she'd take him over to Click-or-Treat so he could use the high-speed connection to e-mail her.

When he was all tucked in, she couldn't resist leaning down and kissing him softly on the mouth. Yes, they fit together as perfectly as the first time. What would happen if she crawled in beside him and spent the night there? Heat shot through her at the idea.

But despite the makeover and despite the pendant, she wasn't that bold. She'd sleep in the guest room tonight, and tomorrow . . . well, tomorrow they'd have to see how they liked each other in broad daylight.

In any case, now she could truthfully say that she'd had a Frenchman in her bed.

Chapter 8

Without the raccoons, Leo would have died of boredom. Sex with Gwen was great, but other than that, Big Knob was a real yawner. After leaving her the night before, he'd played until dawn, slept through the day, and now he was back at it. He planned to take a break around Gwen's normal bedtime to have a quick session with her. Then he'd return to the game.

The poker games were even more fun after they'd raided the Big Knobian and hauled out several cases of beer from the back storeroom. The storeroom wasn't the tidiest place in the world, so Leo doubted the beer would be missed right away. And there was nothing funnier than a drunk raccoon.

Poker had become Leo's new passion, and he was working those raccoons, letting them win often enough that they wouldn't suspect he would take it all before he left. Thanks to their games with that dopey dragon, they had quite a stash of gold coins.

Leo didn't need the money. He'd have more than enough once he became king, and with Gwen coming along so nicely that was a done deal. He was in it for the thrill.

And the beer. He'd lost count of how many he'd

had tonight, and he might want to slow down. Booze might interfere with his technique.

Hell, one more wasn't going to turn him into a loser. He popped the top and settled in for the last hand before he headed off to Gwen's. Yeah, the Frenchman was due in, but Leo wasn't worried.

The dweeb had a hotel reservation in Evansville, which proved how wimpy he was. In his shoes, Leo would have made sure he was in residence the whole three days, baby. More opportunity for nookie.

Obviously the guy was slow on the uptake. Too bad for him, because when he finally got around to making a move on Gwen, Leo would have conditioned her to the kind of outstanding sex that would make her spurn the Frenchman. She wouldn't give Jean-Marc Chevalier the time of day. . . . Or night.

Leo folded his pocket aces and let one of the raccoons take the pot. That way they'd be more eager to bet big when he came back in an hour. He slipped off into the woods to the little cave he called home for the time being. Good thing he'd thought to bring the fantasy costumes to Big Knob, because they got the right reaction from Gwen.

As he dressed in the military uniform he'd decided on for tonight, he had a little trouble with the buttons. The beer must have made him a little fuzzy. No matter. He didn't need to be completely sober to slip into Gwen's dream and accomplish his mission. Not this fairy prince.

He had some trouble concentrating as he prepared to transport himself into her bedroom, but finally he made it. Next time he'd have one less beer.

The bedroom was dark, as usual, and the house was quiet. He could hear her breathing, and wondered if she had a cold because her breathing was heavier than normal. Fortunately fairies couldn't catch colds. Some good sex would fix her right up.

Focusing his thoughts on her, he prepared to enter her dream. Gwen's dream state was soft and cushiony, like the bed she slept on. Maybe she really was sick, because tonight her dream state was rougher, with more hard edges.

Something about this didn't feel quite right, but he blamed the beer. Next time he'd definitely cut back. Firmly planted in her dream, he stepped toward the bed. "I'm here."

"Who the devil are you?"

Sheesh, she must have a terrible sore throat. She sounded almost like a guy. "You know me. I'm the one who gives you incredible orgasms."

"Excuse me?"

"Your lover." Leo wasn't used to her being so dense. After all, this wasn't exactly a brand-new routine.

"My *what?*"

"May I make love to you, sweet Gwendolyn?"

"Who?"

"You're not yourself, but I can make you feel so much better." Leo drew back the comforter and ran his hand down her—wait, this wasn't . . .

"Get the hell away from me!" roared the person in the bed, the person who was *not Gwen.*

Leo pulled his hand back as if he'd been burned. Then he threw the comforter back in place. Shit! Someone was running down the hall. It sounded like a woman's footsteps, so that meant the person in the bed was . . .

Marc. Marc Chevalier was in this bed, and Leo had just put his hand on—no, not *really.* He'd sort of patted, not stroked, and certainly not *caressed.* He had to concentrate, had to get himself back to the forest.

His brain was mush. *Concentrate, idiot!* He managed the transfer a split second before Gwen burst into the room.

Ah. He was safely back in the forest. Hades, but he needed a beer.

Marc heard someone calling his name and fought his way out of a deep sleep. Groggy and disoriented, he struggled to a sitting position. About that time two stained glass lamps flicked on.

When he saw Gwen standing in the doorway, he began to put everything together. He was in Big Knob, in Gwen's house, and in her bed, apparently. She had not joined him, or he hoped not, because he had no memory of making love to her.

He recalled trying in vain to get a text message through to Josette. During the process he had given in to the temptation to fool with the BlackBerry while lying down. That was the last thing he remembered.

Until that dream.

Gwen hovered in the doorway. "Are you okay?"

Glancing over, he noticed what he had missed seeing before. She was wearing the pendant and a nightgown the color of new leaves. The bodice laced up the front, which made for an interesting peekaboo effect with her cleavage. Judging from the way her nipples puckered under the material, she was naked under the nightgown.

He swallowed. The memory of their kiss returned, and in no time he was erect. "You should not have given me your bed." *You should have allowed me to take you to bed.*

"I don't mind. But I heard you cry out, and I wondered if you'd had a nightmare. Or if you needed something."

He needed some*one*, and she was standing less than

ten feet away. Yet nothing had changed on the condom front. They were still in his suitcase, which was still in his rental car two blocks away.

"Marc? You look dazed. Is there anything I can do?"

He couldn't help the moan that escaped. His defenses were down. He needed more sleep in order to rebuild them.

"Oh, dear." She hurried to him and sat on the edge of the bed. "Do you have a fever?" Surrounding him with the scent of roses, she laid her hand on his forehead.

Pure reflex took over. He captured her hand and brought it down to his lips, where he placed a kiss in the center of her palm.

She shuddered. "You're not . . . sick."

"No." Still holding her hand, he looked into her eyes. "I am not sick. But I do seem to have a problem. I want you so much it is killing me."

Her breath caught.

"That is barbaric, considering that I just arrived in town, but I cannot seem to help myself." He kissed her palm again, this time tracing a small circle with his tongue.

"Marc." Her voice sounded strangled.

"I should stop." He pressed his lips against her pulse, which beat wildly against his mouth. The rose scent of her skin weakened his resolve even more.

"We only met a few hours ago." She seemed to be reminding herself.

"I am aware of that." He allowed his gaze to roam her face, which was scrubbed clean of makeup and rosy from sleep. He longed to place kisses on her forehead, her cheeks, her eyelids, and most of all on her mouth. . . .

She cleared her throat. "I was thinking . . ."

"Yes?" He wondered if it was anything close to what he was thinking.

"Now that you're awake, you could get undressed." She gulped. "I mean, get more comfortable. Ack." She raised her eyes to the ceiling. "Everything I say sounds suggestive, and I swear I'm not trying to—"

"Voulez-vous couchez avec moi?"

She met his gaze, and her cheeks flamed bright pink. She moistened her lips and a fine tremor passed through her, making the pendant quiver. "Yes," she murmured. "Yes, I will."

His heartbeat thundered in his ears. Women had agreed to go to bed with him many times, but not once had his heart beat this fast at the prospect. He cupped her face in both hands. "Thank you."

"I don't have—"

"I know. I do not, either." He feathered a kiss over her mouth. "We will be very careful."

Her sigh of surrender signaled such trust that he almost lost control then and there. But he would not lose control. If all went well, she would, but not him.

Kissing her gently so he wouldn't rub her face raw with his whiskers, he drew her down beside him. Tonight would test his skills as never before, because he was determined not to come. Asking her to lie with him made no sense, because pleasuring her would only make his unfulfilled needs greater.

So be it. He smoothed his hand over the silk covering her breasts and listened to the change in her breathing. "I have to be careful. I could scratch you with my beard." He continued to keep his kisses light.

She gasped as he cupped her breast and rubbed his thumb over her peaked nipple. Her reply was breathless, intense with desire. "I don't care."

"I do." He outlined her mouth with his tongue. "I said I would protect your reputation."

"To hell with my reputation." She cupped his face in both hands and tried to pull him closer. "I don't care about that, either."

He chuckled as he resisted her attempt to tug him downward. "You will care in the morning." Ducking away from her grasp, he eased her onto her back and moved over her.

Closing his eyes and releasing his breath in a long sigh, he allowed himself to settle between her thighs. If only . . . but no, that would not be possible tonight. He never intended to take his clothes off.

Her eyes darkened as his erection nudged her. "Are you sure you don't have any . . ."

"Not with me." He preferred not telling her they were in his suitcase. She might think he had planned this.

"Not even in your wallet?"

"That is an American custom." He ran his tongue along the line created by her necklace until he reached the pendant. "Why did you wear this to bed?"

Her breathing grew shallower. "I don't know."

"I think you like the feel of it against your skin." He sucked it in and then deposited it, glistening and smooth, between her breasts. "I think you are a very sensuous woman who loves soft sheets, silk night-gowns and pendants that rest in your cleavage."

"Maybe."

"I am sure of it." He settled his mouth over her silk-covered nipple and bit down gently.

"Ahhh." She arched upward. "I want the night-gown off."

"I will irritate your skin." He could easily undo the laces and have her breasts free in no time, but he would leave her chafed. This was better. Pressing his mouth against the silk, he rubbed his tongue back and forth, teasing her through the thin material.

Moaning softly, she clutched handfuls of his shirt.

"That is not so bad." Lifting his head, he gazed down at the damp silk and could almost see her nipple through it. Loving her like this while protecting her soft skin was a novelty for him, and he found the experience wildly exciting.

"Not bad . . . at all." She gulped in air.

"You have such beautiful breasts." Splaying his fingers, he stretched the silk over her nipple. Then he leaned down and began to suck in a slow, steady rhythm.

She writhed beneath him, her breathing growing increasingly ragged. Her movements caressed his trapped penis and threatened to bring about disaster. Unable to take it another second, he released her breast and rolled to his side. He might not be able to find nirvana, but she could.

Her nightgown had ridden up around her hips and he had no trouble sliding his hand under the bunched hem. He groaned at the softness of her thighs as he sought the moist territory where paradise lay.

When he discovered how ready she was for the thrust of his aching cock, he regretted not following the American custom of carrying protection in a back pocket. Maybe the French could take a lesson from the Americans, after all.

She was so wet, so ready for the climax he longed to give her. He wanted to gaze into her eyes while he did that, but she had closed them tight.

"Regarde moi." He stroked her without penetrating. When he gained entrance, he wanted her to be looking at him, aware of who was touching her so intimately.

Her eyelids fluttered, lifted. Her eyes were liquid chocolate, rich with desire.

"Oui, cherie. Keep your eyes open. Stay with me, be with me when I make you come."

"Yes." She was panting, now, and her hips moved

restlessly against the mattress. "Please, Marc. Oh, please."

He smiled. *"S'il vous plaît?"*

"S'il vous plaît!"

"Bon," he murmured, slipping two fingers deep and rubbing his thumb over her trigger point.

She shuddered and lifted her hips, pushing against his fingers. He had been right. She was very sensuous, very responsive. Giving her this would be pure heaven.

And pure hell. The more she whimpered and undulated against the sheets, the more he longed to open his trousers and plunge into her. It would be so good, so very good.

He could not do that. She trusted him not to.

Tamping down his own response, he pumped his fingers in and out, increasing the pace as he put more pressure on her sweet little clit. *"C'est la."* He curved his fingers to reach her G-spot.

She closed her eyes and groaned. "Yes! There!"

"Look at me." He switched to English to make sure she stayed with him. "Look into my eyes."

She opened her eyes to reveal twin flames of hunger. She wanted this, and she was reaching for it, grasping for her reward as he stroked faster, faster. . . . He held her gaze and pressed down harder with his thumb.

There! Her climax widened her eyes and lifted her hips. With a glorious cry of release, she came, the spasms squeezing his fingers and dampening the sheets.

She gasped for breath and trembled uncontrollably, but all the while she kept her gaze locked with his. In doing as he had asked, she had allowed him to see her vulnerability and her neediness. That took strength, the kind of strength he admired. She would not play games.

Gradually he withdrew his fingers. Then, still holding her gaze, he licked them. "You taste wonderful," he murmured.

Her cheeks turned pink, but she looked straight at him. In fact, she seemed fascinated by what he was doing.

He had told the truth. She tasted sinfully delicious, and the scent of her juices mixed with her natural rose scent was driving him crazy. He had never craved a woman with this kind of intensity.

Maybe it was still jet lag. Maybe it was going without food for at least twelve hours. But he suspected it was Gwen herself. Pheromones. She got to him in ways that no other woman had.

Her pendant had slid from between her breasts and now lay on the sheet. He was entranced by that pendant, especially when it was nestled against her skin. Wanting to see it back there, he picked it up and rearranged it so that it graced her cleavage once more.

Then he adjusted the laces of her nightgown. He made sure they would not loosen and make her breasts available to him. That kind of temptation was beyond his ability to resist, and he would rub her raw.

"Thank you." She gazed up at him. "I seem to be saying that quite a bit tonight."

"I want to give you reason to say it even more." She was so incredibly responsive, and he hoped this interlude would last a very long time.

"You feel good, Marc."

He had felt her hands caressing his back, but he had not allowed himself to consider the full implications. Such as, she could caress other parts of him with similar enthusiasm.

With all the wiggling around, his shirt had come out of the waistband of his trousers and she had slipped her hands under it. If he took off his belt and unfast-

ened his trousers, she could . . . no, that was expecting
too much.

Or was it? He wanted this to continue, wanted to
make her come again. After that, if he was a very
lucky man . . . but he could not automatically expect
that of her. Not yet.

He gave voice to one of his heated thoughts and
kept the rest to himself. "I want to taste you, really
taste you. I want to bury my face between your thighs
and take you with my tongue."

Her breath caught. "Sounds good."

He laughed. She was so refreshingly sweet, so unin-
tentionally sexy. "But I do not want my beard to
scratch your thighs."

She swallowed. "It's not like that would damage my
reputation. No one would be able to tell if my thighs
were chapped."

"I suppose not, but it makes it painful to walk. And
I would not knowingly hurt you."

"I'm willing to chance it, okay?"

He could eat her up. In fact, he would. All he had
to do was take off his shirt and tuck it around her to
cover strategic spots. The night was young.

Chapter 9

"It's not fair," Ambrose grumbled as Dorcas piloted her broom over the town of Big Knob. "Fairies don't feel the cold. Why can't we have that power?"

"Because we have others!" Dorcas had to shout so her answer wouldn't be carried away on the wind. Ambrose was getting on her last nerve. How could she expect George to stop complaining about the unfairness of things if her own husband insisted on doing it?

At least the snow had stopped falling, thank Goddess. Flying a broom through a snowstorm wasn't her idea of a good time. Flying it in the middle of an Indiana winter wasn't a rose garden, either. She had to keep brushing ice off the handle.

This time they wouldn't land a distance away and creep up on the poker game. With the super hearing of fairies, that was a bad plan. From the previous night's raid they'd developed the coordinates for the clearing where the poker games were held, and they were going to attempt a preemptive strike.

Ambrose had brought his wizard's staff, and she had brought her wand. She'd have to create the first spell to keep Leo from miniaturizing himself, because Ambrose would need a few seconds to screw his staff together. He'd decided to convert it to a two-piece model, which made transporting it easier, but his on-the-ground effectiveness was hampered.

She still thought they could make the plan work well enough to detain Leo and question him about his activities in the Whispering Forest. She'd practiced with her wand for a couple of hours before takeoff. Ambrose hadn't practiced a lick, but that was normal. That wizard believed he was invincible.

The cold aside, Dorcas loved flying on her broom. She'd bought it in Peru, and the handle was carved with various Kama Sutra positions. In the many long years she and Ambrose had been married, they'd tried nearly all the positions, but they'd never tried them on a broom.

She knew some witches and wizards who claimed to have done that successfully and had created the Mile-High Broom Handle Club. Dorcas wondered if they were all a bunch of liars. You could get killed doing that nonsense.

Still, she was intrigued. Maybe she and Ambrose could practice on the broom while it was suspended over the bed, in case one or both of them fell off.

"Dorcas, you passed the clearing."

So she had. And she'd been worried about Ambrose's level of concentration. She banked the broom in a sharp U-turn that had Ambrose shrieking with dismay. Even after all this time, he didn't trust her driving, especially on a high-powered broom like this one.

Glancing down, she easily pinpointed the target by the light from the lanterns hanging in the trees. The sound of laughter and the high-pitched chatter of raccoons floated upward from the poker game. She could spot a few of the raccoons, but not Leo, because of the way the trees obscured the view.

No matter. That laughter hadn't come from a raccoon. She tapped Ambrose on the thigh, which was the signal that she was going into her dive. He hated this part, but they needed to do it if they expected to maintain the element of surprise.

Besides, she loved going into a dive. Adrenaline pumping, she pointed the broom's nose at the ground. Whoosh! Like a falcon diving for prey, they hurtled silently toward the clearing at a speed that blew off her hood and brought tears to her eyes. The snowy clearing came at them fast. They clipped an evergreen branch on the way down and were sprayed with snow, but it blew off immediately as they plummeted downward.

Landing was the trick. Dorcas had to pull up the nose of the broom at precisely the right moment or they'd fly right into the ground. Ambrose was always sure they would do exactly that, but Dorcas had practiced this hundreds of times.

She registered the startled bandit faces of the raccoons and the surprise on Leo's handsome face right before she brought the broom's nose up and set them down neatly in the clearing. Unfortunately she also caught the guilty look in the red eyes of the dragon sitting on his regular seat of three tree stumps roped together. George had succumbed to temptation. Again.

The raccoons melted into the shadows as Dorcas pulled her wand out from under her coat. Leo wasn't moving quite as fast as he had the night before, fortunately. She gave credit to the pyramid of beer cans behind his seat.

She pointed her wand at him. *"Corpus status quo!"*

"Whatever." Leo shrugged. "I'm not afraid of you two. You can't even make a dragon toe the line, so why should I be worried?"

"It's his fault." George pointed a claw at Leo. "He

made the raccoons come and get me. They were all *Dude, we have a guest in the forest. You need to make him feel welcome.*"

"Never mind that now," Dorcas said. "Leo, why are you here?"

Leo picked up his beer and took a sip. "I don't have to answer that."

"Yes, you do." Dorcas glanced over her shoulder. "Doesn't he, Ambrose? Ambrose, what are you doing? Where's the other part of your staff?"

"I think I dropped it on the dive." He tramped through the snow, surveying the clearing. "That drop was too extreme, Dorcas. It's easy to lose things."

Dorcas couldn't look at Leo for fear he'd be laughing. Without the power of Ambrose's staff to freeze Leo in place until he confessed, they had no chance of forcing him to share anything he didn't choose to tell them. Her spell would keep him from minimizing himself and flying away, but he didn't seem inclined to do that, anyway. He was too interested in his beer.

Speaking of that, she thought she recognized the type he was drinking. The Big Knobian stocked quite a bit of that brand. "Where did you get the beer?" she asked.

"Found it." He took another swig.

"The dragon drank *no* beer," George said. "Just so you know. I'm beerless. Zero beer. Nada. No imbibe-o the beer-o."

"Okay, George. I get it." Dorcas sighed. "You're a victim of circumstances."

"Exactly!" George sidled over to her. "Care to take a spin around the dance floor, toots? I learned some new moves. I'm leee-thal!"

Dorcas didn't have to look at Leo to know he was laughing. She could hear him.

"Hey, Dorcas," Leo said. "It is Dorcas, right?"

"*Ms. Lowell* to you, sir. As the caretaker of this dragon, I have the right to inquire what your intentions—"

George bellowed in protest. "Caretaker? Dudette, that sounds way too much like *babysitter*, and we all know I don't need a babysitter. A hot dragon lady, now we're talkin'. She'd dig me 'cause I can dance. Chicks like dancin' dudes." George began wiggling his way around the clearing.

"My purpose for being here is benign," Leo said. "So don't get your undies in a bunch, Dorcas."

She gritted her teeth and wondered how his mother could even consider putting him on the throne. He was arrogant, careless, and self-absorbed. Oh, wait. That described the bulk of the world leaders. He'd fit right in.

"Your purpose may or may not be benign, but I'm concerned about the poker games in the forest," Dorcas said. "Ambrose, have you found the other part of your staff yet?"

"Still looking, my love," Ambrose called from the underbrush.

"What's wrong with a friendly game?" Leo asked.

Dorcas eyed his stack of chips and the considerable mound of gold pieces on a stump behind him. "The raccoons have been taking advantage of George's social nature to steal him blind."

"I resent that!" George bellowed. "I win my share of hands, I'll have you know." He blew out a puff of smoke.

"You can't think I'm here for treasure," Leo said. "Atwood is one of the wealthiest fairy kingdoms in existence."

"Ah, but you're not in charge of that kingdom yet, are you?" Dorcas decided to try and needle the truth out of him.

"I will be." Leo remained unruffled.

Or maybe he was just smashed. If he'd stolen the beer, that could cause some problems in a crime-free town like Big Knob. Dorcas glanced over her shoulder. "How are you coming along back there, Ambrose, my love?"

"Still searching," he called back.

With a sigh, Dorcas turned back to Leo, who regarded her with a supercilious grin. "If your purpose here is benign, then you shouldn't mind telling me what it is."

"It's personal. Very personal."

"Does it involve anyone in town, magical or otherwise?"

"Could be." Leo crunched the beer can in his fist.

She decided to try a veiled threat. "The Wizard Council won't be happy that you're camped out in the Whispering Forest, corrupting the dragon we're working with."

"They may not be happy, but they don't have a right to keep me out. They don't have jurisdiction over fairies, and you know it."

"But the Wizard Council and the Fairy Council have been working in harmony for years. I'd hate for anything to change that."

Leo smiled. "You're shadowboxing, Dorcas. You know as well as I do that the Wizard Council won't take on the Fairy Council over a pain-in-the-ass dragon living in a strategically unimportant forest."

"Hey!" George stopped dancing and stepped toward Leo. "You take that back!"

"Which part?" Leo looked unconcerned.

"Both parts, buddy boy. I have fire, and I know how to use it." Swishing his tail, he took another step toward the poker table.

Leo glanced up at the twelve-foot dragon and apparently reconsidered his stance. He held up both hands. "Didn't mean to insult you, dog. I just think if you want poker games, you should have poker games. I don't know why you let a witch and wizard tell you what to do."

"They don't tell me what to do." George slid a glance at Dorcas. "Exactly. They're helping me get my golden scales."

Leo gazed at the cases of beer as if debating whether to open another one. "And what's so great about golden scales?"

"Nothing," Dorcas said, fuming, "unless by chance you want to make a contribution to the world instead of using it as your own personal playground. But you wouldn't understand that concept, Leo, so I'm wasting my breath. Ambrose, have you found it yet?"

"No. Sorry."

"Then let's blow this taco stand."

George blinked. "Hey, dudette, I've never heard you talk like that."

"That's because I've never been this frustrated before." Dorcas stomped through the snow and retrieved her broom.

"Wait a minute," Leo said. "You can't leave without removing the *corpus status quo* spell."

"Let it wear off." Dorcas straddled the broom and glared at Leo. "I'm keeping an eye on you. And we *will* find the other half of Ambrose's staff. When that happens, look out." Mounting the broom, she motioned for Ambrose to climb on behind her.

With a vigorous kick, she sent the broom skyward.

"That didn't go well," Ambrose said.

"No, it didn't."

"I'll take a guess that you aren't in the mood for a little warm-up session in the marital bed."

"You would be guessing right, Ambrose."

The jury was in, and Gwen could say without reservation that a flesh-and-blood lover was far superior to a fantasy man. For one thing, she was awake for the festivities. When Marc had draped her thighs in his silk shirt, the party had proceeded in a most gratifying fashion. He'd given her two more amazing orgasms.

For another thing, he was really into cuddling, something her dream lover hadn't bothered with. Cuddling with him now that he'd taken off his shirt was very satisfying.

"For a professor, you sure have a lot of muscles." She stroked his chest, loving the masculine feel of the hair sprinkled across his pecs.

"I must keep in shape for the research trips."

"Those trips sound dangerous." She brushed her fingers over the nipples hidden beneath the hair and felt them tighten.

"*Oui,* they can be *formidable,* but I enjoy challenging myself out in the field." He sucked in a breath. "*Cherie,* maybe you should not do that."

She stopped teasing his nipples. "You don't like it?"

"I like it too much."

As she allowed her gaze to travel below his belt, she could see that. He'd been so good to her. Wasn't a little reciprocity in order?

Besides, she was curious about what lay in burgeoning splendor beneath the fly of his jeans. Unless he'd stuffed a sock in his underwear, which she seriously doubted, he had much to offer in that department. She wanted to take the mystery out of it.

Of course, being somewhat inexperienced at these things, she wasn't sure how a woman went about suggesting what she had in mind. His use of language had been so exciting, especially delivered with that dreamy accent. He'd made it sound as if he loved her American accent, but she couldn't imagine that her delivery would be as effective as his.

Neither could she imagine herself saying the words without stammering. The phrasing equivalent to what he'd said to her would be *I want to take you with my mouth and make you come.* Could she speak that sentence without messing up? Probably not.

Yet she couldn't lie there and let him suffer. After all, he was a guest in her house. She hadn't been able to feed him dinner, so at least she should offer him a blow job. But she wouldn't be able to use those words, either.

Maybe she could be subtle. Slowly she walked her fingers down to his belt buckle.

"Gwen? What are you doing?"

She started working on the buckle. "I was thinking that in the interest of hospitality . . ." She left the rest unsaid. He was a smart man. He'd figure it out.

"Hospitality?" Laughter edged his question. "Would it be something you feel obliged to do?"

She got the belt unfastened. "I prefer to think of it as a cultural exchange." She glanced up at him. "Interested?"

"Extremely."

"Great." She returned her attention to his belt. "Then let me—"

"I will." He caught her hand. "Believe me, I will. In the shower."

"Uh, I have a hand-held and a claw-foot tub, and that's the story in both bathrooms. You're probably used to a regular shower."

He cupped her face in his hand and guided her close for a tantalizingly brief kiss. "I am used to a hand-held and a claw-foot tub. I am from France, remember?"

As if she'd ever forget. "Then you've come to the right place."

He caressed her cheek with his thumb. "I agree."

Chapter 10

Leo couldn't coax the raccoons back to the poker table, and George seemed to have lost interest, as well. This gig had rapidly gone downhill in the past few hours. The night before he'd had it all—the girl, the beer and the poker game.

Tonight, however, he'd almost kissed a man, although he was doing his best to block that memory. The only positive spin he could put on the incident was remembering that the Frenchman had been alone in the bed. Gwen must have been sleeping down the hall.

But the Frenchman wasn't supposed to be in residence at all. Apparently the damned snowstorm had stranded the guy, so Gwen had given up her soft bed to the stranger. That fact made Leo's jaw clench. He didn't like the idea of anyone besides him enjoying those smooth sheets and that fluffy mattress.

On top of that irritation, he'd had to deal with the witch and wizard. He wasn't in the mood to miniaturize himself, but it grated that he couldn't until the witch's spell wore off. He shouldn't have let her get the drop on him, but he had to admit the beer had slowed him down some.

He still had the cases of beer, but he wasn't a fairy

who liked to drink alone. And the witch and wizard had put a serious crimp in his poker plans. Maybe the raccoons would come back eventually, and maybe they wouldn't. That broom dive had been enough to scare the fur off those little bandits.

He should probably bag this program, take the gold he'd won so far, claim success with Gwendolyn and go back to Atwood. He could say that Gwendolyn now had a man in her bed, which was true. His mother, refreshed after her vacation jaunt, might buy it. Spring was a good time for a coronation.

So why not do that? Because he wasn't ready to stop having sex with Gwendolyn, that's why. He'd missed out tonight, and he was feeling cranky about it.

She'd become an enjoyable habit he'd like to continue a while longer. He could give her up any time, of course, but why should he deny himself when she was possibly the most responsive partner, magical or otherwise, he'd ever had?

The answer was simple. He would give her up when he was good and ready, and not one minute before.

The bathroom off the master bedroom was tiny, which made Marc feel right at home. He had always thought he would get lost in the gigantic bathrooms he had heard were commonplace in American homes these days. Besides, the lack of space meant he had to stay very close to Gwen, and he liked that very much.

She stepped over to the claw-foot tub with its curved shower curtain rod and shower head mounted on a gliding pole. He noted with satisfaction that the bathroom might be small, but the tub was built for two. He approved.

"It might take a minute for the hot water." She leaned down to turn on the faucet.

Meanwhile, Marc admired the way the silk nightgown draped her sexy bottom when she reached for the faucet. His penis twitched. If he had condoms, he could bend her over the pedestal sink and . . . but he had no condoms. Or a razor, which was another impediment he was unaccustomed to.

"Do you have a razor I may borrow?"

She turned. "The kind I use for my legs."

"I am not particular." He rubbed a hand over his scratchy chin. "My beard grows very fast, and I . . . I want to kiss you properly."

Smiling, she opened a hand-painted cupboard hanging on the wall above the toilet. "I'd rather you kissed me improperly."

He sucked in a breath as her breasts jiggled under the pale green silk and the pendant shifted, then settled back into her cleavage. She was driving him crazy with unsatisfied desire. He wondered if she had any idea the iron control he was exercising to keep himself from taking her, and damn the consequences.

"You do not have any condoms somewhere in the back of that cabinet, do you?" He doubted it, but no harm in asking.

She handed him a pink razor and a small can of shaving cream with flowers on it. "Believe me, I wish I did."

"Are you taking birth control?" He was becoming a desperate man. He knew he had no health issues, and he doubted she did, so if she was on the pill . . .

"No." She blushed. "I haven't—um, well, there's been no reason for a while."

"I did not mean to pry," he said quickly. "I just—"

"I know." She glanced down at his trousers where the bulge was obvious. She lifted her gaze. "Me, too."

He groaned softly.

They were so engrossed in each other that they might have stood there until one of them spontaneously combusted. The steam swirling around seemed appropriate, considering the heat in her eyes and the fire raging in his veins.

But when he could barely see her through the fog, he decided maybe they should do something about the situation. "I believe the water is hot now."

"Oh!" She spun back to the tub. "Are you ready for the shower, or would you rather shave first?"

"Fill the tub. A bath will do, as well, and I will shave while you run the water."

"That works." She had to lean way over to retrieve the rubber plug sitting on a little shelf mounted next to the tub.

God help him, he ogled. There was no other word for the way he concentrated on the hem of her night-gown and watched it rise higher as she reached down to insert the plug in the drain. Dear God. Another inch and he would be able to see . . . everything.

She straightened slightly while she adjusted the flow of water and tested it with her hand. The view was not quite as agonizingly wonderful, but heart stopping just the same. He imagined lifting the silk and caress-ing her smooth butt cheeks before he sought the moist spot that was barely out of sight. He trembled at the thought.

But if he gave her another climax now, he would not shave, or if he tried shaving, he would cut his throat. He wanted to shave, wanted to be able to use his mouth on her without worrying about harming her skin. With a supreme effort, he turned toward the sink.

The mirror above it was fogged. A man with a cleft in his chin needed to be able to see. Taking a hand towel from a nearby rack, he wiped a clear space in the mirror. Then he squirted some of the floral cream on his hand, smoothed it over his face and began to shave.

The razor was curved in a way that caused him some difficulties, frustrating his attempt to make quick work of the job. He felt her watching him and suspected she was perched on the closed toilet lid, waiting.

He decided against glancing over to confirm the fact. Looking at her and visualizing what might happen soon with that sweet mouth of hers only made the delay worse. He could hear her soft breathing and even catch her scent, despite the flowery shaving cream overwhelming his sense of smell. But he was not going to look at her.

Finally he reached the tricky part, shaving around the damned dimple. Women might like it, but it was a royal pain in the ass every time he took a blade to it.

"What brand of condom do you like?"

Zip! He cut himself. He swore softly in French.

"Marc, you're bleeding!"

Yes, he was, and no styptic pencil to stop the flow. How romantic he would look with a piece of toilet paper stuck to his chin. He splashed cold water on the nick and willed the blood to stay inside his body. As if that would work.

"Let me help."

He turned to her with blood dripping down his chin. What a suave Frenchman he was.

Holding a tissue in one hand, she grasped him by the back of the head. "Lean closer."

"I feel like a fool." He stooped so that she could reach him better.

"I'm sure it's hard to shave there." She stood on tiptoe and got within two inches of his face as she dabbed at the cut.

"You cannot imagine." He was close enough to study her full mouth, and the longer he did, the more he ached to kiss her again.

She dabbed some more and squinted at the cut. "There. It's stopped now."

"I think you really do need those glasses."

"For small things, yes." Her eyes sparkled with mischief. "So I doubt I'll need them in the tub."

His bark of surprised laughter was followed by an intense desire to finally kiss that saucy mouth in the fashion it deserved. "This is what you get for taunting me." Without preamble he grabbed her and planted his lips firmly over hers. Nothing else mattered but her mouth and his insatiable hunger.

He delved deep, wild with excitement at finally being able to fully enjoy the experience again. Ah, this was good. She had lips made for kisses—his kisses. He could not get enough of her.

He was vaguely aware that she was fumbling with the fastening of his pants, but he became fully aware when she reached inside his silk boxers. He groaned and lifted his mouth a fraction away from hers. "Be careful."

"Your skin is hot," she murmured as she wrapped her fingers around his cock.

"Quelle surprise." He outlined her lips with his tongue as his heart galloped frantically in response to her touch. "If you continue, my skin will also be wet."

"Ready for your bath?" She squeezed gently.

His vocal cords were tight from the effort of holding back. "I thought you would never ask."

She withdrew her hand and efficiently shoved his boxers and slacks to the floor in a show of eagerness. He liked that in a woman. As he stepped out of the puddle of clothes, she stood aside and made a slow survey of his attributes.

He was used to being naked in front of a lover, but he had never worried overmuch about their opinion of his body. Gwen's opinion mattered. "Am I acceptable?"

Her brown eyes flared with desire. "I'm surprised the women of France let you out of the country. You must be a national treasure."

He flushed, ridiculously pleased with the compliment. "I think not." He gazed at her. "And now it is your turn."

She started to take off the pendant.

"Please leave that on."

Hesitating, she closed her fingers over the smooth stone.

"The water will not hurt it," he said. "The chain is gold."

She still seemed uncertain. "But I've never worn a necklace into the bathtub. And it doesn't belong to me."

"You said Madame Lowell loaned it to you."

"Yes, and she insisted I wear it today. Or yesterday, considering it's two in the morning."

Marc wondered if Madame Lowell would sell the pendant, because he wanted to buy it for Gwen. "It is perfect for you, *cherie*. When I see the stone resting in the valley between your breasts, I envy it. I want to be that stone."

"What a beautiful thing to say."

"Please leave it on," he said softly. "There is nothing sexier than a woman wearing a necklace and nothing else."

She gazed at him for several long seconds. Slowly the fire intensified in her brown eyes. Her back arched slightly and her breasts lifted, as if in deliberate invitation.

He watched, fascinated, as she took on the unmistakable bearing of a temptress. She might claim to be unsophisticated, but she looked quite worldly standing before him at this moment.

"Well, then." She reached for the laces holding the lapels of her nightgown together. "It will be my pleasure to give you that visual." Slowly she pulled on both ends of the ties until the bow came undone. Loosening the laces, she gradually pulled the nightgown over her shoulders.

Holding his breath, he waited for the garment to fall and expose the breasts he had fondled, kissed, and never seen. The silk moved with glacial slowness as it descended, revealing creamy mounds that made his mouth water. Then the nightgown caught briefly on her nipples, leaving two rosy half crescents of areola visible.

He moaned. She gave a shimmy, and the nightgown fell to the floor.

As a Frenchman, he prided himself on never being at a loss for words. Yet when confronted with her generous breasts, her small waist, and the downy patch marking the entrance to all things feminine and wonderful—he was speechless. The pendant glowed against her skin and made her look like a regal goddess who had descended from Mount Olympus to grace mere mortals with her presence.

"Am I acceptable?" There was laughter in her voice. Apparently she could see the thunderstruck expression on his face and knew full well that she had achieved her goal of seducing him senseless.

His brain still refused to produce coherent speech, and his tongue felt thick and unwieldy in his mouth. That had never happened in his adult life. He had always been ready with the right comment. Gwen had reduced him to the level of a witless fool who could only nod and continue to stare at her. His dick, however, spoke volumes.

"Then it's bath time." She held out a hand.

How he managed to climb in without stumbling, he would never know. Instead of watching what he was doing, he was consumed with watching her. She climbed in with him and began to wash his pheromone-charged body.

He told himself to snap out of it, to take control of the situation and act like the proud Frenchman he was. Instead he let her caress him with the soft washcloth until he thought he would go out of his mind. He missed the moment when she reached back and pulled the plug. Some of the time he had his eyes closed and was sure he was whimpering with pleasure.

But as the water gurgled down the drain, she leaned forward until her pendant dangled against his rock-hard penis. Then she caught the stone in one hand and rubbed it along the sides of his jutting cock. She continued that sweet torture as he lay propped against the tub in a state of orgasmic lust, hypnotized by the sway of her breasts each time she moved.

He was amazed that he had not come yet, but she seemed to know how far to push him before letting up. At last she rose to her knees and kissed him on the mouth. "Sit on the edge of the tub with your back against the wall," she murmured.

Because he guessed her intention, he found the energy to move. That request could mean only one thing. He struggled to his knees and levered himself into the position she had described.

And then—dear heaven, did life get any better than this?—she took his penis into her mouth. Time stopped. It seemed for a second that his heart stopped. But it started up again, racing at breakneck speed as she caressed him with her lips and tongue. She gave him the full treatment, massaging his balls as she tended to a climax that loomed ever closer.

When he came, his bellow of gratitude rang in the tiny bathroom. Fiercely he gripped the edge of the tub, determined not to topple over and crush her. That would not be a gentlemanly thing to do.

"You . . . are wonderful," he was able to choke out.

Smiling, she helped him out of the tub and clumsily they dried each other off. At last they tumbled naked into her bed.

"You truly are amazing," he said again as they cuddled under the covers.

She snuggled next to him. "You know, I'm beginning to think I am."

Chapter 11

While Ambrose was out shoveling the walk at dawn the following morning, Dorcas tracked down Sabrina to her hidey-hole under the stairs and took off the diamond-studded collar. Ambrose was shoveling, rather than waiting for darkness so he could spell the snow away, because he wanted Dorcas to take pity on him and let him out of the doghouse. He'd headed out there before breakfast, even before coffee.

He was playing the martyr role. She knew it, and she suspected he knew it, too. They'd been married long enough to read each other pretty well.

The heavy snowstorm had been a blessing, though, and she'd already taken a pre-dawn walk to ascertain that Marc's rental car sat in the same spot where he'd parked it the night before. But if Ambrose hadn't remembered at the last minute to turn on the exit sign, Marc might not be in Big Knob at all.

The combination of the exit sign incident and the lost section of Ambrose's staff had ticked her off sufficiently that she wasn't in a particularly loving mood. So she would let him shovel, which wasn't a bad idea, because they needed to keep the neighbors calm. A walk that was snow-covered one day and clean the next, with no evidence of shoveling, could stir up the locals. They wouldn't take kindly to discovering they had a witch and wizard in their midst.

Carrying the collar down to the cellar, she used a butane lighter to ignite her ceremonial candles. Then she tucked the collar in her pocket while she filled the cauldron with water.

Sabrina followed, of course, complaining in high-pitched meows about the loss of her cherished adornment. Sabrina's attachment to the collar only solidified Dorcas's belief that it contained an entitlement charm.

"If you want your collar back, you have to come into the circle and help me." Dorcas dumped the last bucket of water in the cauldron and turned on the gas logs underneath. Then she added a few select herbs and one of Sabrina's whiskers. Whenever Sabrina lost one, Dorcas scooped it up and saved it in a Ziploc bag for future magical use.

Sabrina jumped up on the CD player sitting on a table next to the wall and nudged it with her nose.

Dorcas noticed but continued stirring the brew with a forked stick. "So sorry. We're not playing the Frankie Avalon CD. That's Ambrose's thing, not mine."

Sabrina gave a little *rrrtt* of protest.

"No. This is a discovery charm, not a matchmaking charm. We don't need to hear 'Venus.' In fact, I don't care if I ever hear it again."

Sabrina looked at her with wide eyes, as if Dorcas had committed heresy.

"You're only sticking up for Ambrose because he bought you this collar." She took it from her pocket and motioned Sabrina over. "If you're getting in the circle with me, any time would be good."

Keeping her attention on the sparkling collar, Sabrina pranced over and sat next to the cauldron.

"Let's do it." Dorcas walked clockwise around the cauldron with Sabrina mincing along behind her, looking generally pissed. Dorcas didn't have time to coddle the cat. Eliminating the entitlement charm on Sabrina's collar was only the first item on her to-do list, and she needed to handle it quickly so she could turn to more pressing matters, like the match between Gwen and Marc and the troubling presence of Leo in the forest.

Muttering the discovery charm, she used the forked stick to lower the collar into the cauldron. Leaning the stick against the pot, she resumed her circular walk while she waited the required number of minutes for the potion to work. If her neighbors could only see her now . . .

Somehow she and Ambrose had been able to keep secret their magical status and the presence of a dragon in the forest. Then there was the lake monster named Dee-Dee who'd surfaced the previous summer in Deep Lake, which was visible from the Lowells' kitchen window.

As the resident witch and wizard, Dorcas and Ambrose had been expected to handle Dee-Dee, too. They'd done so by transporting a mate to the lake. Dorcas broke out in a cold sweat remembering the dangers inherent in that maneuver.

They'd succeeded, though, with the help of the town's founder, Isadora Mather. If the townspeople would freak over having a witch and wizard living in their midst, they'd go postal if they ever learned that their beloved town was founded back in the early 1800s by a certified witch who currently resided in San Francisco.

Isadora had made an incognito visit last summer and had helped transport Dee-Dee's true love, Norton, from North Lake. Dee-Dee had been absolutely no problem since. Next spring Dorcas wouldn't be surprised to see a pair of baby lake monsters swimming in the moonlight.

Yes, there were gratifying moments. And then there was George. Sometimes Dorcas felt as if she were juggling punch bowls filled with that awful sherbet-and-fruit-drink concoction that was served at most events here in Big Knob. One false step and she'd be covered in broken glass and icky slop.

Other times she realized she'd fallen in love with the quirky little town and its even quirkier inhabitants. George gave them a convenient excuse to stay on.

In the time they'd lived here, she'd made two converts to magic—Maggie Madigan was their assistant and would return to work soon with little Daisy in tow. Annie Dunstan was working as a correspondent for *Wizardry World* magazine, which was why she was currently in Scotland instead of at home helping Gwen through this soul mate business.

Other than Maggie and Annie, no one else in Big Knob had a clue as to the magical events going on under their collective noses. Dorcas planned to keep it that way. Nonmagical people tended to get nervous in the presence of spells and potions.

She checked her watch. "Ready for the bad news, Sabrina?"

Sabrina sat down, tail twitching, and stared up at the steam rising from the cauldron.

Using the forked stick, Dorcas lifted the collar out of the water. "See? I knew it!" The collar glowed red, a sure sign of an entitlement spell. It was a powerful spell, too. A light pink would have been something she could undo in a few minutes, but this deep red would take hours to counter. She didn't have hours.

Sabrina gazed at the collar and let out a plaintive yowl.

"You can't have it, kitty cat." Ignoring Sabrina's meows of protest, Dorcas balanced the collar on the stick as it gradually cooled. Finally she was able to slip it back into her pocket.

Then she turned to Sabrina. "Once life settles down, I'll see what I can do. It's a pretty collar, but I can't let you wear it like this. You'll become insufferable."

Sabrina glared at her without blinking. She was obviously not happy. But maybe she wouldn't be expecting to have her pillow fluffed during happy hour, either. At least Dorcas had accomplished that much.

Closing the circle, she walked over to the valve and turned off the flame under the cauldron. If Ambrose had finished shoveling the walk, she might relent and allow him a little before-breakfast treat. They hadn't used their sex bench in a while. After Maggie's husband, Sean, had built them such a sturdy one, she hated to see it go to waste.

Gwen didn't have much experience with morning-afters, but Marc seemed to have enough experience for both of them. The phrase *charmed the pants off her* could have been invented to describe Marc. He'd smiled at her upon waking and assured her he'd had the best night of his life.

She doubted that, but he was sweet to say so, especially when she woke up with bed head. After her makeover she'd felt more glamorous than ever in her life, but she wasn't exactly holding the glamour card this morning. One look in the mirror told her—even without her glasses—that she'd morphed back into the old Gwen, with the exception of the gold streaks.

But to hear Marc talk, she was his angel of the morning. He combed his fingers through her tangled hair and pronounced her beautiful. The sun was just rimming the hills on the far side of town, and they

had to sneak out to the Whispering Forest before anyone was around who might question them. She
couldn't even let him go across the square to his car
to get his suitcase for a change of clothes.

Although she figured he could do without sex and
clean clothes temporarily, she couldn't expect him to
go without a decent breakfast. He'd suffered through
many long hours without food, so he readily agreed
with the plan. He also helped her make omelets without being intrusive, which was a miracle in itself.

By adhering to a hands-off policy so they wouldn't
get distracted, they made it out her back door in less
than thirty minutes. A cold blue sky and mounds of
snow greeted them. The sun barely made a dent in
the frigid temperature, and their breath fogged the air.

Because of the fogging issue, she'd tucked her
glasses into the pocket of her coat. Or maybe it wasn't
only the fogging issue. His praise of her beauty had
made her reconsider getting contacts, or at least
glasses that suited her better than these.

She realized now that she'd never thought enough
of her attractiveness to buy a nicer pair. The pendant
she continued to wear seemed to demand that she
think about how to look good instead of dismissing
that as a lost cause. When she'd had to pick an outfit
out of her closet this morning, she'd concluded that
her wardrobe needed a major overhaul.

The quality of Marc's clothes underlined that
thought, although he wasn't nearly the fashion statement now that he'd been yesterday. He was, however,
better prepared to face an Indiana winter day.

Gwen had loaned him her father's navy goose-down
jacket, thermal gloves, and an old pair of fur-lined
boots, items Andre Dubois had left for his rare winter
trips back to Big Knob. The boots fit, but the jacket
was a little small. Marc didn't complain, but Gwen

wondered if his fashion sense was insulted by the loaner clothes.

She thought he'd look yummy no matter what he wore. Or didn't wear. That train of thought had to be derailed *tout suite*. They had things to do before they could consider doing each other.

Nevertheless, she'd have to be made of ice not to anticipate their next sexual encounter, whenever it might be. As she started down the narrow path leading into the woods, she glanced back over her shoulder. "You know that question I asked that made you nick your chin?" She'd noticed this morning that he had a tiny scab at the edge of his dimple to commemorate that moment.

"I remember it well."

"You didn't answer me."

"I was too busy bleeding."

She hoped she wasn't being too forward, but the subject needed to be broached. "We can buy condoms in town today."

"I told you that I would protect your reputation."

"Forget my reputation. Protect me from getting pregnant and I'm good."

"I am serious, Gwen." His footsteps crunched through the snow as he followed her. "You have lived here all your life. I am not willing to suddenly appear and ruin the good name you have worked years to build."

"What makes you think I have a good name?"

"Everyone in the bar hovered around you, trying to help when you had your coughing fit. You are obviously beloved in this town."

She'd never thought about it that way. "They'd treat anybody like that."

"I do not believe so. That Madame Loudermilk would not have people hovering over her."

Gwen smiled. "Clara would never put herself in a

position that required hovering, but I understand what you're saying."

"I need to stay in Evansville for the next two nights."

"What?" She stopped and turned around. "You must be joking."

"No." He cupped her face in his gloved hands, and his gaze was endearingly earnest. "There will be enough talk when everyone learns that I spent the night at your house, but the snowstorm will excuse it. If I stay the rest of the time, they will know something is going on between us."

"First of all, you're supposed to be my cousin—"

"Which I am sure nobody believes."

"And second of all, what's wrong with me having a man stay in my house all night if I want to? It's not like I'm some vestal virgin. I'm an adult woman, and if I want to have sex, that's my—" She would have continued the rant if he hadn't called a halt by kissing her.

As a conversation stopper, it was a beaut. No woman in her right mind would continue talking when she could be kissing Marc Chevalier. As he thrust his tongue into her mouth, she could swear the temperature surrounding them rose by a good ten degrees.

Her hood fell back, and he tunneled his fingers through her hair to hold her absolutely still for his kiss, which was turning into quite a production. She would give it five stars, easy.

The longer he kissed her, the less she cared about the opinion of her friends and neighbors. If he wanted her to agree that abstinence was the way to go, he had a funny way of shoring up his argument. She was beginning to wonder if it was true that snow was a good insulator, and if so, how fast they could build themselves a makeshift igloo.

When he came up for air, they were both breathing

hard enough to create a little cloud layer right where they stood.

She gulped for air. "And your point is?"

"I care about you, *cherie*."

The cold must have been making her eyes water. Surely she wasn't tearing up because he'd told her he cared. Well, yes, she was. She'd never imagined that a guy who looked, acted, and kissed like Marc would say that to her.

He brushed at her cheeks with his gloved thumbs. "I did not mean to make you cry."

"You didn't." She sniffed. "It's the cold."

"Oh." He smiled as if he didn't believe a word of it. "If I did not know better, I would think you are not used to hearing a man say that."

"Sure I am. I hear it so much it's old hat now."

He studied her face. "You do not know how beautiful you are, do you?"

"Of course I do." She sniffed again. "Red nose and chapped lips. What could be lovelier?"

He shook her gently. "Stop that."

"Stop what?"

"Denying your own beauty. I am French. I know beauty when I see it."

"We're talking inner beauty, right? Because I'm all over that. I have the most gorgeous insides you ever saw."

"If my penis could talk, I am sure it would agree with you."

She laughed at the mental image of a talking penis. She pictured it in cartoon form on YouTube, although it was probably too X-rated a subject for that venue. "Would your penis have a sexy accent, too?"

His blue eyes sparkled. "Ah. Mademoiselle, she loves zee ac-*cent*," he said, deliberately emphasizing it. "I must keep zee ac-*cent* com-*ing*."

"Which will keep *me* com-*ing*. Seriously, Marc. Tell me you're not planning to stay at the Holiday Inn for the next two nights."

"I am. But we can still have sex. We just need to be creative. And we have proven we are good at that."

Her beautiful insides, already primed by his kiss, heated another notch or two. Still, she hated to give up two long, glorious nights with him in her fluffy bed. "You do realize I have to work in the shop most of the day, right?"

"I expected that. I can amuse myself."

"If you insist on this Evansville thing, you leave us with so little time. Don't worry about gossip. Stay with me."

"For dinner, yes." He gave her a lingering kiss.

"And dessert?" she murmured against his warm mouth.

"Mm. *Oui.*"

"And a second dessert?" All this talk of her beauty was giving her confidence in her seductive powers. She rubbed against him and gazed into his eyes. If they hadn't been layered in all sorts of winter gear, the rubbing-bodies part might have been more effective.

His blue eyes darkened. "I will enjoy as many desserts as you care to serve. But I will be leaving your home by ten."

"Spoilsport." Privately she plotted how to keep him there. Sessions in her claw-foot tub seemed to work pretty well. She'd just see about this proposed curfew of his. She finally had a Frenchman in her bed, and she didn't want to miss a moment of all that French culture.

"The sun has risen," he said. "Our sneaking-to-see-the-plants plan may soon be compromised."

She sighed with reluctance. She'd been so excited about showing him the plants, but compared to standing in the snow, kissing him, or returning to her bedroom to kiss him some more, viewing the plants didn't seem all that significant.

She'd read about passions this all consuming, but she'd never experienced one firsthand. Now she understood why perfectly sane women turned into blithering idiots. She was in danger of doing that herself.

She would consider closing the shop for the day, but he probably wouldn't let her do that, either, for fear of the talk that would cause. "You still haven't answered the condom question." She was nothing if not persistent, and he might as well discover that now.

"Condoms are not a problem."

She looked into his eyes and saw uncertainty there. She hoped it didn't mean that he was giving up on the concept of having a complete sexual experience with her. "Aren't you planning to indulge in anything that requires them?"

"I did not say that."

Perplexed, she studied him for several seconds. Finally she understood. "You brought them!"

"I debated the question for a long time. I hated for you to think that I—"

"That you hoped we'd get it on? Oh, Marc, that might be the nicest compliment you've paid me so far, and you've paid me a bunch."

"You are not offended?"

She gazed up at him. "I'm flattered. Flattered to think that somehow, through e-mails, without exchanging pictures or personal stats, you were intrigued enough to think we might connect, that we might choose to have sex."

"By French standards, it is too soon. I should have spent more time, prepared the groundwork for what happened. In France, a woman is not rushed into bed."

"Not even if a man is overcome by his desire for

her?" That was the part Gwen loved. If they'd connected as he'd hoped, then he'd planned for a slow seduction. But he hadn't been able to hold back.

"There are exceptions, of course, but generally speaking, a Frenchman—"

"I adore being the exception to the rule." She kissed him quickly and stepped away. "Now let's go check those plants. As we say in America, we're burning daylight."

Chapter 12

"**W**e should use this sex bench more often." Magnificently naked, Ambrose straddled the bench, and Dorcas, equally unclothed, straddled him. They'd managed a simultaneous orgasm, something they were infinitely capable of, but they hadn't put that kind of care into their sex life recently. This morning they had, and she felt satisfied on many levels.

"We will, I promise," Dorcas said. "But now we should probably shower and get dressed." They could magically shower and dress in an instant, but the older they got, the more often they chose the nonmagical way. Dorcas had become quite fond of hot showers and towels warmed by a heated rack.

"I suppose we do need to get going. We haven't even had breakfast yet."

"No, and there's plenty to do today." She gave him a quick kiss and disentangled herself. "We need to find the rest of your staff, for one thing."

"I know." He sounded like a little boy who'd lost one of his mittens.

"Then we also have to check on Gwen, Marc and the plants, not to mention George, who has definitely regressed."

"Looks like it. By the way, thanks for finding that

entitlement charm on Sabrina's collar. The guy's obviously a liar, which I find hard to believe. He was so sincere."

"Uh-huh." Dorcas's irritation with Ambrose had evaporated. Her husband was guilty of wanting to buy something special for the cat he loved, which wasn't a crime. If he tended to believe the best of everyone, that wasn't so terrible, either.

"I will get a full refund once he's back. Or else."

"Oh, don't bother fooling with that. Sabrina loves the collar, and I'll bet I can get that charm off. I just need a free evening to work on it."

"Those are in short supply these days."

"I know." She started toward the bathroom. "I'd better take the first shower so I have time to do my hair."

"Will those burgundy streaks wash out?" Ambrose called after her.

"Nope!" She went over to the tub and turned on the water.

"At least the sparkles will be gone, right?"

She stuck her head around the door frame. "I bought more sparkles."

"Oh." He glanced down at his lap. "I have sparkles on my dick."

"How festive."

He rolled his eyes. "Dorcas, could you *please* change your hair back to the way it was?"

"Negative. Look at it this way, Ambrose. With this hairstyle I feel twenty years younger."

"So?"

"So a woman who feels twenty years younger should be more interested in sex, don't you think?"

His expression changed from annoyed to hopeful. "Really?"

She nodded.

He climbed off the bench. "In that case, how about a quickie in the shower?"

She couldn't help smiling. He was so predictable. "How could I possibly resist a wizard with sparkles on his dick?"

Marc had seen many unusual plant behaviors in his years of botanical research, but finding a species of tropical plant growing in the snow was a first. He took some preliminary pictures with his BlackBerry, but he would come back with his digital camera later.

Once he had some shots, he crouched down next to one of the plants. "So the Lowells discovered these?"

"Right. Not many people go into the Whispering Forest other than Dorcas and Ambrose. Jeff Brady, the guy who owns the Big Knobian, snowshoes in here sometimes, but he stays on the road. I didn't go in here myself until this thing came up about the plants."

Marc fingered one waxy leaf. Then he glanced up at her. "Do you believe the woods are haunted?"

"No." She hesitated. "I mean, not logically, but I grew up hearing stories of people who swore they heard someone whispering, but when they turned, no one was there. And others say they saw disembodied eyes through the trees."

Marc stood and glanced around him. "Practical jokes, perhaps?" He pulled his borrowed gloves from the pockets of his borrowed coat and put them back on. It was damned cold out here.

"Not many practical jokes last for more than a century," she said. "The stories go back further than that, actually. Lucy Dunstan has some old diaries where the pioneers mentioned the same phenomena. I'm sure there's some reasonable explanation."

Marc was becoming more intrigued by the minute. Nature-based religions fascinated him. He had seen several varieties along the Amazon, and he could be standing in a hotbed of another variety right here in Big Knob.

The street grid, the founder's name and now the haunted forest were making him wonder what might be bubbling under the surface of this supposedly quiet little town. If a secret Wiccan community had flourished here ever since the early 1800s, the members might find it to their advantage to perpetuate the haunted forest myth.

He would love to have time to explore the area and see if he could find any evidence that the forest was used for conducting Wiccan rituals. All his reading had convinced him of the gentle nature of Wicca, but most people did not share that view. They thought witches were scary creatures who wore pointed hats and rode on broomsticks.

But he already knew Gwen would rather avoid talking about the possibility of Wiccans having lived here, perhaps still living here. He might have to go elsewhere for his information. "You mentioned that Lucy Dunstan has some old diaries," he said. "Who is she?"

"The town historian. Her son, Jeremy, owns Click-or-Treat."

"Jeremy is married to your best friend, Annie."

"Right. He owns the Internet café I've been using to e-mail you, the same place where you can get high-speed access and e-mail Josette."

Josette. He kept forgetting about her. Some big brother he was. She was going through a crisis in school, and he needed to make sure she was okay. After that he could look into this other matter, which he believed was somehow connected to the out-of-place bromeliads.

Then there was Gwen. His time with her was limited, especially if he insisted on his plan of sleeping in his hotel room in Evansville. His sense of responsibility, his innate scientific curiosity and lust were pulling him in different directions.

Josette had to be given top priority, though. He had neglected her long enough. "How soon does the café open?"

Gwen looked at her watch. "We have another thirty minutes or so. We could be there in about fifteen minutes if we continue along the walking path around town and cut in where Fourth and Fifth intersect."

"At the point of the star."

"Yes."

"This walking path . . ." He hated to upset her again, but his curiosity was killing him.

"Connects the points of the star," she said with obvious reluctance. "I thought of that last night."

"So there is a circle around the star, after all." He was becoming more excited with every new detail.

"Yes, but it doesn't mean anything. Over the years people created the obvious shortcuts. That's all the walking path is—shortcuts."

"I am certain you are correct." But he wanted to talk to Lucy Dunstan and find out more about Isadora Mather. He could also Google Isadora while he was on the Internet. Gwen would not approve. She would not appreciate his wanting to poke around in the forest, looking for ritual circles, either.

He could hardly blame her. She had grown up with a certain set of beliefs about the town where she had lived all her life. He, however, had been exposed to many different cultures and ways of thinking.

But more than that, his parents' deaths in an avalanche during a skiing vacation had taught him that nothing stays the same, no matter how much you might want it to. Their deaths had forced him to embrace change instead of resisting it, but Gwen obviously enjoyed the predictability of Big Knob. She had no interest in hearing that it might not be quite so predictable.

Yet even as he recognized how different they were, he was drawn to her in a way he had never been attracted to another woman. Others had needed to stage an all-out seduction in order to interest him. Gwen had only to glance at him a certain way, or dampen her lower lip with her tongue, or draw in a sharp little breath, and he was filled with an unquenchable thirst for her.

Three days would never be enough to slake it. He already knew that, already was planning how to get her to Paris or make another trip over here. Whatever linked them was powerful. He smiled to himself. Almost like magic.

"You still think the town was laid out by witches, don't you?" Her gaze held a mixture of fear and defiance.

He stepped toward her and took hold of both her hands. "I do not know what to think. You must admit it is intriguing to have a town arranged this way and stories of ghosts in the woods."

"The forest isn't haunted." Her chin lifted, as if daring him to contradict her.

Instead he was blindsided with a dose of lust. He tamped it down. Now was not the time.

He noticed, though, that she had chosen to talk about the haunted forest instead of the street grid. He had a feeling she was no longer so ready to do battle on that front.

Maybe he should leave the subject alone, but he could not. "If the forest is not haunted, how do you explain the stories about disembodied eyes and whispering continuing all these years?"

"People are naturally superstitious." Her tone was

cool and logical. "They were probably even more superstitious a hundred and fifty years ago. Wind became whispers, and the eyes of animals in the dark became disembodied. The myth was passed down and grew more entrenched."

He nodded. "That makes sense. So why not walk in the woods on a regular basis, even at night?" He wanted to know what she was telling herself about these superstitions.

She looked sheepish. "After hearing these things from the time I was old enough to understand, I can't come in here without getting a little spooked. I would never come here at night. I know that's illogical, but—" She went very still and her eyes widened. "Did you hear something?"

Now that she mentioned it, he did. Someone or *something* was coming, its footsteps crunching against the snow. Ghosts would not crunch, he told himself, but all this talk had spooked him a little, too.

"I didn't tell you about the rock," she murmured. Looking scared, she edged closer to him. "Something dropped a rock on one of the bromeliads the night before last."

The hairs on the back of his neck prickled. "That rock over there?" He tilted his head toward a good-sized boulder.

"Yeah. There were five bromeliads out here after Dorcas and Ambrose dug one up."

The crunching grew louder. "That is a big rock." He tried to imagine the strength it would take to move it, and adrenaline spiked through his system.

"Dorcas thought maybe a bear might have wandered over from Ohio."

"Judging from the size of the rock, it would be a big bear." He tried to remember what little he knew about bears. About all he could recall was that they were very fast. They could outrun humans. "If it is a bear, you run and I will distract it," he said.

She squeezed his hands. "Fat chance."

"I am serious, Gwen. You must—"

"Hello!" called a male voice.

Gwen's shoulders slumped in obvious relief. "It's Ambrose," she said. "Dorcas and Ambrose must have come out to check on the plants. We're here!" she called out.

Dorcas and Ambrose. Marc was beginning to believe it was more than coincidence that the Lowells had found the plants. He knew from Gwen's e-mails that the couple was relatively new in town. He vaguely remembered Gwen mentioning they had moved here from Sedona. And unlike the locals, they enjoyed hiking around in the Whispering Forest.

Marc added Sedona as something else to Google once he got the chance. He would like to pay a visit to the Lowells' house, too. Madame Lowell had invited him and Gwen for dinner, but considering the way things had turned out, he was glad they had stayed at Gwen's.

He still disliked the idea of spending hours with them when he could be alone with Gwen. But he would consider going over for a cup of coffee. With the research from his student days, he would know what to look for.

Madame Lowell came into the clearing first, followed by her husband. They looked almost like Parisians with the understated elegance of their fur-trimmed silver jackets, slim black ski pants and fur-lined boots. Marc felt a sharp pain in the vicinity of his heart. Had his parents lived, they might look something like this now.

Dorcas smiled at them. "Monsieur Chevalier, I'd like you to meet my husband."

Marc stepped forward, hand outstretched. "I am glad to meet you at last, Monsieur Lowell."

"Call me Ambrose." His grip was firm and his gaze was clear and assessing.

"All right."

"And please call me Dorcas," said Madame Lowell. "I feel as if we're friends."

Or accomplices. Marc might have been an unwitting one, but he could not complain, considering how everything was turning out with Gwen.

He smiled at Dorcas. "But of course. And my friends call me Marc." He had met Dorcas the night before, but his jet lag had kept him from noticing how attractive she was. Ambrose was a perfect match for her, with his square jaw and touches of gray at his temples.

Neither one of them looked as if they belonged in a little town like Big Knob. They appeared to be a middle-aged couple who had done well and were now easing into a comfortable retirement. He could picture them in a home on the French Riviera, maybe, or the American equivalent, which was probably somewhere along the California coast.

But instead they were here. Maybe if you were a successful couple involved in Wicca, you preferred little out-of-the-way towns with a forest nearby that was purported to be haunted. Maybe the Lowells had been brought here by the Big Knobians who were descended from Isadora Mather, the woman who had inspired her husband to create a town along the lines of a Wiccan symbol.

"I assume you never made it to Evansville," Dorcas said.

"Bob advised against it," Gwen said quickly. "I have a guest room, so—"

"Gwen is a wonderful hostess," Marc said. "I am not such a wonderful guest. I am afraid travel weariness kept me from being very entertaining. I slept like the dead."

"Jet lag's no fun," Ambrose said. "We have some wine from Sedona that's a cure-all for anything that ails you. If you'd like to stop by sometime today, we'd be glad to give you a bottle."

Gwen cleared her throat. "Thanks, but I don't think we—"

"That would be wonderful," Marc said. "I would love to try one of the American wines, especially one that you recommend. When would you like us to stop by?"

"Why not come around five?" Dorcas said. "We can offer you a glass of the wine so you can decide if you want a whole bottle. I'll make a few appetizers."

"Really," Gwen said. "That's nice of you, but Marc and I have several things to take care of."

"We can finish them by five," Marc said.

Gwen laid a hand on his arm. "But—"

"We can manage an hour." Marc squeezed her hand. For some reason Gwen was trying to avoid this couple, and yet they were the whole reason Marc was in Big Knob. He needed to find out more about that, and he was very curious to see the inside of the Lowells' house.

"We'll look forward to it," Ambrose said with a smile.

"Oh, by the way, Dorcas," Gwen said. "I have your pendant." She started to unbutton her coat. "I can return it to—"

"Or I was wondering if you might be willing to part with it? I would like to purchase it for Gwen." Marc glanced at Dorcas. "I do not know if you would consider selling it, but it looks beautiful on her. I am sure it looks beautiful on you, too," he added quickly. "I only hoped that perhaps—"

"Actually, I decided last night that I wanted to give Gwen the pendant," Dorcas said.

Gwen blushed. "Oh, no, I couldn't take it. I'm sure it's extremely valuable."

Dorcas gazed at her. "Would you deprive me of the pleasure of giving you a gift?"

"Well, no, but there are gifts and then there are *gifts*. This one's too much."

Walking toward Gwen, Dorcas laid a hand on her arm. "I have no daughters of my own, no one to pass things down to. That pendant seems made for you, and I want you to have it."

Nicely done. Marc admired the way Dorcas had taken charge of the situation. She had a great deal of personal power. He also suspected that she considered the pendant a talisman of sorts. It probably was.

"What is the name of the stone?" he asked.

"Larimar," Dorcas said.

"I have never heard of it, but it is beautiful. Where does it come from?"

Dorcas trained her amber eyes on him as if he were a precocious kid who asked far too many questions. "The Dominican Republic, I believe."

Marc was convinced she had far more information on Larimar than she was giving him, especially when she turned away and gestured to the plants in an obvious attempt to change the subject.

"What do you think?" she asked.

"Bizarre," Marc answered truthfully. "When did you first notice them growing here?"

"Right after New Year's," Ambrose said. "Naturally, we dug one up and took it to Gwen for an ID."

Marc listened carefully. Unless he had lost every ounce of his intuition, Ambrose was withholding information, too. "Had you been to this clearing before?" he asked. "In other words, could they have been here all along, and you never noticed?"

"It's possible," Dorcas said. "I'm not sure we'd been to this clearing before. What do you think, Ambrose?"

Ambrose glanced at her as if looking for direction. *They are making this up as they go along.* Marc knew, without being able to describe the whys and wherefores, that Dorcas and Ambrose had put these plants there and then supposedly *discovered* them. The motivation was unclear, but once he had a chance to talk with Gwen alone, he would probably find out what their purpose had been.

He decided to ask another question. "Have you ever noticed the unusual layout of the streets in Big Knob?"

Beside him, Gwen drew in a sharp breath.

She might not be happy that he had asked, but if he was right about what was going on in Big Knob, she would ultimately want to know. Ignorance was bliss until you were disillusioned by the truth. He would rather not have that happen to her.

Dorcas gave him the same quelling glance as before. "According to the people who've lived here all their lives, the star shape is to honor the wife of the founder, who said she was his shining star."

"We're history buffs," Ambrose added. "We read all about it, and Isadora Mather must have been something special."

"Gwen told me about her assistance with the small-pox epidemic, but I cannot help thinking there is more to the story. Are you aware of the Wiccan symbol, a five-pointed star surrounded by a circle?"

Ambrose shifted his weight. "I've heard something about that, yes."

"I believe I have, too," Dorcas said. "I don't understand all the significance attached to it, though."

They were lying. Marc was as sure of that as he was of his ten fingers and ten toes. They knew a lot more about the five-pointed star than they were telling. But he would not press the issue because he could feel waves of anxiety rolling off Gwen.

"The five-pointed star is a common shape, though," Dorcas said. "After all, little children learn to draw stars that way when they're in kindergarten." She laughed. "They can hardly be creating Wicca symbols, now, can they?"

"Certainly not." Marc decided to let it go for now. "I merely thought the street arrangement was intriguing."

Ambrose nodded and gave him a man-to-man look. "Makes driving a bitch."

And the founder a witch. Marc almost smiled at his rhyme, but he dared not. Until he had more information, he had to pretend he was still in the dark.

"Driving is a challenge here, but I guarantee Paris is worse," he said. Then he glanced at his watch. "I hope you will excuse us, but Click-or-Treat is nearly open, and I must e-mail my sister."

"And I need to open up Beaucoup Bouquets," Gwen said. "It's getting late."

"It is, at that," Dorcas said. "We don't want to hold you two up. We'll expect you at five."

"We will see you then," Marc said.

Chapter 13

"He's figuring it out," Dorcas said as they trudged back to where they'd parked the scooter. "He's going to blow our cover, and it's our fault, because we decided to find Gwen's soul mate."

"But that's what we do. We find soul mates. It's our raison d'être."

"Pardon me if I'm not in the mood for French. So it's our reason for being. I agree with that, but why did we have to work on Gwen's problem right now? Couldn't we have worked on somebody else's soul mate, maybe a person without a curious bone in his body?"

"It's going to work out. . . . Somehow."

That was so like Ambrose, to leave it up to chance. She wasn't constitutionally capable of that. She turned the problem over in her mind, considering it from every angle.

Perhaps she should have anticipated this, but she'd never imagined a botanist would recognize the town's symbolic street grid. She obviously hadn't placed enough importance on Jean-Marc's love of the unusual or his yearning to explore the unknown. As a result, she couldn't escape her final conclusion. "We have to tell him."

"Everything?" Ambrose glanced at her in shock.

"Enough to satisfy him."

"You can't mean that."

"If he's going to leap to conclusions, I'd rather beat him to the punch."

"You're mixing your metaphors, Dorcas, darling."

She sighed. "That's hardly important at a time like this, Ambrose, *love*."

Ambrose started walking faster, which was his habit when he was agitated. "I don't like the idea of telling him. He's not the type to settle down in Big Knob. We'll never be able to keep tabs on his comings and goings. He travels all over the world."

"So right before he leaves town, we'll find a way to give him a memory potion so he'll forget what he learned." They'd walked far enough down the road that she could see the hated red scooter standing in stark relief against the white snow.

Why couldn't Ambrose have bought something cool like a midnight-black Harley? No, scratch that. He could barely drive the scooter. He'd kill them both on a Harley.

"Counting on a memory potion always makes me nervous," Ambrose said. "It feels like a morning-after pill. And what about Gwen?"

"She doesn't have to know. If I'm reading her right, she doesn't even want to know. She likes her current view of the world."

"So we have to find a way to separate them."

"That might be fairly easy, if he decides to stay at Click-or-Treat for a while and she has to open up her flower shop. Don't you have to check your MySpace page?"

"Not really. There's nothing—"

"Ambrose."

"Oh. You mean we should stop by Click-or-Treat because Marc will be there."

"The thought crossed my mind." She happened to know that Ambrose had a genius IQ, much higher than hers, but when it came to the uptake, he could be dumb as a box of rocks. Dumber, actually. Rocks could send out some incredible vibrations.

As she climbed on board the scooter behind Ambrose, she thought about one particular rock, the Larimar she'd given Gwen. It seemed to be helping the situation, judging from the sparks flying back and forth between Gwen and Marc.

But Marc had been too blessed curious about the Larimar, too. She would have pretended not to know what the stone was, except that she'd broadcast its name at the Bob and Weave yesterday. Besides, a man like Marc would have tracked down the identity of the stone eventually. All she could have done was slow him down.

"Here's how we'll work this," she said to Ambrose as they picked up speed on the main road. "If Marc's alone at Click-or-Treat, great. I'll find a reason to talk with him. But if Gwen's there, too, and seems to want to hang around, then show her one of those silly videos you're always telling me about."

"You mean, go on YouTube?"

"YouTube, MySpace—whatever you do to get these things. I don't keep track of all that terminology."

"Maybe I'll show her the dancing hamster one. And I could show her *Potter's Puppets*. She's read all the Harry Potter books. She'll like those videos."

"Just so she doesn't eavesdrop on me and Marc."

"Leave it to me, dear one."

She would have to. The Internet was not her forte. But damage control certainly was, and they were in desperate need of some.

As Gwen led Marc along the curving path that

joined two points of the star, she tried not to think that her cherished hometown would look like a Wiccan symbol from the air. Witchcraft should stay in novels, where it belonged, not come poking out into everyday life. She'd loved every one of the Harry Potter books, but they were make-believe.

She was perfectly willing to let Marc trash her personal reputation, but she didn't want him messing with the reputation of Big Knob. She wasn't sure how to tell him that, though. He seemed so interested in the subject that her reluctance looked provincial next to his big-city curiosity. So she walked along in silence.

"*Cherie*, you seem upset," he said in his wonderful French accent.

"Not really." She wished they could collect his suitcase and go back to bed. Then he would forget all about this Wicca business.

"I could tell you did not want to go to the Lowells' home for a drink. Is that it?"

It wasn't, but she'd go with it. "How do you feel about professional matchmakers?"

"I do not understand."

"Dorcas and Ambrose are marriage counselors, but they also offer matchmaking services."

Marc laughed in obvious surprise. "People actually *hire* them to do that?"

"Apparently, although I haven't heard of anyone actually paying them for it. They . . . wanted to give me advice before you arrived."

"I see."

"I didn't hire them!" She spun around so fast he bumped into her.

"Hey." Smiling, he grabbed her by the shoulders.

She cleared her throat. "Please don't think I'd do something like that."

"As you said about the condoms, if you hired them, I would be flattered, not angry."

"Okay, but I didn't." She loved looking into his blue eyes and could easily forget the point she'd been about to make. She forced herself to concentrate. "The thing is, it doesn't seem to matter, because they're hovering over us as if I *did* hire them. It's embarrassing."

"If it is their profession, maybe they are driven to do that. Do you ever long to rearrange other people's floral centerpieces?"

"How did you know?"

He shrugged. "When I walk by a garden where someone is weeding, I want to interfere because nothing is a weed as far as I am concerned."

She let out a breath. "I'm probably overreacting."

"Not necessarily. They do behave as if they have a stake in us getting together."

"That's sort of weird, don't you think? I mean, I know them, but it's not like we're superclose. I don't go over there for coffee every morning. I'm trying to remember if I've ever been in their house."

Marc rubbed his hands up and down the sleeves of her coat. "I know this sounds unlikely, but is there any way they could have brought those plants in themselves and then claimed to have found them?"

"You mean it's a hoax? A practical joke?"

"No, not a joke. But what if they wanted to find you a nice botanist? What would be better bait than bromeliads growing in the snow?"

She thought about that for several seconds. Finally she shook her head. "It's an interesting theory, but the process would be too labor intensive. I don't care how dedicated they are at matchmaking."

"They seem to have time on their hands, and they like coming out here."

"Marc, they'd have to practically live out here. You

know as well as I do that keeping those plants alive in such a forbidding climate would take round-the-clock monitoring. They'd need some sort of portable plastic dome to protect them at night."

"I say they could be doing all of that. It could be a game to see if they can pull it off. If we came out here late at night and found a protective covering over them, we would know."

"Yes, we would." She smiled at him. "But you'll be in Evansville, won't you?" *Gotcha.* "Want me to check on the plants and report to you in the morning?"

He gave a little growl of frustration. "I suppose I could stay a little later than ten. But I *will* be gone before midnight."

"So I won't see your rental car turn into a pumpkin?"

"If I could manage that stunt, I could definitely stay all night. A pumpkin is easier to hide than a Pontiac."

"So all you're worried about is having people see your car? We could hide it in the woods and walk back to my place."

He shook his head. "No, we could not. Sneaking around is not my idea of fun. I will leave town tonight, right after we check to see if someone is covering the plants."

"You're a stubborn man."

"I do tend to stick with something once my mind is made up."

The way he said it warmed her all over. She had the distinct feeling he'd made up his mind about her, and that they'd be seeing a lot more of each other in the future. She couldn't believe that Dorcas and Ambrose had gone to the amount of trouble he was suggesting to bring them together, but if they had, the plan was working.

She didn't like being manipulated, but she couldn't argue with the results. Marc was the lover she'd dreamed of ever since learning about the difference between boys and girls. He outshone by a mile that costumed figment of her imagination who had been visiting her at night.

Thinking of her dream lover reminded her of how Marc had cried out in his sleep last night, which had started a whole chain of events she was most grateful for. But she'd never asked him about what must have been a nightmare. "Marc, did you have a bad dream last night?"

He seemed to be looking inward, as if trying to remember. "There was something, yes." Gazing down at her, he took her by the shoulders and turned her around to face forward. "But you reminded me of what happened *after* the nightmare. If we stand here another second, I will kiss you."

She liked knowing she tested his self-control, but she didn't want to keep him from e-mailing his sister, so she did as he asked and started down the path again. "You seemed pretty upset by that nightmare," she said.

"There was a man, and he . . . oh, it is not important. It is too improbable."

"What is?" She wondered how he'd react if she told him the dreams she'd been having before he came to town.

"Oh, there was this blond man in a police uniform, and he—ah, never mind. Forget about it."

She had the distinct impression that Marc was embarrassed to tell her the content of his dream. The man in a police uniform reminded her of . . . but no, that would be too crazy. Because Marc obviously didn't want to talk about it, she let the matter drop.

*   *   *

When Marc and Gwen walked into the Internet café about ten minutes later, Marc was not surprised to see Ambrose and Dorcas there, too. Ambrose made some excuse about remembering he needed to check his MySpace page on the way home, and Dorcas had claimed to crave some of Jeremy Dunstan's coffee, but Marc thought they were there to keep track of their latest matchmaking scheme.

He pretended not to know that, though, and greeted them as if he had not expected to see them again so soon. Gwen introduced him to Jeremy and Jeremy's Irish wolfhound, Megabyte, who sprawled next to the counter like a dog-shaped rug.

After insisting that Marc call him by his first name, Jeremy efficiently set him up at a nearby computer terminal. This time of the morning, Jeremy explained, the café was fairly quiet because the high school kids were all in school.

No sooner had Marc signed on than Ambrose called Gwen over to his terminal to look at some of the crazy videos that populated the Internet these days. Marc noted with amusement that Gwen slipped on her glasses to look at the videos. Her glasses made no difference to him, but she acted as if he would lose all interest if she wore them. As they said in America, fat chance.

But he had to quit watching her or he would never make contact with Josette. He turned back to the screen and downloaded his messages, four of which were from his sister. As he started to open the first one, Dorcas sat down at the vacant computer station next to him.

The fact that she made no move to use the computer confirmed what he had thought from the beginning, that she was there to talk with him. He glanced over and smiled. "I need to send a quick message to my sister. She probably thinks the plane crashed and the authorities are slow to notify her."

"That's fine," Dorcas said in a low voice. "It would probably be better if you continued to type while I talk with you, anyway. I don't want to arouse anyone's curiosity about our conversation."

Marc's hands stilled on the keys, and his heart rate spiked. "You are Wiccan, yes?"

"I'm a witch, yes."

"I was right!"

"Keep your voice down, and keep typing."

"Of course." Marc opened the first e-mail from Josette, which was all in caps. *WHERE ARE YOU?????*

"Ambrose is a wizard," Dorcas said.

Taking a deep breath, Marc typed *I am in Big Knob, safe and sound. More later. Love, Marc.* Then he hit the Send button. "Is there a coven here?" he asked Dorcas as he opened the next email from Josette.

"No. Just the two of us."

Josette's next e-mail was also in caps. *E-MAIL ME!!!!!* Because he had just done that, he felt no need to respond to that one. "Were there more of you here previously?" he asked Dorcas without looking at her. He felt as if he had found the entrance to the Temple of Doom.

"No, only Isadora Mather, who is . . . uh, *was* a witch. You were on the right track. Her husband, Ebenezer, was descended from Cotton Mather. He had no idea he was married to a witch, and she loved the irony of it. She talked him into the star pattern."

Marc was so excited he accidentally deleted Josette's third e-mail. He hoped it was unimportant. "But the townspeople think—"

"What Ebenezer told everyone, that he wanted a tribute to his wife, his shining star. It's a myth that's held up for nearly two hundred years. Isadora created the walking path, too, claiming that it made for an excellent shortcut around town."

"Incredible." He gave Dorcas a quick glance. "But why are you and Ambrose here?"

"We needed to keep an eye on things."

"What things?"

Dorcas hesitated. "Marc, I don't know you very well. This is sensitive information, and if the residents ever suspected that we're—"

"I would never speak of it." He was dying to tell someone, but he knew that many people still feared the idea of witches and wizards. A person had to be careful about sharing that kind of information.

Dorcas and Ambrose seemed to like living here, and they would probably have to move if word got out. If the townspeople ever discovered the origin of their street grid, no telling what they would do. Bulldoze the town pentagon/square, probably.

"You can't even tell Gwen," Dorcas said.

That would be difficult. Gwen was the sort of person he wanted to share everything with.

"I can see you're involved with her," Dorcas said. "You'll be tempted to discuss this with her, but if you've noticed, she isn't comfortable with the concept."

"No, she is not." He admitted that with reluctance. He wanted her to be. He wanted a partner who shared his curiosity about—hey, wait a minute. *Partner?* Was he that far along in his thinking?

"Here she comes," Dorcas said. "Hi, Gwen! Marc's trying to convince me to become an Internet fan like the rest of you, but I can't seem to get into it."

Marc hoped Gwen would not be focusing too closely on his expression when he turned around. "The Internet is not for everyone," he said.

"True." Gwen had taken off her glasses again, and

she squinted slightly as her gaze swung from Marc to Dorcas and back to Marc again. "But the dancing hamster video is pretty funny, Dorcas. Get him to show you that before you leave."

Marc had become sensitive to Gwen's moods, and he could tell she suspected more was going on between him and Dorcas than an Internet discussion.

"Dancing hamsters?" Dorcas stood. "I can't pass that up, now, can I?" She walked over to Ambrose's computer terminal.

"I need to open Beaucoup Bouquets," Gwen said. "I'm not sure what your plans are after you finish here, but—"

"If I may borrow your house, I would like to gather my suitcase and change clothes." Marc noticed that Monsieur Loudermilk had come through the door and his expression had brightened when he spied Marc there.

"Let me give you the key." Gwen reached in her pocket and took out a key ring. Sliding one off, she handed it to him.

"Thank you. I am tired of these clothes after spending twenty-four hours in them." He said it loud enough that everyone in the café should have been able to hear.

Dorcas and Ambrose could think what they chose, but he would not supply any information proving that he had been sexually involved with Gwen. For the benefit of Jeremy and Monsieur Loudermilk, he wanted to suggest that he had stayed fully clothed all night. Some people thought men were not gossips, but Marc knew better.

"I'm sure you're eager to get that suitcase." Gwen's tone was nonchalant, but the look in her brown eyes was anything but casual.

"Certainement." Marc held her gaze. "Do you close the shop for lunch?"

"From twelve to one." The heat in her eyes turned up a notch.

He knew exactly what she was thinking, and it had nothing to do with food. Ah, but that would be sweet. He loved daytime sex.

Then he noticed Monsieur Loudermilk was edging closer, obviously eavesdropping. A lunch rendezvous would be noticed by half the town. "Then we can meet at the Hob Knob Diner for lunch at twelve," Marc said.

Gwen's disappointment was so obvious he had to hold back a smile. "I understand the food is wonderful," he added.

"It is, but I happen to have plenty at home. There's homemade soup, home-baked bread, apple tarts for dessert. . . ."

"Sounds *délicieux*. We can save it for dinner, when we have time to enjoy it." With luck they would have more privacy to enjoy each other, too. There seemed to be little to do in Big Knob on a winter evening except go home and stay home. He had only to make sure his rental car was gone long before dawn.

"Excuse me, Mr. Chevalier." Monsieur Loudermilk obviously was becoming impatient.

Marc glanced past Gwen. "What can I do for you, Monsieur Loudermilk?"

"I noticed you're on the Internet, and I was thinking you might know about some good sites for checking out bra designs."

Keeping her back to Monsieur Loudermilk, Gwen glanced at Marc and rolled her eyes. "Gotta go," she said. "I'll meet you at the Hob Knob at noon, then."

Marc wondered if he could go that long without

seeing her. "Perhaps I will wander over to the shop before then. I would like to see it, if you are not too busy."

She smiled. "Things are slow this time of year. I'd be happy to show you around anytime." Then she turned and left.

"I didn't mean to interrupt your conversation." Monsieur Loudermilk sat down in the chair recently vacated by Dorcas.

"We were finished."

"I thought so. I heard Gwen say she had to open the shop, so I thought maybe you'd be available to give me some advice."

"I am willing to help, but I really have no expertise, monsieur."

Monsieur Loudermilk winked at him. "Don't give me that. Every man alive knows something about the subject. A Frenchman should know even more."

"About women's underwear?"

"Hell, no. I'm talking about *breasts*. At first I was only interested in holding 'em up, but now I want to show 'em off." He reached into a pocket of his overalls and pulled out a folded sheet of paper. "Take a look at this beauty." He spread the sheet out on the desk area between the two computers.

Marc stared in amazement. He had never seen a schematic of a bra before. Monsieur Loudermilk had noted all the points of stress and how the design would counteract gravity while maximizing cleavage.

"I'm not much for lace." Monsieur Loudermilk tapped a pudgy finger on the paper. "So I'm thinking silk, but with cutouts in a daisy pattern."

"I like silk better than lace, myself." Marc was amazed at the artistic detail in the illustration. "Have you taken many drawing classes?"

"Nah. Just drafting. But I've always loved to draw.

Used to do nudes by looking at pictures of those Greek statues."

"You have a good eye," Marc said.

"What do you think of the bra?"

"It looks sexy." He thought about the one Gwen had put on this morning—a plain cotton style that was fine, but . . . this would be a thousand times better.

"That's what I'm going for."

"You do not have a prototype yet, I expect?"

"Still working on it," Monsieur Loudermilk said. "I'm trying to decide what size to make it." He leaned closer to Marc and lowered his voice. "With the first one I used Clara's size, but I can't make this type for her. She's not built for a model like this."

"Then I suggest you make it a size 95-C," Marc said. Monsieur Loudermilk was right that Marc knew a lot about breasts, and he would be willing to bet that size would fit Gwen like a glove.

"Ninety-five? Oh, that would be metric measurements." Monsieur Loudermilk gazed at Marc and slowly nodded. "I can convert that, no problem. You got it."

Marc was afraid he had given himself away. "It is an average size in France," he said.

"Right." With a smile, Monsieur Loudermilk rose from the chair. "I'll let you know when I've put it together. Then you can see if Gwen likes it or not."

Chapter 14

Ever since New Year's, business had been slow at Beaucoup Bouquets. Not today. Gwen had no sooner unlocked the door and taken off her coat and boots than Peggy Anglethorpe came in.

"I need a vase of flowers for the front window." Peggy unzipped her quilted jacket and pushed back the hood, which had messed up her short, permed blond hair. "Something bright and cheerful, that you can see from the street." She finger-combed her hair back in place.

Peggy had never ordered such a thing that Gwen knew of, but she wasn't about to question the customer. "I'll be happy to fix that up for you." She took a medium-sized vase from under the counter. "Like this?"

"Bigger."

Gwen pulled out the next-larger size. "Like this?"

"That should work."

Gwen set the vase on the table she used for making arrangements and walked over to the refrigerated case where she kept her cut flowers in water. "By the way, I appreciate you and Bob offering to put Marc up for the night."

"The boys were disappointed he didn't come over.

They wanted to ask him if he knows Lance Armstrong."

"But Lance Armstrong lives in Texas." As Gwen placed several stalks of iris in the arrangement, she thought about the paperweight Marc had given her with its fleur-de-lis center.

"I know, but the boys connect him with the Tour de France, and they think everyone in France probably knows him." She hesitated. "So what's he like?"

"Lance Armstrong?"

"No, silly. Your French guy."

Hot. But Gwen couldn't very well say that. "He's . . . nice." *Very* nice, indeed.

"I've heard he's really cute."

Cute was too tiny a word for him, in Gwen's opinion. *Gorgeous* was more like it. "He's attractive, I guess," she said. "If you like the type." Personally, she loved the type. Dark, wavy hair, dark blue eyes, square chin with a small cleft, hands that knew how to stroke a woman, and male equipment that made her want—

"Um, Gwen?" Peggy gave her a funny look.

"What?"

"You're the flower arranger and all, but are you sure a big ol' pussy willow looks good in the middle of those roses and such?"

Gwen glanced at the arrangement and discovered a very phallic, sausage-sized pussy willow sticking straight out of a vase that was otherwise packed tightly with every variety of bloom in her case. She'd obviously been shoving flowers in there until the vase was ready to crack down the middle from the strain. Then she'd added the phallic symbol for good measure.

"You're right," she said to Peggy. "That doesn't go at all." She plucked it out and returned it to the case. "In fact, I think this arrangement looks a little crowded."

"I was thinking the same thing, but I didn't want to say. I'm not artistic. But I wanted something pretty in the front room, in case . . . well, if your Frenchman happened to stop by for a visit. I mean, the boys would love it. I—"

"Gwen!" Madeline Danbury, who waitressed at the Hob Knob, charged through the front door of the shop, her cheeks pink and her frizzy white hair tousled by the breeze. "We just heard over at the diner that the Frenchman will be having lunch there today. We need little bud vases of flowers on every table."

"For Marc?" Gwen blinked.

"That's his name?" Madeline frowned. "I'd heard something different."

"His full name is Jean-Marc Chevalier," Gwen said, "but I call him Marc."

Peggy sighed. "How manly."

Gwen said, "It's what all his close friends call him." Then she realized that put her in the close friends category, and she blushed. "I mean, his family members."

"We know what you mean," Madeline said. "It's no secret that you've been hoping to meet up with a French guy for years. That 'cousin' story never fooled anyone. We're happy for you, aren't we, Peggy?"

"I'd be happier if I could lay eyes on him," Peggy said. "I do believe I'll eat at the Hob Knob today. The boys are in school and Bob's working, so why not treat myself? I'll bet Denise would like to have lunch over there. I'll ask Cecily, too."

"You might want to make a reservation," Madeline said. "Francine and Sylvia called over from the Bob and Weave and reserved themselves a table, and Edith Mae Hoogstraten called to say she wanted us to save her a seat. I'm putting her with Billie Smoot, because we don't have enough tables to let folks sit by themselves."

Gwen listened, openmouthed. She probably should warn Marc that he was the floor show at the Hob Knob today. But in the meantime she had ten bud-vase arrangements to make.

As she took a quick inventory of her supplies to see if she had enough bud vases, her phone rang.

"Gwen, this is Francine. Sylvia's doing her hair up in a special arrangement, and she wants a couple of small, peach-colored roses to work into the design. Do you have anything like that?"

"I do, out in the greenhouse."

"Then I'll be over in a few minutes to pick them up. Come to think of it, I'll take some white ones, too. Sylvia's inspiring me, and I might try the same thing."

Gwen turned away from Madeline and Peggy, who were debating how to say *hello* in French. "Francine," she murmured, "has the entire female population of Big Knob gone bonkers?"

Francine laughed. "Pretty much. It's not often we get someone like your Frenchman in town. Once the word was out that he'd be having lunch at the diner, the stampede began. But don't worry, toots. We're only ogling. We know he's yours."

"No, he's not."

"I'd keep that to myself, if I were you. If Sylvia thinks you don't want him, she'll be all over that boy."

Gwen took a deep breath. "I want him."

"I never doubted it. I'll see you in a few."

Marc needed advice, and the first person he thought of was Gwen. She was a woman. She might know what he should do.

He had finally had a moment to read Josette's last e-mail, which unfortunately referred to the deleted one. The last e-mail said *Sorry to unload on you like that, but I wanted you to know why I am dropping*

*out of school. So sorry if I have disappointed you.
Love, Josie.*

He had e-mailed back, admitted to deleting the critical e-mail by accident and asked her to resend. Josette
had answered, but had chosen not to include her origi-
nal text. *Just as well you lost it. I was embarrassed to
have sent it in the first place. I am fine. I am waiting
tables at a café and I plan to support myself. Love, Josie.*

Marc hauled out his BlackBerry to see if he could
make a call to her, but he had no reception. *Merd!*
He would be stuck here right when Josette was self-
destructing. She had no business waiting tables.

He scrubbed a hand over his face. His parents had
meant for her to use the trust fund so she could concentrate on her education without having to earn
money. By allowing things to deteriorate to this point,
Marc had let them down.

Jeremy came by with a coffee carafe in one hand.
"Problems with the server?"

Marc glanced up at Jeremy. He had liked the guy
instantly when Gwen had introduced him. Sincere and
very bright, Jeremy was the sort of person who would
make a good friend. Marc even liked Jeremy's dog,
who was as well-mannered as Parisian dogs.

Still, Marc had known Jeremy less than an hour.
Confiding his family problems did not seem right or
fair.

He shook his head. "The server is fine. I am still a
little tired, is all. I need to collect my suitcase and
return to Gwen's so I can shower and change clothes.
I should feel better after that."

"Then I suggest you hotfoot it out of here right
now. I've had several calls asking if you were here
checking e-mail."

"Who is calling?"

Jeremy nudged his wire-framed glasses back into

place. "Curious citizens of Big Knob. They wanted to come by and say hello, and I tried to convince them you needed some privacy to answer your e-mail. No one's shown up yet, but the longer you hang around here, the more likely you'll get trapped."

"Am I that much of an oddity?"

" 'Fraid so. We don't get many folks from Paris in this town. Come to think of it, I can't remember a single one." He glanced out the window. "Your car's over at the Big Knobian, right?"

"*Oui.* I mean, yes."

Jeremy laughed. "I understand *oui.* It's the verb conjugations I never managed to master. Anyway, the more I think about it, the more I doubt you'll make it to your car and over to Gwen's without being stopped a million times. It could easily take you an hour to make the trip."

Marc groaned.

"Listen, my wife and I have an apartment upstairs. I can offer you a shower and a change of clothes. I think we're about the same size."

"That is way too much to ask of you."

"I can understand if you don't want to," Jeremy said. "But I'd be glad to do it. Any friend of Gwen's and all that."

Marc could hear the affection in Jeremy's voice when he spoke of Gwen. "You have known her a long time?"

"All my life. She's a terrific person."

"Yes." Marc envied Jeremy his long-term relationship with Gwen. "Yes, she is. I am lucky to have met her."

"I'd agree with that. Anyway, do what you want, but I'll be happy to loan you the clothes."

"Thank you." Marc decided accepting Jeremy's generosity would be a good thing to do. People were more familiar with each other in this small town than he was used to in Paris, but he wanted to be friendly. "I accept."

"Okay. Let me get rid of this carafe and I'll show you where everything is."

Moments later, as Jeremy handed Marc some serviceable briefs, a long-sleeved T-shirt, and jeans, Marc noticed a wedding picture on a dresser in the bedroom. Jeremy was in a tuxedo, and a beautiful blonde who must be Annie, Gwen's best friend, was looking at Jeremy lovingly. Marc realized he had yet to meet Annie and wondered where she was.

"Your wife is very pretty," he said.

"She's amazing." Jeremy's expression reflected adoration as he looked at the picture. "She's in Scotland. She has a job writing a series of articles on mythical creatures. I can see Annie being the one who finally exposes the Loch Ness Monster as a hoax. Anyway, she's due back next week."

"She is a journalist?" Marc had noticed a small newspaper office on the square, but the *Big Knob Gazette* looked too small to be able to send reporters to Scotland.

"Before we got married, she worked for the *Chicago Tribune*. I was all set to relocate to be with her, but then the Lowells told her about this organization that needed writers for a huge project on popular myths. You know, like Bigfoot and so on. I'm sure they'll eventually publish her findings in book form."

Marc's instincts went on alert. "The Lowells are interesting people."

"Yep. I don't have a clue why they moved here, but they seem to like it. I'm grateful they did, because they had that connection, which meant Annie and I could live here instead of moving to Chicago. I would've done it for Annie, but I'm not that crazy about city living." He glanced at Marc. "No offense."

"None taken." Marc decided to find out if Jeremy had any inkling about the town's origins. "Has Annie ever suggested writing about the town of Big Knob?"

"Big Knob?" Jeremy chuckled. "That would be one boring story. The most exciting thing that happens here is Friday afternoons at three, when eighty-seven-year-old Edith Mae Hoogstraten drives into town for her weekly early dinner at the Hob Knob and we all hold our breath to see if she'll hit anything."

Marc thought Jeremy was mistaken about that. There probably were far more exciting things going on than some old woman's erratic driving. Annie Dunstan might be one of the few who knew that, but her husband obviously had no idea. And Annie, who was also Gwen's best friend, was not in town. Too bad. Marc would have loved to ask her some questions.

Gwen had hoped Marc would come into the shop some time during the morning, but as the female population of Big Knob continued to arrive in a steady stream, she realized having Marc show up might not be such a great idea. Her customers were either using a floral purchase as an excuse to pump her for information about him, or buying flowers to make themselves look more attractive for their lunch at the Hob Knob.

Lunch would be a mob scene. She would have loved to save him from that, but he hadn't wanted to take her suggestion of a private meal at home. Little did he know that protecting her reputation was becoming a lost cause.

So far, every woman who'd come into Beaucoup Bouquets seemed to believe that Gwen's story about Marc being a cousin was a smoke screen and that she'd hooked up with him through some international online dating service. They all assumed she was having sex with him, and their logic made perfect sense. What woman in her right mind wouldn't try to seduce a man who looked like Marc?

Well, she wouldn't be doing much seducing at the Hob Knob, but she'd promised to meet him there, so she might as well go. Her business had trailed off by eleven thirty, and as she glanced out at the snowy square, she noticed that it was empty. She'd bet that everyone who could spare the time was holding down all the available seats at the Hob Knob.

She wondered if there would be a place for her or if she'd have to go home to eat. Maybe both she and Marc should drive to Evansville tonight. It might be the only way she'd ever have him to herself again.

Closing the shop at five minutes before noon, she bundled up in her coat and boots and cut across the deserted square to the diner. She wished Marc hadn't brought up all that stuff about five-pointed stars and Wicca, because now she looked at the square and the streets around it differently.

She even looked at the bronze statue of Isadora Mather differently. Marc had implied that the pioneer woman might have been Wiccan, but that couldn't be right. Gwen had intended to check out some of Marc's gonzo theories with Lucy Dunstan, but she'd reconsidered doing that. No reason to stir up trouble.

Marc just needed to spend more time in Big Knob. Then he'd see how ridiculous his ideas were. She hoped he'd plan to come back. Once the novelty had worn off, people wouldn't be so desperate to spend time with him.

They apparently were desperate now, though. All the parking spaces in front of the Hob Knob were taken. Edith Mae's old Buick was angled in such a way that it effectively occupied two spaces. Gwen recognized Angie Jankowsky's silver SUV and Donald Jenkins's truck with the Big Knob Dairy logo on the door panel. Old Calvin Gilmore and his wife, Rachel, had driven their well-worn sedan, and there was Candice Merriweather's little sports car.

Many others had walked, no doubt. Most people lived a few blocks from the square, and in winter walking made more sense than driving on the icy roads. Even before Gwen opened the door, she could hear the racket inside. It was noisier than the school gym during a basketball game.

Once she was inside, finding Marc didn't take much effort. She could see the top of his head, but the rest of him was obscured by the Big Knobians crowded around his table. He might as well have been a celebrity holding a press conference. Poor Marc.

She wondered if she could rescue him somehow. Nothing brilliant occurred to her. She'd have to push her way through the crowd to let him know she was here. Talking to him would be out of the question, but she wanted him to know that she'd kept their lunch date. So had three-quarters of the town, unfortunately.

The diner was swelteringly hot with all the bodies inside it, and Gwen took off her coat. She'd probably be putting it right back on again, because there was little chance she'd be staying. She rebelled at being just another groupie.

Her bud vases filled with miniature carnations looked festive on the tables, although she doubted anyone had paid the slightest attention to the flowers. Joe and Sherry rushed to fill orders as quickly as possible.

Gwen was trying to figure out how to wedge herself through the mass of people when the door opened behind her, letting in a welcome blast of cold air.

"This looks like the wrong place to have lunch today," said a male voice that sounded vaguely familiar.

"No kidding." She couldn't quite place the voice, but as she turned, she expected to see another one of her neighbors who'd come to rub shoulders with a genuine Parisian who spoke actual French.

Her breath left her lungs. Looking into those icy blue eyes, she felt her world shift. Now she knew why his voice had sounded so familiar. She'd heard it in her dreams for the past week.

This couldn't be happening. It defied everything she'd ever believed about herself and the nature of reality. She blinked, but he was still there, staring down at her.

"I don't believe we've met." He extended his hand.

Oh yes, we have! You've made passionate love to me every night for a blessed week! Frozen with the improbability of what was happening, she couldn't manage even the barest response. All she could do was stand and stare.

"I'm Leo Atwood." The man lowered his hand again. "I was passing through town and thought I'd stop and get something to eat, but this is nuts. What's going on here?"

Closing her eyes briefly, she swallowed. When she opened her eyes again, she'd regained a measure of composure. Of course this man wasn't her dream lover.

He looked something like him, true, and he sounded a bit like him, but many guys probably looked and sounded something like him. Her dream lover had always shown up in some sort of costume, but this guy wore normal clothes—jeans and a gray sweatshirt under a black quilted ski jacket.

Feeling more confident, she noticed that his hair was shorter than in her dreams and his aftershave smelled nothing like the ocean. She'd been under a strain with this visit from Marc approaching. She'd overreacted.

"Is something wrong?" He peered at her. "You look like you've seen a ghost."

Clearing her throat, she struggled to speak normally. "I . . . uh . . . I'm sorry to be rude. I haven't been sleeping well lately, and . . . you remind me of someone."

He smiled. "I hope it's a good memory."

That smile. Her heart raced, and she grabbed the nearby counter for support as dizziness threatened to knock her off her feet. Forget logic. Forget plausibility. *It was him.*

Chapter 15

"**T**hat man who just walked into the diner looked like Leo!" Dorcas walked faster, her stylish boots plowing through the slush on the sidewalk.

"Oh, I hardly think so, Dorcas." Ambrose hurried to catch up with her. "Probably just somebody who looks like him."

"How could it be? No one in town looks like him, and you turned off the exit sign, so nobody should have come into . . ." She stopped in the middle of the sidewalk and spun to face him. "You *did* turn off the exit sign, didn't you?"

"Uh, I will, my love, as soon as we get home again. I've been worried about losing part of my staff, and I'm not firing on all cylinders."

Dorcas moaned in frustration. "So it could be a stranger who looks something like Leo. We certainly don't need that, if it is, but I think it was him. He had that Leo swagger." She started down the sidewalk again.

"I don't know why he'd be going into the diner." Ambrose fell into step beside her.

"He has business with someone in there, that's why. I'll bet it's no coincidence that he showed up in the area a week before Marc was due to arrive. I haven't put it all together yet, but I will. Now that he's decided to walk around town like a regular guy, I'll smoke out his motivations. See if I don't."

"I have every faith you will, dearest."

Dorcas kept her eye on the diner's front door. "I wonder if my *corpus status quo* spell is still working. That might be why he's resorted to skulking around town as a tourist. He can't minimize himself and do reconnaissance that way."

"I thought you said he was swaggering."

"He was sort of skulking and swaggering."

"Sounds hard to do, Dorcas."

"You're too literal, Ambrose. Mark my words, he's on a reconnaissance mission."

"Reconnaissance for what?"

"Didn't you hear what he said last night? He has something he needs to do here, something of a personal nature. I'm going to guess that Queen Beryl gave him a task that he must complete or he doesn't get the throne."

"That would be a relief, actually," Ambrose said. "Queen Beryl is good people, or good fairies, as the case may be. If she gave Leo a job, it would be a noble task. Am I right?"

"You probably are," Dorcas agreed, "but giving a noble task to a responsible person—or fairy, in this instance—is not the same as giving it to a shithead."

"Dorcas! Watch your language!"

"I can't help it. I'm extremely frustrated. We spent most of the morning looking for the other part of your staff and still couldn't find it. How are we supposed to operate effectively without your powers?"

"I could wear Sabrina's collar."

"Very funny." She paused in front of the door to the diner. Sure was noisy in there. She turned back to Ambrose. "Put on your game face."

Ambrose started to laugh. "I don't know where you get these things without being online."

"I read."

"Celebrity gossip magazines."

"That, too."

"Come on, Dorcas." He opened the door for her. "Let's get you and your game face in there so we can find out what's what."

Dorcas composed her expression and walked into the diner. Ambrose could make fun all he wanted, but she *did* have a game face, and she'd need it if Leo was in that restaurant.

Which he was. He was over by the cash register, talking to Gwen. He glanced over when the door opened but gave no sign of recognition.

Dorcas narrowed her eyes at him. Ambrose might not have found the rest of his wizard's staff, but Leo didn't have to know that. She wanted him to be very afraid.

Sadly, he seemed arrogant as ever. Once he'd noticed who had come in the door, he turned away, dismissing them neatly as he refocused his attention on Gwen.

Gwen, however, spied them and hurried over, panic in her eyes. She clutched her coat in her arms as if needing something to hold on to. "Dorcas and Ambrose, hi!" She sounded manic. "I'd like to introduce Leo Atwood. He's passing through town."

"Really. How nice." Dorcas held out her hand to Leo. She wished she had one of those trick buzzers in her palm to give him a shock. "I would be Dorcas, and this is Ambrose." She inclined her head in her husband's direction.

"I figured that out." Leo shook Ambrose's hand and looked bored. "Interesting little burg you have here," he said with lazy indifference. "I was hoping to get a ham sandwich, but it doesn't look promising."

"I'd try Evansville," Dorcas said. "Or better yet, go into Illinois. Springfield has some good restaurants."

Leo's smile made him look like a shark trolling for chum. "Something tells me I couldn't make it by lunchtime."

"Oh, you never know with the Interstate system," Dorcas said. "It seems as if you can be somewhere instantly. Right, Ambrose, darling?"

"It can seem that way," Ambrose said. "What brings you this way, Mr. Atwood?"

"Business." Leo gestured toward the corner where everyone was crowded around Marc. "I understand this French botanist is the one causing the traffic jam in here. Isn't that what you told me, Gwendolyn?"

Gwen gasped. "What did you call me?"

"Isn't that your name? I could have sworn you said that it was—"

"Gwen," she said, her face pale. "I said it was Gwen. I never said Gwendolyn."

"My mistake. I like old-fashioned names, so I probably made the leap to Gwendolyn."

He seemed to hold some sort of spell over Gwen, Dorcas noted. She'd bet her bottom dollar that whatever Leo was assigned to do in Big Knob, it related to Gwen in some way. She couldn't imagine how, but she was determined to find out.

She turned to Gwen. "Have you talked with Marc yet?"

"No." Gwen looked nervous. "I was about to work my way through the crowd when Mr. Atwood came in. We've been . . . talking." She sounded scared to death.

"Call me Leo."

Dorcas didn't think she imagined the flash of predatory interest she saw in Leo's eyes when he looked at Gwen. *Oh, no, you don't. That woman's spoken for.*

"Let's get you over there, Gwen." Grabbing her by the hand, Dorcas started working her way through the mob. "Marc will want to see you."

"I wouldn't mind meeting this Frenchman myself," Leo said. He followed.

Dorcas didn't want him to follow, but maybe if she gave him some rope, he'd hang himself.

"I'll go along, as well," Ambrose said.

The procession reminded Dorcas of a conga line snaking through the mass of people, but she kept forging ahead and eventually made it over to Marc, who sat at a table with three women. Sylvia and Francine wore elaborate hair arrangements with roses tucked into them, and Edith Mae Hoogstraten sported one of her many outrageous hats. This one included tiny flags from various countries, but the French tricolor was stuck in the crown on top.

Other townspeople had gathered around the table, but somehow Sylvia, Francine and Edith Mae had scored ringside seats.

Edith Mae was talking about *Les Misérables*, which she pronounced, "less *miz*-erables." She'd seen the show back when her husband had been alive and they'd made a trip to Chicago. "I don't get the title," Edith Mae said. "Those people in the show certainly weren't *less* miserable as things went along. If anything, they became even *more* miserable."

Marc appeared to be wearing Jeremy Dunstan's clothes, which Dorcas found interesting. She recognized the long-sleeved T-shirt as one she'd seen on Jeremy several times.

Marc had managed to keep a straight face through the whole *Les Misérables* discussion, but his face relaxed into a happy smile when Dorcas stepped aside and revealed Gwen standing behind her. "I found your lunch date trapped in the crowd," Dorcas said.

Marc gazed at Gwen as a man dying of thirst might gaze at a case of bottled water. "I thought you had forgotten."

Gwen shook her head. "It's just very crowded and I couldn't get through."

"Can you believe this?" Sylvia gestured around. "We arrived at eleven so we'd be sure and get a spot. Marc showed up soon after we did, so we didn't want the poor guy to be lonely while he waited for you."

"I don't think lonely is an issue." Gwen returned her attention to Marc. "What a coincidence. Jeremy has a T-shirt just like that."

"It is not a coincidence," Marc said. "This *is* Jeremy's T-shirt. I never made it back to your house, so he loaned me clothes and let me borrow his shower."

Dorcas wasn't too pleased about that scenario. No doubt Jeremy had proudly mentioned that his wife was an investigative journalist researching mythical creatures like Nessie. He even might have said that Dorcas and Ambrose got Annie the job.

"So you never got your suitcase," Gwen said.

"No." Marc looked unhappy about it, too.

Dorcas wondered if it bothered him that much to be wearing someone else's clothes. She'd taken note of the dress shirt Marc had arrived in, and it was primo stuff. She hoped he wasn't a clothes snob, especially considering how little Gwen seemed to care about how she dressed.

"I'm sure you can grab it later," Gwen said.

"Do not worry, I will." He sounded resolute.

Dorcas began to fear that he *was* a clothes snob. That might not be a huge conflict in the relationship, but it could set up some initial irritations right when Dorcas wanted everything to run smooth as water over polished marble. Maybe she'd loan Gwen a few more outfits.

As she mentally sorted through her wardrobe, Leo edged his way up to the table and stuck out his hand to Marc. "Leo Atwood," he said.

Marc seemed startled, and he hesitated a fraction of a second before reaching out to shake Leo's hand. "Jean-Marc Chevalier. Do I know you from somewhere?"

"Not likely. I'm only passing through. Saw all the commotion and thought I'd check it out. So you're from Paris, huh?"

"Correct." Marc kept eyeing Leo, as if trying to place him.

"And where are *you* from?" asked Sylvia, looking Leo up and down.

"He's not from around here," said somebody in the crowd huddled around the table.

"I'm from Seattle, actually." Leo gave Sylvia one of his carefully crafted smiles. "I'm down here on a business trip."

"That's a long way to go for business," commented another onlooker.

"You have business in Big Knob?" Sylvia asked hopefully.

He winked at her. "That might be arranged. But I hear there's no hotel in town."

"That's true." Dorcas wondered if Leo planned to pose as a traveling salesman and hang around town instead of living in the forest. That wouldn't be all bad. At least she had a better chance of keeping an eye on him. "My husband and I have a spare room, if you'd like to stay there."

"Dorcas and Ambrose have a cat," Sylvia said quickly. "That can be a problem if someone's allergic. I have a spare room and no pets whatsoever."

"As it happens, I am allergic to cats." Leo gave Sylvia another of his patented smiles. "I would hate to put you out, though."

"Believe me, it's no trouble, no trouble at all." She pushed back her chair. "I'm finished eating, and my next appointment's not until two. Why don't I show you the place?"

"Great." He turned to leave with Sylvia.

"Monsieur Atwood," Marc said, stopping him. "Were you at O'Hare airport yesterday? We might have met on the concourse or at the rental car booth."

Leo glanced over his shoulder. "No, I wasn't at O'Hare yesterday. You must be confusing me with somebody else."

"I suppose." Marc frowned.

As Leo left with Sylvia, Ambrose leaned over and murmured in Dorcas's ear, "Same old Leo."

She nodded absently, preoccupied with trying to figure out why Marc thought Leo looked familiar. It could be a coincidence, but she was gathering all the clues she could surrounding the presence of Prince Leo here in Big Knob. She didn't think his task had anything to do with Sylvia. That match-up had been too spur-of-the-moment.

Leo had walked into the diner, looking for someone, perhaps the person who was part of his assigned task. When Dorcas and Ambrose arrived, he'd been talking with Gwen, and she'd been freaked out. Dorcas needed to talk with Gwen, too, but not here.

She took inventory of the situation. The mob scene at the Hob Knob was to be expected, considering that a Frenchman didn't come to town every day, but enough was enough. Somebody had to break up this logjam or Marc and Gwen wouldn't have any time together.

Dorcas looked upward, hoping for inspiration.

There it was, a beautiful sprinkler system, installed to meet the fire code and guaranteed to accomplish her purpose. Dusting off a charm she'd learned years ago, she mentally apologized to the owners, Sherry and Joe. Then she turned on the sprinklers.

In the general pandemonium that followed, she linked an arm through Gwen's. She called to Ambrose to latch on to Marc, and, bless his heart, he was a step ahead of her. In the confusion, no one noticed Ambrose and Dorcas whisking Gwen and Marc out the diner's service entrance in back. They were all soaked, but Dorcas had a plan.

"Come to our house," she said. "We'll get you dried off." *And give you some of the wine a few hours early.*

"Thank you," Marc said. "No one will think to look for me there."

Gwen's teeth chattered. "B-but what ab-bout my shop?"

"Leave it closed for now," Ambrose said. "Half the townspeople just got drenched. I doubt they'll soon be out buying flowers."

Dorcas congratulated herself as the four of them made their way down the alley running behind Fifth Street and entered the Lowells' Victorian by the back door. At last she and Ambrose had their current project under their own roof. Let the magic begin.

"You're tired from all your traveling." Sylvia pulled the sheet over both of them and gave Leo a comforting pat on his arm. "You'll do better after you've rested up."

Leo was too pissed to comment. This sort of thing didn't happen to Prince Leo of Atwood. He was always ready to perform. *Always.* Sure, he'd burned the candle at both ends for the past several nights, but he'd done that before and still managed to have a stiff wick whenever that was required.

Sylvia slid out of bed. "I have to go to work, but I recommend you stay right here and sleep. I get off at five, and then we can try this again." She walked into the bathroom.

Leo watched, observing without interest the perky tilt of her breasts and the inviting sway of her hips. Ordinarily the sight of a good-looking naked woman sent his flags flying. He'd expected a romp with Sylvia to make up for that humiliating incident the night before.

Instead he'd experienced sexual disaster for the first time in his life. He hated it. Add one more humiliation to the first one where he'd accidentally groped a *guy*. Yuck!

Damned if the Frenchman hadn't recognized him, too. So far Frenchy couldn't remember where he'd seen Leo, but eventually it would come to him.

Maybe this bright idea to appear in town and meet Gwen in broad daylight hadn't been so bright. He'd thought she'd be excited to see him. Didn't women want a man who stepped right out of their dreams? According to popular songs, they did.

Gwen hadn't been excited. She'd seemed confused and terrified. He'd hoped for time to calm her down, but then the stupid Lowells had arrived, breaking his concentration. Sylvia's offer, both the spoken and unspoken one, had sounded like the home run he needed to even the score.

Instead he'd struck out.

Chapter 16

Marc sat in a red armchair in front of the fire and towel-dried his hair. Dorcas had spirited Gwen upstairs to give her the benefit of a blow dryer and some styling gel. That was fine with Marc, because Ambrose was also toweling his hair dry while sitting on a purple sofa next to a glossy black cat who had been introduced as Sabrina. Marc had questions for Ambrose that he could not ask in front of Gwen.

The Sedona wine Dorcas had promised them sat open on the coffee table, along with four goblets and an array of crackers and cheese that Dorcas had set out before going upstairs with Gwen. The men had promised to wait for the women before partaking. Gwen had said she would probably pass on the wine, but Marc hoped she would change her mind.

A glass of wine would help them both relax. Then if Gwen kept the shop closed and he could get to his suitcase without being waylaid, the afternoon might end very nicely. In the meantime, he had a chance at an up-close-and-personal view of a house that belonged to a self-proclaimed witch and wizard.

From the minute he had come through the back door of this house, he had been observing like crazy. The black cat who had come to greet them and now lay regally on the sofa was almost a cliché. Even her name, Sabrina, was straight out of a Hollywood movie about witchcraft.

Marc had expected the scent of incense, and it was there. The brightly colored furnishings were a surprise, though. For some reason he had expected everything to be black. He saw no symbolic pieces anywhere, but he noticed that Ambrose had quietly laid a broom across the front doorsill.

Marc had read somewhere that a broom across the door would keep out unwanted influences, including people. Maybe they just tripped over the thing. However it worked, anything to discourage visitors was fine with Marc. He had experienced enough social interaction in the past hour to last him a lifetime.

Although the bold colors were eye popping, the most fascinating thing in this Victorian parlor was the stained glass piece hanging in the side window, away from the street. Weak winter sunlight shone through the colored glass, making it glow faintly. At first Marc had thought it was simply a pretty design, but then he had taken a closer look and discovered the "design" was a couple having sex.

Focusing on that artwork was liable to make him a little too eager to be back at Gwen's, lying naked in her fluffy bed, so he looked away. But much as he tried to ignore the stained glass couple, he found himself returning to look again. And again.

If Dorcas and Ambrose conducted their marriage counseling sessions in this room, they probably had a great success rate. Between the rich colors of the furniture and the suggestive stained glass, Marc was becoming aroused by the whole concept of pleasure through sex.

"We brought that piece from Sedona," Ambrose said.

"Very nice."

"We like it." Ambrose laid the towel on the arm of the sofa and finger-combed his hair. Then he gazed longingly at the wine. "No telling how long the women will be. Ever since Dorcas changed her hairstyle, it takes her forever to fix it."

"How long have you two been married?"

Ambrose stroked Sabrina, who purred loudly. "Many years."

"Smart answer." Marc grinned. Most of his friends lost track of those details, too. "I would bet Dorcas knows exactly how many."

"Dorcas knows *everything*." Ambrose leaned back against the sofa cushions. "But don't tell her I said so."

"Would never dream of it." The statement jolted a memory, and he suddenly knew who Leo Atwood looked like—the guy in his nightmare, the one who had come on to him until he apparently realized Marc was a man.

But that had to be some sort of wild coincidence. Now that he knew why Atwood looked so familiar, he would just forget about it.

Following Ambrose's example, Marc laid his towel on the chair arm and leaned back. He had used the coat, or rather Gwen's father's coat, to repel the sprinkler water. By grabbing it from the back of the chair and throwing it over his head, he had stayed fairly dry. Not having his own clothes was not a problem, but he sure missed those condoms.

"You and Gwen seem to be getting along well," Ambrose said.

"Very well." *And we would get along even better if I could snag my suitcase.* But Marc did not want to talk about Gwen right now, much as he enjoyed the subject. "Pardon, but I assume you are aware of what Dorcas mentioned to me this morning."

Ambrose's expression gave nothing away. "I believe she planned to fill you in on a few things."

"So you are a . . . wizard?" Marc found it harder to say that than he had expected. It was the kind of question you would ask a child playing dress-up in a cape and star-spangled hat, not a question you would normally ask an adult.

"I am," Ambrose said.

"Can you elaborate?"

"What do you mean?"

This discussion was not exactly flowing downhill. "What do wizards do?"

Ambrose continued to stroke Sabrina. "Well, we don't go around casting spells and brewing up potions all the time. In general we lead a fairly normal life."

Marc gulped. "You cast spells?"

"Why, yes."

"I suppose it is all symbolic."

"There is symbolism involved." Ambrose scratched behind the cat's ears.

"Of course there is." Marc chuckled in relief. "After all, nobody can cast a spell and actually make things happen. You simply perform a ritual and hope for the best."

Ambrose gazed at him. "Just what did Dorcas tell you?"

Marc recounted this morning's conversation. "And she also stated that you were here in a supervisory role, but I did not understand that. Is Big Knob some sort of Wiccan version of Mecca?"

Ambrose smiled. "Uh, no."

"Then what are you here to supervise?"

Ambrose hesitated for a few seconds as if considering his answer. "The residents of the forest."

Understanding dawned. "Ah. Of course. You are a nature-based religion, and that would certainly make you conservationists. If you perpetuate the myth of a haunted forest, there is less chance of hunters and loggers coming in, so the forest and its inhabitants remain safe." He waited for Ambrose to applaud his logical thinking.

Instead, the wizard's jaw dropped as if he had stumbled upon a deep, dark secret. "Great Zeus, that's true! All this time, when we thought George was shirking, in a way, he's actually been . . ." Ambrose leaped up from the sofa so fast Sabrina nearly rolled onto the floor. She had to hang on with both front paws and pull herself back up.

"Who is George?" Marc pictured a Wiccan man living in the forest in a hovel.

Ambrose ignored the question. "Excuse me a moment. I need to tell Dorcas. We should have new paperwork drawn up, new criteria established." He started for the stairs. "Dorcas! Whatever you're doing up there, I need to see you immediately!"

"Who is George?" Marc called after him. He got no answer, but he had a hunch if he found George, he would know a lot more about the secrets of Big Knob.

"I'm curious about that man who came into the Hob Knob," Dorcas said as she used a round brush and a blow dryer on Gwen's hair. "The one who went home with Sylvia."

"Leo Atwood." The sensual feel of the brush and the blow dryer relaxed Gwen, and Dorcas's motherly attitude was wearing down her resistance to Dorcas's matchmaking plans. Dorcas had insisted on giving Gwen an outfit to wear in addition to restyling her hair.

Consequently, Gwen had once again become Cinderella going off to the ball, this time wearing a bronze-toned tunic and matching bronze palazzo pants. The clothes were silk and made Gwen feel sexier than sin.

The Larimar pendant was her only piece of jewelry, but it was enough. The scooped neckline of the tunic allowed the pendant to dangle, once again, in Gwen's cleavage.

"Yes, Mr. Atwood," Dorcas said. "Do you know him from somewhere?"

Gwen hesitated, but she desperately needed to tell someone about this strange situation, and it couldn't be Marc. "This is going to sound very weird," she said.

"Try me." Dorcas continued to stroke the brush through Gwen's hair in slow, soothing motions.

Gwen told her about the dreams. After keeping them to herself for so long, it was a huge relief to have someone to confide in.

"So then, this guy shows up, and he looks *exactly* like my dream lover," Gwen said. "He even has the same sexy smile. How is that possible?"

Dorcas didn't answer right away as she continued working on Gwen's hair. "Does Marc know about these dreams?" she said at last.

"God, no. I'd be embarrassed to tell him. This is some bizarre coincidence, right? I mean, you can't conjure up some imaginary lover and then have that person show up in real life."

"Not usually," Dorcas said. "So, how do you feel about Marc?"

"He's terrific."

"And you wouldn't want to be with this Leo person instead?"

"No! You saw him. He's a horn dog. Five minutes after meeting Sylvia he was headed off to her place, and I doubt they were planning to have tea and crumpets."

Dorcas's knowing smile was reflected in the oval mirror of her dressing table. "I'm glad you picked up on that."

"Who wouldn't? When he first walked in he was

coming on to me, but once Sylvia noticed him, he switched his focus to her."

Dorcas turned off the dryer. "Let me get something." Walking over to a velvet jewelry case, she opened it and took out a sparkly bracelet.

"No more jewelry, Dorcas. The Larimar is already more than I feel comfortable accepting."

"I'm not giving this to you," Dorcas said. "But I'll loan it to you for a few nights. It . . . well . . . it might help keep those dreams away."

"I thought dream catchers did that, those spider-webby things. Not that I believe in that sort of thing."

"I know you don't, but humor me."

Gwen eyed the bracelet. "Are those diamonds?"

"Yes. And the links are platinum."

"Good grief! What if I lose it?"

"I'm not worried about that. Try it for one night. If it doesn't work and you still dream about a Leo Atwood look-alike, then you can give it back tomorrow."

Gwen had to admit she was freaked out about the dreams. Maybe a little superstitious nonsense would help calm her nerves. At least she'd be doing something. "I'll try it." She held out her arm, and Dorcas fastened the clasp.

The bracelet looked very elegant, and from the moment it touched Gwen's skin, she felt as if she deserved to wear this kind of jewelry. In fact, she deserved a hottie like Marc, too.

"The bracelet suits you," Dorcas said.

"I wouldn't have thought so, but it goes with these beautiful clothes you've insisted I take. I appreciate your generosity, Dorcas."

"Well, you're involved with a Frenchman." Dorcas wound the cord around the handle of the blow dryer. "And Marc does seem to care about clothes."

"I haven't noticed that. He's running around in borrowed stuff and it doesn't seem to bother him."

"Then why is he so eager to get his suitcase?"

Gwen laughed. "That's not about clothes. That's about condoms."

"He brought some?"

"Yes, and they're in the suitcase, which is still parked in front of the Big Knobian. If he goes over to get the suitcase, he'll be mobbed again. I'm sure that's why he's in Jeremy's clothes. He didn't want to risk walking across the square. I could go buy some, but he's worried about my reputation."

"I see." Dorcas looked amused.

"Do you happen to have any?" Gwen couldn't believe her own boldness, but the words had just slipped out.

"Unfortunately, no. Ambrose and I don't require them."

"Oh." Gwen wondered if they ever had. Dorcas had sounded wistful about not having a daughter to pass on jewelry to. "That was probably an insensitive question. I mean, you don't have kids, so maybe . . . um, I'll quit before I make it worse."

"Heavens, I'm not offended. We could have had children, but we chose not to." She tapped the bracelet on Gwen's wrist. "Let me know how this turns out."

"I definitely will. You're the only person I've told, and it's great to get another opinion. I—" She was interrupted by Ambrose, who called out for Dorcas and sounded as if he was coming upstairs.

"Don't tell Ambrose about the dreams," Gwen said quickly.

"All right. But here's my advice, for what it's worth. Concentrate on Marc and forget about the dreams."

"I feel as if I can do that now."

"Good." Dorcas surveyed her. "You look fabulous. You'll wow that Frenchman."

"I hope so after all your work, but . . . don't you think men should take us as we are? Our hair and clothes shouldn't matter."

"In a perfect world, you're right. But this isn't a perfect world, and there certainly aren't any perfect men."

Ambrose came bounding up the stairs. "What was that, my love?"

"I was just telling Gwen that there's only one perfect man in the world, and I'm married to him."

"Why, thank you, dearest."

Gwen smothered a laugh. Only a man would accept that extravagant line of BS as being true. "I'll head on downstairs so you two can talk," she said.

"I appreciate that," Ambrose said. "Something Marc said gave me a very important insight." He glanced at his wife. "Perhaps we should have Marc and Gwen go ahead with the wine and the cheese and crackers while we discuss this?"

"Of course." Dorcas glanced at Gwen. "Please, have some wine and cheese."

For a brief moment Gwen thought about whether she needed to skip the wine so she'd be in shape to reopen her shop later. Nah. She'd given her customers 110 percent this morning. She deserved to take the afternoon off and have some of the Lowells' vino she'd heard so much about.

"Go on." Dorcas made flapping motions with her hands. "You look beautiful. Doesn't she look beautiful, Ambrose?"

"She does," Ambrose said. "I didn't realize you brought a change of clothes, Gwen. And they aren't creased at all."

Dorcas winked at Gwen. "They're mine. I gave them to her."

"They're yours?" Ambrose frowned. "I've never seen you wear that outfit."

"I've had it on dozens of times."

"Was I there?"

"Yes, dear."

Ambrose shook his head. "I don't recall it at all." He peered at Gwen. "That bracelet you're wearing looks a lot like—"

"Yes," Dorcas said. "I loaned it to her."

Ambrose exchanged a quick glance with his wife. "Okay."

"Doesn't it go great with the outfit?" Gwen held her arm out for Ambrose to admire how the bracelet looked on her.

"Yes, it does. I'm delighted that Dorcas loaned it to you. Now go have a glass of wine with Marc. The poor guy needs it."

"I'll bet. We'll save some wine for you." With a smile of gratitude directed at Dorcas, Gwen turned and descended to the main floor, feeling like a debutante. By being careful, she was able to manage the stairway without her glasses. The minute she had some extra time, she was getting contacts. She deserved them.

Damn, but she felt pretty. Until this week, she'd never had anyone teach her about clothes and makeup. Her mother, who was not French, had no real fashion sense. Although her father was French, he hadn't lived in France since he was six, so he didn't know much about the subject, either.

In high school Annie had tried to help, but Gwen had known she'd never be able to rise to Annie's level of beauty. Her teen self had found it far less stressful to go in the opposite direction and establish her identity as a brainy girl who knew everything about plants. Dorcas, however, had refused to accept that version of her, and now Gwen had a whole different opinion of herself, too.

She realized that Dorcas was satisfying her matchmaking urge by helping Gwen look good. Dorcas wasn't getting paid for it, either. But now that Gwen had finally seen the inside of the Lowells' house, and she realized Dorcas had enough money that she felt no compunction about loaning out diamond bracelets, the idea of not paying her for her help didn't trouble Gwen so much. She'd figured out that Dorcas didn't make matches for the money.

She was ready to quit fighting the Lowells and their impulse to bring people together. If she ended up with Marc as a result, she couldn't argue with their methods. Maybe they'd somehow planted the bromeliads in the forest and had tended them constantly, as Marc had suggested, to keep them alive. She had a hard time imagining someone going through all that trouble, but matchmaking was their passion, so maybe they had.

When she walked into the parlor, Marc stood and his gaze roamed over her. *"Magnifique,"* he murmured.

She met his gaze without blushing. "Thank you." For the first time in her life, she accepted a compliment without attempting to minimize it.

Marc seemed to be completely engrossed in studying her, as if she were the *Venus de Milo*. It occurred to her that he'd probably seen the actual *Venus de Milo*, and the *Mona Lisa*, too. Surely he'd walked along the Seine and stopped to admire the majesty of Notre Dame.

She would do that someday. She'd always wanted

to visit Paris, and she didn't need Marc to get her there, either. If he chose to spend time with her during her visit, so much the better, but she was going regardless. She deserved it.

"Dorcas and Ambrose told us to go ahead with the wine and cheese."

"Bon!" Marc leaped on the suggestion and walked over to the coffee table. "I could use a glass of wine and something to eat, since we were not able to enjoy lunch at the Hob Knob."

"I know." She gazed at the bottle of Mystic Hills red wine. It looked ordinary enough, and Annie had said it was very good. She'd also said that she'd fallen in love with Jeremy over a bottle of wine just like this one. The rumor was that Sean and Maggie Madigan's experience had been very similar.

Marc poured one goblet full and glanced at Gwen. "You are having some wine, yes?"

Briefly she thought about the fact that it was only two thirty in the afternoon. She'd never had a glass of wine that early in the day. But a Frenchman wouldn't care what time it was. The French drank wine 24/7, near as she could tell.

The bracelet Dorcas had loaned her rested against her wrist bone, reminding her that at this present moment, she was a woman wearing diamonds. Such a woman wouldn't worry about the time of day when offered a glass of wine by a handsome Frenchman. Such a woman wouldn't worry about the consequences of drinking said wine, either. Such a woman would look that Frenchman in the eye and say . . .

"But of course."

Marc grinned at her. *"Certainement, mademoiselle. Certainement."*

Chapter 17

Once Gwen was headed downstairs, Ambrose closed the bedroom door. His gray eyes glittered with excitement. "Dorcas, we could be out of here in a matter of days!"

"Out of here? You mean leave Big Knob?" Instead of feeling jubilant at the idea, as she should have, she felt a pang of sadness.

"Yes! Before you know it we'll be basking in the sunshine of Sedona instead of shivering in the cold of an Indiana winter."

"I don't understand. George isn't even close to earning his golden scales."

"That's because the criteria is wrong! We need a new set of specs!"

Dorcas shook her head. "You're making no sense whatsoever. Stop talking like an engineer and start talking like a wizard."

"All right, let me lay it out for you." Ambrose began to pace. "The job description of a Guardian of the Forest. What is it?"

"To protect the forest and its inhabitants. And George is falling far short of that. He's not patrolling on a regular basis, and he's setting a bad example by playing poker with the raccoons. He needs to be a

creature who demands respect, and he can't fill that
role until he grows up and gets serious about his
duties."

Ambrose nodded. "I understood it that way, too.
The paperwork they gave us spells that out quite
clearly. George is supposed to stop scaring the folks
who wander into the forest with his spooky whispering
routine and the disembodied-eyes trick."

"Right. And he's still doing those things, although
I think Leo's been adding to the mix recently by en-
couraging George to be irresponsible."

Ambrose swung around to face her. "But the
spooky whispering and disembodied eyes have convinced everyone the forest is haunted."

"So?" Dorcas had never seen her husband this
worked up about something that didn't involve getting
naked with her.

"Loggers and hunters don't go into a haunted forest. He's been protecting the forest all along!"

Dorcas frowned. "Well, inadvertently, but—"

"Doesn't matter."

"I think it does."

"That's because you're going by the paperwork we
were given. If we wrote up new specs and included
George's tricks as legit ways to guard a forest, then
he's already fulfilled the requirements. Once the Wizard Council approves the new specs, bingo, George is
a True Guardian without doing anything different
from what he's always been doing."

Dorcas sat down on her dressing-table stool to
think. She could see the logic, but she wasn't sure this
would actually work. Worse yet, she wasn't sure she
wanted it to. If George remained a problem, she and
Ambrose would have an excuse to stay in Big Knob.

She glanced up at her husband. Clearly he wanted
to return to Sedona, or he wouldn't be so overjoyed

by this new concept. "What about his golden scales?" she said. "If he's already a True Guardian, even though he doesn't realize what he's doing, why aren't his scales gold by now?"

"I've thought about the scales issue. My theory is that he doesn't think he deserves golden scales. If we convince him he does, I'll bet his scales will turn like that." Ambrose snapped his fingers.

"I guess it's worth a try." Whether or not Dorcas wanted to stay in Big Knob, she owed it to both Ambrose and George to test this new theory. When she looked at the situation objectively, she conceded that keeping hunters and loggers out of the forest was the bottom line. George had done that, even if his reasons had been selfish instead of noble.

She'd be even more selfish if she stood in the way of George earning his True Guardian standing just so she could have a reason to hang around town. Besides, that wasn't fair to Ambrose. Apparently he really missed Sedona.

"Great!" Ambrose rubbed his hands together. "I'll start on the paperwork today, just as soon as Gwen and Marc leave to do . . . whatever it is they're planning to do."

"They're somewhat handicapped at the moment."

Ambrose acted as if he hadn't heard her. He began pacing again. "In the old days this could take weeks, but now we have the Internet. Once I've completed a draft, I can e-mail it to everyone on the Wizarding Council. We could have a decision in a matter of hours."

"I suppose that's true." How depressing.

Ambrose made another circuit of the oval rag rug on the bedroom floor. "I don't suppose we can rush our guests out the door, but I'm very eager to get started on this."

"I know a surefire way to get them out the door in short order."

Pausing in his circuit, Ambrose glanced at her. "What? Just tell me and I'll do it."

"Go into town and buy Marc some condoms."

Ambrose gaped at her. "Did you just tell me to buy condoms for another man?"

"That's what would prompt them to leave so you could get to your paperwork." Dorcas shrugged. "But if you don't want to, then—"

"Why doesn't he buy his own?"

"You saw the scene in the Hob Knob. He can't go anywhere in town without being the center of attention. Besides, he doesn't want the town gossips to know he and Gwen are having sex."

"He should have brought some from Paris, then. The French invented the condom concept, so I'm sure they're widely available over there."

"He did. They're in his suitcase, which is parked in front of the Big Knobian. But he can't—"

"Right, right." Ambrose scrubbed both hands through his hair. "He'll get set upon by the locals. So I'll go get his suitcase."

"And blow his cover as you roll it down the street to our house. I don't think so."

Ambrose wore the expression of a trapped animal. "I don't know the first thing about buying condoms. We've never needed them."

"No one here would know that."

"People our age don't generally use them, so it would seem odd." He sounded desperate.

"Speak for yourself. My new hairstyle makes me look forty. Forty-year-olds can get pregnant."

"So *you* buy them."

She just looked at him.

"Okay, okay, bad idea. I'd come off as a schmuck

for not taking care of it. But, Dorcas, I don't understand the sizing or anything. I think there's ribbed and nonribbed, so which to choose? I suppose there's a difference in the materials that go into them, too. He could be allergic to—"

"So ask him before you go shopping."

"Dear Zeus."

"Look at it this way, Ambrose. You further the cause of our matchmaking project and, as a by-product, you get time to compose the revised True Guardian specs. Two birds with one stone."

Ever since this morning, Marc had wanted to ask Gwen for her advice about Josette. Gwen might have some insight into the problem, insight he desperately needed. But when he saw her coming down the stairs in that bronze silk, he ceased to be the responsible big brother. Josette's situation was not what he wished, but changing it would take . . . well, no telling what it would take, but her life could not be turned around in a matter of hours.

On the other hand, if he spent the next few hours with Gwen, that could change his life and hers. All he needed was his suitcase. He could worry about the suitcase later, though. First order of business: share a glass of the wine that Dorcas and Ambrose had offered them.

Wine was a part of a Frenchman's seduction technique, but current airline regulations had kept him from bringing a couple of bottles as a gift to Gwen. The paperweight had been his alternative. Gwen had seemed appreciative, but he would have preferred bringing wine.

Fortunately, the Lowells had stepped up with a wine from their hometown, and Marc was grateful. Wine before sex was the French way. Now that he had a glass of wine in his hand, he felt more in control of the afternoon's events.

Dealing with the crowd at the Hob Knob had been surreal, and meeting the guy who looked so much like the Midnight Groper had really put a dent in Marc's comfort level. But thanks to a defective sprinkler system and the Lowells, he and Gwen had escaped that. Things were looking up. Sooner or later, Marc would find out who George was.

In the meantime, he planned to spend the afternoon with a beautiful woman. Maybe it was the clothes, obviously borrowed from Dorcas, and her refreshed hairstyle, which might be compliments of Dorcas, too. Whatever the reason, Gwen carried herself with more confidence than she'd had since he had arrived. He found that very sexy.

He handed her a full goblet. If Dorcas and Ambrose had a cellar of this wine, they could probably run down and get another bottle, if necessary. He had the impression that the wine was intended as a matchmaking tool, anyway. The Lowells would want him to be generous with the pouring.

He touched his glass to hers. "A toast to pistils and stamens." He got the reaction he wanted when she laughed. "Old botany joke," he said. He tasted the wine and was pleasantly surprised. "This is very good."

She took a tentative sip and her eyebrows lifted. "Yes, it is. I'd heard that it was wonderful, and it lives up to its reputation."

"We should probably sit down instead of standing in the middle of the Lowells' colorful parlor."

"I have to say, this color scheme took guts. I like it."

"So do I." Once they were seated, Marc planned to point out the stained glass and hope it affected Gwen in the same way it had affected him.

Gwen glanced over at the purple sofa with the red throw pillows lined up along the back. "The cat seems to have commandeered the sofa. We probably can't both take the wingback."

"We could try."

Instead of blushing, Gwen gave him an arch look. "Could we, now?"

A potent image flashed into his mind—him sitting in the plush red chair with Gwen straddling him. But this was not their parlor. "We should probably move the cat and sit on the sofa."

"I'll move her." Gwen set down her wineglass and walked around the coffee table. "What's her name again?"

"Sabrina."

"That's right. Sabrina. Is it my imagination, or is she staring at this bracelet?"

"Maybe because it sparkles."

"Is that right, Sabrina?" Gwen stooped down. "Are you fascinated by bright, shiny things?"

Sabrina regarded her with unblinking green eyes. Her tail twitched rhythmically, thumping against one of the red pillows. Marc could swear the cat looked royally pissed, but maybe that was just her normal expression.

When Gwen reached for her, she wiggled out of Gwen's grasp and stalked to the far end of the sofa.

Gwen turned back to Marc. "She doesn't want me to pick her up."

"At least she moved." Marc gestured for Gwen to take the middle, the spot nearest Sabrina. He sat on Gwen's other side.

As he picked up her wineglass, he pressed his lips to the rim before giving it to her.

Meeting his gaze, she pressed her lips to the same spot as she took a drink. "Mm."

He could hardly believe this was the same woman who had nearly choked to death in the bar because she was so nervous about meeting him. After their glass of wine, they could take the walking path to her house so no one could see them. He might not have his condoms, but he was ready to improvise again.

Lifting his wineglass from the table, he slid his arm around her and drew her against the cushions.

She sighed and nestled against him. "I can't believe you've been in town less than twenty-four hours."

"I know." He leaned down and nuzzled her neck. "I feel as if I have known you forever."

"Am I different from the women you've dated in Paris?"

"Oui." He nipped gently at her earlobe. "And I love those differences, *cherie.* I want to take off that beautiful silk outfit and celebrate those differences."

Her breathing grew unsteady and she rested her hand on his thigh. "You're turning me on."

"I can tell. Your touch burns right through the denim."

She lifted her gaze to his, and her brown eyes were hot with desire. "That may be, but we're in Dorcas and Ambrose's parlor, and they will be down any minute. I can't speak for you, but I'm not into exhibitionism."

"Neither am I. Once we finish our wine, we can go to your—"

"Yikes!" She sat up straight and put her wineglass on the table. "Bad cat."

Marc glanced over and noticed Sabrina had crept

closer and was eyeing the bracelet intently. Her tail twitched back and forth.

"She tried to bite the bracelet! I almost spilled my wine all over this outfit." Gwen turned the bracelet on her wrist. "Good thing this is so sturdy. There's not much damage she can do, but still."

"It must look like a toy to her. Are those real diamonds?"

"Yes." Gwen kept her eye on Sabrina as she picked up her wine again. "The bracelet's on loan. Dorcas thinks it might help with my—help with sleeping."

"You have insomnia?"

"No. Just strange . . . dreams, especially lately. Do you see the way Sabrina's staring at me? Like she's mad about something?"

"I see no reason why. She appears to be living in comfortable luxury here. Then again, I know virtually nothing about cats. I always had dogs."

"Do you have one now? I don't remember you mentioning a dog."

"Not now. Josette has two bichons, Victor and Hugo." Marc looked into the cat's green eyes. That was a glare if he had ever seen one. "She is not purring, and her tail keeps twitching," he said. "The set of her ears looks angry, too. Change places with me and let me sit next to her." He stood.

"Be glad to. She's making me nervous." Gwen scooted over to the far end of the sofa.

Marc placed himself between Gwen and the cat and picked up his wine again. Soon after that, Sabrina hopped to the back of the sofa and walked behind him to perch right near Gwen's shoulder.

"That's it." Gwen stood. "I'm not sitting on the same piece of furniture as the cat, at least not while I'm wearing this bracelet. She has designs on it, for some reason."

Marc heard steps on the stairs. "Dorcas and Ambrose are returning. Maybe they will know why she is upset."

"How's the wine?" Dorcas said as she walked into the parlor.

"The wine's excellent," Gwen said. "But Sabrina is after your bracelet. While I was sitting on the sofa, she tried to bite it."

"Really?" Dorcas seemed to be trying to keep from laughing. "Must be the sparkles."

"Sabrina does love sparkles," Ambrose said as he came in the room behind Dorcas. But his expression was less merry than his wife's.

Marc wondered if the discussion upstairs had not gone Ambrose's way. "May I pour you some of your wine?"

"Yes, please." Ambrose sounded as if he really needed that wine, for some reason.

Maybe Ambrose was worried that Marc would reveal their secret to the residents of Big Knob. If so, Marc would find a way to quiet his new friend's fears. Pouring two more glasses of wine, he handed one to Dorcas first and then turned to Ambrose. "You were right. This is every bit as good as French wine."

"Thank you." Ambrose took the goblet from him and tossed back a hefty swallow.

Marc winced. Wine, especially a fine one like this Mystic Hills label, should not be gulped. But it was Ambrose's wine, so he could drink it however he wanted. He must really be stressed.

Ambrose finished the glass in about ten seconds. Then he took a deep breath and glanced at Marc. "Could I see you in the office for a moment?"

"*Oui.*" Well, that confirmed it, Marc thought as he followed Ambrose across the hall into the office they probably used for their matchmaking business. Ambrose was afraid Marc would reveal too much and cause problems.

Ambrose closed the door, and before he had a chance to turn around, Marc began his speech. "Do not worry about my discretion," he said. "You are obviously concerned, but I want to assure you that everything you have told me about your purpose in Big Knob goes no further. I would never jeopardize your standing in the community."

Ambrose faced him. The guy looked as if he had just stepped in front of a firing squad. "I'm not the least worried about that."

"*Non?* Well, something is bothering you, judging from how fast you drank your wine."

"Dorcas has advised me . . ." Ambrose stopped to clear his throat. "That you are in need of condoms."

Marc stared at him. He had never expected *that* to be the subject under discussion. Now it was his turn to clear his throat. "You . . . uh . . . have some?"

"No." Ambrose turned a dull red. "I'm about to go into town to buy some, and I need to know . . . your, uh, your size."

Marc nearly choked. No telling which of them was more embarrassed. He was so taken aback that he forgot the English word. "*Grande,*" he said in a strangled voice. He hoped to hell Ambrose understood that, because he would not repeat himself.

Chapter 18

Gwen couldn't imagine what had transpired in the office between Ambrose and Marc. Neither of them had made any reference to it when they'd come out, and they'd looked very ill at ease with each other. Then suddenly Ambrose was off to check his MySpace page at Click-or-Treat, leaving Dorcas, Marc and Gwen to finish the bottle of wine and eat the cheese and crackers.

Dorcas filled a small plate with crackers and cheese before crossing to the red wingback. Marc settled with Gwen on the sofa. Sabrina continued to crouch behind Gwen as if ready to pounce at any moment, so Dorcas finally scooped her up and closed her in the office.

"What did you and Ambrose talk about?" Gwen asked while Dorcas was out of the room.

"I will explain later." Marc helped himself to a cracker and a piece of cheese.

"I don't pretend to understand the MySpace culture," Dorcas said when she returned, "but apparently it's of utmost importance that Ambrose post something this afternoon. I hope you'll excuse him."

"MySpace is an amazing presence on the Internet." Marc directed his comment to Dorcas, but he seemed to be avoiding eye contact with her.

Stranger than strange, Gwen thought. It was almost as if Dorcas and Marc knew something she didn't. "I don't have a MySpace page," she said. "I never thought to ask if you do, Marc." She picked up a cracker and placed a piece of cheese on it. Her stomach was pretty much empty, so if she planned to drink more wine, she should eat.

"No, I do not have a MySpace page," Marc said. "My sister has one, however."

"Oh, Josette! I completely forgot." Gwen turned to him. "Did you get an e-mail through? Is everything okay?"

"Well, no. I did e-mail her, but . . . I could use some advice."

"What's wrong?"

Marc picked up a cracker and a piece of cheese with great care, as if buying time while he gathered his thoughts. "She is quitting school."

"Oh." Gwen knew that must be killing him. When they'd e-mailed each other every day he'd told her how worried he was about Josette's future. "Do you know why?"

"Unfortunately, I managed to delete the critical post where she explained her reasons in detail, so the only information I have is the post saying she was quitting school and taking a café job to support herself." Marc crunched down hard on the cracker. He was obviously not a happy man.

But Gwen could see the situation from Josette's perspective, too. She might crave some personal freedom to choose her own path.

Taking a sip of wine, Gwen glanced over at Marc. "You know, if that's what she wants . . ."

"That is just it." Marc sat forward, his body rigid. "She does not know what she wants."

Dorcas put down her plate and focused on Marc. "It sounds as if she knows what she doesn't want."

"Oh yes, there is a complete list of what she does not want—medicine, engineering, law, accounting. But how can she evaluate?" He set the wineglass on the coffee table with a decisive click. "She never gives anything a chance. She is in and out so fast she cannot possibly have explored the potential."

"But that's her right." Gwen reached for more cheese, a white Vermont cheddar that was her favorite. "She shouldn't have to continue with something that doesn't fit her personality."

"Perhaps, but in the meantime she is running through the money our parents left in trust for her education. It is up to me to—"

"No, it's up to *her*." Gwen didn't know where this assertive attitude was coming from, but she had no inclination to mute it. She was all about autonomy, all about exercising a person's right to choose the life they wanted. She bit into the cheese.

"Who picked those areas of study?" Dorcas asked quietly. "You or her?"

Marc shifted in his seat, as if aware that his answer might not be the right one. "I did. But she had no direction, so I started suggesting things. All I want is for her to have some goals. But she has none that I can tell."

"Is that really your problem?" Gwen asked.

His dark blue eyes flashed. "I believe that it is. I am the only family she has. If I do not watch out for her, who will?"

"You could consider trusting her to watch out for herself." Gwen sat forward, too, and she was ready to take him on. Gorgeous or not, he was trying to run his sister's life. "A person is entitled to pursue her own dreams and make her own choices, for good or bad."

"But I cannot sit by and watch her ruin her life," Marc's jaw tensed.

"Might I offer a suggestion?" Dorcas said.

Gwen glanced at her and registered her conciliatory tone. If Dorcas had been waving an olive branch in front of their faces, Gwen wouldn't have been surprised.

Frankly, Gwen was amazed at herself. She was taking a side, voicing an opinion, disagreeing with a man she had every intention of going to bed with later on. That was so unlike her.

"I would appreciate a suggestion." Marc sounded weary. His unspoken implication was that a suggestion was preferable to a confrontation, which Gwen was giving him.

Gwen pulled in her horns instantly. She didn't want to romp all over a guy when he was already down for the count. She still thought he needed to let Josette figure things out for herself, but she'd say so more gently.

Dorcas took another sip of her wine. "Maybe Josette needs to get to know herself better. What does she like to do in her spare time?"

"Nothing that would allow her to make a living," Marc said. "She writes poetry, plays the piano, paints watercolors." He looked over at Gwen. "And before you tell me she should set up an easel beside the Seine, let me tell you that those artists struggle to survive. It all sounds very romantic, but in reality it is a tough life."

"I wasn't going to say that." But she had been thinking it.

"Your sister sounds like a very creative person," Dorcas said.

"Yes, she is." Marc swallowed the last of his wine and set the glass on the coffee table. "And I believe a person should have hobbies. But she needs a career."

"Do you have hobbies?" Gwen asked.

He looked uncomfortable. "Well . . . no. I have not felt the need for them at this point. I love my work, and I—"

"Exactly," Gwen said. "I don't have hobbies, either. I was lucky enough to grow up in the florist business, a profession I happen to love even more than my parents did. You latched on to a career you loved, so you don't feel the driving need for hobbies, either."

Dorcas got up to pour the last of the wine in Gwen's and Marc's glasses. "In other words, it's better to have work you love than work you tolerate so you have the money for your hobbies."

Marc groaned. "Of course it is. I only wish she would learn to love something that paid a decent wage. I hate that she is dropping out of school. And I wish I knew what she had said in the e-mail I deleted."

"I can guess." Gwen took another swallow of her wine and picked up a cracker. The more wine she had, the less she wanted to fight with Marc and the more she wanted to jump his bones.

"I can guess, too," Dorcas said. "I'm afraid your success intimidates her."

Gwen nodded. The wine and excellent cheese had mellowed her stance considerably. "Not that it's your fault, but you must be a tough act to follow. Josette can't compete, so she's giving up." Gwen knew all about that, although she'd given up in a different arena. She'd let Annie be the pretty, popular one.

"It should not be a competition." Marc's expression revealed pure frustration.

"Drink your wine," Gwen said gently. "Have another piece of that terrific cheese. It'll make you feel better."

"Then I probably need a case of wine and a wheel of cheese to help me with Josie." With a sigh, he picked up his glass and took another square of cheese.

Settling into the red wingback, Dorcas gazed at him with compassion. "She could also feel she's not living up to your expectations."

"She would be correct." Marc swirled the wine in his goblet and stared at the red liquid sliding down the inside of the glass. "At the very least, I expect her to stay in school."

"But she knows she's wasting your parents' money," Gwen said. "Until she figures out what she wants to do, quitting makes a lot of sense. I say don't worry about it."

"Easy enough to say, but very difficult to do." But he took another sip of wine, and his jaw relaxed a little. He ate the cheese before turning to her. "Perhaps you could help her sort this out."

"Me?"

"*Certainement.* She is afraid to try new things, but you could give her courage. You were acting shy when I first met you, but less than a day later, look at you." He swept a hand to include her hair and her outfit. "Confident enough to argue with me." He didn't sound too upset about it. In fact, there was a certain amount of excitement in his tone.

Awareness zinged through her. Marc found confidence sexy. Why not? So did she. "To be honest, I'm not sure how that came about."

"I am." Heat simmered in Marc's eyes. "You held your breath and jumped in."

That did describe the past twenty-something hours. She seemed to be learning how to be assertive by doing it. The more confident she acted, the more confident she felt. "But there's no reason your sister would want to confide in me," she said. "I don't even know her."

Marc continued to hold her gaze. "You will."

A surge of anticipation left her quivering. If she'd ever worried that this was a fling for Marc, if she'd ever worried that he was a botanist with a girl in every floral shop, those worries were over. He wanted her to meet his sister.

As she savored the idea of that, the front door opened. "I'm back!" Ambrose came into the parlor, his cheeks ruddy from the cold.

"All set with your MySpace page?" Dorcas asked.

"All set." Ambrose's cheeks should have started to lose their pink color the longer he was indoors, but instead they got brighter.

Gwen was no psychic, but she didn't think Ambrose had gone into town to check his MySpace page. She also thought the front of his parka stuck out at an odd angle, as if he had a package inside. Obviously he didn't want to show it to everyone, because he didn't unzip his jacket.

Instead he glanced over at Marc. "Can I see you in the office for a minute?"

"Yes." Marc popped off the sofa as if he'd been sitting on a spring, and both men disappeared into the room across the hall.

Gwen heard some manly chuckles, and what sounded like a hearty backslap. She looked at Dorcas. "What's going on?"

Dorcas acted as if she could barely contain herself. Her amber eyes sparkled. "You'll find out. But if I tell you now, Ambrose will kill me."

Marc came out of the office and walked back to the

kitchen, for some reason. Ambrose opened the door to the basement and his footsteps could be heard descending the steps.

Gwen turned back to Dorcas. "What the hell's going on?"

"I'm guessing Marc went to fetch your coats and boots."

Obviously she was right, because Marc was back in no time. He already had his boots on and his jacket was zipped. Now the bulge beneath the coat belonged to Marc instead of Ambrose.

Marc held Gwen's coat in one hand and her boots in the other. "If you do not mind, I would like more time to examine that potted plant in your kitchen. If we go out the back door and take the walking path, we should be able to avoid the curiosity seekers."

All of a sudden the picture clicked into focus for Gwen. Ambrose had gone shopping for condoms. That was what he'd smuggled in under his jacket, and what Marc had tucked in his jacket right now. She should be terrifically embarrassed that Ambrose had been pressed into service, probably by Dorcas. Instead, Gwen was thrilled.

Finishing the last of her wine, she walked over and slipped into the coat Marc held for her, and shoved her feet into the boots.

A little out of breath, Ambrose came through the cellar door, carrying another bottle of Mystic Hills wine. "Here. Take this."

"Merci." Marc took the wine and glanced at Gwen. "Ready?"

"Let's go."

Marc supposed the scenery at this end of town was picturesque, but the only scenery he cared about in-

cluded indoor views of Gwen stretched out on her
feather bed. That view could take a while to materialize, considering the distance they had to walk.

In order to get to the path circling the town, they
headed in the direction of the lake. It was frozen at
this time of year, and the evergreens surrounding it
were covered in snow that sparkled like white Christmas lights in the afternoon sunshine. Pretty, if you
wanted pretty. Marc wanted naked.

Gwen walked quickly toward the path and turned
right. "Ambrose bought condoms this afternoon,
didn't he?" She flung the words over her shoulder
without breaking stride.

"Oui." They had to go single file on the narrow
trail, so, being a gentleman, he followed her. He saw
no human footprints other than hers, but the forest
animals must have used the path today, because there
was a rut through the new-fallen snow just wide
enough for a person to walk.

"I can figure out that the second meeting in the
office involved transferring the box from him to you."

"Oui." That second meeting had gone easier than
the first. Ambrose obviously had been proud of himself for completing the assignment. He had felt comfortable enough to tease Marc about putting all his
condoms in one suitcase, sort of like putting all his
eggs in one basket.

"What was the first meeting in the office about,
then?"

Marc cast around for a distraction so he could avoid
the question. Birds flying in a V formation caught his
eye. *"Alors!* Look up! Canadian geese!"

"Uh, right. We get them flying over a lot."

"I saw a program on television about them and their
migration patterns. *Incroyable."*

"They are, but I'm a lot more curious about that first time Ambrose called you into the office. Surely he didn't ask you to give him the money to buy them."

"No." Marc groaned. "And I should have offered. *Sacre bleu!* I will need to remember to give him money the next time I see him."

"Then what *did* he want?"

"My size." Marc hoped never to live through a moment like that again. Gwen would probably laugh herself silly when she pictured that scene.

But he did not hear any laughter coming out of her. She bowed her head, as if trying to control herself, but she did not actually laugh, for which he would be eternally grateful.

"But, um—" She paused to clear her throat. "What if the sizing is different over here? What if they don't fit?"

Marc muttered a few choice swear words in French.

"What was that?" Gwen called, laughter bubbling through her words.

"I said I will make them fit, *mademoiselle!*" His voice echoed through the trees, and a blue jay squawked and flew away.

Gwen stopped on the trail and turned around, her cheeks flushed from her obvious attempt to control herself. "Pardon me for giggling, but this is about the funniest situation I've ever been in."

"I agree. It is ridiculous."

"I love your accent when you say that word." She attempted to mimic him. "Re-dic-u-loose."

He could not resist her. Sticking the wine in a snowbank beside the trail, he took her face in his gloved hands. "I love your mouth when you try to imitate a French accent." Then he finally gave in to the urge that he had been fighting ever since this morning, and kissed her.

Bad mistake, if he expected to get all the way around the walking path. She tasted of wine and cheese, a combination guaranteed to please a Frenchman. And she was kissing him back with great enthusiasm. His penis responded immediately and joyously to her little moan of pleasure when he thrust his tongue into her mouth.

Much more of this and he would not be in very good shape to walk. But he could not seem to stop. Delving hungrily into her warm, wet mouth, he pulled her closer, and the condom box dug into his ribs.

Stupid box. He was not about to give up her delicious lips, so he continued the kiss, but he did let go of her long enough to unzip his jacket and pull out the box. Holding it in one hand, he wound both arms around her and pulled her in tight enough that he could feel her heat, even through the layers of clothes.

He wanted her with a fierceness that amazed him. He tried to unbutton her coat with his free hand, but the borrowed gloves made doing so awkward. The thought penetrated his lust-fogged brain that he needed the glove off, so he dropped the condom box in the snow so he could remove both gloves, which also landed in the snow.

Gwen pulled back a fraction. "What are you doing?"

"Removing my gloves."

"Why is that?"

"So I can unbutton your coat."

"Marc . . ."

"I know." He worked on the buttons. "It is cold, but I will keep you warm. I need to touch you, hold you." He gazed into her eyes. "It is essential, like breathing. If I cannot get closer, my heart will stop beating."

"That's so romantic."

"I mean very, very close."

"How close?"

"As close as a man can be to a woman."

Her eyes widened. "Now?"

"*Now*. Take pity on me, *cherie*. I will never make it to the cottage."

Her low laughter filled the cold air between them, creating an intimacy that told him she was willing, even before she softly said, "Okay."

"Ah, *cherie*."

"But you'd better pick up that box you just dropped in the snow."

He nodded, not yet believing that she would let him do what he had in mind.

She gestured toward a tree a few feet into the forest. "Up against the trunk would work, don't you think?"

He could not think. If he had been thinking, he would be urging her down the trail to her house and into her very civilized, very centrally heated, bedroom. But logical thought had evaporated from his brain like water in a boiling teapot. She would do this for him.

Consequently he found himself ripping open the box of condoms and grabbing one before taking her hand and leading her through several snowdrifts. Considering how much he was shaking, he managed to get her pants and panties down to her ankles in record time. He thought about the silk dragging in the snow. . . . Then completely dismissed it as irrelevant.

He was too busy opening his fly and rolling the condom on to worry about potentially damaged silk. "Have you ever made love outdoors?" he asked, gasping for breath.

"No." She was breathing hard, too. "You?"

"Yes. But never in the snow. Hold on to my shoulders."

She followed directions well. She gripped him so hard he could almost feel her nails through the coat.

Mentally thanking all those hours at the gym, he grasped her bare bottom and lifted her up against the snowy trunk of the tree.

Almost there. "Is your back all right?" He prayed her coat was enough cushion, because he could not stop now.

She gulped for air. "Back's fine. Concentrate on front."

"Front?"

"Do me, Monsieur Chevalier. Do me now!"

He did. Sliding into her was the easiest motion he had ever known in his life. Finding the right rhythm was child's play. A feather bed was not needed to make love to this woman. All he needed was privacy and a condom.

It seemed as if he had anticipated this moment for years instead of mere hours. She looked into his eyes, choked out his name, and climaxed within seconds.

He felt his orgasm galloping toward him at a pace most uncharacteristic for a laid-back Frenchman. He certainly was not in control of it. Surrender was his only option.

With a bellow of ecstasy, he gave himself to the intense pleasure of her tight vagina. His last thrust must have been vigorous enough to shake the tree, because at the exact moment when his climax roared through him, changing the world as he knew it, a layer of snow fell from a branch and landed on his head. With angels singing and trumpets blaring, he hardly noticed the impact of a little snow.

Chapter 19

Leo had spent the rest of the afternoon watching ESPN and talking to his dick. When Sylvia came home from work, his buddy boy was going to perform, or else. Lying down on the job was simply not acceptable. For the past week he'd been a real stud with Gwendolyn, so how could he lose it that fast?

Sylvia walked through the door a little after five. She looked hot in her short leather skirt and tight black sweater, so why wasn't he hard? She was the kind of woman who would be willing to do all kinds of interesting things. This afternoon she'd tried the basics, fondling and a little mouth-to-cock resuscitation.

She'd probably be willing to get more exotic than that. Leo pictured some light bondage courtesy of the leggy blonde, but even that mental image left him limp. He wondered if his father's old book covered this condition. But the book was tucked away in the castle at Atwood, and Leo was left with . . . ol' floppy.

Sylvia tossed her coat on a chair, pulled something out of her shoulder purse and sashayed over to him. "I've been thinking about you." She ran her tongue over her lips. "And what I'd like to do to you."

Ordinarily a comment like that would have turned

him into a seething mass of lust. Instead he felt nothing whatsoever down below. Mostly he was wishing she'd move so he could see the TV. He was pretty sure the Sonics had just gone ahead, 85 to 84.

She wiggled a box under his nose. "Chocolate-flavored condoms."

"You found those in—" He stopped himself before saying *this hick town.* "Big Knob?"

"In case you hadn't noticed, Big Knob is a very sexually oriented community. We don't spend a lot of time talking about it, but with that big hunk of granite to inspire us, we spend a lot of time doing it. The drugstore has a ton of choices."

"Good to know." He wouldn't be telling her that condoms were extraneous with a fairy prince who was not only able to vaporize his sperm, but was immune to giving or getting communicable diseases.

"You might also like to know that I *love* chocolate. I could nibble on it forever."

He gave her a leer because she obviously expected one. "Got a sweet tooth, babe?" By moving a little to the left, he caught the score. Outstanding. The Sonics were ahead.

She leaned down and cupped his crotch. "You have no idea."

He felt the faintest of stirrings, which gave him hope. Brushing his knuckles over the spot where her nipples pushed against the sweater, he favored her with one of his killer smiles. "Then let me be your personal candy bar."

"I was hoping you'd say that." She eased away from him. "I'm going to change into something more . . . accessible."

"Don't take too long." He wasn't sure he could sustain this semierection he had going.

"I won't," she called from her bedroom. "Guess

who was in the drugstore buying condoms the same time as me?"

Something about that statement niggled at him, pulling his attention away from the game. Then he realized what it was. If that Frenchman had been stocking up on condoms, then Leo would need to interfere with whatever plans the guy had. "Who?"

"Ambrose Lowell."

"You're kidding." Ho-hum. Leo went back to watching the game.

"I know. Surprised me, too. When a couple gets to be their age, they usually don't need to worry about such matters, if you know what I mean."

Along came another niggling thought, and when it finally got Leo's attention, he sat up so fast that the remote hit the floor. "You're sure he was buying condoms?"

"Very sure. He wasn't very accomplished at it, either. He kept changing his mind about which ones to get. In the end I advised him to go with the ribbed. Dorcas will thank me."

Zeus's balls! Leo jumped up, all thoughts of sex with Sylvia gone. Ambrose didn't need condoms. A witch and wizard had much more sophisticated birth-control methods than that, but Leo would guess both Dorcas and Ambrose were past child-bearing age, anyway.

Of course they were. They'd made the decision that those of their kind were given to make—kids or long life. They'd obviously chosen long life over diapers and teething.

Good choice, in Leo's opinion. Too bad fairies weren't given the same option. He'd take it and convince his mother to give him the throne because he'd live for a very long time.

But he was stuck with a normal lifespan of some-

thing like eighty years, which was why he was expected to produce an heir. If witches and wizards
chose that route, their lifespan would return to the
normal average.

The bottom line to all that was, Ambrose hadn't
been buying the condoms for himself. Dorcas had
been acting all mother-henish with Gwendolyn at the
Hob Knob today. She and Ambrose were probably
doing their matchmaking thing with Gwen and Chevalier.

That left an obvious candidate for the little rain-
coats Ambrose had purchased today. Leo's jaw
clenched. He was not about to allow some Frenchman
to move in on his territory.

"What do you think?" Sylvia appeared in a black
corset that barely covered her nipples, a black garter
belt attached to fishnet stockings, a skimpy black
thong and five-inch black stilettos.

Leo noted with great concern that his penis didn't
so much as twitch, let alone stand up and take notice.
What in Hades had happened? He'd been completely
fine two nights ago!

An image of Gwendolyn lying in her feather bed
hovered in the back of his mind. His penis began to
throb. With a sense of immense relief, he focused on
Gwendolyn and how she'd looked that last night he'd
slipped into her dream.

He pictured her satin skin, flushed from the orgasms
he'd given her. He remembered her nipples had tightened when he touched them. By concentrating really
hard, he could almost hear her soft moans.

And he had liftoff! His penis strained against the
material of his slacks. A glance at Sylvia reversed the
effect, however. Only thoughts of Gwendolyn seemed
to rescue his buddy from Flaccidville.

That made life easy, now didn't it? He required

Gwendolyn to keep his penis happy, and that meant preventing any interference from the condom-wielding Marc Chevalier. He couldn't hang around Sylvia's a minute longer.

He walked over to the closet where he'd left his coat.

"You're not leaving?"

He made the mistake of looking at her. Maybe he was going soft in the head as well as in the cock, because her sad expression got to him. He wasn't into mercy missions, but on the other hand, she'd dressed up just for him. He probably could spare ten minutes.

"Sit on your kitchen counter," he said.

"Ooo-kay." She walked into her kitchen and hopped right up there. "It's not the most romantic proposition I've ever had, but I like the way you think."

"Just wanted to give you something to remember me by." Leo was fairly certain he'd never done this without expecting reciprocity afterward. Self-sacrifice had never been his thing, and he hoped this wasn't a trend.

Kneeling between her outstretched thighs, he ripped away the thong and gave her the best tongue job he could manage, all things considered. She seemed to like it, judging by the way she whooped and hollered.

He stood, leaving her collapsed back on the Formica. "Now I really have to go."

She was gasping for breath. "You're welcome to come back . . . anytime."

"We'll see." Maybe a session with Gwendolyn would fix him and he'd be back to his old self. Then he'd take Sylvia up on that offer. She was undeniably hot.

Grabbing his coat, he left her apartment. The *corpus status quo* had finally worn off, so once he was out the door, he minimized himself and flew in the direction of the town square. He would dream up an even better costume tonight. But first he had to do a little reconnaissance and find out what was going on.

Right away he noticed that Chevalier's rental car hadn't been moved from its parking spot in front of the Hob Knobian. Maybe the Frenchman was inside having a brewski. A guy who couldn't bring himself to buy his own condoms probably needed some Dutch courage before he attempted the deed.

What a wimp; but then again, he was a professor of some dorky subject like botany. Hardly a stud. Hardly any real competition, either, but Leo couldn't take chances. His penis would be served.

After checking through the Big Knobian's windows, Leo had to conclude that Chevalier wasn't in there, after all. He might be with Gwendolyn, softening her up with a nice meal. It wasn't six yet, so they could be over at the Hob Knob.

That was fine with Leo, because he didn't think a meal by itself would be enough to convince Gwendolyn to go to bed with a wuss like Chevalier. She'd need several glasses of wine, and the Hob Knob didn't serve booze. Leo had checked that out when he was in there this afternoon, because he'd thought of ordering a beer with lunch.

As things had turned out, he hadn't ordered lunch at all. Sylvia had fed him cold pizza in bed, thinking maybe hunger had kept him from getting it up. He'd been willing to believe that, too.

But the cold pizza hadn't worked. The cold beer hadn't been any help, either. He'd even tried dipping her nipples in it to make them taste better. They'd definitely tasted better flavored, but sucking on them had done nothing to pump life into his buddy.

Nipples had always been a mainstay of his routine. Gwendolyn's had been a real treat, one he was eager to have again. If she was eating dinner with Chevalier at the Hob Knob, he'd follow them to wherever they went afterward. Chevalier was not getting a chance to use those condoms. No way.

But Gwendolyn wasn't at the Hob Knob, and neither was the Frenchman. Leo hated to think of them alone in the cottage, but he took heart in knowing that Chevalier hadn't been man enough to buy the condoms himself. His seduction techniques probably sucked the big one, too.

Soft lights glowed from the cottage windows, but no smoke rose from the chimney. Ha. Maybe Gwendolyn didn't think enough of this schmuck to build a cozy fire for him.

She might be tearing her hair out trying to entertain this boring dude with something deadly dull like Scrabble. She probably had no idea Chevalier was packing condoms. Maybe she was tolerating him to be polite, doing her bit for international relations.

Leo put his wings on hover speed and peeked in the kitchen window. Nobody was there, but somebody had been there. He saw a wine opener lying on the counter, along with part of a loaf of French bread and a cheese wrapper.

Okay, so they were having happy hour in the living room. That didn't mean they were happy. Enough wine, though, and they might get that way.

Leo didn't think for a minute that Gwendolyn would go to bed with this loser when she was stone-cold sober. But no telling what she might do when she was blitzed. Chevalier might be a dweeb, but he was smart.

Putting his wings back into zoom mode, Leo rounded the house and managed to find an opening in the living room curtains. The room was empty. A sick feeling settled over him. There was only one other place to check. Maybe he wasn't too late.

The bedroom curtains were drawn tight, but Leo didn't have to see inside to fear the worst. His fairy hearing picked up on the noises within the room. He knew how Gwendolyn cried out when she was nearing a climax because he'd made it happen often enough.

Finally he found a spot where the curtains didn't quite meet. Peering through the tiny slit, he could see just enough to make him yell in outrage. When he was this size, it came out as a squeak.

That was one of two reasons he didn't like going the miniaturized route. Squeaking wasn't manly. The other reason had to do with his penis. He was always afraid when he went back to full size, he'd lose something in the transition.

The slice of the bedroom available for viewing included Gwendolyn's creamy thighs. The Frenchman's head was buried between them, and she sounded way too happy about that. No fair. Leo could do that little maneuver for her better than Chevalier. Way better.

He just . . . hadn't. The satisfaction of burying his cock in her had been so fulfilling that he'd sort of bypassed the frills. Now he realized that might have been a serious omission.

The Frenchman seemed to be all about the frills. He kissed her everywhere, including the spot that nearly made her levitate. Then Leo had a cheery thought. Maybe Chevalier had the same humiliating problem with Gwendolyn that Leo had experienced today with Sylvia. Maybe that was why Chevalier was spending so much time with the peripheral stuff.

Ha. That could be it. The poor slob was compensating for his ED, as they said on the TV commercials. Eventually Gwendolyn would pick up on that and send him straight back where he came from.

Ambrose could buy condoms until the cows came home, but they were useless if there was nothing solid to put them on. So much for the efforts of those meddling matchmakers. Leo would emerge the victor.

He had half a mind to wait here until Gwendolyn figured out she was in bed with Mr. Impotent. She would hate that, and he'd love watching her kick Chevalier to the curb. Then Leo would . . .

Wait a minute. The kissing and nuzzling had stopped. Was this the moment Leo had been waiting for, when Gwendolyn asked for more than her bed partner was able to give?

The Frenchman reached toward the bedside table. Whatever he was after, Leo had a bad feeling that he didn't want to know. His view wouldn't allow him to get a good look at Chevalier's movements, but when the guy assumed the missionary position, Leo wanted to break something.

If only he had a fairy trick to stop this! One probably existed, but he hadn't paid much attention to his royal tutors. Once he'd learned to fly and minimize himself, he hadn't bothered with much else until puberty, when he'd learned sperm evaporation and the technique to invade a woman's dreams.

Gwen wasn't exactly dreaming. No, she was wide awake, moaning loudly, and lifting her hips to meet the Frenchman's thrusts. Leo didn't want to think she was more vocal now than when he'd been in that position, but he feared it was true. He also feared that when a woman consented to sex in real life, she was more involved than when she consented to dream sex. Shit.

As he listened to their enthusiastic horizontal cha-cha, he kept hoping for a miracle. Premature ejaculation would be good. If one or both of them could bang their head on the headboard, that could put a crimp in the proceedings. Maybe the Frenchman would throw his back out.

Sad to say, the episode continued without a hitch. Chevalier outlasted Gwendolyn, for which Leo gave him grudging respect. He knew how difficult that could be with a woman so lush and responsive.

Leo's wings began to wobble. He'd been hovering a long time, and his mental state wasn't the best, either. Rather than fall into one of the large snowdrifts under the window, he chose to fly over to the swing on Gwendolyn's back porch.

He still could hear the sounds from the bedroom, but not as clearly, which helped some. Finally it was quiet, which meant they were cuddling in the aftermath. He'd wanted to do that with her. Hades, but he was depressed.

As he sat with his chin in his hands, he reviewed his options. On the positive side, he'd completed his assignment. Gwen's self-confidence seemed more than fine, and Leo was prepared to take all the credit.

The Frenchman had come in on the tail end of the project and was currently reaping the rewards. In any case, Queen Beryl would be over the moon about her son's accomplishments. Leo would look selfless as hell. He could go home to Atwood and assume the throne.

Except, and this was a really big except, he'd developed a thing for Gwendolyn. That could be why his dick would only respond to her. After all these years, it had decided to be faithful. What rotten timing.

Gwendolyn wasn't faithful, but he could hardly blame her. He'd created himself as a figment of her imagination. Although he'd hoped that seeing him in the flesh would gladden her heart, it had produced the opposite effect. He'd freaked her out.

She'd probably put it down to weird coincidence—dreaming of him and then running into a man who looked so similar. He needed to talk with her and convince her that she wasn't crazy. Her dream lover was real and very willing to have sex with her when she was awake.

Once she realized that, she'd ditch the Frenchman. And then . . . this was the part that had only just come to him . . . he would take her back to Atwood to be his queen.

Yes, it was unusual, a human becoming the wife of a fairy, especially a fairy prince. But he'd known of at least two cases where a human and a fairy had married and had children. Some of the children had inherited fairy traits and some had not.

Producing an heir had seemed like such a boring project, but it wouldn't be boring if Gwendolyn was involved. If the first few children had no fairy leanings, they'd just keep trying. He got hard thinking about that, which illustrated why this was the only answer. His penis must be served.

As he was working all that out, he heard Gwendolyn and Chevalier again. This time they were having an actual conversation instead of the primitive moans and groans he'd been subjected to earlier. His wings had rested enough that he could fly back to the window and hover while they talked.

"I am going to drive back to Evansville tonight," the Frenchman said in his irritating accent.

Yes! Leo jabbed a fist in the air. *Get outta town, loser. Make way for the first string!*

"That's silly," Gwendolyn said. "Please stay with me. I love having you in my bed."

Leo's wings lost a beat. He definitely didn't need to hear that.

"I love being in your bed," the Frenchman said.

Leo made gagging noises. What a suck-up.

"Then stay." Gwendolyn lowered her voice to a sexy purr. "You know I don't care what people say. Let them talk."

Leo ground a few millimeters off his back molars.

"I care," the Frenchman said in such a sickeningly compassionate voice that Leo gagged again.

"Stay. Please, please, stay."

Was she *begging*? What was wrong with that chick? Guys like Chevalier were a dime a dozen. Fairy princes, on the other hand, weren't all that thick on the ground. Clearly she needed to be educated about the possibilities, and he was just the fairy to do it.

"I must go," the Frenchman said.

So leave, already.

"What about the plants?" Gwendolyn asked. "Didn't you want to go into the forest tonight and see whether Dorcas and Ambrose have been covering them?"

Leo had noticed the stupid plants and now he understood. The matchmaking duo had stuck them there to attract this genius, hoping to hook him up with Gwen. Leo would take pleasure in messing with that program.

"I am convinced Dorcas and Ambrose created the entire plant scheme to bring us together," the Frenchman said. "We do not need to tramp out in the woods at night in below-freezing temperatures to prove it."

"I think you're right," Gwendolyn said. "I was only looking for a way to keep you here."

"I will be back in the morning," the Frenchman said.

"Your last day." Gwendolyn sounded really sad.

Leo, on the other hand, was tickled shitless. Good riddance.

"Tomorrow will not be the last time I see you," the Frenchman said, globs of sincerity oozing from his words like jam from a sandwich.

Oh, yes, it will. If Leo had anything to say about it, tomorrow would be the last time anyone in Big Knob would see Gwendolyn. He would have her as his fairy queen.

Chapter 20

Wearing her terry robe and nothing else, Gwen closed the front door behind Marc and leaned against it. She listened for a soft knock and his voice saying he'd changed his mind and would stay with her tonight.

Instead she heard his footsteps crunching through the snow on her unshoveled path as he walked toward the square and his rental car. He'd promised to call her when he'd arrived at the Holiday Inn in Evansville. She wasn't crazy about him driving on icy roads with little sleep.

But he'd insisted this was the right way to do things. Too bad he was so damned noble. Then again, that was something she cherished about him.

She might even love it about him, but she was a little nervous about throwing the *love* word around so soon. Even counting their online relationship, they'd known each other a very short time.

Walking back to the bedroom to pick up the empty wine bottle, the glasses and the bread basket, she thought of how important he'd become to her in that short time. How strange that her parents didn't even know of his existence. She'd decided not to tell them, in case the whole visit became a fiasco.

She should tell them now, especially because she wondered if he could be the future father of her children, her mate for life. He had so many qualities she admired—focus, intelligence, humor, compassion. On top of all that, he was French. Her dad would love that.

Marc's Frenchness was part of his appeal, but she was well aware it could also be a stumbling block. She had told him how much she liked all things French. She hadn't told him that she also loved all things Big Knob. Both the town and her flower shop suited her. She didn't want to give up either.

She hadn't realized how much they suited her until he'd talked about Paris tonight, in between making incredible love to her. He'd painted a vivid picture of bustle and sophistication, possibly to pique her interest. He obviously loved it there. Although she could handle a large city for brief visits, a permanent move was out of the question.

Would he consider living in Big Knob? She found that hard to imagine. He seemed to relish his teaching job at the Sorbonne and his trips to exotic places in search of rare plants. Paris provided a world-class university and an international airport. Big Knob had neither.

Returning to her kitchen, Gwen rinsed the wine bottle and decided to save it. No matter how things turned out, she'd want a souvenir of this night, a night when she'd felt like the most beautiful woman in the world, even when she wasn't wearing the pendant or the bracelet. She didn't need either of those things when she was in Marc's arms and he loved the living daylights out of her.

But he wasn't here, and without the adrenaline rush of being near him, she realized how tired she was. She hadn't slept much at all the night before. Neither had he. She decided to get ready for bed so that once he'd called to let her know he was safe, she could get some rest.

The phone rang as she slipped on one of her silk nightgowns. She picked up the bedside cordless with the ridiculous hope that he'd tell her he was on his way back, that he couldn't bear to be apart from her.

"I am in Evansville," he said without preamble.

"And they gave away your hotel room. What a shame. You'll have to come back."

"*Ah, non, cherie.* They have plenty of rooms. It is not busy this time of year. Let me give you the number in case you need me."

"I need you. Come back."

"I wish I could, *cherie.*"

"Then do it. Sneak into town. We'll find a way to hide your car in the woods behind my house."

He laughed. "And then?"

"We'll pick a good time midmorning to transfer it into my driveway."

"People would notice us driving a car out of the woods behind your house. Even in the short time I have been there, I can see how everyone keeps track of things. It is a small miracle that no one saw us having sex in the forest."

"Unless you're planning to hotfoot it back here, you'd best not be reminding me of sex in the forest. A girl can only take so much frustration, you know."

"What are you wearing?"

She glanced down at her ivory nightgown. Two could play this game. "Nothing whatsoever."

"I do not believe you. You are not the kind of woman who walks around naked for no reason."

"I wasn't before, but that doesn't mean I haven't changed."

His voice grew husky. "You have definitely changed. I love . . ."

Her breath caught. *Not on the phone. Don't say it on the phone.*

". . . your boldness," he finished.

She let her breath out slowly, so he wouldn't be able to tell she'd been holding it. "And I love . . ." She hesitated deliberately. ". . . your cock."

His surprised bark of laughter gratified her. She'd managed to shock him, this sophisticated Parisian, a little. He cleared his throat. "That is good to know, but I hope you realize the condition you have created. I will be taking a cold shower tonight, thanks to you."

"I won't be taking a cold shower." She'd never felt so sexually powerful in her life. "I'll be soaking in a warm tub. I might even make use of that handheld shower to have a little fun, seeing as how you're not here."

"Gwen."

"Then I plan to sleep naked. And you won't be here to enjoy that, because you're in Evansville, watching out for my reputation."

He groaned. "You are killing me."

"That's the idea. Are you driving back over here or not?"

There was a long pause followed by a deep sigh. "No, I am not. Let me give you the number for my room."

"The room number? There's a thought. I could drive there!"

"You would be missed, you know this. Here is the phone number." He said it slowly.

"You're absolutely no fun." She wrote it down on a pad of paper next to the kitchen phone. "Maybe I'll crank call you."

"I know you do not agree with me. But you will thank me later."

"I doubt it. I'll bet nobody even noticed you leave town."

"Oh, *oui*, they did. When I went to pick up my car Monsieur and Madame Loudermilk were coming out of the bar. We talked about Monsieur Loudermilk's new prototype, and I also told them I was driving to Evansville. As I drove away, I looked in the rearview mirror, and they watched to make sure I was headed in the correct direction."

No point in telling him that she didn't care what Clara Loudermilk spread all over town. Marc was going to protect her, whether she wanted him to or not. "All your noble sacrifice will be ruined when I seduce you in the middle of the square tomorrow morning."

"Ah, there is a picture."

"Hold on to it, 'cause it's gonna happen." She wouldn't exactly get naked with him there, but she wasn't above planting a big old kiss on his gorgeous mouth, just so no one in town would have any doubt that something was going on with Gwen Dubois and her French visitor.

"Bon nuit, cherie," he said softly, a smile in his voice.

"Think of me naked."

"Do not worry. I will." With a gentle click, he ended the call.

She thought about taking off the nightgown, just to keep herself from being a liar, but what was the point? She'd been taught from a young age that you should wear something to bed in case the house caught on fire and you had to run out in a hurry. Conditioning like that didn't disappear overnight, no matter how sexually confident you became.

If Marc were here, she would be more interested in

the fire going on inside her than a potential fire in the house. She'd happily stay naked all night long. But Marc wasn't here, so going starkers didn't make much sense.

She'd invented the part about soaking in the tub and using the handheld shower, too. When a girl had been treated to primo lovemaking from the likes of Marc Chevalier for several hours straight, she couldn't get too excited about a shower head.

Consequently she brushed her teeth and climbed into bed. The sheets smelled of sex, which was nice, but would probably give her wet dreams. As she thought about that, she climbed back out of bed. She'd promised Dorcas she'd wear the bracelet to bed. Where had she put it?

When she couldn't find it anywhere, she ended up crawling around on the hardwood floor. Her clothes still lay on the floor where she'd flung them once she and Marc had made it to the bedroom. The session in the woods had been deliciously exciting, but they'd both known that the best would be here in this room, in her bed. And it had been incredible.

Finally she spied the bracelet lying under her little antique chair. That's where it must have landed when she got rid of it after it caught on Marc's chest hair. Once that happened, she hadn't wanted to wear anything, not even the Larimar pendant. Marc had worn nothing but a condom. They'd made the ecstasy last, drawing out their responses until they couldn't stand it another second.

Later on, they'd taken a break for wine and French bread before falling back into bed and pleasuring each other in ways that made her hot all over again as she remembered Marc's hands, his lips, his tongue. . . . The physical part of the relationship had been amazing.

She didn't believe it was all technique on his part,

or all physical craving on hers. From the beginning, their emotions had been involved. Every touch and every kiss only deepened that emotional connection. She had no doubt they were falling in love.

Briefly she considered whether the wine had anything to do with that. Then she quickly dismissed that idea. There had been no wine the first night, and that's when they'd discovered the undeniable heat they generated together.

Picking up the bracelet, she wondered if she'd need it. Dreaming about someone else seemed impossible now that she'd made love to Marc. But she'd promised Dorcas she would wear it.

It felt clunky around her wrist as she climbed into bed and switched off the light. She considered removing the bracelet, but she was so tired that even that small effort seemed like more trouble than it was worth. She slept.

"Gwendolyn, wake up, my darling."

She tried to rouse herself, thinking Marc had returned. But that couldn't be right. She hadn't given him a key, so he would have had to ring the doorbell.

Forcing her eyes open, she saw a man standing beside her bed in the flowing robes of a sheik. His head was covered in a turban, so she couldn't see the color of his hair, but his eyes were the icy blue of her dream lover.

Crap. She was dreaming of *him* again, even though she was wearing the bracelet, even though her heart and her body belonged to Marc Chevalier. Her tongue was thick with sleep, but she had to get rid of this unwelcome presence in her dream.

"Go away," she said as clearly as possible. Her dream speech was so much slower than her real speech.

His blue eyes registered disappointment. "You can't

mean that, Gwendolyn, after all we've been to each
other."

"You're not real."

"Ah, but I am. Let me show you." He took off his
turban and tossed it on the bedpost. "I'm the same
man who came into town today."

"No, you're most certainly not. That was . . . someone else." She felt the uneasy beginnings of dream
panic, when she wanted to run but couldn't make her
legs move. "It was someone who looks like you."

"No, it was me. I can inhabit both dimensions, your
dream state and your reality state."

"I'm dreaming now, right?"

"Yes, my beautiful Gwendolyn. And we're going to
have wonderful sex in your dream, the way we've always had. I want to remind you how good it can be."
He began unfastening his robes.

"Don't take anything off. I don't want you to do
that."

"Of course you do. Remember how many times I
made you come?" The robes dropped to the floor,
and there he stood with his magnificent body and his
very hard penis.

He was, she realized with a pang of disloyalty, a
finer specimen of manhood than Marc. Marc's abs
weren't quite as tight and his pecs not as fully developed. This man was beautiful.

Not so long ago she'd secretly, somewhat guiltily,
relished her imaginary encounters with him. He'd
given her orgasms and told her she was beautiful. At
the time, she'd desperately needed that. No more.

Because now she understood that this dream lover
was the opposite of Marc. This phantom of her imagination was all technique and no heart. He prided himself on his abilities as a stud and had put on quite a
performance. That was the right word for it, too—

performance. She could see that he thought, first and foremost, about himself.

Apparently she'd created this dream lover, which was a chilling prospect. How could she have thought this was the kind of man she wanted? Yet she must have thought so, to have had him return night after night.

"May I make love to you, sweet Gwendolyn?"

"No, you may not. I've outgrown you, and I want you out of here."

"You're teasing me, aren't you? Playing hard to get."

"Try *impossible* to get."

He smiled and shook his head. "That's not the Gwendolyn I know. I'm sure you're hot and wet, like you always are when you see me." He leaned down and slid his hand under the covers, touching her breast.

"No!" She shoved his hand away. Even though this was a dream, his hand felt warm and strong.

He grasped her wrist. "Wearing diamonds to bed, are you?"

"Yes, because I deserve them." She wrenched her wrist free. "Now go away."

"You want me, Gwendolyn. You know you do."

"I don't want you. I love someone else."

His eyes narrowed. "The Frenchman?"

"Yes. I love Marc." She glared into her dream lover's icy blue eyes. "Now get out of my dream."

"You're kicking me out of your dream? Are you serious? No one's ever done that before." He looked genuinely hurt.

"Then let me be the first. Don't let the door hit you on the way out."

"Okay, so you don't like sheiks. I could be something else. How about a mountain man? Give me a few minutes and I'll—"

"It's not the costume, buddy. It's you I don't want in my bedroom. Vamoose."

"I have to say, you're making a doozy of a mistake." He picked up the robe. "Come on, Gwendolyn. Work with me, here. You won't be sorry."

"You will be, though, if you keep hanging around in a dream where you're not wanted. I deserve better than what you were giving me. I deserve to be loved."

"I can love you. I think."

"You *think*? That's almost funny. Now *leave*."

"See what you're doing to me with your rejection?" He swept a hand downward. "I'm losing firmness."

"That's good news to me. I'm sick of looking at that thing. Bye, dream lover, whoever you are. I'm closing my eyes, and when I open them again, I want you and your male equipment gone."

"All right. The rules of dream engagement are very clear. I can't stay in your dream if you don't want me there."

"Good deal."

He put on the robe. "I think it's time I told you my name."

"Who cares?" She kept her eyes closed tight.

"You should care. I'm Prince Leo of Atwood. Remember that, Gwendolyn, because we will meet again."

A chill ran down her spine. Leo Atwood. This was too crazy. "Which I hope is never!" she cried out. Then she opened her eyes and switched on the bedroom lamp, heart pounding.

No one was in the room. But something was hanging on the bedpost. When she saw it, she pinched herself, certain that she was still dreaming. The pinch hurt, but she couldn't believe she was awake. Climbing out of bed, she grabbed her terry robe and shoved her feet into furry slippers.

Those props had always comforted her in the past, but they weren't enough now. She checked the bedroom window. Locked from the inside. Marching through the house and flipping on lights as she went, she examined every window lock and they were all secure.

She noticed that a light snow was falling outside, which gave her another idea. With a good grasp on a heavy flashlight, she unlocked the front door and quickly passed the light over the front stoop. No footprints. She repeated the exercise for the back door. The snow was undisturbed.

Although she could be asleep, this was the most detailed dream she'd ever had. There was one way to make sure she was awake. She walked into the kitchen, picked up the wall phone and dialed the number she'd written on the pad next to it.

Marc answered on the second ring and he sounded groggy.

"It's me," she said. "I had to call and make sure I'm awake." She picked up the other item lying on the counter, the paperweight he'd given her. Looking at it grounded her.

"You sound very awake," he said. "I am not. Give me a moment, *cherie.*"

"I don't know if I have a moment to give. I need you to drive back here, and it has nothing to do with sex."

His voice sharpened immediately. "What is wrong?"

She quickly told him about the dreams she'd been having, although she soft-pedaled how satisfying they'd been. No need for Marc to know that, because she would never allow them to take place again.

"You wish me to come back because of a bad dream?" Marc sounded confused.

"No, there's more. This morning a guy who looked exactly like him showed up at the Hob Knob." She glanced at the clock and saw it was after midnight. "I mean, yesterday morning."

"Leo Atwood."

"Yes." The name made her shiver.

Marc was silent for several seconds. "Do you remember the nightmare I had the first night at your house?"

The hairs on the back of her neck stood up. "Of course." That nightmare had been the cause of them making love for the first time. She'd never forget that.

"A man who resembled Leo Atwood was in that nightmare. In the dream, he acted as if he expected to find a woman in the bed and instead found me."

Gwen's heart beat so fast she could barely breathe. "Are you saying . . . we weren't dreaming? That he really was there?"

"I do not know what to think."

"He couldn't have been there." She was desperate to prove that. "I ran in from the guest room the minute you cried out. He would have had to go past me to get out either door, and the windows lock from the inside, so he didn't leave that way."

"It makes no sense."

"I know that. Worse yet, he came again tonight, dressed as a sheik. I ordered him out of my dream, and when I opened my eyes, he was gone, but . . ."

"But what, Gwen?"

"He left behind a turban."

Marc drew in a quick breath. "Call Bob Anglethorpe."

"And tell him what?" Gwen fought panic. "I

checked outside both the front and back doors for footprints. There weren't any."

"You should not have opened those doors!"

"Yeah, yeah, I know. Don't go in the basement because the killer's waiting there. I've seen all those movies. But I had to know, and I didn't get murdered as a result. All I can say is that no one came through either of those doors. No one real, anyway."

"You should still call Bob."

"Marc, if you think my reputation will be ruined by your staying overnight, what will happen to it if I report seeing ghosts in my bedroom?"

"Do you have anything you could use as a weapon?"

"A heavy flashlight." She picked up the gift he'd brought. "And your paperweight."

He muttered something in French that sounded like curse words. "Make sure everything is locked up tight. Drink coffee until I get there. I will have my cell phone if you—"

"They don't work here, Marc. Just come."

"I am on my way."

Chapter 21

Leo was totally bummed by Gwendolyn's reaction to his sheik schtick, but he wasn't giving up. Royal blood flowed through his veins. More important, royal blood flowed to his penis whenever he contemplated sex with Gwendolyn, who was becoming more of a babe every minute.

He might never understand why he could get it up with Gwen and not with Sylvia, but he had a hunch Gwen had more depth of character. His penis had never cared about that before, but it might be developing some discrimination. Maybe, now that he was about to become a king, his penis knew more than he did about the quality of woman he required.

He'd left the turban behind on purpose, to give her something to think about. Minimizing himself, he'd flown back to his cave for supplies. If Gwendolyn liked Chevalier's look, then he'd copy it.

He emerged from the cave wearing jeans, a long-sleeved white T-shirt with a Mariners logo on the front, and a black leather jacket. He'd added black leather boots, a departure from the Chevalier outfit, but he needed the boots so he could tuck his jeweled fairy dagger in one of them.

Because he was a lover, not a fighter, he'd never

actually drawn the silver dagger out of its sheath. He didn't much like the weapon, which released a deadly poison when the blade pierced anything, even a loaf of bread.

You didn't dare shave with the thing or use it to slice a wedge of cheese. But he took it whenever he left the Kingdom of Atwood, because it seemed like the thing to do. Until now, it had always stayed in his suitcase.

His father used to own it, so Leo had inherited it at sixteen. According to Queen Beryl, her husband had never drawn the blade, either. For all Leo knew, the guarantee on the poison had expired long ago and the dagger was just a pretty knife.

In any case, it seemed that if he ever planned to carry it, now would be the time. A fairy prince going in pursuit of his queen should carry some kind of weapon, just on principle.

A sword would be more dramatic, but harder to disguise. Besides, he'd never learned how to fence. He'd been too busy learning how to vaporize his sperm. So the dagger would have to do.

Once it was tucked inside his boot, he visualized himself into her living room. It was a homey place, but nothing compared to the Great Hall in Atwood Castle. He settled into one of the overstuffed chairs by the fireplace and waited.

If he'd paid more attention to his tutors, he'd be able to command a cheerful fire to welcome her when she came into the room. But he couldn't remember how to do that, and it would be a waste, anyway. Both of them would be leaving soon.

She walked out of the kitchen wearing a bathrobe and slippers that did nothing for her figure. He'd burn those when he had the chance. No way was she wearing an outfit like that around the castle.

She stopped in the hallway when she caught sight of him. Whatever she'd been holding in her hand, she slipped into the pocket of her ugly robe.

He stood. "Hello, Gwendolyn." He hated her terrified expression, but that would change when she realized how lucky she was. She just didn't get it. When she did, she'd cover him with kisses and they might even be able to have sex before starting the journey to Atwood.

He'd already figured out they'd have to take public transportation. He might be able to travel through visualization, but she couldn't. Getting a human to Atwood was tricky but doable.

She was trembling, but she lifted her chin and looked him in the eye. "How the hell did you get in here?"

Time to start dazzling her with his magnificence. "I'm a fairy prince. I have the ability to materialize anywhere I choose."

"Yeah, and I'm Angelina Jolie. You can pick locks, can't you?"

"No. I don't need to."

"Of course." Her voice dripped with unbecoming sarcasm. "Because you're a frigging fairy prince. Like I'm going to believe that nonsense."

"Want to see my wings?" He'd never shown them to a human before, but for Gwendolyn, he'd make an exception. She'd have to get used to them, anyway.

"Oh, right. I'm so sure you have wings."

"I do. They're retractable, but if I take off my jacket and shirt, I can—"

"You take off a single item of clothing and I'll scream the house down. I still haven't figured out how you get through the door without leaving footprints, but for all I know you studied under David Copperfield."

"David Copperfield only pretends to do magic. I really can." In truth, he wasn't much good at magic, but he could be. With Gwendolyn for inspiration, he'd turn into the most magical guy around.

"Listen, Prince Whack Job. I've called for help, and it's on the way. Unless you like the idea of being in a padded cell for the rest of your life, I suggest you leave by whatever means you came in here."

He was impressed with her chutzpah. She thought she was dealing with a crazy person, and she was keeping her cool. She would make such an excellent Queen of Atwood. "You know, my mother is going to love you."

"Did you embalm her and prop her in a rocking chair in an upstairs room of your creepy old house?"

He laughed. "*Psycho.* I have it on DVD. No, my mother, Queen Beryl, is alive and well. She's the one who sent me to Big Knob. I didn't want to come here, to be honest. But I have to say, you've been a pleasant surprise."

"And you've been a nightmare. Literally."

"Picture yourself sitting on a throne, dressed in velvet robes."

"Picture yourself sitting in a courtroom in an orange jumpsuit."

Leo sighed. This wasn't getting them anywhere, and he had no doubt Chevalier was riding to the rescue behind the wheel of his galloping black rental car. Leo had no choice but to cast a spell on her, rusty as he was at those things. He'd never had to bespell a woman into submission.

Searching his memory, he came up with what he thought would work. He took a step forward and pointed a finger at her. *"Hypnosis ad nauseam."*

She stared at him. "What?"

Maybe that wasn't quite it. He drew closer and pointed at her again. *"Hypnosis ad hoc."*

"You are seriously delusional. But if you come any closer, you're going to be very sorry. I have a gun." Her hand moved inside her bathrobe pocket, as if she might be getting a firmer grip on whatever was inside.

He knew she didn't have a gun. Guns weren't round, which was the shape of whatever she was fondling in her pocket. But she was obviously planning to bean him with the object if he came closer. He was strong enough to keep her from doing that, but he didn't relish having to carry her, kicking and screaming, out the back door. That might attract attention.

He edged closer as he dug frantically through the dusty recesses of his brain for the right spell.

A pulse was beating rapidly in her throat. She was scared, but she stood her ground. "I'm warning you. Come one step closer, and you're a dead man."

What spirit! She'd have the kingdom at her feet. He raised his hand and pointed again. Everyone said the third time was a charm, and he needed a charm desperately. *"Hypnosis ad infinitum!"*

He watched in fascination as the spell began to take effect. She was fighting it, and she lifted the object out of her pocket as if to hurl it at him. Her diamond bracelet flashed in the lamplight, and for a moment, he was afraid she'd beat back the spell.

Then her brown eyes glazed over, and the object, some kind of crystal paperweight, fell from her slack grip onto the hardwood floor.

There would be a dent in the floor, but better that than a dent in his head. "Sorry about this, Gwendolyn." He stepped forward and took her limp hand. "One of these days you'll realize that I'm doing you a huge favor. You'll thank me for saving you from a boring botanist."

She merely stared at him.

He missed her sassy comebacks and her fighting

spirit, but the spell would wear off in . . . It came to him that he had no idea how soon the spell would wear off. That meant he'd better boogie, because for all he knew it was a twenty-second spell.

Leading her back to the bedroom, he glanced longingly at the bed, but there was no time for sex. Besides, she wouldn't be any fun in her current state. Still, he had a moment of lust when he took off the ugly bathrobe and her hideous slippers, leaving her wearing only a cream-colored nightgown and the diamond bracelet.

He remembered that nightgown. She'd had it on the first time he'd entered her dream. That night he'd discovered that helping her to become more self-confident wouldn't be much of a chore, after all.

Teaching her to love her role as his queen wouldn't be that tough, either, once he got her to Atwood. Women loved castles, crowns, moats and shit like that. She would be able to have a hundred diamond bracelets. Once she understood her good fortune, she'd want to kiss his feet, but he'd direct her to aim higher up.

Yes, this was going to be excellent. But she needed traveling clothes for the plane. The bronze outfit on the floor looked better than anything he'd seen her wear, but it was wrinkled and the pants were water stained, as if she'd hiked through some serious snow.

He had no choice but to take the boring stuff in her closet. He found a small rolling suitcase in there and packed it quickly. Everything she owned except her nightgowns was cotton, but in no time he'd have her in silk and velvet full-time. He grabbed a pair of what his mother called sensible shoes.

Finally the suitcase was ready. She'd need a coat and boots to go outside, but fortunately those were in the bedroom, too. The boots lay there as if she'd kicked them off, and the coat was in a heap in the far corner of the room.

She wasn't normally this casual about her clothes. He knew that from his many visits to this room. It bugged him that she'd been so motivated to get naked with the Frenchman that she'd thrown clothes everywhere and hadn't even bothered to pick them up after he'd left.

Maybe it was the oral sex that had impressed her. Leo vowed to get with that program ASAP. But first he had to get her back to his cave, where he'd proceed to convince her that he was the one she wanted.

At the last minute he remembered to take her purse. She'd need identification to get on a flight. Luckily he'd brought his fake ID with him on this trip, for some unknown reason. Maybe he was getting psychic.

He turned off all the lights. Then, because he had her purse and her keys, he locked up the place. No reason to leave it open and make things easier for Chevalier when he arrived.

At last they were ready to start out. Navigating wasn't easy on the narrow path that led into the forest. He put one hand on her shoulder to guide her so she'd walk in front of him. At least in her hypnotic state she was like a wind-up doll. Point her in one direction and she kept going.

He slung her purse over his shoulder and pulled the rolling suitcase behind him. Several yards down the trail he realized that the tracks they were leaving would be like a neon sign to anyone with half a brain. Chevalier had a pretty good brain, as evidenced by his taste in women.

"Stop, Gwendolyn." He squeezed her shoulder and she came to a halt. The trance he'd put her in was kind of creepy, like a horror movie with zombies in it. Those had always scared the pee out of him.

He'd be glad when the spell was gone and she'd come to realize that she was the luckiest girl in the world. He might have physical possession of her right now, but it didn't feel like a victory.

"Hold your purse." He hooked it over her shoulder. He could have done that in the first place, but she was acting so dazed that she might have dropped it. She'd need the purse for traveling, plus he didn't want to leave that behind as evidence, either.

Setting the suitcase next to her, he broke off an evergreen branch and returned quickly to her back porch. Walking backward down the path, he swept the snow to erase both sets of footprints and the double line made by the rolling bag.

Thinking of the rolling bag gave him an idea. He could attach the branch to the bag using the little strap intended for briefcases and small carry-ons. Then as he pulled the rolling bag, the branch would automatically sweep behind them.

Brilliant concept. People always underestimated him, especially his mother. He was a lot like Thomas Jefferson—leader, inventor, stud. Leo thought he had the potential to be the best king Atwood ever had, especially with the right queen.

Because he was walking backward and thinking about his future reign of excellence, he didn't realize he'd reached the spot where he'd left Gwendolyn until he bumped into the suitcase and knocked it over.

"Whoops." He turned, thinking the suitcase might have banged into his future queen. And it might have, if she'd been standing there. Instead she was gone.

Marc took some chances on the drive back to Big Knob, both with the road conditions and the highway patrol. He skidded once and managed to pull out of it without hitting anyone or anything. Fortunately there were not many cars on the interstate at one in the morning.

The only police car he passed was headed in the opposite direction and did not appear interested in turning around to give him a ticket. Marc was not sure what he would do if anyone tried to stop him. He would probably shove the gas pedal to the floor and hope the car had enough speed to outrun a pursuer.

Luckily, he did not have to test that. He arrived on the outskirts of Big Knob without incident. As he drove down Fourth toward Beaucoup Bouquets, the town looked peaceful and innocent under its new veil of white snow. His were the only tire tracks. The businesses on the square were closed and dark, even the Big Knobian.

But something was going on in this town, something that had the hairs all over Marc's body standing at attention. He did not know if the town's Wiccan heritage was somehow connected to the bizarre dream scenario. He did not believe in paranormal events, and yet . . . nothing else would explain Gwen's dreams, or his one experience with her dream guy.

She had left out the details of those dreams, for which Marc was grateful. He had experienced sex dreams before, so he had a fair idea of what Gwen's had been like. She had called them *realistic*, but he did not want to think too much about what that could mean.

He parked in one of the empty spots in front of her flower shop, got out quickly and started around back. Immediately he knew something was very wrong. As scared as she had been, she would have left all the lights on. The cottage was dark.

Heart pounding, he rang the doorbell. He was not surprised to get no answer. His breath clouded the air, but sweat trickled down his back. This was not good.

Running around the house as fast as her father's boots would allow, he got to the back door and pounded on it. Nothing. To hell with it. He was breaking in.

Only thing was, he was a botany professor, not a thief. He had never broken into a house before. He checked out the windows and they were all sturdy double-paned. Both doors had dead bolts. He thought again about Leo Atwood, and whether he had been able to somehow get inside and make Gwen think she was dreaming.

That made no sense, though. Although Marc was not a woman, he had to believe if a woman woke up in the middle of the night with a real man in her bed, she would certainly know it. She would not imagine she was dreaming and accept the situation. She would scream bloody murder and struggle to get away.

In the end, Marc figured out that the only glass that was not double-paned was the bay window in the kitchen that she used as a mini greenhouse. He had to dig a suitable rock out of the snow so he could break the glass. The job was harder than he thought. By the time he had enough glass broken away to hoist himself up and crawl in, he was bleeding from several cuts on his hand.

He could not worry about that. He also could not worry about the herbs he squashed on his way though the bay window. Ironically, he knocked over the pot holding the bromeliad, the plant that had started this whole saga.

It fell to the floor, its clay pot shattering on impact. Marc spared it one quick glance, which was when he noticed that the roots were glowing.

Dear God. His chest tightened. "Gwen!" No answer. He started through the house, turning on lights as he went and calling her name. If anything had happened to her, if that Atwood character, whoever or whatever he was, had harmed her . . .

He found the paperweight in the living room on the floor, where it had dented the hardwood. Panic threatened to engulf him. She would not have left the paperweight on the floor unless she had been powerless to pick it up.

"Gwen!" He started down the hall toward the bedroom almost in a crouch, afraid of what he might find. When he turned on the jeweled lamps in the bedroom, he knew she was gone. Her bathrobe and slippers were still there, but her coat and boots were missing.

Tearing back to the kitchen, he wrenched open drawers and cupboards until he found what he needed: Big Knob's thin little excuse for a phone book. Although he'd told Gwen to call Bob Anglethorpe, Bob wasn't the answer to this crisis. Marc had to face the possibility that witchcraft was involved.

That meant only two people in town could help. In seconds he was dialing Dorcas and Ambrose's number.

"Gwen is missing," he snapped when a sleepy Ambrose answered. "I believe Leo Atwood took her."

"We'll be right over," Ambrose said.

"Who is this bastard, Ambrose?"

But Ambrose had already hung up.

Chapter 22

Gwen had no idea why she was stumbling along a path in the middle of the forest, wearing her coat over her nightgown and carrying her purse over her shoulder. She just knew she had to keep going, had to get deeper into the forest and hide. Thinking was difficult. Her brain seemed clogged with dryer lint, as if she'd been drugged.

Even so, she was positive that something or someone was after her. She just couldn't remember who or why. If only she could clear her head, then she'd know how to protect herself.

By day she knew this forest pretty well, but she didn't come here at night. She didn't really believe it was haunted, but she wondered if someone had an interest in making it seem that way. If so, that someone wouldn't be above scaring her to death if she ventured in here after dark.

What had happened to put her here on this cold night? She fought backward through the fuzziness and tried to piece it together. Marc. Where was he? Oh yeah. He'd left and driven to Evansville.

Then she'd gone to sleep, but . . . *he* had shown up. Then it came back to her in a rush—the sheik costume, the turban, the call to Marc, and Leo Atwood appearing as if by magic in her living room.

He'd been trying to convince her that he was somebody special, a fairy prince, of all things. Then he'd started throwing around Latin phrases. That was the last thing she remembered until she found herself here, with an urgency to continue down the path into dark woods that intimidated her.

But something more intimidating was behind her. She thought it was probably Leo, who seemed determined to take her somewhere. He couldn't have possibly put a *spell* on her, could he? No, such things didn't exist.

Then she heard him calling her. It had to be him, because he was the only person who refused to use her nickname. She'd never liked Gwendolyn, and now she hated it with a passion.

She picked up the pace and dug in her purse for her keys. In college she'd learned the self-defense trick of holding your keys with the points sticking out through your fist. She'd never expected to have to use the technique once she returned to Big Knob.

Heart pounding, she riffled through the junk in her purse, searching for the damned keys. Finally her fingers closed around the comforting metal. As she pulled them out, she became aware of the bracelet on her wrist, the *diamond* bracelet. Nothing was harder than diamonds.

The nut job called out again, and he was getting closer. Ducking into the trees, she found a little path that was no more than an animal trail. She paused just long enough to unclasp the bracelet and wrap it around her knuckles.

All righty. Bring it on. She had keys sticking out of one fist and diamond-studded knuckles on the other. This girl wasn't going down without a fight.

But if she could avoid him completely, that would be better. She pushed farther into the woods along the narrow trail, and snowy evergreen branches slapped her in the face. She welcomed the sensation, because it helped counteract the groggy feeling.

He must have drugged her, but how? She'd had nothing to drink besides the wine that she'd shared with Marc. Leo couldn't have forced something down her throat or injected her somehow. She'd remember that.

He'd only touched her once, and she'd been dreaming then. Hadn't she? The lines were blurring between dreams and reality. She didn't like that one damned bit.

As she continued to elbow her way through the overgrown trail, she became aware of a glow off to her right. A campfire? That sounded cozy and welcoming. Where there was a campfire there would be campers, normal people who would be happy to help save her from a crazy guy who thought he was a freaking prince.

Camping in the forest in the middle of winter wasn't all that bright, but she wasn't interested in finding high IQs. She was hoping for rugged outdoorsy types in buffalo-plaid jackets who chopped their own firewood with a sturdy ax. Yes, a sturdy ax sounded terrific right now.

As she drew closer, she realized the light came from a couple of kerosene lanterns hung in the trees. That was still okay. The campfire wasn't a necessity, only the rugged campers armed with at least one ax.

She heard chattering, but couldn't make out any words. Unfortunately, the campers didn't sound like manly men. She'd met hefty guys with high-pitched voices, though, so she wasn't giving up on the buffalo plaid and the sharp ax.

"Awesome river card, dude!" The voice was the first one she could understand clearly. "Check out these beauties. Pocket aces!"

So the campers played poker. She had no problem with that, especially if they had an ax in addition to a deck of cards. She'd really started to count on the ax.

Mentally she rehearsed her story as she drew close to the clearing. She'd say that a man had broken into her house, and she'd managed to grab her coat and boots before escaping out the back door. The man was following her, and he was probably loony tunes.

Okay, the story sounded plausible enough. She peered into the clearing. Blinking, she looked again. She didn't know whether to laugh or groan. She was still dreaming.

While knowing that gave her some relief, she would love to wake up and get the hell out of this nightmare. Instead she was smack-dab in the middle of it, staring at a dragon playing poker with five raccoons. Because a light snow continued to fall, they'd strung a tarp over the poker table.

So none of this had been real—not the sheik in her bedroom, the phone call to Marc, the return of Leo Atwood. She had a monster imagination, that was for sure. She could smell the pine fragrance of the trees and the kerosene burning in the lamps.

She could even smell the dank scent of the raccoons, whose coats were damp from the snow that blew in under the tarp. The breeze felt icy on her cheeks and nose. Yessiree, this was one detailed dream, and she wanted to wake up *now*.

"The dragon always loses." Leo's voice came a split second before he grabbed her from behind, his arm going around her waist and pulling her tight against him.

Gwen wiggled in his grasp and tried to punch backward with her two weapons, but he was very strong. She should have realized that after seeing his muscles up close and personal.

Holding her viselike against his hard body, Leo pried the keys out of one fist and tossed them into the bushes.

"Hey! I need those!" Even knowing this was a dream, she hated the thought of losing her keys.

The chattering stopped and the raccoons all looked in her direction like a collection of little bandits. The dragon looked, too, his red eyes more curious than menacing. He was a greenish-brown color, although the tips of his scales were gold.

This dream got wilder and wilder, because she could swear the dragon had a white iPod around his neck. The earbuds were dangling there, too, because he needed to hear while he played poker. Of course he did.

She wanted to remember this dream to tell Marc. He'd laugh his head off, especially at the part about the dragon. She couldn't bring herself to be afraid of the creature, probably because he was playing poker and wearing an iPod.

The dragon got up from his seat, three tree trunks roped together, and peered at the spot where Gwen was being held captive. "Leo, is that you hiding in the bushes, dude?"

"It's me, George." Leo wrestled Gwen out into the clearing, and the commotion they made scared the raccoons, who scattered and melted into the shadows.

Gwen tried to use the opportunity of being walked into the clearing as a way to punch Leo with the fist holding the diamond bracelet. Instead she dropped the blasted thing. Fortunately this was only a dream, because it wasn't her bracelet and she'd promised to return it to Dorcas.

The dragon, who seemed to be named George, had to be at least twelve feet tall standing on his hind legs. Logically, Gwen should have been terrified, but she wasn't. She didn't even flinch as George lowered his head to study her.

"Who's this dudette, Leo?"

"Gwendolyn, the future Queen of Atwood."

"My name's Gwen, nimrod!" With a growl of frustration, she tried to kick Leo in the shins.

George scratched the top of his head with one long claw. "I hate to break it to you, but she doesn't act all that excited about the program."

"She just doesn't know what she's missing. Ouch! Stop that!"

Gwen had managed to connect with one kick and she was working up to another. "Let me go, and I'll be happy to stop kicking your royal prince-ness!" She swung her booted foot back and felt it connect with Leo's leg again.

George tilted his massive head this way and that, as if surveying the situation from all angles. "Up to you, dude, but she doesn't seem to want this queen thing. I'm thinking you need a new approach. Candy, maybe a few flowers, a little jewelry."

Gwen decided the dragon was an improvement over dealing with Leo, and because this was only a dream, she had nothing to lose. She glanced up at the creature. "Hello, George."

"Hidey-ho, dudette. How's it hanging?"

"Not so well, I'm afraid. Prince Fathead here thinks I'm going to be his queen."

"Hey!" Leo said. "Don't call me names. I'm a royal."

"A royal pain in the ass," Gwen said. "George, do you think it's right to force someone to be your life partner?"

George frowned. "No. 'Cause then they could creep up on you while you're sleeping and brain you with a frying pan."

"Well said." Gwen tried to pry Leo's arm from around her waist. "Leo, let me go."

"Sorry. No can do."

"Why not?"

"Yeah, why not?" George echoed. "Grab a clue. Find a chick who actually likes you, dog."

"Gwendolyn used to like me, and she'll like me again once we're alone." Leo put his mouth close to Gwen's ear. "Think oral sex."

"Eeeuuuwww."

George leaned closer. "I didn't catch that."

"Trust me, George, you're better off not knowing." Gwen made a face. "It was gross."

"You know what?" Leo said. "This conversation is boring me. Gwendolyn and I need to get back to my cave for a little one-on-one."

Gwen tried to fight him, but she was no match for all those muscles. Before she realized what had happened, he'd turned her around and flung her over his shoulder. She kicked with her feet and beat with her fists, but he acted as if he didn't feel it.

When struggling didn't help, she started yelling as loud as she could. She didn't know if anyone could hear her besides George and the raccoons. If this was a dream, she'd wake up soon and none of it would matter.

But she wasn't having sex, even dream sex, with Prince Leo of Atwood. Not this girl. Marc was her main man, and she would be true to him no matter what.

"I'm not sure this is right, dude," George said. "I mean, you're my poker buddy and that's been awesome, but she's all 'Help, he's kidnapping me!' That

makes her, like, a damsel in distress. And seeing as
how she's in my forest, then—"

"*Your* forest? Hey, lighten up, George. You don't
have to take responsibility for this piece of woods.
Don't let them lay that on you."

"George!" Gwen continued to scream at the top of
her lungs. "Be a man! I mean, a dragon! Don't let
him haul me off to his icky cave!" She wished she
could see what was going on, but from the sounds
of heavy footsteps she thought that George might be
moving into position so he could block Leo's escape.

"Don't be an idiot, George," Leo said. "Get out of
my way."

Yes. George is going to help me. "George, George,
he's our dragon! If he can't do it, no use naggin'!"

"Awesome cheer, dudette. Nobody's ever given me
a cheer before."

Leo gripped her tighter. "Cheer, schmeer. Look,
dragon breath. I'm a fairy prince. I have connections.
If you don't want trouble with the Fairy Council,
you'll mind your own business on this deal."

"I'm not letting you take her, dude."

"Neither am I," said an incredibly welcome male
voice. "Put her down, Atwood."

Hallelujah! Her knight in shining armor had arrived.
"Marc! You came!"

"And he didn't come alone. Ambrose and I are
here with him."

Gwen recognized Dorcas's voice. "I dropped your
bracelet over there in the bushes," she said. "I know
this is just a dream, but I still feel bad about it."

There were at least three seconds of silence in the
clearing. Finally Marc spoke up. "*Cherie*, it is not a
dream."

"Yeah, right. Raccoons playing poker, an iPod-
wearing dragon, a fairy prince who claims to have

wings. I'm supposed to buy all that?" More silence. She could imagine them all exchanging glances. "Marc?"

"We will talk about it later," Marc said. "Atwood, put her down. This has gone far enough."

"Indeed it has," Ambrose said. "You can't fight all of us, Leo. Release Gwen and we'll forget this ever happened."

"I will never forget," Marc said.

That's my man.

"Let's put it this way." Leo stooped down, and for one glorious moment, Gwen thought he planned to let her go. Instead he grabbed her by the arm as he pulled something out of his boot. "This is a fairy dagger. Does everyone know what that means?"

"No," said Marc, "but if you so much as nick her skin, I will have your head on a platter."

"You'd better listen to him," Gwen said. "He's French. They invented the guillotine." Now that she was back on her feet, she was able to see the man she loved standing a few feet away, poised to jump Leo.

His face was unshaven and his eyes bloodshot. His shirttail hung out below the hem of his black jacket, and his jeans were filthy with mud and snow. He was the most gorgeous sight she'd ever laid eyes on.

Dorcas and Ambrose stood behind him, and they didn't look any better. The normally elegant couple appeared as if they'd thrown on whatever clothes were handy with no regard to color, style or even gender. Dorcas was wearing a red jacket that was too big for her and probably belonged to Ambrose. Ambrose had on a ratty old wool coat with oil stains on it and a knit cap that was too small for him and probably belonged to Dorcas.

They all looked like that because they'd rushed to

her aid and she loved them for it. Even though none of this was real, she appreciated the effort.

Marc stepped toward her. "Atwood, I told you to let her go."

"Be careful, Marc," Ambrose said. "If that's really a fairy dagger, and it looks genuine to me, one cut with the thing is deadly."

"Bummer, dude! Those daggers are bad news."

Gwen glanced over her shoulder and saw George backing away.

Marc, however, held his ground. "Dorcas and Ambrose, talk to me." He kept his attention on Leo. "Can you two counteract the effects of this fairy dagger?"

"I'd have a slight chance if I had both parts of my staff," Ambrose said. "Which I don't."

"It would take me hours to brew a potion," Dorcas said. "Even then I'm not sure it would work. I'm scandalized that Queen Beryl turned him loose with one of those. No fairy should own one unless they know the proper spells to neutralize the poison, and I can't believe Leo has that kind of knowledge." She hesitated. "Of course, it could be a fake."

Leo waved the knife around. "Anybody willing to take that chance?"

"Certainement." Without warning, Marc threw himself at Leo.

"I'm with you, dude!" George charged from the rear.

"Fools!" Leo lashed out with the knife, but he loosened his grip on Gwen.

Quickly she twisted away from him. She was free! But as she turned, she saw Marc stagger back, a gash across his neck.

It's only a dream. But Gwen couldn't stop the cry of agony that rose in her throat as she ran to Marc,

who had already dropped to his knees. *Only a dream!*
It wasn't a deep cut, but blood dripped from it, and
when she pressed her fingers there, it felt like real
blood.

"Mon Dieu," Marc murmured. *"Je suis fatigue."*

"He got me on the belly," George said. "But I'm a
dragon! I'm cool. I'm . . . feeling sick. Woozy city."

"Leo, you reckless imbecile!" Dorcas sounded desperate. "Reverse the effects of the poison! Reverse it
right now, or so help me, your life will not be worth
living!"

Holding on to Marc, Gwen turned and gazed up at
Leo. She no longer could separate dreams from reality, and this felt way too real to suit her. Against all
logic, she believed if she didn't find a way to save
Marc, he would die.

According to Dorcas and Ambrose, Leo was the
only one who could save him. "Please," she whispered
through cold lips. "Please help him. Help both of
them."

Leo stood holding the bloody knife. "If you'll be
my queen, I will."

There was no other choice. Marc was slipping away,
and the poor dragon was down, too. "All right, you
slimy bastard. I'll be your queen."

George's voice came faintly across the clearing.
"Don't forget about the frying pan."

She didn't intend to. Someday, somehow, Leo
would pay for this.

Chapter 23

Leo had the leverage he needed. He hadn't meant to actually cut either Chevalier or George, but accidents happened. This accident would work out well if he could figure out the reversal spell, because then Gwendolyn would be his queen.

If he couldn't figure out the reversal spell, then Gwendolyn would probably kill him, so the spell would be a good thing to have right now. It had been in the list of instructions that came with the knife, but he wasn't sure what he'd done with those instructions.

Think, Atwood. Okay, hold on. It was coming to him. He'd shoved that little piece of paper in the sheath, in case of emergencies, like actually using the blasted thing. If it hadn't fallen out somewhere, he was in business.

Plunging the knife into a nearby snowdrift, he pulled the sheath out of his boot and stuck his finger down into it, hoping to touch the folded instructions.

"What in Hades's name are you waiting for?" Ambrose walked over to him. "You said you'd do the spell, so do it!"

"Cool your jets. I'll do the spell." If he didn't have the instructions in the sheath, he wouldn't be doing shit, but he wasn't about to admit that if he didn't have to.

"We need that spell, and we need it now, Atwood." Ambrose gestured toward Dorcas, who'd packed snow around the Frenchman's wound and was now doing the same with the dragon. "She can slow the progress, but that's only a temporary measure."

"Be right with you." Leo turned his back on Ambrose as his finger touched the edge of what could be the paper containing the instructions. He hoped they were in English. If they were in English, he hoped they'd been written by a native speaker.

But first he had to get the instructions out of the sheath, and they appeared to be wedged in there. Leo began to sweat. His fingers weren't quite long enough. . . . The blade! He could use that to pry them out.

Turning, he pulled the silver knife out of the snow-drift.

"Put that down." Ambrose seemed to appear magically in front of him. "You can't be trusted with that." He looked prepared to try to wrestle the knife away from Leo.

Ambrose wasn't strong enough to do that, but one of them could get hurt in the process. Lethally hurt. Leo was forced to explain himself.

"The instructions for reversing the effects of the poison are inside this sheath. I'm trying to get them out and I thought I'd use the knife."

Ambrose groaned. "I don't know whether to be horrified that you need written instructions or thrilled that instructions exist so we can all look at them."

"They're stuck." Leo began to probe inside the sheath with the point of the knife. "But I have to be careful or I might cut myself."

"No joke. Didn't you have to pass an exam to be allowed to carry that thing?"

"Yeah. I found my dad's old cheat sheet. Hades, I can't get this stupid piece of paper out!"

"Dorcas," Ambrose called. "Can you take a break and bring your wand over here?"

Dorcas stood and hurried over. "A wand isn't going to reverse the effects of that poison."

"No, but I'll bet you could get the instructions out of the sheath. They're wedged in there."

Dorcas stared at the two men. "Why didn't you tell me that earlier? Move that knife. Stick it back in the snow."

Leo was only too glad to get rid of it.

Dorcas pointed her wand at the sheath. *"Erupit!"* The sheath split in half, revealing a crumpled piece of yellowed paper.

They all reached for it at once, ripping the paper so they each ended up with a piece of it.

"Hold out your pieces," Dorcas commanded. As they did so, she pointed her wand again. *"E pluribus unum."* The three pieces united in Dorcas's hand.

Leo blinked. "Aren't those the words on a dollar bill?"

"Yes, which makes them easy to remember. And they work just fine. Let me look at this." Pulling a pair of jeweled glasses out of her jacket pocket, Dorcas slipped them on and consulted the instructions.

Leo and Ambrose crowded around and read over her shoulder.

"Any day now!" Gwendolyn's voice cracked. "Both of them are fading!"

Dorcas handed Leo the paper. "You have to do this because you're the official fairy. But I'll coach you."

"Right." Leo took a deep breath.

"Step one," Dorcas said. "Face the victim. Or in this case, victims."

"Doing it." Leo turned so he could see both George

and Chevalier. George's scales had turned a muddy brown, and Chevalier's face was pasty. Neither of them looked good.

"Step two, ask the victims for forgiveness for your unintentional and rash act. Say their full names and titles."

Gwendolyn was crying and could barely talk. "Marc's full name is . . . is Jean-Marc Chevalier, Professor of Botany, Sorb-bonne University, P-Paris."

Leo managed to say all that, but then he glanced at Dorcas. "What's George's full name? I only know him by George."

Dorcas didn't look all that steady, either. "His full name is George, the True Guardian of the Whispering Forest."

Ambrose touched her arm. "I didn't get the paperwork approved. He hasn't officially earned—"

"The hell he hasn't!" Dorcas's eyes shimmered with tears as she glared at her husband. "Did he not just risk his life to save someone who was in danger within the confines of this forest?"

"Yes, he did." Ambrose cleared his throat. "Most certainly. Proceed."

"And George, the True Guardian of the Whispering Forest," Leo said. "I ask forgiveness for my rash and unintentional act."

"It was supposed to be unintentional and rash," Ambrose said. "He got it backward."

"I doubt that matters," Dorcas said. "This isn't like one of your computer codes, Ambrose. It's the intent that matters, not the exact order of the words." She consulted the paper again. "Step three, bestow a kiss on the cheek of the victim and wish the victim a long and prosperous life. Use the full name and title again."

Leo made a face. "A kiss? How about a handshake? Wouldn't that be the same intent?"

"It says a kiss." Dorcas fixed her gaze on him. "In this case, no waffling. There's no substitute for a kiss."

Leo hesitated. Then he saw the tears streaming down Gwendolyn's face and knew he had to do it, icky though it would be. He chose the dragon first as the lesser of two evils.

The dragon didn't smell good under normal circumstances, but now that he was turning color and losing life, he smelled even worse. Leo hoped he wouldn't puke as he crouched down and pressed his lips against the scaly cheek. Ugh.

"George, the True Guardian of the Whispering Forest, I wish you a long and prosperous life."

"Now do Marc," Dorcas said.

Leo stood. "I'd appreciate it if you'd rephrase that."

"Oh, for Hera's sake! Now *kiss* Marc."

Leo had never kissed a man on the cheek with the exception of his dad, when he was a little kid who didn't know any better. This would take fortitude.

He glanced at Gwendolyn. "This is for you." Then he got to his knees in the snow and kissed Chevalier's bristly, very chilly, cheek. "Jean-Marc Chevalier, I wish you a long and prosperous life." Then he leaped up and backed away, wiping his mouth on his sleeve.

"Step four, sing 'Imagine' by John Lennon."

"I don't know all the words!"

"I'll help you," Dorcas said. And she began to sing in a clear voice.

Leo couldn't carry a tune in a bucket, but he stumbled along with Dorcas, anyway. He could see color was returning to both the dragon and the Frenchman, so he sang louder. Yes! They'd done it!

Chevalier was the first to sit up and glance around,

while Gwendolyn knelt beside him, sobbing and kissing the wound that was already healing.

"Ce qui s'est passé?" the Frenchman mumbled.

"N-nothing," Gwendolyn said as she smoothed his hair back from his forehead. "Just a b-bad dream."

"Hey, dudes and dudettes!" George struggled to his feet. "I feel awesome!"

More than happy to stop looking at Gwendolyn fawning over the Frenchman, Leo turned his attention to the dragon. Whoa.

"George," Dorcas said, her voice hushed. "Your scales."

"What about 'em?" Then George glanced down at himself. "Cowabunga! Gold city!"

"Yes!" Dorcas shoved both fists in the air.

"Party down!" George began to dance and sing something he seemed to be making up on the spot. "It's good to be gold, so good to be gold, now I can be bold, 'cause I am all GOLD!"

Soon Dorcas joined him, dancing around the clearing, and then Ambrose joined in. Leo stared at the three of them acting like crazy fools and shook his head. He didn't get it.

By now Chevalier was standing and looked pretty healthy for a guy who'd almost died of a poisoned fairy blade. Gwendolyn held his face between her hands. "I'm so glad you're alive."

"That makes two of us." He wound his arms around her waist. "Gwen, we must talk."

Leo didn't like watching them get all kissy-face. It made him sort of sick.

"I keep thinking this is only a dream," Gwendolyn said. "But even so—"

"It is not a dream." Chevalier looked very intense for a boring botany professor. "That is what we need to talk about."

"The thing is, I can't talk to you anymore. Not in this dream, anyway. I made a promise to Leo."

Damn straight! You're my woman, now! Leo preened, knowing that she was about to tell this bozo adios.

"What promise?" The Frenchman looked worried.

"To go with him. He healed you and now I have to go with him to . . . wherever. Some fairy kingdom. And even though I'm sure this is a dream, I'm scared stiff, because I don't think I'll ever see you again."

"You are not going." Chevalier's jaw tightened and he glanced over at Leo. "I am sorry, Atwood. You cannot take her."

"Yes, he can." Gwendolyn pushed away from Chevalier, but she seemed to be in agony over it. "I promised." She turned to Leo, and her eyes were leaking water again.

She walked over to him as if about to meet her death. "I'm ready. Let's go."

He could see she'd be a barrel of laughs if she stayed in this kind of mood. He had a bad feeling that she might be in love with the botany professor. Shit. He shouldn't care about that. He had his penis to think about.

But Gwendolyn looked miserable. He wished she'd sass him, but the fight seemed to have gone out of her. She was resigned to her fate, which was him.

He sighed. "Ah, fugettaboutit," he said. "Stay with the Frenchman if it makes you happy." What a chump he was, and his poor penis was SOL, but the words were out now, and he couldn't very well take them back.

He'd shocked Gwendolyn all to Hades, though. She was staring at him as if she couldn't believe he'd said that. He could barely believe it himself.

"Well done, Prince Leo," Dorcas said.

He turned to find her smiling at him. He hadn't noticed that she and Ambrose had stopped dancing with George, but now all three of them stood watching him. In their eyes he saw something he wasn't particularly used to—respect.

He shrugged, not sure how to deal with something like that. "No biggie."

"It's a biggie," Ambrose said.

"My curiosity is killing me." Dorcas gazed at him. "Did you come here to convince Gwen to be your queen?"

Leo started to say that he'd been sent to do a good deed and boost Gwen's self-esteem, but that wouldn't make Gwen feel very good. "You bet." He decided to embellish on the lie. "I noticed her on a flyby during Christmas and decided I needed some of that for the Kingdom of Atwood."

"I wasn't here over Christmas," Gwen said. "I was in Yuma."

"That's exactly where I was flying," Leo said. "Yuma."

"I see." Dorcas didn't look as if she was buying it, but she seemed to be willing to let it go. "I have to say that I'm more at ease with you taking over the throne after this episode. I'm sure your mother will be, too."

"I guess." Yeah, he'd probably get the throne now. But providing an heir might not be all that simple. He might go down in fairy history as King Leo of the Limp Dick.

"Thank you, Leo." Gwendolyn came over and gave him a quick kiss on the cheek. A sisterly kiss. How depressing.

"I do have wings, you know," he said. "I'll show you."

Her eyes widened as he stripped off the black

leather jacket. "Leo, for heaven's sake. It's freezing out here!"

"Fairies don't feel the cold." Stripping off the T-shirt, he arched his back and his retractable wings unfurled.

She gasped.

He took some satisfaction in that. Those white wings were pretty impressive. Maybe she'd have a little twinge of regret. He glanced over, but she didn't look as if she regretted anything. He had her attention, but she hadn't let go of the Frenchman.

Oh, well. If he couldn't have the girl, he'd at least go for the dramatic exit.

Except he couldn't think of a good exit line. *We'll always have Paris?* No good. *Frankly, my dear, I don't give a damn?* That didn't quite fit, either.

He was losing the moment. He flapped his wings. "*Hasta la vista,* baby." It wasn't great, but he'd go with it so he could get the hell out of there. He flew upward into the swirling snow.

An hour later, Marc sat across from Gwen at her kitchen table. Both of them held on to mugs of steaming coffee as if they were life preservers. Marc let go of his long enough to touch his throat where the fairy blade had cut him and nearly ended his life. There was nothing there now, not even a scar.

"I just know I'm going to wake up any minute." Gwen had said something similar several times in the past hour. She had taken off her coat and boots and put on her furry robe and slippers, as if trying to return to the moment before Leo had appeared in her living room.

"It is a lot to take in all at once." But Marc was determined to help her do it. The world was not as either of them imagined, but that meant the possibilities were larger and more amazing, too. He was exhilarated by the prospects.

Gwen did not seem to share that emotion. Dorcas had taken him aside to say that if Gwen wanted to believe she had dreamed all that had happened, he should let her do that. Some people were not able to accept the world of magic, according to Dorcas. Gwen might be one of those.

But Marc wanted Gwen to be in on it with him. He wanted her to acknowledge the incredible phenomenon they had glimpsed, even if it contradicted every no-nonsense bone in her body. Marc had not processed it all thoroughly himself, but he was not trying to deny it. She was.

"A dragon." Gwen shook her head. "That's so ridiculous."

"I know. But he is not a trick. He exists." Marc planned to make one more trip out to talk with George before leaving for Chicago. He had considered skipping the conference, but that would leave them without a main speaker. Even so, he was toying with the idea of staying here.

Right now, though, both he and Gwen needed to rest and regroup, let the adrenaline rush wear off. Dorcas and Ambrose obviously had recognized that. Once Leo was gone, they had suggested everyone call it a night.

Before leaving the forest, Dorcas and Ambrose promised George a party the next night, because he wanted to celebrate his newfound goldness. The dragon also discovered a new sensitivity to his environment. Now that he was a True Guardian, he could tell when anything was out of place in the forest.

In no time he plucked the diamond bracelet out of the bushes and handed it to Dorcas. Then he proudly located the missing part of Ambrose's staff and produced Gwen's keys. He also agreed to talk to the raccoons about returning some cases of beer they had borrowed from the Big Knobian.

After they left George, Dorcas and Ambrose had returned to Gwen's house briefly so that Dorcas could repair Gwen's destroyed kitchen window. Marc had hoped Gwen would be as fascinated by that as he was. Instead she managed to be in another part of the house while it happened.

Dorcas had also quietly put Gwen's clothes and suitcase back in her closet. Gwen paid no attention to what Dorcas was doing in that regard, either, as if shutting out the truth would make it go away.

She does not want to know what she knows. But Marc could not imagine how she could deny what she had seen. She had heard, smelled, tasted and touched magic tonight. She had to acknowledge that, did she not?

He reached across the table and covered her hand with his. "Are you all right, *cherie?*"

She met his gaze. "We should go to bed."

"That is a good idea." He wanted desperately to hold her. If she was willing, he would make love to her, too. He would try anything to help her acknowledge what had happened to them.

She pushed back her chair. "The sooner we go to bed, the sooner we will wake up and realize this was all a crazy, crazy dream."

Surely she would not be able to convince herself of that! In a way, he wished Dorcas had not repaired the window and put away Gwen's clothes, so he would have evidence he could use to make his point. Maybe that damned turban was still hanging on the bedpost. Much as he hated to think of Leo's involvement with Gwen, he almost hoped the turban was there.

Chapter 24

In the bedroom, Gwen looked around and could see no evidence of a fairy prince who could sprout wings and fly away. She must have imagined it all, because winged fairies didn't exist and neither did golden dragons. Magic wands couldn't repair windows, and Marc hadn't really been about to die from a dagger's wound.

Marc had no wings or dragon scales. He didn't use wands or magic spells. He was simply a man.

Hungry for that kind of normalcy, she stripped off her nightgown and climbed into bed with him, needing his warmth and his strength. If this was dream sex, at least Marc hadn't shown up in a fantasy costume or called her Gwendolyn.

Most of all, she could sense that he cared for her, that this wasn't simply a game or a chance for physical release. Marc wasn't touching some generic woman's body; he was caressing hers. In the short time they'd been lovers, he'd learned the spots that triggered a response in her, and now he kissed them all—behind her ear, beneath her breast, inside her elbow and behind her knee.

His beard scratched a little, and that was fine with her. It was a reminder that he was flesh and blood, not some creation of her dream world. He wasn't the smoothest lover in the world, but he was an honest one.

Even the condom he unrolled was a testament to his human traits. She was reassured by the ordinariness of it all as he snapped the condom into place.

But there was nothing ordinary about joining her body with his. She knew how quickly she could be swept away and wondered if she was too fragile right now to handle the intense feelings he generated within her.

As if sensing her hesitation, he rolled to his back and invited her to take him, instead of the other way around. He gave her the most precious gift of all— control. She was thirsting for it.

She straddled him, stroked herself lightly over his erection, and found the exact spot where one down-ward movement would lock them together and begin the dance. Yet she held herself slightly apart from him, not quite ready to make that commitment.

Although she was throbbing and wet with desire, still she swayed above him, unsure. "It scares me how much I want you," she confessed.

"I know, *cherie*," he murmured. "I am scared, as well."

"You've become so important to me."

He bracketed her hips in his large hands. "And you to me. But we can give each other courage."

With a groan of surrender, she impaled herself, tak-ing him up to the hilt. Yes, this was right and true. She could believe in this connection with Marc.

Slowly she began to move, listening to his breathing, hearing the catch as he drew closer to his release. The tension built within her in tandem with his response. She didn't have to work at it, didn't have to orches-trate anything. They were in tune, and that was all that mattered.

"Marc, I love you." The words spilled out before she could censor them.

His fingers dug into her hips, holding her tight, stopping her movement. *"Pardon?"*

She couldn't take it back and didn't even want to. "I love you."

His intense blue eyes held hers as surely as his hands kept her from moving. "And I love you. You were prepared to sacrifice yourself for me."

"It was only a dream."

"But it felt real, did it not? The sacrifice felt real."

She couldn't deny that. "Yes. I thought you were dying."

"I was." He held her, but his eyes darkened. "I am alive because of you."

She started to deny it, but then she felt him pulse within her, and her womb answered. With a cry he surged upward, his gaze locked with hers. She was helpless to stop the orgasm that rolled through her in perfect rhythm with his.

She'd never known anything like this moment— each of them giving the other all that was in them, all that they knew, all that they were.

As the intensity gradually ebbed, she felt a moment of unease. If the rest had been a dream, then this moment couldn't be real, either. She desperately wanted it to be.

Dorcas and Ambrose cuddled in bed, spent after celebrating George's transformation with a round of hot sex.

"I glanced at that set of instructions for reversing the dagger's poison," Ambrose said. "There were only three steps. I didn't see a thing about singing John Lennon's song."

Dorcas laughed. "I threw that in. After all Leo put us through, I decided he should have to complete as many embarrassing moves as I could dream up. I was trying to come up with a step five, but I could tell George and Marc were reviving and I wouldn't get away with it."

"Looks like our soul mates are in love."

"Yes, but it's not a done deal." Dorcas laid her head in the curve of Ambrose's shoulder. "Marc wants her to accept the magic and she's resisting. I advised him to let her opt out, but that's not the kind of partnership he wants."

"Did you tell him we have two mixed couples in town already?"

"I started to, but Gwen interrupted our conversation. But how other couples handle it wouldn't matter to Marc. Both Annie and Maggie are happy keeping their husbands in the dark. Maybe it's because they're women."

"Hey." Ambrose gave her a pinch on the butt.

"Kidding. Sort of. It might have nothing to do with gender, but Marc definitely wants his life partner to share his enthusiasm for the unknown. Scientific adventure is part of his DNA."

"Could it be a deal-breaker?"

Dorcas sighed. "I hope not."

"I hope not, either, because once we wind up the Gwen and Marc project, we're free to leave Big Knob."

"I wouldn't mind hanging around to see Dee-Dee's baby lake monsters born." Dorcas made it sound like a casual request.

"That could be months."

Exactly. Dorcas was prepared to stall the move for as long as possible. "Maybe not. Oh, and we have to make sure Maggie has another job lined up. We can't leave her stranded with nothing. She needs the money and the mental stimulation."

"I've already thought of that. She could work with Clem Loudermilk to market his new line of bras. He's planning to sell them himself instead of leasing the patent to a major company like he did before."

Dorcas tried to picture Maggie working for Clem. She couldn't imagine Maggie being happy there. "We'll see." She hadn't figured out a way to convince Ambrose to stay, but now that George had his golden scales, she'd have to find something *tout suite*, as Marc would say.

She didn't want Marc and Gwen to have problems with their relationship, but on the positive side, problems would give Dorcas an excuse to hang around town a while longer.

Waking up next to Gwen was even more wonderful the second morning than it had been the first. For a few moments Marc simply watched her sleep. He wanted her again, but he also knew they had a few hurdles to face and they were running short on time.

Making love all morning sounded *merveilleux*, but she would want to open her shop after keeping it closed half the day yesterday. He had to decide whether he was truly going to Chicago. If not, he owed the conference committee a phone call at the very least.

He thought through his options. He could e-mail the organizers his notes for his talk and have someone else deliver it. They would be unhappy about that, but Marc was in the process of rearranging his priorities.

One of those was still his sister. From his new perspective of nearly dying from magic the night before, he could see how relatively unimportant a university degree was. He'd been overbearing and overprotective with Josette, and he needed to tell her that, but he wanted to do it in person.

He also wanted Gwen to come to Paris. That was another whole discussion they needed to have. He loved her, and he knew she loved him. But that would not make the next steps either easy or simple.

As plans began to swirl in his head, he was unable to lie there another moment. Gwen seemed to be sound asleep, so he slipped out of bed, grabbed the clothes he had worn the night before, and walked into the kitchen.

On his way he searched for the dent in the floor where he had found the paperweight after breaking into the house. Dorcas had fixed that, too, and had set the paperweight back on the kitchen counter. The kitchen window looked perfect.

Marc supposed it was second nature for Dorcas to go around doing these things so the nonmagical people of Big Knob would not suspect a thing. He wished she had been less thorough this time, though. The bromeliad he had knocked over was back in its pot.

Then he remembered what he had seen when he knocked it over. The roots had glowed. They could still be glowing. He could show that to Gwen when she woke up. Then again, maybe it would be unnecessary. Maybe she would be more open to the idea of magic this morning.

He was dressed, had coffee brewing, and was rummaging in the refrigerator when she came into the kitchen. He glanced up and his heart ached at how beautiful she looked all rumpled from sleep. He loved the way the furry bathrobe and slippers hid all her curves, making her look like a package ready to be unwrapped.

Her tousled hair fell in thick, shiny layers, stopping

just below her chin. Her cheeks were still rosy from sleep and her mouth looked so kissable that he closed the refrigerator door and walked over to avail himself of the opportunity.

She kissed him back with enough enthusiasm that he reconsidered his ambitious morning plans. Maybe staying in bed until noon was a good idea.

He lifted his head and gazed into her eyes. "I hope I did not wake you."

She shook her head. "I was awake. I was just . . . thinking."

"Pretending to sleep, were you?" He smiled.

She did not smile back. "Marc, I had a really weird dream last night. There was a dragon living in Whispering Forest, and a fairy prince tried to kill you." She watched him quietly, obviously waiting for his reaction.

He knew the safe route. If he laughed and said that sounded like the result of too much wine and too little food, she would relax and they could go on from there. They could talk about his sister and maybe even about the trip to Paris.

He took a deep breath and continued to hold her. "That was not a dream, *cherie*. Big Knob is filled with many magical happenings."

Her pupils widened. "You're scaring me, Marc. Either I'm crazy or you are. There are no such things as dragons and fairy princes."

"Yesterday I would have agreed with you. Today I cannot." He rubbed her back, hoping to ease the tension he felt there. "Have some coffee. We will talk."

She perched on the edge of a kitchen chair while he poured her a mug of coffee. She looked like a wild animal ready to bolt at any moment.

Maybe he should start with the easy subjects first. "I have been considering what you said about Josette." He set the mug of coffee in front of her and poured one for himself.

She looked blank for a moment.

He could understand if she needed prompting. So much had happened since then. "You advised me to let her find her own way and not worry that she has dropped out of school."

"Oh, right." Some of the tension eased out of her expression, as if she appreciated the normal topic. "You can't force someone into living the life you want for them."

He wondered if she meant that to cover his behavior with her, too. Was he forcing her to be someone she was not, pushing her so far out of her comfort zone that she would run from him in fear?

"You are correct about Josie," he said. "When I return to Paris, I will tell her that I will support her decisions, however she chooses to handle her future."

"Good."

"Which brings up the question of our future." And that made the difference, he thought. Josie had only herself to consider. If he and Gwen loved each other, they had to consider each other and what a shared future would look like.

Was it his imagination, or did she tighten up again? He became less sure of himself. "At least, I hope we have a future," he said softly.

She met his gaze. "I would like that, but . . . I can't figure out how it would work."

"You have said that you love France." Now that he was about to suggest his solution, anxiety twisted in his gut. "Move there with me."

Her expression was still troubled.

"I did not say that correctly." He grasped both her hands. "Please marry me and live with me in Paris."

The anguish he was feeling seemed reflected in her eyes. "Oh, Marc, this isn't easy."

"It could be very easy. Marry me, move to France, have babies with me, grow old with me."

Her deep sigh seemed to come all the way from her toes. "I can't imagine living in Paris. I can't imagine giving up Beaucoup Bouquets and the cozy security of this little town." Defiance flashed in her gaze, as if she were daring him to contradict her image of Big Knob.

He could not argue with her. Even with all the magic going on, Big Knob was still cozy and secure. Dorcas and Ambrose saw to that. Now that George was a True Guardian, he would be a legitimate part of the security system instead of an accidental one.

Navigating this discussion without stepping on a land mine would require care. "I am certain you have strong ties to this town," he said.

"I didn't realize how strong until I listened to you describe life in Paris."

That was discouraging. He had been trying to excite her about the city. "I might not have described it well. You would love Paris, Gwen. Come see for yourself. Do not reject the idea without giving it a chance. You could certainly have a flower shop there."

She watched the coffee swirl as she rotated the mug in both hands. Then she glanced up at him. "But mine wouldn't be the only flower shop."

"No. No, it would not." *But you would be with me. We could be together.* He could not say that. He refused to pressure her into this, refused to treat her in the heavy-handed way he had apparently treated Josette.

"I know better than to ask you to relocate to Big Knob."

He could not imagine it, either. But he would be willing to spend more time here if he could interact with the magical elements while he was in town.

Under those circumstances he could see staying two or three months.

But he hesitated to suggest that kind of compromise as long as she denied the existence of all they had seen and heard in the past twenty-four hours. He was not going to spend months here sneaking out to the forest or over to see the Lowells.

Finally he decided to tackle the big issue. "Gwen, are you thoroughly convinced that nothing strange or magical happened last night?"

A pulse beat in her throat. "Yes."

"You are unwilling to believe that Leo Atwood was able to invade your dreams because he is a fairy prince?"

"Yes, I am. That's ludicrous."

"D'accord." He pushed back his chair and walked over to the bromeliad. "What if I could prove to you that this plant has magical properties?"

"I can't imagine how you'd do that."

He glanced at a door on the far wall. "Is that a pantry?"

"What does that have to do with anything?"

"Come in the pantry with me." He picked up the pot and walked over to the door, but she had not moved. "Please."

She looked frightened, but she put down her mug, stood and came to stand beside him.

"Watch." Marc opened the pantry door, went inside and pulled Gwen in with him. "This will prove that the magic exists." Once they were enclosed in darkness, he reached down and yanked the plant out by the roots.

"How?"

"Perhaps it takes a few seconds." He waited, but nothing happened. The roots were just roots. "I do not understand."

"Marc, what's going on?" Gwen sounded very nervous.

"Last night, when I tipped this pot over, the roots were glowing. I thought if you saw that . . ."

"But they're not glowing now, are they?"

"There must be an explanation," Marc said. "Perhaps it is a nighttime phenomenon. Perhaps—"

"Perhaps you dreamed about the glowing roots, and now it's daytime and you're not dreaming." Gwen pushed open the pantry door. "There's no magic, Marc. I know it and you know it."

"I do not!" He walked out of the pantry, holding the plant in one hand and the pot in the other. He trailed dirt on her hardwood floor.

Gwen stood gazing at him. "It's been an intense couple of days."

"Yes."

"Maybe we both need some perspective."

No, he needed her, as a lover and a life's companion, one who shared his new belief in the power of magic. But he would not force her to admit something she did not want to see. And he would not let her know she was breaking his heart in pieces that no magic spell could restore.

"Perhaps we do," he said quietly. "I must leave for Chicago soon, anyway."

"And I should be getting ready to open the shop."

"Yes. I will . . . call you."

Last night she had been sobbing at the thought of leaving him to go with Prince Leo. This morning she was dry-eyed at the idea they might never see each other again. "Just remember cell phone reception is terrible here," she said.

"I will remember." He wondered if she had ever considered why that was so. There was no logical reason for it. But there could be a magical one.

Chapter 25

In the days that followed, Gwen took refuge in a comforting routine of tending her plants, her shop, and her little French cottage. She was biding her time until Annie Dunstan came home. Annie would help her figure this out. Gwen desperately needed someone to talk to, someone she could trust.

Marc had been gone five days when Annie came home. Her friend had actually arrived the night before, but Gwen wasn't about to interfere with the homecoming celebration between Annie and Jeremy. Jeremy had promised Annie would come by Beaucoup Bouquets first thing this morning.

Other than dropping by Click-or-Treat to ask if Annie could come to see her, Gwen had avoided the Internet café. She was still so conflicted about Marc that she had no idea what she'd say to him in an e-mail.

She was almost willing to believe he'd been part of the dream, too, except several people had asked her about him and whether he was back in Paris. They wanted to know if he had plans to visit Big Knob again, or if she'd be going over to see him.

They made it all sound so simple. They didn't know that Marc was asking her to uproot her life. But more than that, he wanted her to go along with the whole dragon-and-fairy scenario. He'd obviously been very disappointed when she'd refused to accept the possibility of magical events in Big Knob.

Yet every morning when she woke up and looked out at the town of Big Knob from the windows of her cottage, she couldn't imagine how those things had been real. No one else believed in that kind of thing, so why should she?

Eventually she'd had to admit to herself that *something* had happened that night. She wondered if Dorcas and Ambrose had cooked up the entire elaborate show as part of the matchmaking scheme. That seemed extreme and not a little bizarre, but maybe they had Hollywood connections.

Annie would have some ideas. She'd been on the trail of the Loch Ness Monster. Maybe she'd exposed that particular myth as a hoax. Now she could work on one closer to home. How she'd laugh to think that someone was trying to pretend there was a dragon in the Whispering Forest.

Two minutes after Gwen opened the shop, Annie came through the door looking her usual blond, gorgeous self, smiling that Miss Dairy Queen smile. She was wearing her hair short these days to make travel easier and the style suited her. Of course, any style would look good on Annie.

She hurried toward the counter. "That haircut and color looks fabo, girlfriend! And where are your glasses?"

"I got contacts." Gwen ran around the counter to give her a hug.

"I go away for a couple of weeks and you transform yourself! Jeremy said I missed all the fun."

"You have no idea. Listen, since no customers are

here yet, I'm going to put up the BE BACK SOON sign so we can go over to the house for coffee."

"Works for me." Annie held up a small bag. "Brought you a present."

"Hey, you didn't have to do that." But she was thrilled, although the moment reminded her of Marc and his gift of a paperweight. Of course, nearly everything reminded her of Marc these days. Couldn't be helped.

"It's just a touristy thing, but I thought you'd get a kick out of it."

Gwen opened the bag and took out a small stuffed version of Nessie. "Cute!" She glanced up. "Did you debunk that ridiculous myth?"

"Uh, not exactly." Annie avoided her gaze.

"Come on, Annie. You and I both know there's no such thing." She needed her friend to agree with her on this before they moved on to dragons and fairies in the Whispering Forest.

"We can talk about that later." Annie walked over to the window, picked up the BE BACK SOON sign from its place on the ledge, and hung it from a suction cup. "First I want to hear all about your Frenchman. And I'm dying for some of your French roast coffee. Coffee in Scotland is . . . different."

"Then let's go." Gwen tucked the stuffed animal back in the bag and grabbed her coat and boots. She wished Annie hadn't ducked the question like that, but she probably was curious about Marc, as everyone was.

A few minutes later, Annie was wandering around Gwen's kitchen while the coffee brewed. "I really love what you've done with this place." She glanced at the pots hanging from the ceiling and the open shelves stacked with pottery dishes. "I want to get a house, but Jeremy says there's no point as long as I'm traveling all the time. He's so damned logical, but I suppose he's right."

"Logic can be good." Gwen had the uneasy feeling that Jeremy might be the one she should have talked to about the magic. He thought like her, while Annie had always been a little woo-woo.

"Logic is wonderful, unless you're dying for a house like this one," Annie said. "You even have a little herb garden in the window. I would never have time to tend one, but I love the idea."

"And then you'd have herbs to cook with." It was a running joke between them that Annie was pretty much at a loss in the kitchen.

"Hey, I'm not saying I'd use the herbs. I just want an herb garden. It's cool. It's savvy."

"Oh, that would be me, no question. Ms. Cool and Savvy, right here." Gwen glanced at the window. The bromeliad was no longer there. It had died soon after Marc left for Chicago. Gwen hadn't gone into the forest to check on the others, but she'd bet they'd died, too. They'd served Dorcas and Ambrose's purpose.

"You are! The hair and contacts look great. Is that new makeup?"

"Francine talked me into it."

"That's a new necklace, too. Did your French guy bring that to you?"

"No, Dorcas gave it to me." Gwen rolled the smooth stone between her thumb and forefinger, something she'd been doing a lot lately. She'd told herself to put the necklace away because it was such a poignant reminder of Marc, but she hadn't been able to make herself do it.

"That Dorcas has good taste. So where did this come from?" She picked up the paperweight from the counter.

"Marc brought it from Paris."

"It's gorgeous. I love the fleur-de-lis in the center. But did you know it's cracked?"

"Yes." Gwen had looked at that crack a million times. She remembered having the paperweight in her pocket when she confronted Leo Atwood in her living room. It hadn't been cracked then.

"Must have happened on the trip over. But it's pretty, anyway."

"No. I dropped it." That was all Gwen could figure.

"Aw. That's too bad. So what's with the French guy? Are you going to see him again?"

"I don't know." Gwen took time out to pour their coffee.

"Uh-oh, you two didn't get along? Jeremy seemed to think you did." Annie brought the paperweight with her as she came over to sit down. She took the chair Marc had used.

Gwen hadn't sat across this table with anyone since Marc left. "We did get along." Gwen gazed at her friend. "Very well."

"Wow. The way you say that tells me we might be talking the L word."

Gwen nodded. No use denying it. Love wasn't the issue. There was plenty of love, plenty of passion. "He asked me to move to Paris."

"Whoa." Annie blew across her coffee and took a small sip. "I don't see you packing."

"No." Gwen looked at the paperweight and wished she could be with Marc now. Right now.

"I totally get that. I enjoyed visiting Scotland, but I wouldn't want to move there permanently. It's not home."

"Where we'd live would be tough to work out, no question. But the more I think about it, the more I realize we could deal with it if each of us made some concessions. No, that's not the biggest problem."

"He doesn't want kids."

"No, actually, I think he does." She could see those dark-haired kids so clearly. They'd grow up bilingual, something she'd never quite managed to do. She'd make sure that happened with any kids she and Marc had. . . . Except their children might never exist.

"Religious differences?"

"Not really. Although, in a way . . ." Gwen hesitated. She was about to make the man she loved sound like a gullible person at best, a flake at worst. But Annie needed to know this. "He believes there's a dragon living in the Whispering Forest."

Annie choked on her coffee.

Gwen got her some water and patted her back, but inside she was smiling. This was the reaction she'd hoped for. Her friend didn't believe in that kind of nonsense, either.

At last Annie pulled herself together and cleared her throat. "Why would he think that?"

"It's a long story."

"Unless you're worried about the shop, I have all morning."

Gwen spilled everything, beginning with the erotic dreams and ending with the scene in the forest with something that looked like a dragon and a person who made it appear that he had wings and could levitate. "I'm sure it's all fake, something created by Dorcas and Ambrose, but Marc believes it's real."

Annie gazed at her for several long seconds.

Finally Gwen couldn't stand the suspense. "What do you think?"

"I'm working on it."

"Want more coffee?"

"Do you have any Bailey's to put in it?"

"Let me look." Gwen went to her liquor stash and found an unopened bottle her parents had given her for Christmas a year ago. "We're in luck." After filling each of their mugs three-quarters full of coffee, she poured in a generous amount of Bailey's.

Annie took a sip. "Ah, better."

"I don't know if I mentioned that the Lowells gave Marc and me a bottle of that Mystic Hills wine."

"You didn't mention it, but it's standard procedure. They were definitely setting you two up. I wish I'd been here."

"Believe me, so do I." Gwen took a drink of her coffee and decided the Bailey's was a very good idea. Between talking to Annie and the Bailey's, she felt much more relaxed. "Is there something special about that wine or is it the power of suggestion?"

"A little of both. But I can tell you this—you and Marc need to work this out or you'll both be extremely miserable. He's the one for you, Gwen. And guaranteed you're his true love."

"How can you know? You've never met him."

"Let's put it this way. When the Lowells bring two people together, they do their research. There's nothing random about the choice. We're talking eHarmony to the tenth power."

"They told you this?"

"I asked. I'm a reporter, remember?"

"True." Gwen savored her coffee and felt more mellow by the minute.

"Have you talked to Dorcas about any of this?"

"No."

"Why not?"

Gwen had consumed a fair amount of her Bailey's-laced coffee, and somehow the truth slipped out. "Afraid to."

"Finish your coffee. Then we'll walk over there together." Annie picked up the paperweight. "And bring this. I'll bet Dorcas can fix it for you."

"Fix it? It's heavy blown glass. You can't just pour some Elmer's on it."

"Dorcas is very good at fixing things."

Memories rose to the surface, of a piece of paper ripping and Dorcas saying something in Latin. Then they'd come home to Gwen's shattered kitchen window. Gwen hadn't wanted to watch, hadn't wanted to acknowledge what was going on, but Dorcas had fixed that, too.

Gwen drained her mug and stood.

Annie followed suit. "Ready?"

"I don't know."

Annie walked around the table and gave her a hug. "You can do this. We'll do it together."

Fifteen minutes later, as Gwen stood with Annie on the Lowells' front porch, she was shaking. If Annie hadn't been there, she would have turned around and left. But Annie was already pushing the doorbell, which chimed Beethoven's *Ode to Joy*.

Ambrose came to the door, wearing a sweatshirt printed with a picture of a bee wearing a halo. Underneath it said BLESSED BEES. "Annie, you're home!" He threw open the door and gathered her into his arms for a bear hug.

"Feeling like a rock star, are you, Ambrose?" Annie hugged him back and then tapped his chest. "You still haven't let me hear you play that bass guitar."

Ambrose blushed. "It doesn't sound like much without the rest of the band."

Gwen watched the two of them, her mouth hanging open. She'd had no idea they were so close.

Ambrose glanced over at Gwen. "Good to see you." His smile was cautious as he ushered them both into the hallway. "How've you been?"

"She's been in a world of hurt," Annie said. "We

need to talk to Dorcas. Both of you, actually. I just wasn't sure you'd be home. Jeremy said you're pretty regular at Click-or-Treat these days, checking your MySpace page."

"I stayed home this morning to help Dorcas work on something. Excuse me a minute. I'll get her." He opened a doorway and started down what appeared to be the basement steps.

Gwen caught a glimpse of candlelight. "Are we interrupting?" She didn't want to know what Dorcas and Ambrose had been working on by candlelight in the basement. An unusual smell floated up the stairs. "Because this can wait. In fact, I should probably—"

"Stay right here." Annie caught her arm and pulled her into the parlor. "Take your coat off. Make yourself comfortable."

Gwen followed Annie's instructions and took off her coat and boots, because if she didn't, she'd look like a complete coward. But she remained standing as memories washed over her.

The last time she'd been in this room, she'd sat with Marc on the purple sofa. Missing him became nearly unbearable as she remembered that afternoon. She'd lapsed back into the habit of figuring the time difference and realized that he could be having dinner now, maybe even at the café where Josette worked.

"I don't see Sabrina anywhere," Annie said. "She usually comes out."

"The last time I saw her, she was after the bracelet Dorcas loaned me. Dorcas had to close her in another room because she seemed ready to attack."

Annie laughed. "She was probably playing. She's not the type to leap on someone."

Once again, Gwen was surprised at how familiar Annie was with Sabrina. "Do you come over here a lot?"

"Fairly often."

"Why?"

Annie sat on the purple sofa. "You're about to find out."

"Annie!" Dorcas hurried into the room, arms outstretched. "How was Scotland?"

Annie got up to give her a hug. "Very productive."

"Good. And how are you, Gwen?" Dorcas's expression was as guarded as Ambrose's had been.

"She's confused," Annie said. "I've told her you'll explain everything."

Dorcas's eyebrows lifted. "You have?"

"I think she's ready."

Gwen wasn't so sure. A movement by the door caught her eye, and Sabrina pranced in wearing the diamond bracelet as a collar. "You gave that to the cat?"

Ambrose followed Sabrina in. "Actually, I gave it to her originally. But it . . . didn't work out at first."

"I hope it does now," Dorcas said. "I'm still not sure we got it all. She looks pretty cocky to me."

"Of course she does." Annie picked up the cat and scratched behind her ears. "Who wouldn't be cocky wearing a collar like this, huh, Sabrina? Come sit with me on the sofa."

The cat purred loud enough to be heard throughout the room. Even Sabrina seemed to know Annie very well.

"Do have a seat, Gwen." Dorcas gestured toward the red wingback. "Ambrose will make us some tea." She walked around the coffee table and sat beside Annie.

Gwen perched on the edge of the chair, her coat in her lap.

"Why don't you show Dorcas the paperweight?" Annie said.

Gwen unfolded her coat and took the paperweight

out of the pocket. "Marc brought this over from Paris."

Dorcas nodded. "I've seen it."

"Did you know it was cracked?" Annie asked.

"As a matter of fact, I did."

"I figured," Annie said. "You don't miss a trick. What would you say to fixing it?"

Dorcas turned to gaze at Annie. "That's a big step."

"I think it's a necessary step."

"All right. I'll get my wand." She left the room.

Gwen's heart raced the way it had when she was a child right before her first roller coaster ride. She'd never learned how to like roller coasters. "Did she say she was going to get her *wand*?"

"Yes." Annie glanced at her. "Gwen, you look scared to death." She settled the cat on the sofa and came over to crouch beside Gwen's chair. "Trust me, it's okay." She took the paperweight and stood. "I want you to see this. You need to know it's not a trick."

Gwen swallowed. "I'd rather believe in tricks."

"I know." Annie gave her shoulder a reassuring squeeze. "But if you're going to be happy with Marc, you need to step up to the plate."

"You were the softball star. I was never good at stepping up to the plate."

"It's an expression."

"I know." Gwen swallowed again. "I'm just babbling because I feel so disoriented."

"I'll be right here."

Dorcas came back into the room, carrying something that could have been a conductor's baton, but Gwen knew it wasn't. It was a wand, the kind that witches used. All the things Marc had said about the shape of the streets and the name of the town's founder came back to her.

Annie held the paperweight in the palm of her hand and stretched her arm out toward Dorcas. Dorcas cleared her throat, pointed her wand at the paperweight and said *"E pluribus unum."*

Gwen had the insane urge to laugh. That was the phrase on a dollar bill! These people were quacks!

Annie clutched the paperweight and peered into it. "Great job."

"You mean it's fixed?" Gwen couldn't believe it. "With some Latin phrase from a dollar bill? You've got to be kidding me."

"I've tested different phrases," Dorcas said, "and some are too complicated to remember. This one works as well as any, and it's easy to say."

"See for yourself." Annie handed Gwen the paperweight.

Gwen took it, and it felt almost hot to the touch. The crack was gone. She kept turning the paperweight over in her hand, sure she'd find the crack, but it wasn't there. Her chest tightened as she absorbed the significance of that.

Slowly she looked up. "Who are you?"

"I'm a witch," Dorcas said.

Ambrose came in carrying a tray loaded down with cups and a steaming teapot. "And I'm a wizard."

"They're in Big Knob because of George, the dragon," Annie said. "And I understand congratulations are in order, by the way. That's awesome about his golden scales."

"We had a party," Dorcas said. "I wanted to wait for you, but he was so eager to celebrate. Maggie came."

Gwen's head was spinning. "Maggie Grady? She knows about the dragon?"

"She'd sort of have to," Ambrose said. "She's our assistant."

Gwen was having trouble breathing. "Who . . . who else knows?"

"Well, Marc," Dorcas said. "And now you. We would have filled you in completely that night, except . . . you didn't seem to want to know."

Gwen held on tight to the paperweight as she gazed up at Annie. "What about Jeremy?"

She shook her head. "It's better if he doesn't know. He'd worry himself sick if he realized I was out there in a boat this past week talking to Nessie. Which reminds me, Dorcas. Nessie gave me a few baby things to pass on to Dee-Dee for her little ones."

"How sweet!" Dorcas beamed at her.

Gwen gulped. "Who's Dee-Dee?"

Annie took one look at Gwen and came back over to put a comforting arm around her shoulders. "She's a lake monster who lives in Deep Lake."

"Oh . . . my . . . God."

"Don't worry, Gwen. You'll get used to this. Having your Frenchman by your side will help. You don't know how many times I've wished I could tell Jeremy, but I don't think he could handle it. Maggie feels the same about Sean."

"I'm not sure *I* can handle it," Gwen wailed.

"Just hold on to your Frenchman," Annie said.

And suddenly, that's what Gwen wanted to do. "I need to fly to Paris."

"Oh, boy." Annie gazed at her in sympathy. "That requires a passport, girlfriend."

Gwen sent a pleading glance in Dorcas's direction. "Can't you make me one with that wand of yours?"

Dorcas shook her head. "Sorry. In the old days, maybe. But with security the way it is now, I'd be asking for a whole lot of trouble. You'll have to do this the old-fashioned way."

"Then I'll have to get it as fast as I can."

"You could start e-mailing Marc again," Ambrose suggested.

Gwen considered that for about two seconds. "No. What I need to say to him shouldn't be said in an e-mail." She looked around the room. "And don't any of you e-mail him on my behalf. He would come straight over here, and I don't want that. It will mean a thousand times more if I go to him instead."

"I think you're right," Dorcas said.

Gwen's eagerness grew as she imagined seeing Marc face-to-face. She had so much to tell him! Then she remembered something that had been said earlier. "Is the lake monster . . . pregnant?"

"Yes," Annie said. "And we're very excited about that. We've never—"

"That means there's *another* one?"

"Oh, right," Ambrose said. "I guess we forgot to mention Norbert from North Lake. We flew him over here last year."

Gwen started making mental notes. She could hardly wait to see the expression on Marc's face when he heard that George wasn't the only magical creature in Big Knob. He would love that.

But she hoped he'd love seeing her even more. There was the slight chance that his feelings toward her had cooled once he'd returned to Paris. She needed to take that risk.

Chapter 26

Marc had taken to working in his office instead of taking a lunch break between his morning and afternoon classes. Food held no interest for him lately, and when he submerged himself in his teaching duties he managed to miss Gwen a little less. Not much less, though.

Ever since returning to Paris, he had picked up the phone a dozen times. He had never made the call. He had no words that would make everything right between them.

E-mail had been another option, but he had hesitated with that, too. He could have e-mailed Ambrose, but that seemed like the kind of thing a schoolboy would do. *Have you seen Gwen? Does she still think of me?*

She might have tried to forget him. After all, he reminded her of that night where she had been part of a world she wanted to deny. He could not forget what he had learned that night, and she did not want to remember.

He was in the middle of grading a batch of exams when his phone rang. The front office informed him he had a visitor at the main gate. He smiled. Probably Josie, come to drag him off to lunch.

Grabbing his coat, he left the office and walked across the open courtyard toward the front gate. He should get his sister a pass so she could come in at will. She had never shown an interest in visiting him here, so he had not thought of it.

But lately she had let slip a few comments that made him think she might apply for the fall semester. Once upon a time she had sworn never to attend a university where he was a professor. Now that he had stopped trying to run her life, she seemed less concerned about being in his sphere of influence.

He thought about where they could go for lunch. There were several small cafés nearby. She was pickier now that she worked in one. The food and service had to be just so or she would complain to the manager.

That made him smile, too. She was becoming more assertive, something she had desperately needed. Gwen had been right about letting Josette find her own way. Doing that was giving her confidence.

As he approached the entrance he expected to see his dark-haired sister talking to the guard. But the woman standing there in a stylish wool trench coat was not his sister. His heartbeat kicked up a notch. He had not seen her in weeks, but he would recognize that profile anywhere.

She caught sight of him and turned, her smile so achingly familiar that he had to control the impulse to rush forward and gather her in his arms. But he did not know why she was here.

"Hi, Marc." Her gaze was warm. That was a promising start. "Or should I say, *Professor Chevalier?*"

"Marc is fine." He stepped through the entrance onto the sidewalk. Confound it, he did not even know if he should touch her. "Hello, Gwen. I had no idea—"

"I wanted to surprise you. Can you get away?"

Get away? For her he would abandon his job and fly to Tahiti, if that would make her happy.

"For lunch, I mean," she said. "I'm sure you're busy."

"Not terribly. Give me a moment." Turning aside, he pulled out his cell and speed-dialed his closest friend in the department. He quickly asked Antoine if he would take all his afternoon classes, and told him where to find his notes. Antoine agreed without asking why, as if he sensed the urgency in his friend's voice. Marc thanked him and hung up.

Gwen stared at him. "Did you just duck out of your afternoon classes?"

"Yes."

"Is that a good idea?"

"It is a very good idea." Deciding he could at least take her arm, he guided her in the direction of an area where they could find food. He did not care whether they ate or not, but she had suggested lunch, so she must be hungry. "When did you arrive in Paris?"

"About two hours ago."

He skidded to a stop. "You have been flying all night?"

"That seems to be the best way to make the trip. My friend Annie knows more about these things than I do, and she helped me set it up."

"Do you have a place to stay?"

"Of course. I wouldn't presume . . ."

He failed to censor his growl of frustration.

Her eyes widened. "Is something wrong?"

"*Oui.* Yes." He stopped and ran his fingers through his hair. "After what we have shared, I would want you to feel free to stay with me." He glanced away, almost afraid of what he would see in her expression. "I would not pressure you for anything. You would be under no obligation to . . . to . . ."

"Make love to you?"

With a sharp intake of breath, he swung to face her. "Are you saying that is a possibility?"

"I hope so." Her smile trembled. "I've missed you something awful."

"Ah, Gwen." He bracketed her face with his hands. "I have been going insane with missing you."

"Then do you suppose you could kiss me hello?"

He let out his breath in a long sigh. *"Certainement."* Slowly he lowered his mouth to hers as anticipation sang through his veins. What a sweet homecoming. Her lips opened under his, and he knew in that moment that he would make any sacrifice to be with her.

If she did not want to believe in dragons, so be it. If he had to find a way to make a living in Big Knob, Indiana, he would do that. All that he needed was here, with this woman.

She eased away from him, her breathing unsteady. "That was quite a greeting."

"We get into the spirit of welcome here in France." He dipped his head to continue where they had left off.

"Wait."

"Why?" He nibbled at her lips, uninterested in the people passing them on the street. "I am making up for lost time."

"I have something important to tell you."

"I have something important to tell you, too." He looked into her eyes. "I love you, Gwen."

Her eyes glowed with happiness. "I love you, too, Marc. Desperately. But that's not what I wanted to tell you."

He stilled. "You are pregnant." He searched her

expression, hoping to find some joy there. Was that why she had come to Paris? Well, he would take it, especially because she had said she loved him. "That is wonderful. We will marry right away."

"No, silly." She laughed and pressed her finger against his lips. "I'm not pregnant. That would be a shame after Ambrose went to all that trouble to get us condoms."

He wasn't sure whether to be sad that she was not carrying his baby or happy that she had come to Paris just to see him. "I would not have minded if you were pregnant," he said.

Her expression softened. "I wouldn't have minded, either. But I'm not." Her gaze searched his. "I came here to tell you that I believe in dragons."

Now, there was a statement he did not hear every day. "You do?" He wondered if it could be this easy, that Gwen would suddenly open her eyes to the possibilities and he could have the relationship he wanted with her.

She nodded. "My friend Annie came home and it turns out she knew all about the dragon. There's also a lake monster named Dee-Dee."

Apparently it was just that easy, if the woman you loved had a trusted friend who would give her the solid truth. Marc felt like dancing a jig, but he did not want Gwen to think he placed too much importance on this revelation. "Is that so?" He did his best imitation of a bored intellectual. "How intriguing."

She jabbed him in the ribs. "Don't give me that. You can hardly wait to see that creature."

"You are correct. I will clear my calendar so we may leave immediately."

"No way!"

"Why not?"

"Because I want you to show me Paris. If we're

going to divide our time between Paris and Big Knob, I should know my way around."

"What type of division are you considering?" He was tempted to pinch himself. She had been so convinced the magical experiences were a dream, but this felt like one to him.

"We'll have to see how it would work with your teaching schedule, but if we could manage fifty-fifty, that would be perfect."

He was already figuring it out. He could teach one semester and ask an assistant to help him with the second one. The Internet would be invaluable for communication while he was in Big Knob.

"The lake monster is having babies this spring," Gwen said. "You might want to be there for that."

His internal jig had expanded to include cartwheels and backflips. "I might, yes." He had an inspiration. "A spring wedding would be nice."

"Very nice." She gazed up at him. "Are we going to stand here all afternoon, or should we get some lunch?"

"I have food at my apartment." Slipping his arm around her waist, he guided her in the opposite direction from where they had been headed. "And my apartment is very close by."

She matched her stride to his. "By the way, do you happen to have condoms in this apartment of yours?"

"I have the same box I brought to Big Knob and never used, but that is irrelevant."

"It is?"

"Yes." He leaned down and gave her a quick kiss. "Let us make you pregnant."

"Marc! Think of what my neighbors will say back in Big Knob."

He hugged her close. "I am thinking of that. And I want to give them something to talk about."

Dorcas begged Ambrose to sit out the next dance. She'd worn her cute shoes and her feet hurt. But she didn't mind her aching feet when she glanced over at the head table and noticed Marc and Gwen gazing into each others' eyes.

Another successful wedding on the town square. And Gwen had confided yesterday that she was pregnant. Dorcas couldn't wait to fuss over yet another baby. She would get to do that, assuming everything worked out as she hoped regarding the news she'd been guarding all day.

"I'd say this case is closed." Ambrose handed Dorcas a flute of champagne. "Dee-Dee's babies were born last week, and George continues to be dressed in gold. Our work here is done."

"I suppose it is." Dorcas nudged off her shoes under the table and sighed with relief. The moment had come for her to broach the subject closest to her heart. "Ambrose, are you aware of the unicorn problem?"

"I heard speculation that they might be added to the Magical Creatures Endangered Species list."

"It's gone beyond the speculation level. They're on the list." Dorcas rubbed one foot against the other to ease the ache. "Most of the known breeding pairs are getting on in years. Besides that, a male and female who are the optimum age for producing young are not matched up."

"Why not?"

"The female's in France near Versailles, and the male lives in the hills of Tennessee. That in itself wouldn't be insurmountable, but the female has no interest in mating. She's too busy enjoying her independence. And even if she were to consider it, she wouldn't want an American unicorn who is . . . a little rough around the edges."

"I see." Ambrose gave her an assessing look. "And how is it that you know all this?"

"Cyril called this morning while you were at Click-or-Treat." She couldn't keep her secret another minute. "We've been so busy getting ready for the wedding that I wanted to save the news until the excitement died down."

"Cyril's forgiven us for screwing up the spell on his brother-in-law?"

"Way better." Excitement fizzed through Dorcas's veins. "The Wizarding Council is planning to honor us with an award for our work with George. They're saying we've accomplished something of a miracle."

"Really? That's nice to hear."

"Isn't it? Not so long ago we were in disgrace, but now the Grand High Wizard is calling to tell us we're about to be honored for our work."

Ambrose beamed. "An awards ceremony would make for a great homecoming."

Dorcas drew in a breath. Now came the tricky part. "That wasn't all Cyril had to say. He has a proposition for us."

"This has something to do with the unicorns, doesn't it? I should have known. You don't bring up a topic for no reason."

"It makes sense for them to ask us to help. We're respected relationship counselors, and by converting George to a True Guardian, we've created the perfect environment for those two unicorns in the Whispering Forest."

Ambrose stared at her. "The unicorns would come *here*?"

"Yes. We'd need to go get them, but the male in Tennessee would be easy. As for the female, I'd love to visit Paris, wouldn't you?"

"Dorcas, I—"

"Marc and Gwen could help us with the operation, and we could meet Josette. Just think of the glory if we could turn those unicorns into a loving couple."

"I'm thinking of the work involved."

She'd saved the clincher for last. "If we succeed, we will each be given a seat on the council."

"We will?" Ambrose's sat up straighter. "Wow, that's huge. No members have been added in almost . . ."

"A hundred years. Can you turn down that opportunity?"

"I'll admit I'm tempted. Those fuddy-duddies need new blood."

"Absolutely." Dorcas forgot all about her aching feet. Ambrose was weakening. She might get to stay, after all. "By the way, George is wondering if he'll get a mate, now that he has his golden scales. Would you trust the job of finding his true love to anyone else?"

Ambrose groaned. "Dorcas, you are one persuasive witch."

"Sexy, too."

"I was just thinking that." He waggled his eyebrows at her. "Do you suppose the reception's wound down enough that we can go home?"

Dorcas evaluated the gathering. "Probably. Are we agreed, then? We'll take on the unicorn project?"

"Ask me again when we're naked."

Dorcas smiled at him. "Don't worry. I will."

Please read on for an excerpt from

BLONDE WITH A WAND

Available from Onyx in March 2010

The night Anica Revere turned Jasper Danes into a cat started out innocently enough.

They'd dated for nearly three weeks, and tonight lust Ping-Ponged across the restaurant table. Anica had anticipated this moment since she first glimpsed this dark-haired Adonis with golden eyes. Although Monday wasn't a common date night, Jasper's favorite restaurant was open and he hadn't wanted to wait for the weekend to see her again. All the signs pointed to finally Doing It.

He studied Anica as if he wanted to lick her all over, which sounded great to her, except . . . she still hadn't mentioned a significant detail, one that could be a real buzzkill. She hadn't told him she was a witch.

With chemistry this strong, she was so tempted not to tell him, but one mistake with a nonmagical man was enough. The image of Edward racing out of her bedroom a year ago still pained her.

He hadn't even bothered to grab his clothes. Sad to say, a Chicago police squad car had been cruising by the apartment building and poor Edward had been arrested using a *Keep Lake Michigan Clean* leaflet as a fig leaf substitute.

She'd heard all about it from her neighbor Julie,

who kept a video camera running from her third-story window in hopes that she'd get something worth airing on her brother's independent cable show, *Not So Shy Chi-Town*. That clip made it on the show, no problem. Thankfully Edward's features had been scrambled so no one except Julie and Anica knew who it was.

"You're frowning," Jasper said. "Anything wrong?"

Good thing he wasn't a mind reader. "No, no. Sorry." She smiled to prove that everything was hunky-dory.

He reached for her hand. "What do you say we get out of here?"

Whoops. She wasn't quite ready to be alone with him. Better to reveal her witch status in a public place, where she could resist the urge to prove that she had special powers.

That had been her biggest mistake with Edward. He hadn't believed her, and she'd worked one teensy spell to convince him and had been inspired by what was at hand, so to speak. Then he'd left before she could explain that his penis would return to its normal color in a few hours.

"I'm fine with leaving," she said. "But there's chocolate mousse on the dessert menu. Let's get some to go. Mousse could be . . . a lot of fun."

"Mmm." His gaze grew hot. "I like the way you think."

As he signaled their waitress, Anica searched for the least threatening way to explain her unique gifts. After her experience with Edward, she dreaded broaching the witch situation. Maybe she should retreat to a quiet place for a few minutes and ask for guidance.

She pushed back her chair and picked up her purse. "I need to make a trip to the ladies' room."

He stood, a perfect gentleman. "Hurry back."

"You bet." All the way to the rear of the restaurant, she thought about how gorgeous he was and how much she wanted him. She imagined how his eyes would darken during sex. So far his lips had only touched her mouth and neck, but she could mentally translate that delicious sensation to full-body kisses. She longed to feel his dark chest hair tickling her breasts as he hovered over her, poised for that first thrust.

Despite her parents' urging her to find a nice wizard boy, she'd always been attracted to nonmagical guys. Because they couldn't wave a wand or brew a potion to create what they wanted, they had to make it through life on sheer grit and determination. She admired that.

She'd noticed Jasper the minute he'd stepped into her downtown coffee shop because he was insanely handsome. She'd become his friend once she'd learned he was suffering from a broken heart. Sure, he probably had the ability to recover on his own, but she wanted to help.

They'd progressed from conversations at Wicked Brew to a lunch date. That had been followed by two dinner dates, and after the last one he'd kissed her until she'd nearly caved and invited him upstairs, rule or no rule.

He had a right to know the truth before the kissing started again, though, and most likely he wouldn't believe her. If he didn't, she had to let him go. No clever little tricks to convince the guy this time. But letting him go would be very difficult.

The bathroom was empty, which pleased her. She'd been hoping for time alone to prepare. Jasper was special and she didn't want to muck this up if she could possibly help it.

Closing her eyes, she took a calming breath and murmured softly, "Great Mother and Great Father, guide me in my relationship with this man. Help me find the best way to tell him of my special powers. May we find a kinship that transcends our differences. With harm to none, so mote it be."

The bathroom door squeaked open. Anica quickly opened her eyes, turned toward the mirror and unzipped her purse as a tall brunette walked in. Moving aside the eight-inch rowan wood traveling wand she carried for emergencies, Anica pulled out her lipstick and began applying another coat of Retro Red.

She expected the woman to head for a stall or take the sink adjoining Anica's to repair her makeup. Instead the woman clutched her purse and watched Anica. Weird. Maybe this chick needed privacy, too.

Anica capped her lipstick, dropped it in her purse, and closed the zipper. Turning, she smiled at the woman, who didn't smile back. Instead her classic features creased in a frown. Troubles, apparently. She looked to be in her late twenties, about Anica's age.

"It's all yours." Anica started toward the door.

"Damn, I can't decide what to do."

Oh, Hades. Anica tended to invite confidences and she was usually willing to listen and offer whatever help she could. But now wasn't a good time. "I'm sorry. I have to get back to my date."

"Jasper Danes."

Anica blinked. "You know him?"

"Yes." The woman sighed. "I stopped by here for a drink, hoping to run into him, because he comes to this restaurant all the time. I should have realized by now he'd be involved with someone else."

Anticipation drained out of Anica so quickly she felt dizzy. She looked into the woman's soft brown eyes. "You're Sheila."

The woman nodded.

In the spot where hope had bubbled only moments

ago, disappointment invaded like sludge. If Sheila was having second thoughts about breaking up with Jasper, then Anica should step aside. What Anica shared with him was mere lust, which might disappear once he found out she was a witch.

She made herself do the noble thing. "We're not really involved." *Yet.*

"I was afraid to ask if it was serious between you two, because it looked as if—"

"We were heading in that direction, but when I first met him, he was devastated over your breakup. If you regret leaving him, then maybe there's still a chance to start over." Anica wanted to cry. Jasper was the first man she'd had any real interest in since Edward and she was giving him back to his ex. Nobility sucked.

"Excuse me, but did you say *I* left *him*?"

"Yes. He said that he begged you to reconsider, but you—"

"Oh, my God." Sheila gazed at the ceiling. "It's déjà vu." She closed her eyes and let her head drop. "I thought I was smarter than that. Guess not."

"I don't understand."

When Sheila opened her eyes to look at Anica, her gaze had hardened. "I didn't understand, either, until now. Tell me, did he say that I broke his heart?"

"Sort of. You know how guys are."

"Apparently I don't know enough about how guys are, but I'll learn. Let me guess what he said." Sheila deepened her voice in a pretty good imitation of Jasper. " 'I thought we had something special. I was all set to take her home to meet my folks in Wisconsin when she lowered the boom. Maybe I should have seen it coming. Maybe I dropped the ball somehow, didn't live up to her expectations. I tried to get her to reconsider, but she was finished with me.' "

Uneasiness settled in Anica's stomach. Sheila had

quoted Jasper almost word for word. What if this woman was a nutcase who'd been lurking in the coffee shop behind a newspaper while Jasper spilled his guts? "That's . . . approximately what he said."

"I'll bet a million dollars that's *exactly* what he said. Because that's the speech he gave me about Kate, his previous girlfriend. It touched my heartstrings, which appear to be directly connected to my libido. A few dates, and we were in bed, where I could mend his broken heart." She blew out a breath. "I didn't leave Jasper. He dumped me three weeks ago."

Three weeks ago Jasper had walked into Wicked Brew for the first time and she'd elbowed her employee Sally out of the way so that she could personally serve him a latte. Jasper had shown up the next morning, and the next, and on the third morning he'd announced that his girlfriend had left him.

But Sheila couldn't be telling the truth about that breakup. Anica prided herself on her ability to read people, and Jasper had been one forlorn guy three weeks ago. If he'd made up that story— No, she couldn't believe that he'd do such a thing.

"I want to hear Jasper's side," she said. "I don't see any reason why he'd—"

"Don't you? He's figured out that women are suckers for a sob story. He hangs with a woman until he finds somebody he likes better. Then he dumps the current girlfriend and works the heartbreak-kid angle with the new one. I fell for it. And the worst part is, if I could have him back, I'd take him, even knowing what I know."

Anica shook her head, still unwilling to accept what Sheila was saying. "I'm sure there's an explanation. Maybe you two misunderstood each other." That still left Anica out in the cold if Sheila and Jasper reunited, but she'd rather see that happen than discover Jasper was a louse.

"It's hard to misunderstand when someone says: 'It's been lots of fun and you're amazing, but it's time to move on.' That's pretty damned clear, don't you think?"

"Did you two fight about something?"

"No. All was peaches and cream. I'm guessing he met you and decided to trade up."

Had Jasper lied to her? Anica couldn't believe it, but there was only one way to find out. "I'll talk to him."

"You do that, and if you decide you don't want him after you find out the truth, let me know." Sheila thrust a business card in Anica's hand. "He might bounce back my way."

Anica stared at her in disbelief. "You'd still want him, even if he lied to you?"

" 'Fraid so. I shouldn't, but . . . he's just that good."